PENGUIN CLASSICS

THE FIVE-AND-TWENTY TALES OF THE GENIE

There are no biographical details available for Śivadāsa, the author of *The Five-and-Twenty Tales of the Genie*. From a careful reading of the text, however, we can glean the following facts: Śivadāsa was a man of great learning, even erudition; he wrote primarily for a certain type of reader – the gallants, well-educated, cultivated men-about-town with a keen interest in the fine arts and beautiful women. Śivadāsa's text is often humourous; he is gently critical and takes a shot at pomposity, pretentiousness and sanctimonious hypocrisy. He poses problems that tease the reader into thought, making his work more than just a retelling of an ancient body of tales.

CHANDRA RAJAN studied Sanskrit from the age of nine, in the time-honoured manner, with a pandit in Madras. She went to St Stephen's College, Delhi, where she had a distinguished academic record and took degrees in English and Sanskrit. Trained early in Carnatic music, she studied Western music in New York. She has taught English at Lady Sri Ram College, Delhi University, and at the University of Western Ontario, London, Canada. Her publications include *Winged Words; Re-Visions*, a volume of verse; and *Kālidāsa: The Loom of Time* published by Penguin India in 1989. Chandra Rajan is currently working on a children's version of the *Pañcatantra* and a translation and critical study of Bāna's famous prose romance, Kādambari, and a series of tales belonging to the Vikramaditya cycle: *The Goblin Tales*, also known as the *Vetālapañćavinśati*. She is also involved in a long-term project for the Sahitya Akademi – a translation of the complete works of Kālidāsa.

ŚIVADĀSA

The Five-and-Twenty Tales of the Genie

(Vetālapañćavinśati)

Translated from the Sanskrit with an Introduction by
CHANDRA RAJAN

PENGUIN BOOKS

PENGUIN BOOKS

Published by the Penguin Group
Penguin Books Ltd, 80 Strand, London WC2R 0RL, England
Penguin Group (USA) Inc., 375 Hudson Street, New York, New York 10014, USA
Penguin Group (Canada), 90 Eglinton Avenue East, Suite 700, Toronto, Ontario, Canada M4P 2Y3
(a division of Pearson Penguin Canada Inc.)
Penguin Ireland, 25 St Stephen's Green, Dublin 2, Ireland (a division of Penguin Books Ltd)
Penguin Group (Australia), 250 Camberwell Road, Camberwell,
Victoria 3124, Australia (a division of Pearson Australia Group Pty Ltd)
Penguin Books India Pvt Ltd, 11 Community Centre,
Panchsheel Park, New Delhi – 110 017, India
Penguin Group (NZ), cnr Airborne and Rosedale Roads, Albany,
Auckland 1310, New Zealand (a division of Pearson New Zealand Ltd)
Penguin Books (South Africa) (Pty) Ltd, 24 Sturdee Avenue,
Rosebank, Johannesburg 2196, South Africa

Penguin Books Ltd, Registered Offices: 80 Strand, London WC2R 0RL, England

www.penguin.com

First published by Penguin Books India 1995
Published in Penguin Classics 2006

003

The translation of Śivadāsa's *Vetālapañćavinśatika* is based on the Sanskrit text edited by Heinrich Uhle, Brockhaus, Leipzig, 1914; and the extracts from Jambhaladatta's *Vetālapañćavinśati*, on the text prepared for the AOS by M. B. Emeneau, 1934.

Printed and bound in Great Britain by Clays Ltd, Elcograf S.p.A.

ISBN-13: 978–0–14–045519–9

www.greenpenguin.co.uk

MIX
Paper | Supporting responsible forestry
FSC® C018179
FSC www.fsc.org

Penguin Books is committed to a sustainable future for our business, our readers and our planet. This book is made from Forest Stewardship Council™ certified paper.

In memory of
the three greatest storytellers
of all times
Vyāsa, Vālmīki, and Viṣṇu Śarma

Contents

Key to the Pronunciation of Sanskrit Words

Vowels:
The line on top of a vowel indicates that it is long.
a (short)as the u in b*u*t
ā (long) as the a in f*a*r
i (short) as the i in s*i*t
ī (long) as the ee in sw*ee*t
u (short) as the u in p*u*t
ū as the oo in c*oo*l
e is always a long vowel like a in m*a*te
ai as the i in p*i*le
o as the ow in *o*wl

Consonants:
k, b and p are the same as in English
kh is aspirated
g as in *g*oat
gh is aspirated
ć as in *ch*urch or *c*ello
ćh is aspirated as in *chh*ota
j as in *j*ewel
jh is aspirated
ṭ and ḍ are hard when dotted below as in *t*alk and *d*ot
ṭh is the aspirated sound
ḍh is aspirated
ṇ when dotted is a dental; the tongue has to curl

back to touch the palate.

ṅ as in ki*ng*

ñ is as in si*n*ge

t undotted is a th as in *th*ermal

th is aspirated

d undotted is a soft sound—there is no corresponding English sound, the Russian 'da' is the closest.

dh is aspirated

ph and bh are aspirated

ṃ is a nasal sound

There are three sibilants in Sanskrit: S as in song, Ṣ as in *sh*ove and a palatal ś which is in between, e.g. Śiva.

Foreword

The *Vetālapañĉavinśati*, as it is generally known, is an important work of narrative fiction, the kathā, belonging originally to the rich, age-old oral tradition of storytelling in India, and later committed to writing. In its popularity and in its contribution to popular tales elsewhere in the world, it is second only to the *Panĉatantra*.

Of the four main recensions of this work of fiction, two are parts of larger wholes and two are autonomous texts, one by Śivadāsa and the other by Jambhaladatta. Śivadāsa's text is the finer of these two and more interesting to modern readers, because it is problematic and raises issues that tease the reader into thought. It is a sadly neglected and little known text. In fact, it is a minor classic as I have attempted to show in the introduction. It deserves to be looked at as a literary text and not simply a collection of amusing tales.

Because the kathā is a very important part of Sanskrit literature, I have devoted some space in the introduction to give a brief account of its distinctive features in both its oral and written expressions.

Texts in the oral tradition are not 'fixed'; they are therefore subject to many changes during the course of transmission. The various recensions of a text that originated in the oral tradition are not identical for this reason. I have therefore tried to give an idea of how different such texts can be in different recensions by translating and including in this volume parts of the other autonomous recension, by Jambhaladatta, in the appendix. I have included the frame story, the epilogue and conclusion, and six tales. Three of the tales, (21, 22, 23), of the Jambhaladatta text are not found in Śivadāsa's recension of the *Vetālapañčavinśatikā* (the last syllable 'ka' expresses dimunition, to convey the idea that the tales are short). The three other tales common to both texts, numbers 7, 11, 20, in the Jambhaladatta text and tale numbers 8, 10 and 22, in Śivadāsa's text are told differently. Śivadāsa often places his tales in a particular context and makes a point by juxtaposing two different points of view or draws an ironic parallel between opposing views, as in Tale 22—the difference between precept and practice. The sermon at the beginning on the worthlessness of earthly pursuits is in contrast to the Brāhmaṇa Nārāyaṇa's entering a youthful body in order to enjoy the many pleasures of life. Jambhaladatta simply tells the tale, as it is.

1 Paush, Vikrama era 2051 — Chandra Rajan
(19 December 1994)

Introduction

I

No monarch in the annals of India's long history has caught and held the popular imagination in wonder and delight as the fabled emperor, Vikramāditya (the Sun of Valour) has. Down the centuries, and throughout the length and breadth of the country, Vikramāditya's magnificence and courage, nobility and wisdom and magnanimity have been proverbial. Warrior and conqueror, an undaunted hero, a scholar and patron of the arts, he was set up as the ideal monarch; a just and virtuous ruler, ever willing and ready to give, to reach out and to help the weak and needy, not counting the cost and without a thought of the greatest risks to his own life. His many adventures and exploits, those brave deeds exhibiting valour tempered by compassion which is the true mark of heroism, was the stuff of which many tales were spun and then collected to form story cycles. The *Simhāsanadvātrimśikā*[1] (the *Thirty-two Tales of the Lion Throne*) is one such work.

In this work, King Bhoja of Dhāra discovered by chance Vikramāditya's lion throne that for want of a worthy successor had been hidden away after the great monarch met his death in a great battle.[2] Bhoja was stopped from ascending the throne by the first of the thirty-two jewelled statuettes that adorned, one at each end, the sixteen golden steps that led up to the gem-studded golden throne. Each of the thirty-two statuettes told him by turns, a tale illustrating the pre-eminent virtues of the dead monarch. Each tale ended with the same statement: that Bhoja could set foot on the step if he truly regarded himself as a worthy successor to the monarch who had occupied the throne with such rare distinction in the past. King Bhoja stood abashed. According to the frame story in this story cycle, the *Thirty-two Tales of the Lion Throne,* Bhoja paid homage to the illustrious monarch, long dead, by worshipping the throne with flowers and other articles of adoration. But he never tried to ascend the throne. Now King Bhoja, a historical monarch (1055 CE), was a great ruler, and a good ruler according to history. He was a renowned warrior and conqueror, an accomplished scholar, poet, mathematician and astronomer, with many books to his credit on these subjects and on poetics; a patron of the arts and a great builder. In short he was rather like Vikramāditya himself, that illustrious monarch who had ruled over that same region, Mālava (Malwa), a millennium before the powerful Pāramāra dynasty of Bhoja held sway. Yet, the storytellers of those times made him bow before the earlier monarch, and accept second place. Such was the incomparable greatness of Vikramāditya's name, and the aura of his immeasurable fame in the popular imagination of that time and of all time. His name was magic.

The Vikramāditya story-complex is extensive and has continued to be part of the living tradition of storytelling to which it originally belonged, circulating at the level of oral transmission, side by side with the written and then the later printed texts.

Besides the *Thirty-two Tales of the Lion Throne,* a cycle of the Vikramāditya tales is to be found in the great Kashmiri work of fiction, the *Kathāsaritsāgara* (*Ocean of Story Streams*), composed around 1070 CE, by Somadeva, who is contemporaneous with King Bhoja. This Vikramāditya story cycle is the concluding portion of the *Kathāsaritsāgara* (vol. 9 Tawney-Penzer).

The most popular and celebrated of the tales that constitute the Vikramāditya story-complex, however, is the cycle of stories that centre around the encounter of Vikramāditya with a vetāla, a genie. A vetāla is a suprahuman being similar to the djinn, a familiar character that we meet in so many of the tales in the *Arabian Nights*, for instance, 'Aladdin and the Lamp'. This extraordinary encounter is the theme of the *Vetālapañcavinśatikā*, the *Five-and-Twenty (Short) Tales of the Genie*, or the *Vetāla Tales*, for short.

Four main recensions in Sanskrit, of this widely popular kathā, have survived, with known authorship. And numerous versions came into existence in other Indian languages over a long period, the most important of these being the versions in Vrajbhasha, i.e., Old Hindi (the *Baitāl Pacīsī*); Tamil (the *Vedālakkadaigal*); and the Marathi version.

Of the four Sanskrit recensions, two are found as parts of larger wholes, set in a mosaic of colourful tales and story cycles within an over-arching frame, and connected by a continuous narrative. These are the two Kashmiri works of narrative fiction of the eleventh century CE that are vast collections of tales then current in Kashmir: Somadeva's *Kathāsaritsāgara* (about 1070 CE), already referred to, and Kṣemendra's *Bṛhatkathāmanjarī* (Blossom Sprays of the Great Tale), 1037 CE, composed some twenty years earlier. Both these works are in verse, Somadeva's being the finer, because he is the better poet, and a skilled storyteller. To these two important works that are justly famous, is owed the preservation of many a fine tale and many a delightful story cycle which otherwise might have been lost forever, a tragedy that has overtaken ancient Indian literary works too often.

It is believed that the *Vetāla Tales* was originally an autonomous work and not part of any other large collection of stories. And we do have two recensions, autonomous, of the work. One is by Śivadāsa in a mix of verse and prose, a literary form known as champu which appears to have been popular in medieval Sanskrit literature. It is possible that the champu is a form derived directly from the oral tradition; from *storytelling* as distinctive from *story writing*. For oral narratives are a mixture of narrative and passages of singing, as can be seen from the performances of contemporary artists in the oral tradition. And the sung passages would tend to be in verse. Initially a transitional literary form perhaps when oral narratives were being committed to writing, the mixed form or champu might have been appropriated by later writers as a new literary form. In narrative fiction that uses a mix of verse and prose, the two styles would be employed for different purposes: the prose for narrative, to carry the story-line; the verse for description and commentary, for authorial observations and non-fictional didactic material. This is how Śivadāsa uses the two styles. And we see the same distinctive uses of verse and prose for different purposes in the *Pañcatantra*.

The other autonomous text of the *Vetāla Tales* is by Jambhaladatta which is wholly in prose with a verse or two thrown in here and there. None of Jambhaladatta's verses, except for the opening ones, have any merit.

However, something of historic interest leaps up from the opening page of Jambhaladatta's text to arrest the reader's attention. In the second introductory verse, he writes:

> Having *heard* these tales of the genie, five-and-twenty,
> filled with fine flavours, from Varadeva's lotus mouth
> —he who was Minister for Peace and War—
> Jambhaladatta in reverence for his preceptor,
> has *set them down in words* few but fitting,
> in order that these tales so fabulous
> would always live preserved in men's memories.
>
> [Emphasis mine]

At some point in the course of oral transmission, works of narrative fiction, the kathā, would have been committed to writing giving rise to several versions, or recensions. Lines

6-7 of the above quotation provide one of the main incentives to do so for they imply that already in the medieval period (the eleventh to the fourteenth centuries CE) 'oral expressions' might have been in danger of being lost. Dates, provenance, authorship and such data are almost impossible to come by in the case of oral texts and rarely do we get to witness the transition of an oral text to a written one. Yet, this is precisely what we see happening right before our eyes, here, in the above quoted verse. Jambhaladatta having *heard* the *Vetāla Tales* has written them down so that they are not lost to posterity. The verse also indicates another characteristic of oral storytelling. The texts are passed on from preceptor to pupil, by word of mouth.

Unfortunately, there is no clue to the dates of these two men, Varadeva, the *storyteller* and his pupil, Jambhaladatta, the *story writer*. Nothing but their names and the fact that they were Ministers for Peace and War, or Foreign Ministers, are given. Jambhaladatta signs himself in the colophon of his text as Minister for Peace and War. But in which kingdom in medieval India of the many kingdoms large and small, weak or powerful, they served as ministers and whether one succeeded the other in the same high post, are facts that will never be known.

A fifth recension extant is of little consequence, being merely a text that closely follows the versions of the *Vetāla Tales* in the two Kashmiri works of fiction already referred to, of Somadeva Bhatta and Kṣemendra.

The four main recensions of the *Vetāla Tales* noted already are of a comparatively late date. They belong to medieval literature of the period of the eleventh to the fourteenth centuries CE, and have been 'set down', i.e., committed to writing, during this period by the four authors whose names appear in the manuscripts in the introductory verses and/or colophon, or at the end of each tale, as in the Śivadāsa text. But the stories themselves are much, much older. They go far back in time. For storytelling in India is indeed an ancient art, and a very sophisticated and polished art at that. Like other well-known works of fiction, the kathā, such as the *Jātaka Tales*,[3] the *Śukasaptati*[4] and that best known, best loved, and most celebrated of them all, the inimitable *Pańcantantra*,[5] the *Vetāla Tales* belonged originally to the rich, age-old oral literature of the country. The poet and playwright, Kālidāsa, who is placed either in the first century BCE, or the fourth century CE—for such is the state of uncertainty in the matter of dates of ancient Indian authors and texts—refers in his beautiful poem *Meghadūtam* to 'village-elders' in Avanti who are 'well-versed in the Udayana-tales' (v.32), and again to 'skilled storytellers', in Ujjayinī, 'recounting old tales' to 'entertain their visiting kin' (v.33a). Incidentally, Udayana is the hero of the first part of the *Kathāsaritsāgara*; Book II contains Udayana-tales, tales of his life and loves (Vol. I Tawney-Penzer).

The *Mahābhārata*, a veritable treasure house of stories, is the earliest surviving work of narrative fiction, besides being much else, for it is a multi-faceted, encyclopaedic text as it has come down to us. We find stories that are often taken out of the *Mahābhārata* used by later writers, playwrights and writers of fiction.[6] It is a text that has suffered much heavy editing during its long course of oral transmission with many additions and revisions made to it but in its initial form of articulation as an oral text without all the accretions that it has acquired over many centuries, the *Mahābhārata* has to be placed in the first quarter of the first millennium BCE, the period that might be characterized as the Heroic Age with its distinctive socio-political structures, economy and values. The text as we have it today probably began taking shape a few centuries later, possibly around the fifth century BCE, to continue to grow and evolve over a long stretch of time.

Certain stories are also common to more than one, if not several works of fiction and not necessarily taken out of the *Mahābhārata*. They are told differently, placed in different contexts, put to different uses and present slight variations in detail.[7] This points to a common source. Presumably, stories that were part of the vast repertory of *storytelling,* as distinct from *story writing,* once formed a body of floating tales that was the common heritage of ancient communities: tales of love and war, romance and high adventure, of magic, the marvellous and horrific; beast fables, moral tales, humorous folk tales; tales of mighty deeds of heroism, loyalty and sacrifice. The *Mahābhārata* also mentions another group of tales that were current: 'the celestial tales, the tales told of devas and asuras' and 'the stories of men, Nāgas and Gandharvas' (the *Mahābhārata* I.4.1-4). It should be noted that here the sage Śaunaka, head of the hermitage in the Naimiṣa Forest distinguishes the 'three worlds' with their inhabitants, of ancient Indian cosmography.

Like the mighty ocean into which rivers and streams from many places and from many directions flow constantly adding to its store of waters, so also, the vast repertory of stories would have been constantly added to, as new tales were brought by travellers of all sorts returning home: sailors, soldiers, merchants, pilgrims all reporting strange sights and stranger happenings. Tale 8, for instance, in the Śivadāsa text suggests just such a possibility. The use of the image of the ocean and rivers flowing into it, might be noted in the title that Somadeva has given to his great work of fiction—*Kathāsaritsāgara* (story-stream-ocean).

These ancient tales would have been told and re-told countless times for entertainment and edification. And in the course of oral transmission, the tales would inevitably have been revised, changed in many ways; minor changes as in changes of locale, names of places and persons, and slight variations in narrative detail; major changes, such as changes in tone and orientation, aims and purposes as well.

Storytelling is an eminently portable art, with few, minimal props: a drum, a stringed instrument and a side-kick. Any place functions as its theatre: temples and palaces, fair grounds and marketplaces, sacred fords and forest retreats and often the shade of the banyan tree in a village. But the audiences are always different. And 'skilled storytellers' feel the pulse of their audience and *revise* with a keen eye to relevance and contemporary appeal. A storyteller has the advantage of getting a feedback, an immediate response so that he can improvise on the spur of the moment. And he does. Narrator and creator, he combines continuity with freshness, bringing the spice of novelty into a well-worn tale to give it a new lease of life. That itinerant storytellers or narrators (kāthakas) and bards (sūtas) carried around the narratives they had inherited, having learnt them by rote from parent or preceptor (the Sanskrit term guru signifies both); that certain versions of tales were passed down the generations from father to son in certain families of kāthakas and sūtas, or in the succession of preceptor-pupil (guru-śiṣya-paramparā); that skilled narrators revised the inherited material; all this is patently clear from certain passages in the opening chapters of the *Mahābhārata* [I.1.10-12; I.5.1-7; I.13.5-7; I.53.27-33].

The frame story of the *Mahābhārata* is set in the hermitage of Śaunaka, in the Naimiṣa Forest. The narrator is the sūta Ugraśravas, who is in the direct line of succession of preceptor/parent/pupil of the ancient narrators of this great saga that is 'the tale of the tribe', the tale of the celebrated tribe of Bhāratas of the Vedic Age. Vyāsa is its first narrator/author, as we know it. It is of interest to note that the sage Śaunaka, kulapati (head) of the hermitage and spokesman for the audience of sages, makes a request from time to time to the narrator asking him to tell them a particular tale, or an account of a special lineage of kings and sages or an episode of interest to the audience. He makes a point as well of instructing the narrator to 'tell' a tale exactly as his father had narrated it to him, and exactly as his father had narrated it before them, the sages of the Naimiṣa Forest, in the past. No changes please, seems to be the concern of this audience. The implication is clearly that bards/narrators often revised the narratives.

It cannot be sufficiently emphasized that the stories comprising the *Vetāla Tales*, or any other work of narrative fiction for that matter, were not invented by the authors under whose names the texts appeared at a later date. The stories are old; they have been re-used. The story material is ancient, inherited; it is re-worked, re-shaped, re-organized and re-articulated. Therefore there is the existence of several recensions of one 'original' text, if one can speak in terms of an 'original', and its derived versions in the case of oral literature.

Somadeva, who has included in his work a version of the *Vetāla Tales* in its entirety, presumably the version that was current in Kashmir before his time, states in the preamble (kathāmukha) of the *Kathāsaritsāgara* that he was only presenting in his work, the *essential Bṛhatkathā* (*The Great Tale*), an ancient work of fiction consisting of thousands of stories that had been lost (*Kathāsaritsāgara* 1.1.3). He adds that his book is modelled precisely on the lost work without any deviation; that he has only tightened the narrative and rearranged the contents so as to preserve the cohesion and intrinsic logic of the tales, 'as far as possible'; and that he has only given to the work *the words* that were needed to do all this [emphasis mine]. What Somadeva is virtually saying here is that his work, the *Kathāsaritsāgara*, is a *re-telling* of this ancient work of fiction, Guṇāḍhya's *Bṛhatkathā* (circa 200 BCE, or the beginning of the first millennium CE).

The *Bṛhatkathā* seems in some strange way to have disappeared from the canon sometime towards the close of the first millennium CE. It is referred to in terms of the highest praise in the works of seventh century writers: poets, writers of fiction, poeticians—Bāṇa, Daṇḍin and others[8]—who view the work canonically and accord its author, Guṇāḍhya, a status similar to or even equal to that of Vyāsa and Vālmīki, authors of the *Mahābhārata* and the *Rāmāyaṇa*. References to the *Bṛhatkathā* are also found in Kampuchean stone inscriptions of the ninth century.

Tradition has a way of creating legends round ancient authors and their works; and to account for the loss of the *Bṛhatkathā*, tradition has provided one. Guṇāḍhya, the court poet of the Śātavāhana emperor,[9] angered by his royal master's curt rejection of his magnum opus (the *Bṛhatkathā*) that he had written during his self-imposed exile in the Vindhyan forests, with his own blood for he had no ink, left the court, and in a moment of hurt pride started burning the leaves on which he had written his book. Fortunately, the emperor relented and sent for him; and Guṇāḍhya was stopped before he had completely destroyed his work. But only a small portion of it, about a seventh, could be salvaged and retrieved.

Presumably, Somadeva used this truncated *Bṛhatkathā*, the Kashmiri version current in his time, re-shaping, re-organizing, re-articulating the ancient fragment. It is to be strongly doubted that the *Vetāla Tales*, which is included in its entirety in Somadeva's great work (vols. 6, 7, Tawney-Penzer, *Kathāsaritsāgara*), ever formed part of the 'original' *Bṛhatkathā* of Guṇāḍhya, or whether any of the Vikramāditya stories that are found in the *Kathāsaritsāgara* (vol. 9. Tawney-Penzer *Kathāsaritsāgara*) belonged to it either. It is probable that the *Vetāla Tales* were tacked on to the Kashmiri *Bṛhatkathā* before Somadeva's time. Their origin has to be sought elsewhere, for it is most unlikely that Kashmir was the provenance of the 'original' *Bṛhatkathā*, or of the Vikramāditya story corpus and the *Vetāla Tales*, for that matter. The Guṇāḍhya legends and tradition place the *Bṛhatkathā* and its author in the Deccan. Guṇāḍhya, according to tradition, was the court poet of the Śātavāhana emperor. The Śātavāhana Empire (circa 200 BCE–300 CE) was a southern empire which at the height of its power controlled the entire peninsula, barring the traditional Chola county in the deep south, and extended up to Ujjayinī (Ujjain, Madhya Pradesh). Both the *Vetāla Tales* and the *Bṛhatkathā* in its Kashmiri versions locate their frame stories in Pratiṣṭhāna on the Godāvarī, the Śātavāhana capital (modern Paithan, near Aurangabad) in the western Deccan. These narratives appear to have migrated a long way from home to Kashmir, carried by itinerant storytellers, and subjected to changes in the process of transmission.

Working from the premise that it is highly unlikely that the *Vetāla Tales* ever formed part of the lost *Bṛhatkathā* in its original form, it is not in any doubt that the *Ur-Vetāla Tales* of some ancient, anonymous storyteller, is lost. All that we have are recensions of this 'original' narrative, long vanished, almost a millennium later. The recensions are *re-tellings* at several removes. Given its protean character that compels a narrative that originates in the oral tradition of storytelling to revise itself continuously, thereby constantly renewing itself, it is a forlorn hope, indeed, that sets out to seek and find its 'absolute beginnings'. What has survived is the *re-telling*; a re-telling that is one of a series of re-tellings that is also lost.

In this connection it is interesting and illuminating to refer to the frame story in the Tamil version of the *Vetāla Tales* which places the ultimate origins of storytelling using a legend, in a world, beyond the world where the ultimate ground of creation, Śiva, abides.

From a conversation of Indra, Lord of the Immortals and the sage Nārada, a courier par excellence and messenger of sorts, we learn that the lord Śiva, narrated the tales of Vikramāditya and the vetāla in private on Kailāsa's peak in the Himalayas, the temporal abode of the divine, to his consort Pārvatī, the Mother of the Universe, who had requested the lord to tell her tales 'never told before'. A certain Brāhmaṇa overheard the narration (how he got there and secured a secret hiding place to listen is not told) but coming down to earth (?), he retailed the very same tales as told by the lord Śiva, to his own wife. Thus what was exclusive and private became public 'intellectual property', gaining common knowledge. Śiva, learning of this transgression of the Brāhmaṇa, cursed the unfortunate man to become a vetāla.

Transported to a wilderness, the Brāhmaṇa-vetāla had to inhabit a corpse hanging on the branch of a murunga tree. However, when the Brāhmaṇa, contrite, pleaded for release, Śiva set a term to the curse saying that he would be freed from the curse when whosoever he told the tales to, listened to them and answered the questions that he as a vetāla would ask the listener. One among the several purposes of the question-answer exercise that concludes each tale in the *Vetāla Tales* is thus indicated, though neither of the autonomous texts of the *Vetāla Tales*, Śivadāsa's and Jambhaladatta's, include the curse.

By positing such a hoary antiquity to storytelling and projecting it far back in time to the quasi-eternal and temporal abode of divinity, and by making the divine pair Śiva and Śakti (Parvati) as the primal narrator and audience, tradition is pointing to a very ancient and undateable origin for it. This apocryphal story underlines what is central to the genre of oral storytelling, and defines its special nature. Storytelling is timeless. Like fire it is brought down to earth for man's use and entertainment. A narrative is a *re-telling* and will always be that. However far back in time it is traced to it always remains a *re-telling*. We are still left, not with an 'original', not with 'absolute beginnings' of a narrative, of any narrative, but with successive *re-tellings*, the one in this volume of the *Vetāla Tales* being the last for the moment, in another language, to new audiences. To place the initial, the original narration on Mt. Kailāsa, in the divine world of the timeless, is simply to state this ineluctable fact in a mythic form.

Since nothing exists before the earliest recensions of the *Vetāla Tales* which form part of the eleventh century Kashmiri works, we cannot even begin to predicate a point in time when the parent text from which the Śivadāsa recension derives, was current; or the versions, oral or written, from which the Tamil and Old Hindi versions derive. At one time, several versions, oral and/or written, of such a widely popular work of fiction as the *Vetāla Tales* would have been current in different parts of the country. In the case of the *Pañcatantra* no fewer than twenty-five recensions[10] have survived, no two versions identical. However, most of the Vetāla-Tale-recensions appear to have been lost.

An oral narrative is like the banyan tree, a tree so distinctive a feature of the Indian landscape; a tree that sends down vital, aerial roots to push themselves deeply into the surrounding soil, take root firmly and put out fresh shoots. In decades and centuries, a whole banyan-tree-complex comes into existence. No two of the siblings are identical and none quite like the parent. Yet, there are unmistakably recognizable similarities. So it is with oral texts.

Since no two of the four main recensions of the *Vetāla Tales* are identical, and since the much later Old Hindi and Tamil versions are also not identical either with each other or with any of the four Sanskrit recensions, it is not in any doubt that they all derive, each from a separate, individual version, oral or written. The two Kashmiri recensions probably had the same parent, namely, some work of fiction or collection of tales current in tenth century Kashmir. But the Śivadāsa recension is clearly divergent, as are the Hindi-Tamil versions. All of the parent versions from which the extant recensions are derived appear to be lost.

It is in the frame stories of the four Sanskrit recensions and the Tamil-Hindi versions of the *Vetāla Tales* that the differences are mainly present. Many of the stories set within the frame are common and reasons for this have already been indicated. But an important fact to bear in mind is that though the paraphrasable contents of the tales might be the same, the stories themselves are told differently; and *how* a story is told is as important as the story itself. On the other hand, the differences in the frame stories are highly significant because the frame story defines the tone of the work as a whole and conveys the vision that directs and orders the narrative. And in the Śivadāsa text the preamble and frame story which together form a kind of prologue, the kathāmukha, are crucial in determining the tone and structure of the work, and in conveying the specific vision of the author. This prologue to his text is the most compelling in its role as a framing-device, compared to the prologues in the other versions of the *Vetāla Tales*. It is a prologue that is problematic and teases the modern reader into thought. Śivadāsa succeeds in doing this by first introducing a tale of the hero Vikramāditya's father and the strange events surrounding the birth of the hero himself that is not found in any other frame story in the other extant recensions of the *Vetāla Tales*, nor in the Hindi-Tamil versions of a later date. And he follows this up by suggesting through structure and language the significance in the text, of an ordeal-cum-test that the hero has to face and undergo successfully before he can fulfil the great destiny that has been foretold for him in the prologue. Because of its crucial importance in the structure of the text, the prologue will be discussed later in some detail. But at this point the identity of the hero, Vikramāditya, has to be examined first.

II

The hero of the *Vetāla Tales* goes under several names: Vikramasena (the king whose armies strode forth victorious); Trivikramasena (whose armies strode the earth three times victorious); Vikramakesarī (The Lion of Valour: Kesarī–lion); Vikramānka (marked out by valour: anka–mark); and Vikramāditya (vikrama + āditya = the Sun of Valour). (The term Vikrama, that is part of all these names, signifies valour, heroism, and the act of striding forth.) The last name, Vikramāditya, is the one that is generally found to be employed in history and legend. Āditya, as one of the many names for the sun, brings in solar association and gives the monarch solar attributes. Vikramāditya is the monarch who blazes like the sun, sustaining as well as destroying. He strides forth in glory in the world like the sun wheeling through space, illuminating the whole world. He is the centre and ruler of the world, just as the sun is the ruler of the universe, and his wheel of glory and justice, like the sun's disc, rolls over the entire earth as the ancient Indians knew it. Rich with all these resonances, the name Vikramāditya, first the given name for a particular monarch, was later assumed by other monarchs in India as a title. And in adopting this title they appropriated the glory and fame of the original possessor of the name. Who was this monarch is the question that has to be asked now.

Who was Vikramāditya? Was he a historical king? Tradition asserts that he was. Many historians argue that he was not and produce half-a-dozen kings who went by that name or adopted it as a title in history. Having done that they finally settle upon Chandragupta Vikramāditya (fourth century CE), the greatest of the Gupta emperors as the real monarch, the Vikramāditya of story and legend.

However, tradition should not be summarily dismissed, as is too often done in discussing problems of dates and data in ancient Indian history, as so much story or legend. Legend, it is true, often surrounds the name and fame of certain historical personages; great monarchs and saints and poets. Legends too often have a basis, however slender, in actual facts and events of history. And it cannot be denied that there is some *story* in *history*; some attempts to mythologize important figures, create legends around them and build images of them, even in our own age that prides itself on its factual objectivity and accuracy in recording events. Tradition asserts that there was a monarch by the name of Vikramāditya, ruler of a vast and powerful kingdom, who lived at the close of the first millennium BCE and whose capital was Ujjayinī; that he was a most illustrious and noble king, just, accomplished, a great warrior and munificent patron of the arts, in short, the embodiment of the very ideal of kingship; that he routed the Śaka invaders, pushed them out and established the Vikrama era in 57 BCE to commemmorate the victory. But most scholars deny this monarch any historicity. Indeed, they relegate him totally to the realm of legend and romance. Since the historicity of this remarkable ruler is in question and as it can neither be proved nor disproved that he was a real monarch, we could perforce be content to regard him as, at best, a quasi-historical figure, like King Arthur of the Round Table or the Charlemagne of story and song and leave it at that. But this is not a very satisfactory way of dealing with the Vikramāditya-problem. An alternative might be suggested. In all probability, the monarch Vikramāditya of tradition, of story and legend, is a composite figure made up of the lives and exploits of more than one historical ruler who was outstanding in one respect or another. Several remarkable monarchs might have come together in the popular imagination and fused into one extraordinary person, an ideal and symbol of the Indian concept of a perfect sovereign. Certain facts support this suggestion. In the Śivadāsa recension of the *Vetāla Tales,* the frame story is located in Pratiṣṭhāna, a great capital of the ancient world situated on the banks of the Godāvarī. The prince born in that city is named Vikramāditya; he is the hero of the *Vetāla Tales*. Pratiṣṭhānapura is modern Paithan in Maharashtra, now famous for its exquisitely woven silk saris, but all its past glory has vanished. However, in the Vikramāditya story cyle that forms the concluding portion of the *Kathāsaritsāgara,* the hero is the ruler of Mālava at Ujjayinī.

As noted already, Vikramāditya is known under several names in the Vetāla-texts. Might it be possible that this rather casual way of using many names for the one hero of the *Vetāla Tales* reflects a successive superimposition of *the image* of several monarchs one after the other on all the rulers who appropriated the name of the original monarch, Vikramāditya, king of the Mālavas? This would produce an amalgam of several notable rulers and of their eminent virtues and their exploits, and present us with a composite figure. As the original tales, or the early form of the *Vetāla Tales* as we now have it, travelled from place to place and from one royal court to another in the early days of its peregrinations, could it be that the tales relating to a particular monarch, a great and noble warrior perhaps, were appropriated with all its associations of adventure and glory by bards and storytellers and attached to the name and fame of their own king whom they served and whose deeds real and imaginary they celebrated in story and song? We might speculate endlessly after this fashion but the probability that something like this did actually take place is high.

It seems very likely that there was an actual historical king named Vikramāditya at the close of the first millennium BCE, who was a ruler of the Mālavas. He might very well have been an exemplary king in many respects. There certainly was a regnal era known as the Mālava era, which might be the same era as the Vikrama era believed to have been established by the emperor Vikramāditya in 57 BCE. This same monarch is in tradition credited with having fought the invading Śakas (Scythians), routed them and pushed them out of the Mālava region. The difficulty, however, that faces us here is that this King Vikramāditya reigned at Ujjayinī, on the banks of the river Śiprā, a tributary of the great Narmadā, whereas our King Vikramāditya of the *Vetāla Tales* in this volume reigned, after the death of his father, Gandharvasena, at Pratiṣṭhānapura, on the banks of the river Godāvarī, which is a long distance from the Narmadā valley.

So much for the riddle of the great hero, Vikramāditya, the king with many names, celebrated for his many noble virtues and kingly qualities and for many a heroic deed. Who is the *real* Vikramāditya? We may never know. As far as the hero in *the world of the text* is concerned, he has to be viewed as the fabled monarch who ruled over the whole earth wisely and well and afterwards became King of the Vidyādharas[11] in their fabled kingdom. While kings whose dates we know for certain, crumbled into dust and are just names in the pages of history, this king who reigns supreme as he has for a couple of millennia in the land of the imagination, is immortal. And now we proceed to examine the structure of works in which his name and fame are enshrined.

III

The structural pattern characteristic of many works of fiction in India consists of a frame story with a number of stories set within the frame and a continuous narrative running through the whole work. This pattern that I shall define as the frame-emboxment structure might be more, or less complex and complicated, but it is the basic pattern created and established very early in Indian literature by the genius of Vyāsa in the *Mahābhārata* (circa 800 BCE). It is followed by later writers of fiction, Viṣṇu Śarma (the *Pañcatantra*), Bāṇa (*Kādambarī*), Daṇḍin (*Tales of the Ten Princes*), Somadeva (*Kathāsaritsāgara*) and others whose works have fewer complications and therefore less complexity as, for example the author of the *Sukasaptati*.

Vyāsa carried the frame-emboxment device to its farthest limits, to compose a multi-dimensional, layered text in the great *Mahābhārata* saga whose structure he further complicated by bringing in several individual story-cycles, introducing many kinds of non-fictional material and weaving it all together into the fabric of the main narrative, the Bhārata War. Vyāsa's great text has no second, although it is paralleled in accomplishment in a much more limited but compact manner in the *Pañcatantra*.

With its multiple levels of narration (and *modes* of narration as well), each set in its individual frame, a sub-frame, and the whole set within the over-arching double frame; with its plurality of narrators, each with his/her own audience, and functioning within the sub-frame, yet related to other narrations and to the central narrative, this was a literary form that offered unlimited opportunities and scope for the writing of fiction. What Vyāsa succeeded in creating was a literary form quite revolutionary in the craft of fiction; a unique form; a new genre which might be viewed and discussed as novelistic. In the *Mahābhārata* saga[12] (and I am mainly referring to a text that can be predicated hypothetically as Vyāsa's text, minus the later accretions, namely, the huge chunks of didactic and philosophical material, the *Anuśāsana Parva* mainly), Vyāsa has at his command an array of literary devices that he uses with superb artistry: flashbacks, prophecies, the curse, recollection (remembrance or smaraṇa) and recognition. These devices serve to effect a fusion of time; to bring time past and time future into the present moment. There are also other devices that Vyāsa employs: metamorphosis, confusion of identity and so on. The employment of these devices extends the range of imaginative responses and opens windows into worlds of aesthetic experience that a simple narration could hardly hope to achieve. Later writers who inherited this unique form had at their command a flexible mode of narration which would enable them to set themselves goals other than mere storytelling for entertainment, which no doubt is a legitimate and valid aim, but one that leaves much to be desired.

The two autonomous recensions of the *Vetāla Tales*, of Śivadāsa and Jambhaladatta follow a simplified form of the classic pattern outlined already. There is the frame story and twenty-four (twenty-five in the Jambhaladatta recension) stories, and the continuous narrative. Three characters only are employed: the hero, the villain and the genie, the vetāla who combines in himself the roles of narrator and actor. This is a far cry from the multivocal texts of Vyāsa and Viṣṇu Śarma where the large number of characters provide multiple points of view. The goals of our two authors of the twelfth-thirteenth centuries are different and limited. Jambhaladatta gives us a text that aims at straightforward, uncomplicated storytelling for the sheer joy of telling a good tale as best as the storyteller can and the reader's delight at reading a good tale well told for the most part. Jambhaladatta's narrative is at times written in a somewhat pedestrian prose and lacks depth. Śivadāsa's text, on the other hand is a finer text; a deeply thoughtful text. It is a text that is troubled at times, burdened by an awareness of the presence of wrongdoing, even evil in the stark sense of the term, and of subsequent moral retribution. There is a strong sense of the ways, often strange and inscrutable, in which these two constants in the order of existence interact to determine human action. The text rehearses the inexorable march of events to its bitter end on a course set in motion by an initial act that on the surface appears to be trifling but, in fact, turns out to be tragic in nature and brings a set of bizarre happenings in its wake. This rather trifling act is the petty revenge that King Gandharvasena, in a moment of pique, wreaks on an unoffending ascetic sitting in silent penance in the forest. The king's action, flowing out of inordinate pride, is an act of wrongdoing unworthy of a virtuous and responsible monarch. It sows the seed of evil. Order is broken; disorder enters. Innocent blood is shed in a gruesome manner and the unnatural act of a father (the ascetic) killing his own little son blazes a trail of evil, of foul murder and deeply-laid plots to commit more 'foul murder', practise deception and villainy, until finally the evil is extinguished by another killing, which is a ritual slaying. Blood pays for blood. Blood washes away blood. And a new dawn sees the re-establishment of order and harmony. The righteous age of Vikramāditya is ushered in. But, it is not all that simple and straightforward, as will be demonstrated in the following paragraphs.

Śivadāsa's text is problematic. It raises issues, poses problems. It hangs the hero, Vikramāditya, on the horns of vexing dilemmas. Questions trouble the readers (and, one suspects, the author himself) as they ponder over imponderables, and tease them into thought. For instance, if we consider the strange events surrounding the birth of our hero, we have first a child killed by its own father; then its triply-fragmented frame produces conception in three women in three different places, *somehow*. But how? The reader trying to figure out this macabre situation savours the fascination of being in a state of uncertainty. He is more than perplexed. He is haunted and senses depths of meaning that he cannot quite get a handle on. However, it is the very essence of folk and fairy tales to present inexplicable situations and *suggest* rather than *state*.

Śivadāsa's strong sense of wrongdoing and the subsequent moral retribution is the imperative that dictates his handling of the inherited story material. He re-shapes the received text, driven by his moral concerns and literary objectives. And we see this in the manner in which he structures his narrative; and, in the language in the gnomic verse, and in two specific passages of description (p. 13 and pp. 17–19).

A couple of examples from the text to illustrate the issues that Śivadāsa raises and the dilemmas he places his hero in, should be useful.

The most important element in the structure of the narrative is the preamble (or prologue) that forms the story of Vikramāditya's father and the ascetic Valkalāśana. This story that rehearses events in the past before the hero, King Vikramāditya, and the villain, the yogi, Kṣāntaśīla are born is not found in the other three recensions of the *Vetāla Tales*. Where Śivadāsa found this particular tale is something that we cannot even begin to speculate about. But that he saw the possibilities latent in the Gandharvasena-Valkalāśana tale is evidence of his artistic sense and his vision. He has seized upon the possibilities contained in the material of this particular story and made skilful use of it to convey his sense of evil and moral retribution; his view of kingship with its conflicting duties and responsibilities; his aesthetic concerns to suggest avenues of exploration of certain elements in the narrative structure, not ethically and philosophically, but imaginatively. For example, the nature of the strange bonds that link the three characters in the text, hero, villain and vetāla, and establish certain relationships; the special status awarded to the question-answer passages at the end of each tale; the significance that the text reveals to the reader of the genie's disappearing act and the hero's repeated return to the tree, both of which enclose each tale, setting apart the storybook-world from the necromancing Kṣāntiśīla's demonic world.

Śivadāsa places the story of the king and the ascetic right at the beginning whereby it gains a special status and crucial importance. The frame story always has the effect of defining the tone of the work as a whole. In this case, Śivadāsa has the story of the ascetic and King Gandharvasena in addition to the frame story which is a normal part of the text in a frame-emboxment-structure. Together they have enormous significance. The effect is particularly evident in the question-answer passage at the end of each tale which seen in the light of the prologue (the preamble and frame story) takes on meaning and purpose to serve as more than a link in the narrative structure providing the *raison d'être* to tell yet another tale. Instead of being a mechanical device it becomes an integral part of the structure. Further, in Śivadāsa's hands, it functions as the vehicle to convey an important aspect of his vision. These passages (the question-answer passage and the authorial interventions at the beginning and end of each tale) are employed to indicate and formulate a test and an ordeal that the hero is subjected to, as it will become evident in the final sections of the introduction.

Next in importance is the frame story itself, where the text proclaims the ideal of kingship implicit in the description of Vikramāditya, who as legend and tradition claimed, *was* the ideal monarch. (In Jambhaladatta's text the description is perfunctory and nondescript.) This long passage describing the fabled emperor on his lion-throne (p.13) ought not to be dismissed as a passage of flowery verse cast in a conventional mode of description. It has a purpose. Śivadāsa is here using theories of the divine origin of kings propounded in treatises on the Law (Dharma Śastras), that characterize the king as compounded of portions of all the gods (*Manusmṛti* 7.1-8). That inheritance is what makes kingship legitimate on earth and gives a king the right to rule. This is an ancient concept. The most important of a king's many virtues are couched in the following lines in the Śivadāsa narrative: ' . . . like the noble ocean / never o'erstepping the bounds set by the Law / ever honoured by the wise and virtuous'; and the concluding lines of this passage are of special importance.

> The due care and protection of the good,
> as well the curbing of the evildoer,
> this was the highest duty and happiness
> of this king in this world and the other.

These lines ought to be linked to the climactic act in the epilogue, the ritual killing of Kṣāntiśīla.

We might note in passing that the father of the hero, King Gandharvasena, is far from being an ideal monarch.

Vikramāditya, on the other hand, is set up right at the beginning in the opening of the frame story as an ideal monarch. However, Śivadāsa follows this initial statement of an *ideal* with the *actual* encounter of king and yogi; and here he lays out the problems of the role of the ideal ruler, as he shows the conduct of Vikramāditya, a wise and just ruler, being caught between conflicting imperatives. A ruler has to balance the often contrary demands of private and public good, of personal honour and the well-being and security of the state and the people. These are difficult decisions for any one holding the highest offices in a state at any time, including our own. Śivadāsa first makes use of the episode of the yogi bringing the king a gift of bilva fruit to make his point. When is a gift not simply a gift but a bribe or temptation?

The king is offered certain gifts. He has to accept them;

he cannot refuse. The yogi has laid his plans very cleverly. Up to the moment of discovery that the fruits contained gems there was a proper exercise of mutual courtesies that was part of Indian social custom. The guest brings fruit, the host offers the guest a seat and the traditional welcome with paan and supari. Now the situation has changed with Vikramāditya seated on the lion-throne and a heap of gems blazing at his feet. He is amazed, even dazzled by the richness of the gift. Feeling much beholden he wishes to make some recompense. How is he to act? The yogi now seizes his opportunity and is ready to make his request. But he is adamant that it has to be made in strict secrecy. Normally, it is the king-in-council, that is the ruler in the presence of his ministers (the cabinet) who meets suppliants, hears petitions, grants requests and so on. The treatises on statecraft lay down such guidelines. But Vikramāditya agrees to the yogi's condition. We might question the wisdom of granting a private interview to a suppliant without checking his credentials. In Tale 4, in Śivadāsa's text, Vīravara, a suppliant seeking the king's employment is interviewed in the Audience Hall, in the presence of the full Assembly, the Sabhā. Yet, day after day, for years, the yogi comes with a gift of bilva fruit, and the king pays no attention to this somewhat strange conduct.

Spies are the eyes and ears of a king, but the king makes no use of them. And further, without any scrutiny of a suppliant who comes from nowhere with untold treasures as gifts, and demands to be heard in private, Vikramāditya agrees. It is a strange request that he hears. Unquestioning, without the least hesitation and without the aid of ministerial counsel, he accedes to the request. On the other hand, as a king and as a man he could not refuse the one thing that the suppliant asks for in return for the fabulous gifts he has made which appears to be something quite innocuous. Or is it? Granted that he was unaware of the true nature of the yogi's request and what was involved in it, yet it must be pointed out that Kṣāntiśīla, the yogi, clearly spells out what his request for the king's help is all about. It is to gain the eight great Siddhis:

> To be minute as an atom, or enormous as a mountain,
> light as air or heavy as rock; to be invisible at will,
> to have all one's desires fulfilled, to subject others to one's will;
> and to have lordship of the world.

But this is asking for a great deal. Īśatvam (in line 4) is supremacy, mastery. And the 'rites', mantrasādhanam, the term used in the text sounds a bit dubious. Mantra signifies holy prayers, spells, incantations. It is possible that holy prayers can be performed even in the cremation grounds. Śiva, the world's supreme yogi and ascetic is associated with the burning grounds, symbolically and metaphysically. Still, there is a bad odour to the whole affair, and Vikramāditya being a very learned and wise monarch should have been alerted to something not quite right in the situation. The truth is that he does not suspect the yogi, and a king ought not to be too trusting. He makes a rash promise and decides to help the yogi without any scrutiny of the latter's credentials. In myth, King Bali made a rash promise to Viṣṇu who came as a suppliant in the form of a dwarf, asking for land that just three of his tiny steps would cover; and for his magnanimity, he lost everything being pushed by Viṣṇu, who had assumed his cosmic form, into the underworld. And Vikramāditya being a very learned monarch would have known all the myths and their meanings. Further, a decision arrived at without proper scrutiny is not the right one. Vikramāditya himself says this, and quite rightly in his answer to the vetāla's question at the end of Tale I. Yet as he is facing Kṣāntiśīla, he does not apply this important dictum that should direct the decision-making of monarchs and men in high office, to his own case. Was he so dazzled by the richness of the yogi's gift that it clouded his judgement?

At this point, attention ought to be paid to the verses (on p.31) that are placed immediately before the vetāla asks his question at the end of Tale I:

> Without vigilant scrutiny act not,
> act only after full investigation,
> lest you reap the fruit of bitter remorse . . .

and,

> Whatever deed Destiny has willed,
> that deed will be as it has been willed;

even the gods cannot change what has been *willed*; and finally we read this:

> At a time when catastrophe is poised to strike,
> a man's judgement forsakes him, as a rule,
> even if he is virtuous and wise.

Śivadāsa has a purpose in the sententiaea, the gnomic verses that he introduces and the point at which he places them. They are guide posts to the reader. The lines quoted above apply to the king Dantaghāṭa in Tale I. But it also reflects on the other king, the hero, Vikramāditya. The first line in this passage that says 'if an artifice is really well-concealed', even the Creator will not find it out, also reflects on the events in the frame story. 'Well-concealed' gems are the beginning of Vikramāditya's problems; they are the necromancing evil yogi's 'artifice'. One other point to be noted in this passage is that Śivadāsa prefaces it with the words, 'As we have heard'. He has set down two different points of view of events that happen in a person's life, that events are pre-ordained and unalterable and that a person has to be vigilant and act; a person has the freedom of choice: it is a matter of Free Will versus Fate. But Śivadāsa disclaims responsibility for both views. He simply states them as two alternate views. There is no authorial comment; no judgement made. The reader is not required to pass judgement either, but to think of each problem that Vikramāditya faces from several points of view.

It is through such skilful use of language and structuring, and by his choice of a literary form, the champu, that Śivadāsa shows the reader ways of *reading* the text. The champu with its blend of verse and prose, each with its distinctive role, enables him to do this. The verse sets the tone and provides an indirect gloss for the narrative in prose. And by employing formulaic expressions such as As it is said', or 'As we have heard', so characteristic of oral storytelling, he avoids imposing authorial constraints of interpretation. At the same time he sets forth different points of view and presents the hero in a dilemma.

An important example of the dilemma that the hero finds himself in, is the situation that obtains in the cremation grounds, when Vikramāditya walks back and forth carrying the corpse, and this will be examined when the significance of the question-answer format at the end of each tale is discussed.

Towards the end of the text after the necromancer, Kṣāntiśīla, has been decapitated and offered as a sacrifice to the vetāla, Śivadāsa places this verse, again not in his own person but distancing himself from the view expressed in it with the phrase, 'And it is also said:

> Pay a man back in his own coin;
> do harm unto him who has done harm to you;
> I see no harm in that;
> adopt foul means towards an evil man.

The placement of this verse at this point raises questions. The idea implied in this verse is one of revenge, not justice. A king dispenses justice and orders punishment. 'Foul means' are used in private revenge, in vendettas. Why is this verse placed here? Where is the need for a defensive statement even if it is not articulated by the author in his own person, when it is followed by the prose passage pointing out that Vikramāditya's slaying of the evil necromancer is blessed by 'the Gandharvas in the World of Light' raining flowers on earth, the moon raising 'excellent cries of victory' to the king and the celestials proclaiming the rightness of his action and offering him a boon? And why is the descent of the Trinity, to bless Vikramāditya and Śiva's special declaration that he was a portion of Śiva's own power and effulgence, distanced by a short prose passage from the previous acclamation of the hero by the Gandharvas, the moon and 'the celestials', meaning Indra and his host of Devas, the Immortals? After Vikramāditya has stated his wish which we presume is granted, that the work the *Vetāla Tales* now concluded be 'celebrated and gain renown' and that he himself be granted the services of the vetāla, the text continues, with a verse beginning with the word *then*, (emphasis mine) Brahmā-Viṣṇu-Śiva descend manifest on earth and bow down to him. Śiva declares that the hero, known as Vikramasena and Vikramāditya is really a portion of the Effulgence, Śiva himself, born on earth. The narrative concludes with the promise of Vikramāditya's glorious future as Lord of the Vidyādharas, who are not of this earth, and whose kingdom is not on this earth. The first benediction assures the hero of earthly sovereignty and power, the second of sovereignty in the future in another sphere of existence.

Śivadāsa appears to deem this proclamation of the hero's divinity necessary at this point, because nothing like this is to be found in the Jambhaladatta text. It sets the reader wondering if Śivadāsa is troubled by the act of shedding blood, once again, even though this time the act is sanctified by being made into one of ritual sacrifice. And going back to what was said about the verse about foul means and paying a man back in his own coin, it seems more certain that Śivadāsa is troubled. By being troubled himself he directs the reader to wonder about ritual slaying and the concept of blood paying for blood. Not that this is not an idea strongly entertained in our own world, today. Capital punishment, the donning of the mantle of patriotism to justify the shedding of blood innocent or otherwise, the just war, these are all no different in essence from the ritual slaying of Kṣāntiśīla by Vikramāditya. They are only deadlier. Śivadāsa is directing the reader's attention to this problematic issue and by doing so he makes his concerns relevant in our own day and age.

The sombre tone set by the preamble and frame story is largely responsible for the questioning and uncertainties roused by the text in readers' minds. We now turn to these two stories and examine them in some depth.

IV

King Gandharvasena causes mortal offence to an unoffending anchorite, Valkalāśana (literally, one who eats bark) who has been performing penance in utter solitude in the deep woods for a thousand years, absorbed in silent meditation; for such are the vows that he has undertaken. The king construes the ascetic's impregnable silence as an insult to his royal dignity and pays a harlot to seduce the ascetic (a classic motif in Indian literature). The son born to the fallen ascetic and the fallen woman (the harlot) dies a gruesome death at the hands of the enraged father who realizes when he is in the presence of the king that he has been tricked into losing the fruits of his penance for no reason other than the whim of an arrogant monarch. The ascetic picks up his infant son by the legs, whirls him around and dashes his little body on the floor in the royal Audience Hall. The child is dismembered. The three fragments that the body breaks into fall in three different places: the head in the palace, the trunk in a potter's house and the feet in an oil merchant's. A strange happening indeed. But stranger still is what follows this extraordinary event. The queen and the wives of the oil merchant and potter conceive that very day and at full term, each woman gives birth to a little boy at one and the same moment. They are therefore born under the same zodiacal sign and have identical natal charts. A bizarre relationship is established; a macabre blood bond apparently unites a dead and dismembered male child and three other male infants born to three different mothers, and presumably to three different fathers. Or, are they born to different fathers? Are the three infants brothers? Who is their real father? Do they all share the ascetic Valkalāśana's blood? (In ancient thought blood and semen are the same.) One last question in our Vetāla-like series of questions: Does the triple fragmentation of the slain child suggest the triple division of the body-politic? And/or a symbolic representation of the three aspects of personality? A fractured personality to be integrated and made whole? Is the text suggesting that the three orders in the body-politic, Kṣatriya (the prince), Vaiśya or trader (the oil merchant), Śudra or artisan (the potter), the three 'brothers' work together for the good of all. But that does not happen.

The text seems to be suggesting a number of ways in which to perceive the fragmentation of the infant. The suggestions are tantalizing and elusive. But interestingly enough, the third 'brother', the oil merchant's son who is innocent and inoffensive but unconscionably sinned against, is in the end the unwitting means to accomplish justice, contain evil and restore order. There is a strong implication in the text that the genie, or the vetāla who speaks out of the mouth of the corpse is the restless spirit of this third 'brother'. The common belief even to this day, especially in rural communities is, that the ātmā (spirit) of a person dying a violent and unnatural death, either through murder or suicide, wanders, hovering in an in-between world that is neither the world, nor the hereafter, finding no peace. The text does not say this is so many words, but suggests that the murdered man, now a mere disgusting shell and voiceless, is given a *voice* by the genie. It is also a common belief that the ātmā of persons dying through violence haunt the spot where the deed was committed, be it murder or suicide.

The dismemberment of the ascetic's little son presents a strange situation where birth, death, blood and fragmentation of the whole exist in an unholy alliance. The riddle of the births of this 'fraternity' as the consequence of the death of another infant, and the questions that rise in the reader's mind like spectres are a kind of grim parody of the riddles posed and the questions asked repeatedly by the genie. Attention ought to be specially drawn to Tale 18, 'Who is Prince Haridatta's Real Father?' There are three possible fathers, the thief, the gallant (the biological father), the king (the foster parent). Vikramāditya's answer is that the thief is the real father, because he is the legal parent. Even as he was dying impaled on the stake, the thief had legally married the future mother of Haridatta, though she was but a child herself at the time.

The strange bond between the sons of the king, the potter and the oil merchant—Vikramāditya, Kṣāntiśīla, and the Vetāla (who is the *real* son of the oil merchant)—is established as the result of a chance encounter of king and ascetic (Gandharvasena and Valkalāśana). The chance encounter leads to wrongdoing on the part of both men, one flowing from inordinate pride and lack of judgement—both serious flaws in a monarch—and the other through uncontrolled lust and anger, both unpardonable flaws in an ascetic practising penance for a thousand years in the hope of gaining everlasting life in the realms of Light, Brahmaloka.

To further complicate the strangeness of the situation, a prophecy is made at the time of the triple births, that one of the infants will slay the other two and become the paramount ruler of the earth. Again, questions rise in the reader's mind; a second set of questions that parallel the genie's questions at the end of each tale. Who should rule? According to the principle of hierarchy, the prince should rule. By birth and opportunity and because the head of the dismembered infant fell in the palace, *his* is the right. The head is the prime member of the body as Vikramāditya declares to the genie at the close of Tale 6—'Of the Young Bride Who Switched Heads' : 'of all the body parts/the head is pre-eminent'. But it seems that the trunk puts in its own claim. The potter's son, evil by nature and consumed by ambition holds that the man who dares and reaches out to seize the crown should be king. And he makes his plans accordingly, in secret. He interprets the prophecy to suit his interests, foully murders the oil merchant's son, escapes the king's justice, spends years learning the arts of magic and hatches his plan to kill the king by offering him as a blood sacrifice to obtain the eight Siddhis which would assure him of unbounded power, dominion and immortality.

The prophecy comes true in its own way; for all prophecies are confusing; they are riddling. They betray those who pin their faith and hopes on them. Vikramāditya, the prince, the head of the dismembered child, becomes the paramount ruler over the whole wide earth. But until the last page in Śivadāsa's text is turned, the brooding sense of impending danger in the form of Kṣāntiśīla, the yogi, and the presence of the evil that was the consequence of the initial shedding of innocent blood, persist as undercurrents beneath the narrative structure. Twenty-four tales, many delightful and happy, some a trifle sad, a few grisly or bawdy are told, as King Vikramāditya walks back and forth through the cremation grounds carrying a corpse. A significant feature of the *Vetāla Tales* is that the tales are narrated in the cremation grounds, a place of dissolution; a place that marks the passage from one life to another and from one world to another. His education is completed by the experience of carrying out a dangerous and life-threatening mission successfully. In a deeper sense, he is 'initiated' He is born again.

V

Vikramāditya is told twenty-four tales, each of which concludes with a question which he has to answer. This question-answer format is an unusual feature of the Vikramāditya corpus being found in all the extant recensions of the *Vetāla Tales* and in the *Thirty-Two Tales of the Lion Throne*, as well.

'Now tell me, O, king . . . ' is the vetāla's inevitable refrain. The vetāla concludes his telling of a tale with a question that demands an answer. Invariably, he creates in each tale a situation that raises a question, poses a problem or riddle. The riddle has to be unriddled, the problem solved, an awkward set of circumstances sorted out properly, a question has to be answered. The initial condition that the vetāla lays down when the lets himself be carted along by Vikramāditya is that if he has the answer, the king should unfailingly provide it. If he knowingly refrains from providing the answer or the solution demanded by his interlocutor, his (the king's) heart would crack and he would die. Incidentally, this motif of the heart cracking or the head shivering to bits is a form of curse found in Indian literature from vedic times.

Now, Kṣāntiśīla had already warned the king about such an event taking place and instructed him to observe complete silence, whatever the vetāla might or might not say (p.16). 'If you speak, the corpse will return to that tree'; and ' . . . bring it here quickly in complete silence disregarding what the corpse might say to you; for it will utter many clever deceitful words,' warns Kṣāntiśīla. On the other hand the vetāla's initial condition looms large as a curse before the king; it is certain death to break his agreement with the vetāla. And more than that, to break his promise to the vetāla is to be guilty of lying and cheating, a most dishonourable way of behaviour in a great king. A monarch such as the celebrated emperor, Vikramāditya, would rather lose his life than his honour. Further, if he did not keep his word to the vetāla, he could not possibly carry it to Kṣāntiśīla's presence and in that case, the king would be guilty of not keeping his promise to the necromancer. And if he did he would also be facing certain death, for as we learn later at the conclusion, Kṣāntiśīla was planning to make the king the human sacrifice in the Rite of the Corpse. This gruesome rite, the crowning act we presume of Kṣāntiśīla's long years of study and mastery of the arts of magic (the text does not mention this fact in so many words) would get him the long desired prize, the possession of the eight Siddhis. The Siddhis are, literally, Perfections. But in the esoteric arts of white and black magic (Tāla and Vetāla) they are the suprahuman powers that Kṣāntiśīla himself lists in the frame story (pp.15–16). The most important (to Kṣāntiśīla at least) is the last power listed, which is lordship, supremacy over the earth. And it is the most menacing to Vikramāditya and more importantly to the world. If Kṣāntiśīla were to succeed, the world would be ruled by an evil man who would institute a demonic order. This is the most important dilemma that the hero faces. There are two sets of imperatives, both binding. Which one is he to choose to follow?

For Vikramāditya, it is a no-win situation. 'Damned if you do, damned if you don't,' sums up the nature of the dangerous quandary that the king appears to have placed himself in because of his rash, though magnanimous, gesture to a total stranger who has come from nowhere as a suppliant to make a strange request. However, Vikramāditya was a monarch who was magnanimous to a fault. At least, this is the prevailing *image* of the monarch. It is also a part of the greatness and nobility, the magnanimity of a king to offer help unquestionably to a suppliant. Or is it? Śivadāsa appears to be concerned about this article of faith in the code of honour of kings and heroes, and probes deeply into the assumptions of the code. He is questioning the code placing 'the image' of an ideal ruler with the realities that governance is involved in.

Further, there is another interesting aspect to the question-answer exercise. The vetāla's behaviour is extraordinary and puzzling. No sooner does the king give the answer or offer the solution required, than the vetāla leaves his shoulders and flies back to the śinśipā tree to hang once again from a branch on it. The king and we are back to square one, at the base of the dreadful tree with the hanging corpse. The whole procedure, arduous and tormenting as it must have been for the king to get hold of his elusive and slippery customer, hauling the corpse over his shoulders and setting out towards the horrible cremation grounds where Kṣāntiśīla was sitting in eager expectation, has to start all over again. And so it goes on and on until twenty-four (or twenty-five) tales have been told.

Considering that whatever answer the king makes, the vetāla flies away to his tree, it is tempting to dismiss the whole exercise as pointless and futile, except to see it as a narrative device, a convenient peg to hang tales from, for pure entertainment, a legitimate enough purpose no doubt. But pure entertainment is not always the sole aim of tales, especially of the Śivadāsa version of the *Vetāla Tales*. There is definitely an ethical and metaphysical dimension in Śivadāsa's shaping and articulation of the material of the *Vetāla* stories centering round the famous monarch, Vikramāditya, that is an integral part of the structure of his text, and this will become clear in the following paragraphs.

Before considering the question-answer format and suggesting a way of looking at it to see what, if any, purpose it serves, certain points have to be made about the king's mission itself, its nature and the time and place marked out for its performance and the manner in which it has to be carried out.

The day and time that Kṣāntiśīla selects for the terrible mission he thrusts upon Vikramāditya is highly significant.

The day is the fourteenth day of the dark half of the

month of Bhadrā that marks the beginning of the dark half of the year, when the sun starts its downward course towards the south. The south is the region of darkness and death; the north of life and light. And the time is midnight on this day of the new moon. It is a special day and night, given over to the reign of demonic forces, especially in and around the place of the dead, the cremation grounds.

The frame story leads the king and the reader out of the splendid Court in the capital, Pratiṣṭhāna, into the murky world of evil and bloody savagery of the terrible cremation grounds outside the great city. There has already been a gruesome murder in the forests edging the cremation grounds, years before the encounter of Vikramāditya and the yogi, Kṣāntiśīla. In a powerful and dramatic passage of eleven verses built of long compound words articulating vivid, evocative imagery (pp.17–19), Śivadāsa paints a landscape of spine-chilling horrors which leads us to the base of the śinśipā tree from whose branches hangs the wasted corpse of the unfortunate son of the oil-merchant murdered by Kṣāntiśīla. This event took place many years before Kṣāntiśīla, having mastered all the arts of black magic and performed severe austerities, comes to the court of King Vikramāditya with murder in his heart.

In this crucial passage of description, one of two, placed for a purpose at these particular points in the text, Śivadāsa paints in bold strokes a scene where demonic forces are rampant, engaged in wild, orgiastic rites and practices. It is a scene reminiscent of the savagery of bloody battles of the epic past. Śivadāsa's writing is highly allusive in this passage, resonant with echoes from the *Mahābhārata* and the *Rāmāyaṇa*, evocative of passages describing the carnage of the Bhārata War, the fierce sacking and burning of the great city of Lankā, the deceptions and illusions that occur in the forests where the exiled Rāma loses Sītā. The passage reaches its high point when Śivadāsa moves from the distant past into the even more distant future, to the end of time and the destruction of the universe. Time (Kāla), in the form of the primal sound of OM annihilates the universe and by implication, therefore, since Time brought the universe into being, we are both at the Beginning when nothing was and at the End when nothing will be. Thus within the narrow compass of a few stanzas, so powerfully articulated, the whole history of the world and of mankind is drawn in. This is the place set as *the place* for Vikramāditya's mission. This passage, it must be emphasized, is not placed here as pure description for its own sake, but forms an integral part of the structure of the narrative. This place, the cremation grounds is the natural habitat of both the vetāla and the yogi, Kṣāntiśīla. So greatly evocative a passage as this is necessary to convey the gravity of the danger that Kṣāntiśīla poses not only to the hero, but to the whole world that he is destined to rule.

As already noted, Śivadāsa uses the intrinsic qualities of the champu form, skilfully: the prose to tell the story, and the verse, capable of both pithiness (in the gnomic verses) and elaborate, allusive richness to create other effects. The former serves to provide the *indirect* comments of the author; the latter creates the ambience of terror as in the passage referred to here; and of earthly magnificence and divine aura as in the earlier passage descriptive of the hero and his virtues, and of the ideal of kingship (p.13).

The landscape that Śivadāsa paints in this passage is fully in keeping in tone with the sinister happenings in the preamble, and it further underlines the daring and courage and steadfastness of purpose of the hero, as well as the dangerous and life threatening character of the mission that he has accepted willingly. This passage leads straight through the cremation grounds to the śinśipā tree standing at its edge—the periphery of Kṣāntiśīla's demonic world—like some sort of marker between two worlds, the demonic world of the necromancer and the storybook world of the genie. On one of its branches hangs the corpse, blue-black, cadaverous, spectral, 'a horrid sight' (p.19).

The tree is an important element in the bitter story of deceit and betrayal resulting in the shedding of innocent blood, told in the preamble. The woods where it stands have been already mentioned twice in the preamble. It is these woods where the bark-eating ascetic, Valkalāśana sat in silent solitude for a thousand years, meditating, in the hope of gaining everlasting life, until he lost all, giving rein to unbridled sexual passion. And it is in the same woods, where one of his triple offspring killed one sibling, was now planning to kill the other.

'Some four miles from here, O king . . . a corpse hangs from the branches of a śinśipā tree . . . ' says Kṣāntiśīla to Vikramāditya. Here, interestingly, Śivadāsa carefully notes the distance from the centre of the cremation grounds where Kṣāntiśīla situates himself to the periphery where the tree of execution stands, and thereby suggests the time it would take the hero to traverse that distance. Yojanārdhe, that is, half-a-yojana is the term in the text. A yojana is roughly nine miles.

Physically, the distance marks the space existing between the centre of the great cremation grounds, its heart of darkness where the evil yogi sits waiting impatiently to perform the Rite of the Corpse, and the other point on the periphery where the tree of death and judgement, the śinśipā tree, stands as a marker. Part of this distance would be traversed in the time-taken to tell each tale.

In a metaphysical sense, this distance measures the space between the murderer, the yogi, Kṣāntiśīla and his innocent victim, now a spectral shape animated by the genie through whom he, the oil-merchant's murdered son, will ultimately redress the wrong done to him.

The genie only appears in the beginning to be wily and capricious, raising obstacles to prevent the hero from accomplishing the mission entrusted to him by Kṣāntiśīla. In the end, it is clear that the genie is in fact the saviour of the hero, and of the world.

In the text, Kṣāntiśīla is referred to as the yogi and 'the naked mendicant'. The terms yoga and yogi (one who practises yoga) have a meaning other than what is normally understand. Yoga, a word signifying the mental and physical discipline undertaken to integrate the self, ātmā. Ultimately, with the supreme self, Brahma (yoga is from the root yuk, to yoke, to unite), also signifies the study and practice of esoteric knowledge, chiefly of the arts of magic and sorcery. It is in the sense of a sorcerer that the term yogi is applied to Kṣāntiśīla. The other term 'digambara' (the naked mendicant) is pejorative.

Kṣāntiśīla is a man who is consumed by lust for total power and dominion. He is aiming at achieving his objectives by performing the rites that would gain him the eight Siddhis.

> To be minute as an atom or enormous as a
> mountain,
> light as air or heavy as rock; to be invisible at will
> to have all one's desires fulfilled, to subject others
> to one's will:
> and to have lordship of the world.
>
> (pp.15–16)

These rites appear to have included a human sacrifice. The accession of such powers would free the possessor from all the bounds of humanness and mortality, make him semi-divine and more, for he would be as a god. It is this unbounded ambition and the terrifying prospect that Kṣāntiśīla might reach his goal that would make him dangerous, a threat to the world that has to be destroyed without delay.

The brooding presence of evil represented by/or embodied in the evil yogi remains a palpable presence throughout the narrative, though Kṣāntiśīla's physical presence is there only in the prologue and the epilogue. The corpse of his victim and the tree to which he bound it are constant reminders of him.

The genie that lives within the corpse and makes the murdered man live again is also bound to the śinśipā tree. As suggested already the genie is probably intended by Śivadāsa to be the ātmā of the murdered oil merchant's son. For, as stated earlier, it is common belief that the spirits of those dying violent and unnatural deaths restlessly haunt the spot where the deaths occurred.

The repeated return to the śinśipā tree is an integral part of the narrative structure. It is inevitable because Vikramāditya (and we, the readers, with him) is inexorably linked to the tree and the genie-in-the-corpse from the moment he makes a firm commitment to Kṣāntiśīla to aid him in the performance of the Rite of the Corpse. The repeated act of walking to and from the śinśipā tree has to go on until the train of events set in motion by the initial act of wrongdoing, the ill-considered action of King Gandharvasena, father of the hero, is broken; until the pattern of crime-retribution is dissolved at the end by the ritual slaying, at which point evil is *contained, in the world of the text*. It is *the world of the text* that is under consideration, although it is related to our own everyday world in many undefined ways and though the problems and concerns of the world in which the text lives and moves are relevant to those in the world we the readers live and move in.

The ritual slaying of the slayer releases the genie from the corpse and its tree home. However, the second boon asked for by Vikramāditya, that the genie be his minister and carry out his orders, is hard to explain. And we should perhaps not try to look for an explanation. A work of art has its own logic. We can try to see *how* it works in its own world, and not ask *why*.

Right through the narrative, the three 'brothers' strangely linked to one another at birth and to the child born of a fallen ascetic and a fallen woman, continue to be linked. The text does not, however, specifically identify the vetāla (the genie in the corpse) and Kṣāntiśīla, the necromancer, as the two other members of this 'brotherhood', the sons born to the potter and the oil merchant and related in some inscrutable manner to the dismembered child of the ascetic and the courtesan. This is a secret hidden in the dark heart of the narrative and known only to the two, the yogi and the genie, until the very end. Even then the identity is not stated bluntly, but suggested. Śivadāsa's art works through suggestion.

As the frame story draws to a close and the storytelling session begins, we leave behind the Kṣāntiśīlan world of murder and mayhem presented in the frame story and enter the delightful storybook world that the vetāla, a witty and capricious but superb teller of tales, creates for the reader and the king. It is a world that mirrors Vikramāditya's world. As already noted, we are periodically returned to the savage world of the śinśipā tree and Kṣāntiśīla, the evil yogi. There is a pause between tales, before the genie takes the king and us once again into its storybook world. In this pause, the narrative situates the question-answer exchange between Vikramāditya and the vetāla.

Many of the tales appear to be constructed with a view to let certain situations emerge at the end giving rise to problems that demand solutions. These problems are not dissimilar to those that Vikramāditya would face in the day-to-day dispensation of justice. It is as if the genie is presenting a case time and time again before the king and asking for a judgement. The answers that the king gives to the genie's questions are not unlike the judgements that he would deliver in his hall of audience. One purpose therefore of the question-answer exchange is to *test* the hero's wisdom and knowledge of the Law (Dharma) in all its aspects; 'ever dedicated to upholding the Law/in its manifold aspects' is how Śivadāsa characterizes the hero (p.13 frame story). But there is a deeper purpose. The hero is tested in a more thorough manner to prove himself as something more than a judge of the supreme court. He has to be in reality the ideal monarch as described in the opening of the frame story (p.13 frame story). The education in governance that he has received as a prince is not adequate, not rounded enough for this purpose. It has left him vulnerable in certain respects, for instance to the crafty manipulations and designs, upon his innate nobility of nature, of Kṣāntiśīla. The education has to be completed now in the hard school of experience.

Śivadāsa prepares the ground carefully and in a subtle manner in the prologue (preamble-frame story) for the purpose of investing the question-answer format with significance. The question-answer exercise, the genie's repeated disappearing act and the walking back and forth through the terrible cremation grounds, yield excellent artistic insights if viewed as a test-cum-ordeal that the hero is repeatedly subjected to.

In many folk and fairy tales the hero has to pass a difficult test and is often required to go through an ordeal, at times life threatening, successfully, before he can claim and be awarded the great prize that he is destined to possess. A tough riddle to be solved, a difficult question to be answered, an intricate knot to be unknotted or a web to be unravelled; a monster to be killed hiding in a labyrinth, a blazing fire or treacherous rapids to be entered a target to be hit under impossible circumstances and so on—these are some of the examples of tests and ordeals that we are familiar with in literature.

Vikramāditya has to undergo a test and ordeal, repeatedly; twenty-four times to be precise. Repetition of a word, a chant or prayer, or an act, is itself a discipline. The hero of the *Vetāla Tales* has to perform the ordeal of walking through the landscape of horrors, the cremation grounds, outside his great capital repeatedly. He does so with unwavering determination and he walks not alone, but with a corpse that he carries on his shoulders and driven by a seemingly implacable demon dwelling within the corpse. The mission that he has undertaken is harsh, extremely arduous, and worse, immeasurably humiliating, even life threatening, enough to drive the strongest in mind and heart crazy. The prize is inestimable, no less than the present sovereignty of the whole, wide earth and the future inheritance of the fabled kingdom of the Vidyādharas. But Vikramāditya is totally unaware of all this. He does not have a clue either that he is being tested and that he is actually involved in an ordeal to prove something—his fitness. Vikramāditya has willingly undertaken this mission, at first totally ignorant of the perils involved, only to keep his promise to the man who had brought him untold riches in the form of priceless gems, and out of the innate nobility and magnanimity in him that never said no to a suppliant. What he promises to do and persists in doing is prompted by duty and not by desire. This is a distinctive feature of the test-ordeal motif in the *Vetāla Tales* which distinguishes it not only from such motifs in other literatures but more importantly from tests and ordeals and challenges accepted by heroes in Indian literature itself. Rāma, Arjuna, Aja and other epic heroes know what is involved and precisely what the pot of gold at the end of the rainbow is. Not so our hero, Vikramāditya, and this is a very significant difference between this and many other texts that depict the great deeds of a hero.

The site of the test and the nature of the ordeal are also singularly different and distinctive. The site is not a gilded court, a splendid tournament. It is literally the wilderness, desolate, an unimaginable place of horrors—the cremation grounds. The hero is tested and judged by a committee of one, the genie, who is deputizing, as we learn at the end, for the whole host of the Immortals and the Trinity (p.181). Once he has demonstrated his pre-eminent fitness to occupy the most coveted post, a post for which Kṣāntiśīla has killed once and is willing to kill again, his election is by general, full-throated acclamation with the supreme lord Śiva bestowing the final benediction in person. Honour and rewards come unsolicited to Vikramāditya. He does his duty as he is expected to without any expectations.

The test is framed to assess qualities in the hero over

and above, though including qualities normally expected and found in great kings: valour and daring, magnificence, liberality, wisdom and so on. A whole gamut of other highly desirable qualities are expected in Vikramāditya, the future ćakravarti (one who turns the wheel of empire) and lord of the Vidyādharas, and found to be present in him and displayed under great pressure: poise and purposefulness, calmness and patience in the face of intense frustration, perseverance despite the tricks of his slippery customer, the genie, who tries his best to foil the hero's best attempts to fulfil Kṣāntiśīla's need for the corpse. The genie has the most commendable reasons for what he does but the hero has not a clue to it. Most important is the absence of sheer rage or even passing impatience in Vikramāditya over the repeated failure of his mission as *he* understands it given his ignorance of the truth of the matter; and the unwavering determination he displays to carry a mission undertaken to its bitter end at whatever cost. Without a murmur, the king simply walks back to the śinśipā tree and goes through what he has done before. 'The king went back once again to the same place . . .' A simple statement of fact expressed more or less in the same words in tale after tale, to indicate the repetition of the same act. No emotion is conveyed; the king does what he has to do, quietly, with no fuss.

Such qualities as these are found sadly lacking in the other king, Gandharvasena, the father of Vikramāditya. Enraged by a trivial incident, the intransigent silence of an anchorite which he misinterprets as an affront to his royal dignity, not understanding the silence to be an essential part of the anchorite's vows, King Gandharvasena sets in motion a train of events that sows the seed of evil and brings death into his world, and by extension, danger to the whole world. His son redeems this parental wrongdoing.

Vikramāditya is first presented by Śivadāsa as the embodiment of ideal kingship (frame story p.13). Is he truly what he is cried up to be? Or is what is said of him simply what bards always said of the monarchs they served? That has to be tested and established beyond all reasonable doubt, for the fate of the world and its peoples hangs on it. Vikramāditya is tried and tested and found true, nothing wanting.

When Vikramāditya passes the test successfully, and only then, does the genie impart to him the truth about the yogi Kṣāntiśīla and his nefarious plans and instructs him in the means to thwart Kṣāntiśīla's evil designs.

The nature of the task laid (literally) on Vikramāditya's shoulders is the meanest, most despicable imaginable for one so great. Highest of the high in the land, 'the jewel among kings', Vikramāditya is asked to perform the lowest of the low menial acts—carrying a corpse on his shoulders that even the hangman would do only out of necessity and with abhorrence. Yet, Vikramāditya does this unquestioningly, without a murmur.

The task is specifically designed to humble and chasten the magnificent monarch. It places him in a situation that he has never been in before. It opens his eyes to realities that he has never known before. It is one thing to face enemies of flesh and blood in person in battlefields with their ambience of glory and wild excitement, with trumpets blaring and drums resounding to the skies, great warriors on prancing horses and gilded chariots, swords glittering and pennants flying, following their magnificent monarch and bards singing his praises. It is quite another matter to walk alone in the darkness of the cremation grounds, the hell on earth if there were a hell and feel the presence of faceless assailants and walk surrounded by nameless persons, real and imagined; all this and more when there was nothing in it for him. This is true heroism. It is like the sun *striding forth* in obedience to the Cosmic Law, Ṛtā, of the Vedas; and it justifies the hero's name, Vikramāditya, a name that means both the Sun of Valour, and the sun striding forth.

Each of the extant recensions of the *Vetāla Tales* concludes each and every tale with a question-answer passage followed by the disappearance of the genie and the other details already discussed. But it is only in Śivadāsa's text that these details of narrative are invested with significance and made integral parts of the narrative structure and employed to convey a vision. It is Śivadāsa's effective use and precise placement where it would have the greatest impact on the text, of the story in the preamble; the two main passages of description in the text: one, the characterization of the king, Vikramāditya, an individual ruler and the ideal of kingship, and two, the powerful description of the cremation grounds packed with epic imagery and mythic resonances that creates a scene of palpable horror; and generally the skilful deployment of language strategies in the text as a whole, that makes his work a minor classic.

VI

Śivadāsa's work, the *Vetālapañčavinśati* is a neglected work, undeservedly so.

We know nothing about Śivadāsa, perhaps not even his name. For the name under which the work goes may well be a *nom de plume,* as in the case of Kalīdāsa. What we know is what we can glean from a careful *reading* of his text.

Śivadāsa is a man of great learning, even erudition. Bits of information from various fields of contemporary knowledge—astrology (preamble, tale 2), medicine (tale 2)—quaint bits of knowledge from treatises on drama (the theory of the nāyikās, or heroines and of the ten stages of being in love, of Bharata Muni in tale 3, subtale-ii; tale 16) from treatises in the amatory arts and on feminine beauty (tale 3, subtale ii, tale 4); central tenets from Buddhist, Jain, Śaiva thought are brought in and fitted neatly into the narrative.

From such passages we might conclude that Śivadāsa wrote primarily for a certain type of reader: the gallants, nāgarikas, well-educated, cultivated, accomplished men-about-town with a keen interest in the fine arts and beautiful women, with a lot of time on their hands and plenty of money in their purses, men who were aesthetes, dilettantes, wrote poetry, painted the pictures of their mistresses, played music, danced, told stories, understood the finer points of writing. Such a readership (or audience, if Śivadāsa did narrate his tales, as he well might have done) would be familiar with tales told over and over again and would expect something a little different in the telling and the writing of the old favourites. Such a readership would look for something to titillate their jaded palates and judge the skill of the author in introducing non-fictional material into the narrative without awkwardness and with artistry. An example would be the delightful paean to the joys of chewing paan and supari and the glories of musk (p.26–27):

> Oh! For a chewy roll of paan leaf
> filled with scented supari
> laced with slaked lime and spices!

and

> Musk! Its birthplace is not a place of note,
> its hue is nothing to write home about;
> at a distance appearing to advantage,
> smeared on the body it is mistaken for mud.

One can imagine the responses to this in an 'arty' salon of handsome, young connoisseurs of literature; the approving nods of the head and amused smiles, the coy looks and giggles of the 'ladies' in the company (not wives).

Śivadāsa is not without wit and humour. The lines quoted above and the whole passage has the ring of a take-off of some contemporary poet or other. In Tale 2, there is unmistakeable irony in the verses describing the grave itemization of symptoms, prognosis and findings of a conclave of physicians summoned by the Brāhmaṇa, Keśava, to cure his daughter, Mandāravatī of snake bite. While the girl is dying, unattended, and the father is desperate to save her, the physicians solemnly exhibit their medical knowledge. There are many such passages in Śivadāsa's narrative of the *Vetāla Tales* where he is gently critical, witty and takes a shot at pomposity, pretentiousness, sanctimonious hypocrisy (Tale 17).

Śivadāsa's text has an ethical dimension as well. Like the *Pañcatantra* it is in part a nitiśāstra; it lays out the main requisites to live wisely and well. But it has less accomplishment and artistry compared to its great predecessor.

A simple and straightforward narrative
pleases some learned readers;
some, wiser, delight in the figurative—
irony, ambiguity, metaphors,
while others love a tale filled with flavours
of fine sentiments plentiful and pleasing.
So there's something here to suit every palate.

It is not an unjustified claim by the author of the *Vetāla Tales*.

Postscript

This introduction would not be really complete without the mention of the latest recension of our own times, of the *Vetāla Tales—Vikram and the Vampire*—composed by Richard Burton during the 'Indian' phase of his long and quite extraordinary career. Predictably, it is more Burtonian than Indian. Burton felt that the bare bones of the Indian narrative needed to be fleshed out. And that is just what he did. It is *his* version of a very ancient cycle of stories about Vikramāditya and a genie (not a vampire) who teased the king, taught him through telling tales, saved him and ultimately became his minister (in our version by Śivadāsa); perhaps a sort of factotum in other versions, begetting a whole host of sons in other storytelling traditions to serve other royal and not so royal masters as slaves and servants; djinns who lived in bottles, in dusty lamps and wherever else they could make a home. Then there was a change of sex. And in the fairy tale world of Hollywood, our wise and witty genie, became *Jeanie* who appeared and disappeared with a nod of her head and a toss of her ponytail. She had a bottle too in which she lived; she married an astronaut and tried hard not to tread on the sensitive corns of a rather quaint and conservative, suburban community that lived at the 'base' where her astronaut-husband worked as a guinea pig for experiments on space travel. A far cry indeed from the banks of the mighty Godāvarī. But tales do travel far and suffer a 'sea change' when they cross the perilous oceans of the world!

About the Title

Who Is the Vetāla?

The *Vetālapañcavinsatikā* of Śivadāsa is named after not the hero but the narrator of the tales, the vetāla, a being that inhabits an ancient corpse hanging from a tree at the edge of the cremation grounds.

Who or what is the vetāla? The word vetāla is of doubtful etymology, notes Monier Williams in his dictionary of the Sanskrit language. That might be because the word is non-Sanskritic in origin. There are many such words in Sanskrit that have come into the language from the other languages and dialects in India; and vice versa.

The word vetāla signifies a being, a power, or divinity that is non-Vedic, non-Brahmanic (I am using the term not for a class, but for a system of beliefs, practices and worship), even pre-Vedic in all probability.

There is a class of divine or semi-divine beings that form part of the vast collection of deities and divinities, major and minor, in Indian mythology: yakṣa, yakṣī, vidyādhara, vidyādharī and others. These were divinities that reigned supreme in the earliest times, honoured and worshipped by the first 'nations' of the land, adored as well as placated. They were symbols of the forces of nature, centres of power and plenitude in the natural world, perceived as givers of riches and prosperity, of fertility to man and beast and the land; naturally beneficent powers that could and did turn hostile and malevolent to man when he transgressed nature's holy laws, rampaging and destroying his environment. These divinities, or powers in the universe, were seen by their worshippers as indwelling spirits of woods and waters; of hills, streams, pools and trees. The existence to this day of tree worship, snake worship and the worship of streams and rivers (waters) points to the existence of these and other forms of non-Vedic, non-Brahmanic religions in the ancient times. The vetāla was one of these divinities. In one of the recensions (southern) of the *Tales of the Thirty-two-Statuettes,* referred to in the introduction, King Vikramāditya, faced by terrible portents in Ujjayini which foretold his imminent defeat and death, addresses the Vetāla who is always at his beck and call, as Yakṣa: 'Listen, O Yakṣa! Go fly over this whole earth and find out who has been born to kill me . . . .' The yakṣas, as already noted, are ancient divinities, honoured and worshipped.

Since the Vikramāditya story cycles including the *Vetāla Tales* are located in the region of the Vindhyas and the areas adjacent to it, it seems most likely that the vetāla was a divinity worshipped by the people of this area; the word probably belongs then to some language spoken by these people.

Like the yakṣa-yakṣī, the vetāla is closely associated with trees, suggesting that it was a divinity related to and controlling vegetation and fertility to whom blood sacrifices, including human sacrifices, were offered. This is a common feature of ancient fertility cults.

The vetāla, and a class of chthonic deities, generally known as bhūtas, were closely associated with Śiva and functioned as his attendants. Śiva and the mother goddess, Devī, known and worshipped under many names, Vindhyavāsinī, being one of them, are associated both with Kailāsa and the Himalayas, and the Vindhyas. Śiva is also associated with cremation grounds, corpses, skulls and all the other furniture of the cremation grounds and the symbols of death and dissolution. Śiva is the power of dissolution as well as the creation and maintenance of the universe. This two-in-one godhead unites opposing aspects in himself; creating-destroying, calm-fierce, benevolent-wild. The vetāla, as Śiva's attendant spirit, is naturally linked to the cremation grounds and corpses; and shares his master's ambivalence—helpful, beneficent, if man lives in harmony with the natural world, hostile and malevolent if, as already pointed out, nature's holy laws are broken (as Kṣāntiśīla does in the text).

Popular belief views the vetāla as a malevolent spirit, waylaying unwary persons walking near certain trees—banyan, peepul, tamarind—and in lonely places, especially if they were women, and 'possessing' them. But this is the result of ignorance, prejudice and misunderstanding. In the *Vetāla Tales*, the vetāla is not evil; he is a saviour of the hero and of the world under threat from the necromancing Kṣāntiśīla who is aiming to possess it by usurping the lordship of the universe.

The vetāla was believed to be brought within the power of a yogi, a sorcerer like Kṣāntiśīla, and controlled through spells, incantations and the prescribed rites and rituals of worship. He would then become the worshipper/sacrificer's agent, helper, and general factotum, to serve him and do his bidding in all missions, good or evil, whenever he is summoned by spells, incantations and so on. But, to possess this power, the person has to undergo severe austerities and study the lore of magic deeply under a guru after being initiated properly into the discipline. All this is but a figurative way of saying that man can control the forces of nature by acquiring a body of knowledge within a specified discipline. Whether, having acquired the powers to control the forces of nature, man uses it in a positive manner for the good of all, or negatively for purposes of exploitation and self-aggrandizement is another matter. Our author, Śivadāsa, is aware of the ethical dimensions of power and knowledge and presents the problems involved admirably in his text.

The relationship between the vetāla and the yogi suggests that something like shamanistic practices existed as part of the rites of worship of divinities like the vetāla. It is present even now in certain communities, where the god's priest functions as the person in whom the power to invoke the deity or exorcise it from any one held to be 'possessed' by the god, is invested.

Now, to come to the title, I have translated vetāla as genie.

In previous translations of the *Vetāla Tales* into English, most of these having been done in the late nineteenth century, the word vetāla has been rendered by a number of words that do not quite fit the bill: vampire, demon, goblin, spectre, sprite. One thing that the vetāla is definitely not is a vampire, a creature that ought to be left to haunt its native country, Transylvania. Our vetāla is not a man who has turned into a bloodsucking incubus with prominent canines and a penchant for young, preferably beautiful females. The vetāla is not a night owl that sleeps in a coffin during the day. Further, it is a power, not a person.

The vetāla is not a spectre either, a word defined as a ghost, an apparition, a phantom, all words that have the faint odour of mortality still clinging to them. The vetāla, on the other hand, is a force of nature and semi-divine, not a mortal.

The term sprite conjures up a rather delicate, winsome creature, a trifle mischievous perhaps, like a pixie. And the goblin is plainly a grotesque sort of creature. Vikramāditya could not have addressed a goblin as 'yakṣa'; as mentioned earlier, a yakṣa is a divinity.

That the vetāla is not a demon but an ancient divinity worshipped by the earliest peoples of the land has been argued at some length.

Since I find all these terms inappropriate for one reason or another, I have not used any of them. I have used the word genie instead for a couple of reasons. Readers are familiar with the terms djinn and genie from their reading of the *Arabian Nights*. Burton, in his translation of this famous work, uses the term jinni, which is employed in Islamic mythology for a spirit, often in a pejorative sense. In the tales from the *Arabian Nights*, a djinn or genie is summoned by the use of a spell or a special act empowered to control the genie or djinn, by a sorcerer or a person to whom the sorcerer has passed on his knowledge and powers over the genie in one way or other. A vetāla is similarly brought within the power of a sorcerer or yogi and he would appear when invoked by an incantation. But our vetāla is not the kind of abject slave like the genies and djinns of the *Arabian Nights*.

The other and more important reason for employing the term genie for the vetāla is its sonic similarity and etymological affinity to the words genius, genii (plural). A genius is a guardian spirit, an attendant spirit. Milton uses the phrase 'Genius of the shore' (Lycidas, line 181) in the sense of a guardian spirit who watched over seafarers. The term genius is employed elsewhere too in English poetry, in conjunction with other words such as spirits and daemons derived from the Greek, daimōn, meaning a divinity or attendant spirit, a being filled with divine power. The same word with the altered spelling, 'demon' has acquired pejorative meanings in later usage that it did not have earlier.

The words genius, genii, come invested with sacrality, signifying beings that possessed divine power. Therefore, the word genie seemed to me to be a better word to use for our vetāla; more appropriate, more meaningful than words such as spectre, sprite, goblin 'and all that'.

The Five-and-Twenty Tales of the Genie

(Vetālapañćavinśati)

---

as set down by
Śivadāsa

PREAMBLE

. . . *'By the seeing of him, all sins will be destroyed. Therefore, before returning home, I ought to seek his presence and pay my respects.' With this thought, he went towards the hermitage.

In that hermitage lived the hermit Valkalāśana. A thousand years had gone by since the day he made that his abode. Firmly resolved to gain the world of eternal light he sat under a nimba tree[1] performing penance, absorbed in deepest meditation. The hermit knew not what physical comfort was. Yoked to penance, his body was as a piece of wood; it did not even perform the excretory functions. At midnight, this hermit absorbed in deepest meditation, ate one single mouthful of the bark of the nimba tree. The next day, at precisely the same hour, he again ate a mouthful of the same. And in this manner, a thousand years had gone by for that hermit living in silence in the hermitage.

Now that king saw the hermit completely absorbed in deepest meditation. Watching him, the king said to himself: 'Well, the moment he comes out of his meditation, I shall bow low with reverence at his feet.'

Still mounted on his horse the king remained silent. Four watches of the day did the king keep his silent vigil. Yet, the hermit remained immersed in meditation. So the king now said to himself: 'Ah! The arrogance he displays towards me! As if to say: "This is how I am." So be it; we'll fix him.'

* The opening sections of the text are missing in the available manuscripts.

And the king returned to his capital.

Seating himself in the Hall of Audience, the king summoned the citizens and made a public declaration: 'Hey there! Is there one among you who is prepared to interrupt the penance[2] of this haughty hermit?'

The citizens listened in silence and made no reply.[3] Noting that not one single person was willing to respond to the king's call, a courtesan spoke up:

'O, king, I shall interrupt his penance. Is it anything to be wondered at that I have the power to enslave him? I shall surely make that hermit infatuated by my beauty and charm. For, whosoever in this city sets eyes on me becomes infatuated straight away. As we have heard it said:

'A pot of butter is woman,
and a glowing coal is man;
closeness makes the pot drip,
(and the harlot's paramour[4] too)
and that is just what can happen
when man meets woman.'

The king proclaimed: 'Well, my lady courtesan, listen to me; if you succeed in interrupting this man's penance, I shall grant you a village.'

'At your bidding, I shall bring him into my power,' she replied and swore an oath to that effect before the king.

She went home, made herself beautiful using sixteen different ways of adornment and set out for the hermitage. She took a look at the silent hermit; then she built herself a tiny, little hut[5] close by and waited.

From dawn to dusk, she saw the hermit immersed solely in meditation and she asked herself: 'How in the world can I bring this man into my power when he doesn't even notice me! Well, let us see. Since I have watched and waited during the four watches of the day, I may as well do the same during the night.' And she sat there in complete silence.

At midnight, the hermit who was given to silent meditation ate a mouthful of the tree's bark. And at that moment, the courtesan got a good look at the silent hermit. Instantly, the thought came into her mind: 'Aha! Now I know that I can get him into my power.' She went straight home, prepared a sweet dish of milk boiled down to the consistency of thick cream with melted butter and crystallized sugar, formed little balls of it and returned to the woods. Having placed one of these sweet balls at the base of the nimba tree, she quietly withdrew and stayed still as a mouse inside her little hut.

At his usual hour, the silent hermit took the sweet ball and ate it. And that day the hermit's tongue knew the taste of sweetness. The courtesan continued placing the sweet balls at the base of the tree and waited, ever watchful. On the third day, the hermit ate four of those sweet balls. In this way, the hermit's consumption of sweetmeats gradually increased, until it reached the count of twenty. And in time, the hermit became nice and sleek and plump; then he lost his power of meditation.

After a while, the hermit's glance chanced to fall one day on the courtesan. He fell madly in love with her. Burning with passion, he burst into verse:

'Ha! For the enjoyment of a woman!
What can give greater pleasure in this world!
No, not even the Elixir of Life!
All senses, altogether, all at once,
find in it their perfect fulfilment!'

So much of the day passed, measured out by wasted hours. Then the hermit went close to the courtesan and asked: 'Who are you?'

Covering her face with the end of her upper garment, the courtesan said softly: 'I am the handmaid of the Lord of the Immortals.[6] What would you have?'

The hermit responded delightedly: 'I have lost my heart to you. Be my wife. Here in these lonely woods we shall live happily, just the two of us.'

The courtesan demurred: 'O, what an improper request, sir! How can I consent to this? When my true home is in the Realm of Light,[7] in the presence of the Lord of Immortals, in attendance upon Him? Pray do not speak like this.'

But that love-tormented hermit repeated his plea, 'O, lady with beautiful eyebrows! Please listen to my suit.'

'Well then,' observed the courtesan, 'I guess I have to stay right here in this very hermitage of my own sweet will.' Since she had consented, the hermit created a divine mansion for her there; and in that mansion he engaged daily in lovemaking with her.

Day after day they made love and in time the courtesan conceived. Day by day she rounded out till she reached full term and a boy was born. The hermit clasped the baby to his bosom and played with him in the hermitage. The baby's urine and faeces dropped on his limbs. Ritual baths and prescribed rites such as libations of water to the gods and ancestors were not performed.

Then one day, when the child had completed his first year, the courtesan spoke to the hermit: 'Now, listen, hermit; pay attention to my words. Let us leave these woods and go elsewhere; because according to the law,[8] a householder's proper place of residence is not the woods. And furthermore, lions, tigers and other beasts of prey roam these woods. How can our child be properly protected here? We should therefore make our home in some city or other.'

The hermit agreed: 'Wherever your fancy takes you, my dear, there shall we go to make our home,' he said.

The courtesan observed: 'Perhaps you have seen my city, O hermit. So, place the cradle with the little boy in it on your shoulders and go with me to my city.'

The hermit lifted the little boy in his cradle on to his shoulders and set out with the courtesan; and walking ahead with the hermit keeping behind her, she proceeded towards Pratiṣṭhānapura and arrived at the city.

She went straight to the Royal Hall of Audience and after presenting the hermit Valkalāśana to the king, stood aside. The king observed that very same hermit now standing holding his son. And the king laughed. Then placing a finger between his teeth, the king addressed the hermit: 'Well, well, hermit, are the penances completed?' To which the hermit replied: 'O, great king, listen to me:

'Lovely face lustrous as the Lord of Stars,[9]
loins shapely as those of the Lord of Beasts,[10]
a gait majestic as that of lordly tuskers—
when such a sweetheart dwells enshrined in one's heart:

What place for prayers intoned!
What place for penance performed!
What place for contemplation!'

The king listened and capped the hermit's verse with one of his own.

'Saffron paste smoothed lightly o'er lovely limbs;
garlands of pearls trembling o'er glowing breasts;
on lotus-feet anklets make music, tinkling
like bell tones of wild geese calling:
A woman of such beauty! If she wills,
lives there a man in this world she cannot enthral?'

Hearing these words of banter the hermit flew into a rage and holding the little boy by his feet, swung him in the air and dashed him against the floor in front of the king. The child's head fell inside the palace; the trunk in a potter's house; the feet in the house of an oil merchant.

That very day the queen consort conceived and the very same day the wives of the potter and the oil merchant also conceived. At full-term three boys were born: one in the palace and one each in the homes of the potter and the oil merchant. There was great jubilation in the palace. As soon as his son was born, the king feasted Brāhmaṇas and bards with sumptuous food and presented them with fine garments and other gifts; he ordered five kinds of drums to be beaten; and summoned an astromancer to prepare the natal charts of the little prince. Having calculated the times and positions of the celestial bodies with the ghatika,[11] the astromancer drew up the charts and then declared: 'O, king, your son is born under an exceedingly auspicious zodiacal sign; five of the planets stand at the apex of their orbits. As noted in the texts:

'Sun in the Ram, Moon in the Bull,
Mercury in the Virgin Venus in the Fishes,
Jupiter in the crab; in these signs,
these five planets in elevation dwell.

'Therefore, O king, this little boy is destined for a great future. This little boy and the sons of a potter and an oil merchant in the city have all three been born the same day under the same zodiacal sign. Now hear the prediction, Your Majesty. Of these three, one will slay the other two; one alone shall remain; he will be the mighty lord of the earth. Your Majesty, signs indicate that your newborn son will display extraordinary valour at a very early age. So let him be named Vikramāditya, the Sun of Valour.'

The king listened to the prediction with great joy and presented the astromancer with cows and gold and other fine gifts. Similarly, the astromancer calculated and drew up the natal charts for the newborn sons of the potter and the oil merchant and made the same prediction: 'Of the three little boys born this day, one will slay the other two; one alone will remain; he will be the mighty lord of the earth.'

After some time, King Gandharvasena celebrated the ceremony of trimming of the locks[12] of his little son, and later, in the prince's sixth year, had the rite of investiture of the sacred[13] thread performed . . . .[14] And as the little prince was growing up, the king arranged for the education and training of his son in gradual stages in the military sciences, in sacred and secular sciences and arts, and in archery.

In the course of time, King Gandharvasena passed away. The council of ministers assembled the leading citizens and together they placed the king's body on a sandalwood pyre and cremated him. They had Prince Vikramāditya perform all the prescribed last rites[15] such as offering of oblations of balls of cooked rice and sesame seeds with sanctified water and so on. This was followed by sumptuous feasting of Brāhmaṇas.

Then the ministers fixed on a coronation date after carefully examining the day, the zodiacal sign governing that day and the auspicious time of day. They placed the mark of sovereignty[16] on Vikramāditya's forehead even though he was a young boy at the time. So, the prince was duly crowned king. The citizens paid him homage and from that day he began his rule as protector of the realm.

One day, the potter's son, sitting by his mother's side heard the events of his birth related. This set him thinking: 'Ah! I see. If the astromancer's predictions were in fact to come true, then indeed I might really become king one day. Once I manage to get rid of the oil merchant's son and kill the king, why then, sovereignty should be mine as a matter of course. It is up to me to make determined efforts for this purpose. For it is said:

> 'To lion-like men richly endowed with enterprise
> comes the goddess[17] of prosperity and success;
> "Ah! Fate is all-powerful," is the coward's refrain.

Strike Fate down; exerting your own strength and power
display manliness; if your efforts fail
though you give of your very best, what blame?

And further:

Apathy, entrenched in the body,
is indeed the greatest enemy.
Perseverance is man's best friend;
stick to it and you'll never be ruined.'

Resolved to act, the potter's son sought out the son of the oil merchant and made friends with him. Daily he plied him with many gifts. Then one day the potter's son said to the other, the oil merchant's son: 'Listen, my friend, will you go with me to the woods to gather kindling for the sacred fire?'

'Certainly, I'll go with you,' replied the other.

And the oil merchant's son went along to the woods with the potter's son. Determined to carry out his foul purpose, the potter's son drew his friend into the most desolate part of the woods and there slipped a noose round the other's neck and strangled him. He then tied a rope round the neck of the dead body and hung it on the branch of a śinśipā tree. Following a secret trail, he quietly returned to the city.

However, the citizens got wind of the matter and went straight to the king to report that the potter's son had murdered the son of the oil merchant. The king listened to the complaint of the citizens and dispatched one of the palace guards to apprehend the criminal. But out of fear of the king the potter's son fled the city and escaped to another land. The guard returned and reported: 'Your Majesty, out of fear of Your Majesty, the man has fled.'

The king, having listened to the report, instantly ordered

that the escaped murderer's house be ransacked, his possessions confiscated and his house and other properties be torn down and razed to the ground.

After this, King Vikramāditya sighed with relief, confident that now his realm was rid of thorns;[18] and he rejoiced in his heart.

FRAME STORY

Salutations to Lord Ganeśa[19]

I bow my head before Lord Vināyaka,
the remover of obstacles, the commander
of Śiva's impish retinue; and this work
I compose for the entertainment of the world.

The base never begin an undertaking
for fear of encountering obstacles;
the mediocre leave off where they begin
faced by obstacles that come closing in;
undaunted, the highest, men of great merit
never abandon what they have once begun
though hemmed in by obstacles a thousandfold.

A simple and straightforward narrative
    pleases some learned readers;
some, wiser, delight in the figurative—
    irony, ambiguity, metaphors.
While others love a tale filled with flavours
of fine sentiments plentiful and pleasing.
So there's something here to suit every palate.

In the southern lands there flourished the fair city of Pratiṣṭhāna ruled by King Vikramasena, the king who possessed armies of heroic prowess. What kind of king was he? Hear!

Blazing with the brilliance of a million suns,
dazzling-bright like flashing lightnings,
he sat on the splendid lion-throne of fabled wonder,
and by his side the band of ministers
    who held him in highest esteem.
In appearance beautiful as Love, the god
who sets the world on fire; like lord Śiva
beloved of all people; like the noble ocean
never o'erstepping the bounds set by the Law,[20]
    ever honoured by the wise and virtuous;
he shone with the cool glow of the moon and white
jasmine,
of brightest dew or camphor; stainless as purest crystal
    and the rays of the autumnal moon.
Ever bounteous, giving gifts manifold,
ever dedicated to upholding the Law
in its manifold aspects.
In anger he was like the fire at the end of time[21]
that causes the dissolution of the universe,
blazing as if lit by million lightning flashes.
His bearing was a blend of captivating charm
and abundant heroic ardour; valorous,
    he strove against all odds.
His person radiated magnificence
in a stream of scintillating rays of light.
The gladdener of a great dynasty was he.
The due care and protection of the good,
as well as the curbing of the evildoer,
was the highest duty and happiness
of this king in this world and the other.

This monarch, who was invested in full measure with all fine qualities was present at all hours in the great Hall of Audience. One day, a naked mendicant monk[22] named Kṣāntiśīla came there from somewhere or other. Holding a fruit in his hand he entered the hall and presented the king with that fruit. The king welcomed him, offering a seat and paan.[23] He accepted the hospitality and after a few moments took his leave and went on his way. In this manner, the naked mendicant monk came daily, to see the king and present him with a fruit.

One day, the fruit happened to slip and fall from the king's hand. It was broken open by a pet monkey and a ruby rolled out of it. Its lustre created a commotion in the hall, for everyone there was greatly astonished.

The king sat in amazement and asked the mendicant monk: 'Hey, ascetic! Why would you bring such a priceless gem as a gift to me?'

And the naked mendicant monk replied: 'O, great king, hear me! It is said in the learned texts:

'One does not visit a king,
a physician or preceptor,
a child or an astrologer,
    or a good friend, empty-handed.
The gift of fruit yields its own fruit.

'O, great king, for twelve years have I placed as a gift in your hand a priceless gem such as this hidden inside a fruit.'

The king, greatly surprised by these words, sent for the keeper of the royal store and said to him: 'Sir, keeper of the store, you remember the fruits that this naked mendicant monk has been gifting to me daily in the past, which I assume you have been keeping in the store-room: pray, bring them all here.'

The keeper of the store brought all the fruits at the king's command and when broken, each one was seen to contain a gemstone. The king was transported with joy. He gazed at the heap of flashing gemstones and exclaimed, 'Hey, naked mendicant monk, wherefore have you brought to me these gemstones of inestimable value, when it is not in my power to pay you the cost of even one of these gems? What is it that you desire in return for such fabulous gifts? Tell me.'

And the yogi[24] responded reciting a verse:

'Even if it be a trifling matter,
if to rulers of the earth it relates,
it should not be uttered, said Bṛhaspati,[25]
in the open assembly.

Magic spells, medicines, matters of sex,
good works, cracks and flaws in one's house and home;
forbidden foods, slander, vital secrets:
a shrewd man doesn't broadcast these to the world.

Heard by six ears, a secret breaks;
heard by four ears, it stays secure;
and not even the Creator himself
can get to the bottom of a secret
that is heard by two ears alone.

Climbing right up to the top of a hill,
going in secret to an open terrace;
in deep woods or in some spot desolate:
in such places is a secret disclosed.

'Your Majesty, I shall disclose my purpose to you in private.'

The king then dismissed everyone; and the yogī explained: 'Your Majesty, the coming fourteenth day of the dark half of the month, in the great burning grounds on the banks of the river Godāvarī, I intend to perform certain secret rites. Once the rites are completed, I shall succeed in attaining the eight great Siddhis, supernatural powers:

'To be minute as an atom,

or enormous as a mountain,
light as air or heavy as rock,
to be invisible at will,
to have all one's desires fulfilled,
to subject others to one's will
and to have lordship of the world;
know these to be the eight Siddhis.

If a brave man and steadfast were to assist,
even a weak man possessed of magic powers
could be a destroyer like Death itself.

No man appears to me so brave,
so steadfast as you; therefore I desire
to have you for my assistant
and you alone, O King.

'Therefore, pray be my assistant. Your Honour must come to me alone at night with only your sword.'

The king promised. 'Yes, I shall do as you ask,' he said. Whereupon, the naked mendicant monk left and went about the business of collecting the articles required for the special rites he was planning. On the fourteenth day, as stated, he resorted to the great burning grounds.

The king too for his part set out at night dressed in dark garments and met the mendicant there.

Seeing that the king had arrived there true to his promise, the naked ascetic thrilled with intense excitement; he then explained what had to be done. 'Some four leagues from here, O King, lies a great cremation ground where a corpse hangs from the branch of a śinśipā tree. Go there and bring back that corpse quickly. (If you speak, the corpse will return to that tree).'

The king listened attentively to the ascetic's instructions. Then that king who was unsurpassed in daring, set out towards the śinśipā tree.

Undaunted, the king reached those burning grounds
that loomed in front, in swirling smoke enveloped,
complete with a whole array of horrors;
the most hideous place imaginable on this earth.

With ramparts rising up of bones bleached white
    smeared with traces of brain;
with bloody guts and organs, and skulls
    that had served as goblets for liquor
all strewn around, littering the ground,
    it seemed Death's very own playground.

Murky with thick pall of smoke and blinding darkness,
uproarious with wild yells of spirits demonic,
thrashed by leaping whips of flames from funeral
                                                                pyres,
it seemed the black, diluvial masses of clouds,
world-dissolving, of Time, the Destroyer,
    who had risen to perform the dance of death,
whirling around decked in long, pendulous garlands
    of entrails pecked out by vultures, was there before
                                                                him.

Shaking with the riotous dance of the Pleiades
—those six mothers who had nursed the god of war—
echoing with eerie whistling of wild winds
whizzing with lightning speed through hollow tubes
of ancient bones, long-decayed;
resounding with the jangling anklets of Yoginīs[26]
                                                    moving about,
it seemed frenzied Time a bacchanalia was staging.

As space in all directions reverberated
filled with the swelling roars of defiance
    of ghoulish bandits,
it seemed as if Time, the Great Ender,

revealing himself in the form
of the Primal Sound—OM—had rung
the knell of dissolution of the triple-world.

Studded with skulls and lopped-off limbs,
decked with row upon row of skeletons
for garlands;
lit sombrely by blazing firebrands, the burning grounds
pictured a second Bhairava,[27]
the Lord's destructive power.

As well a second Bhārata war as well,[28]
its killing-fields tumultuous
with Karṇa and Śalva's[29] defiant howls;
and awesome Bhīmas[30] strutting, replaying
Duhśāsanas'[31] cruel slaying.

Unpredictable as fights with the rolling dice,
hard as women's hearts of stone;
like the undiscriminating mind
that houses hatchets of fears and misgivings
constantly hammering away at it;
such was the sight of the burning grounds.
It seemed as if it were Janasthāna[32] itself
haunted by the mighty Khara
and Śūrpanakhā, the terrible,
lurking at its fringes;

Like Daṇḍaka forests[33] in whose dark depths
Mārīća stood skulking, trembling with fear:
And Dhūmrākṣa, Meghanāda, Vibhīṣana,
Lankā's great barons, reeling astounded;
Lankā burning, Rāvaṇa himself, her demon-king,[34]
born as her tragic fate, still living:
such was the scene the burning grounds presented.

A lair for a host of sorrows it was,
invaded by mobs of ravening ghouls,
and embraced by numerous dreadful dangers;
a place of gathering for ghosts; and seen there
was a variety of ghouls, genies, ogres,
their mouths gorged with flesh,
    their faces flushed with drink.

Walking up to the śinśipā tree, the king climbed it, cut the rope by which the corpse was hanging and let the body fall to the ground. What was this corpse like?

Dark blue as a rain cloud,
the hair on its head standing erect,
goggle-eyed, no trace of flesh on its frame,
marked with the signs of a ghost,
it was a horrid sight.

No sooner had the king climbed down than the corpse was up again hanging on a branch. Again the king climbed the tree, placed the corpse on his shoulders and set out on his journey back. The corpse was possessed of a genie and as the king walked along, the genie spoke: 'Listen, O king!' it began.

'Time passes for the intelligent
in the enjoyment of poetry and martial sports;
but for the foolish and ignorant,
in sleep, mischief or vicious pursuits.
What good is good fortune[35] without discipline?
    What good is night without the moon?
Without true wisdom, what good is skill with words?

'So, listen, O king, while I regale you with a tale,' said the genie.

TALE 1

Of Vajramukuta and the Beautiful Padmāvatī

There is a great city named Vārānasī where King Pratāpamukuta reigned. His son was Vajramukuta. One day the prince rode far into the dark woods with the minister's son Buddhisena, to hunt. There the two enjoyed their passion for the chase to the fullest and at noon they chanced upon a lake. A charming lake indeed it was:

Teeming with wild geese and mallards; studded
prettily with bright-plumaged sheldrakes; overspread
with lotus-filaments and round green lotus-leaves;
covered with white lilies and red and white lotuses;
dotted with water-dwellers: turtles and fishes.
Pretty awnings of trees with thick foliage,
edgings of clumps of screw-pines embellished the lake.
Overflowing with the murmurous hum of greedy bees
drawn by the fragrance of Kadali-blossoms
and with a confused blend of bird calls,
gallinules, loons and peacocks
and partridges that feed on moonbeams;
enchanting with varied melodious sounds,
resonant with the cooing of sweet-throated koels;
thronged by waterfowls; laced by scallops of sarus cranes;
the lake presented a charming picture.

When the prince and his friend had dismounted from their horses and washed their hands and feet and faces, they noticed a little shrine. Entering it they bowed and worshipped the god. For it is said:

In travel or in battle,
with a friend or a powerful foe,
with a sage or a lump of earth,
on a bed of flowers or of rock,
on a straw mat or with a woman,
the days of my life pass alike,
prating—'Śiva, Śiva, Śiva'—
in some sacred woods or other.

In the abyss or the firmament,
in the ten directions of space,
in the skies, in the seas,
on all mountains;
in ashes, in wood,
or in clods of earth,
on land and water and air,
in the still and the moving worlds,
in the seeds of all herbs,
in the path of demon or god,
in the petal of a blossom,
on the tip of a blade of grass,
this Śiva, the great lord, All-Pervading,
abides. There is no other god.

As the prince sat worshipping the divinity, a certain lady,[36] surrounded by her companions arrived at that lake to bathe. Having finished her bath and completing the rites of worship to the goddess Gauri and other customary rituals, she was on the point of leaving when she noticed the prince. Their eyes met and they gazed intently at each other. She was stricken to the heart by Cupid's arrows, the five arrows that make a person languorous, infatuated, inflamed, passion-driven and obsessed. So was he.

The lady conveyed her feelings through mime, by means of a series of gestures. She removed a lotus from her hair and placed it at her ear; then she took it from her ear and placed it between her teeth; removing it from her teeth she put it against her heart; and then placed it under her foot. Having done this she departed. The prince sat as if dazed. Thinking of her, his whole body appeared to have become all crumpled and worn down.

The minister's son noticed him in this appalling state and asked: 'Look here, my dear friend, why do you appear so dazed? Tell me the reason.'

The young prince, reeling under love's onslaught, confided his pain to his friend. 'Ah! My dear friend, I saw a lady exceedingly beautiful by the lake; but I know nothing of her whereabouts. All I know is that only if she becomes my bride will I live; otherwise I shall surely die. This is my firm resolve.'

Listening to these disturbing words, the minister's son asked the prince: 'Dearest friend, tell me, did she say anything to you that I might ponder over and find some consolation for you?'

The prince asked rather surprised: 'And how will you know?' To which the minister's son replied:

'Even animals grasp what is clearly expressed;
spurred on, horses and elephants advance;
but what is unspoken, the scholar infers;
to make sense of hints thrown out by others,
    is the advantage the intellect confers.
By looks, by hints, by gait and by gesture,
by words one speaks and the way one speaks them,
by changes of face and eyes: by these
are known the innermost, most secret thoughts.

'So tell me what she did, whatever it might be.'

And the prince said, 'Well then, I shall describe to you the way she acted; though I myself do not comprehend any of it. She took a lotus from her head, placed it at her ear, then removing it from there, she gripped it with her teeth and then placed it next to her heart. Finally, talking it from her bosom, she put it under her feet. After acting this way she departed.'

The minister's son thought for a while and then said to his friend: 'Listen, this is what she was saying: by removing a lotus from her head to place it by her ear she was saying: "Karṇakubja[37] is the name of my city"; by gripping it with her teeth she was saying: "I am the daughter of Dantāghāta[38](Bite)"; and by placing the lotus next to her heart she was saying: "You alone are dear to me as life; you live in my heart"; by placing the lotus under her foot, she was saying: "Padmāvatī[39] (Lady Lotus) is my name".'

Having heard what the minister's son told him, the prince declared: 'If I obtain her, then I shall live; if not, I die. Get up, my friend, let us go there where she is who is dear as life to me. I shall not eat until I reach that place.'

Leaving the lakeside, the prince and his friend reached Padmāvatī's city. They stopped at the home of an old woman who lived in seclusion, a wandering female mendicant, for it is said:

A strolling nun, an actress, a wet nurse,
  a washerwoman, a neighbour:
protect your wives from these women
  for they serve as a go-between.

The prince now asked the old recluse: 'Listen, old mother, have you always lived in this city?'

And she replied: 'Yes, I have always lived in this city.'

'Is there a princess by the name of Padmāvatī in this city?' asked the prince.

'O, yes,' replied the old recluse. 'The daughter of King Dantāghāta is named Padmāvatī. I visit her daily.'

The minister's son said at the point: 'Today you should visit her.'

The recluse agreed. 'Yes, I shall,' said she.

The prince now sat down to weave a garland of flowers, while the old recluse was dispatched on some other business. And when she returned after performing her task, she took the flower garland and set out to visit Padmāvatī. Before she left, the prince said to her privately: 'Look, tell Padmāvatī this: "That young prince, whom you saw at the lake, has arrived and is living here".'

'All right, I shall tell her,' said the recluse.

The recluse now went to the palace and reported everything to Padmāvatī, though the princess had already guessed it all, by the way the flowers had been strung. However, she pretended to be furious. Dipping her hand in pale, liquid sandal, she slapped the old recluse on both cheeks. Further, she spoke severely to the old woman, saying: 'If you dare speak to me in this manner ever again, I shall kill you; now go.' The old woman was driven out.

The old woman returned to the prince crestfallen. Seeing her face, the prince became disconsolate. The old woman reported what had happened. And the prince said turning to his friend: 'O, my friend, what do we make of this?'

But the minister's son reassured him. 'Do not be discouraged; there is a reason for her actions. When the princess slapped the woman with a hand smeared with pale sandal paste, she was in fact saying: "Wait for ten days, until the dark half of the month begins."'

At the end of ten days, the old woman was dispatched once more to the princess, Padmāvatī. Seeing the old woman before her, Padmāvatī dipped her hand in a bowl of moist, red saffron, slapped the old recluse's cheek with three fingers and pushed her out. When the prince saw the old woman returning, he fell into deep despair. Turning to his friend he remarked: 'O, my friend, what is to be done now? Today is definitely the day of my death.'

But the minister's son consoled him, saying: 'Be of good courage; there is a reason here; for it is said:

'On the first day of her courses,
a woman is as good as an outcast;
on the second, a hateful murderess;
    on the third day, a woman
    who washes dirty linen;
on the fourth day she becomes cleansed.[40]

'My lord, the princess is at present in her courses; on the fourth day she will have the ritual bath that removes impurity.'

At the end of four days, the old woman was sent again to visit Padmāvatī. When Padmāvatī saw her approaching, she took a strong rope and bound the old woman, seized her by the throat and pushed her out by the western entrance.

The old woman returned in an ugly mood and reported what had happened.

The minister's son thought over this and then observed: 'My lord, tonight you should go to the princess, entering by the west gate.'

Once he had heard this, the day dragged on for the prince like a hundred, long years. It was night at last. The prince was dressed to kill and went to the west gate with his friend. There, the attendants of the princess pulled the prince up with strong ropes, while his friend returned home.

This was the prince's first meeting with Padmāvatī. They began conversing and enquired after each other's health and well-being. The prince was treated to a perfumed bath; dinner was served; fine clothes and beautiful jewels were put on him; he was rubbed with fragrant creams such as sandal, aloes and others; and after accepting scented paan to chew, the prince sat at ease on a soft, luxurious bed. He then made passionate love to Padmāvatī in four different ways.

When husband and wife, lying side by side,
bodies straight, parallel, pressed tightly together
in close embrace make passionate love,
it is known as union in 'low-position'.

The girl lying below, the man above her,
a mode well-known, practised the world over,
  is favoured by rustic lovers.

When a woman gratifies a lustful man,
riding him, it is known as the 'inverse mode',
a mode that pleases all lustful lovers.

Where a woman gratifies a lascivious man,
crouching like a beast on all fours, that mode,
bestial, pleases experts on amatory arts.

Breasts pressed tightly in close embrace,
hair on the limbs upspringing,
passion's delicious nectar outpouring,
the splendid garment slipping down her loins—
'No, don't, O giver of honour![41]
don't do this to me—enough . . .'
thus she breathes out faint syllables fading away—
What! Is she asleep? Is she dead?
Or, melting into my heart, is she lost?

Oh! For a chewy roll of paan leaf
filled with scented supari,
laced with slaked lime and spices!
Piquant and tart and tangy, sweet-and-hot,
  astringent and alkaline,
calming wind, dissolving phlegm, routing germs,
driving away foul odours, cleansing the body;

paan enhances the beauty of lips,
and briskly kindles the flames of passion!
Ha! The thirteen fine virtues that the paan has
are hard to find even in paradise, my friend!

Properly blended aromatic fillers
generate passion's glow;
nut in excess makes passion wane,
leaf in plenty diffuses a fine fragrance,
and excess of aromatic fillers
takes away the freshness of the breath.

Musk! Its birthplace is not a place of note,
its hue is nothing to write home about;
at a distance appearing to advantage,
smeared on the body it is mistaken for mud.
Even so, it surpasses in fragrance
every other sweet-scented substance.
Who truly knows the fragrant properties,
Ha! Of the real thing, essence of musk!

Having enjoyed passionate love-sport, the prince sat relaxed. Padmāvatī now put a question to him: 'So, my lord, you understood what my true feelings for you were.'

And the prince's answer was: 'Oh! I understood nothing; it was my friend who understood it all, using his intelligence.'

'Ah! Is that so? How pleased I am with your friend!' observed Padmāvatī. Then she added: 'In the morning I shall have a nice spicy dish specially prepared for him.'

Dawn broke and the prince hastened home to his friend and told him everything that had gone on at night, saying:

'She gives and she receives;
she confides her secrets and asks for mine;
she gets pleasure and she gives me pleasure;
in these six ways she shows her affection.

'And now listen to this, dear friend, she will be sending you the midday meal, specially prepared for you.'

The minister's son, having listened attentively remarked: 'O, she will, will she, my lord? Poisoned laddus[42] specially prepared for me will arrive, I have no doubt.'

Even as he made this remark, a maidservant was seen approaching, with a salver of poisoned laddus in her hands. The minister's son looked at the sweets, picked one up and threw it to a dog that was standing by. It ate the laddu and instantly dropped dead. Seeing the poor creature lying dead, the prince exclaimed angrily: 'This girl desires the death of my dearest friend! I shall not touch her with a barge-pole. Never.'

And his friend said quietly: 'Ah! My lord, listen: the lady is head over heels in love with you; it is her love that has prompted her action; for, you must have heard this:

'Parents and country, kith and kin,
riches and life itself: women
devoted solely to any one special man,
do not care a straw for such things.

And it is also said:

When one has stayed in someone's house
    and shared a meal with him,
it is only right to have good thoughts about him
    and do him good by word and deed.
The wise laud that goodwill
that is the equal of milk-and-water;
in it water becomes as milk;
that milk protects in fire.

'But why talk at such length? What I now say ought to be done at once. My lord, today at midnight, indulge in such raptures of passionate sport that it leads Padmāvatī to a pitch of fevered excitement and leaves her overpowered and languid. Then, make three marks on her left thigh with a sharp point of your nail, relieve her of her fine garments and jewels and come to meet me.'

The prince duly followed the instructions of the minister's son and taking Padmāvatī's things went to meet his friend who was sitting in the great burning grounds in the garb of an ascetic. The prince saw him,

Seated in the lotus pose, eyes barely open,
observing total silence; hair matted and twisted,
and piled high in a crescent-shaped coil adorned
by a chaplet of flowers shaped into a half moon.

The minister's son gave Padmāvatī's ring to the prince to take to the bazaar and sell. When the prince showed the ring to the goldsmiths there, they scrutinized it and exclaimed: 'What! This is one of the jewels belonging to the princess.' They took the prince straightaway to the Keeper of the Royal Treasury and reported his possession of the princess' ring.

The Keeper of the Treasury seized the prince and questioned him saying: 'Hey, you are a warrior, bearing arms. How did you come by this ornament?'

'My guru gave it to me,' replied the prince. The Keeper of the Treasury marched the prince along to where his guru was, and now questioned the guru: 'Say, worshipful ascetic! How did you come by a jewel marked with the royal name?'

The venerable sage answered promptly: 'On the fourteenth night of the dark half of the month I saw a band of yoginīs[43] marking out a magic circle[44] with red flowers and worshipping there, after which they tore a male victim limb from limb and started eating him. I picked up my trident and darted towards them. Seeing how outraged I was, they fled in all directions. However, one of them was hit by my trident on her left thigh as she fled. So terrified was she that her clothes and jewels fell off her. I picked them up.'

The Keeper of the Treasury now went to the king and conveyed to him what he had been told. The king heard the report with attention and sent for the portress of the Inner Apartments[45] and ordered her thus: 'Go to Padmāvatī's chambers, strip her and see if she has any marks on her left thigh.' The portress went at once in obedience to the king's command and examining Padmāvatī's body noticed the aforesaid marks. Returning at once to the king she reported what she had seen. 'Your Majesty, what the Keeper of the Treasury has conveyed to you is absolutely correct. But such information should not be made public; for it is said:

'Loss of wealth, rifts and dissension,
questionable conduct in the home,
matters of deceit or disgrace:
the discreet do not broadcast these to the world.'

The king addressed the Keeper of the Treasury: 'Sir, Keeper of the Treasury, you had better go to that eminent sage and ask him: "What is the proper punishment for an act such as you described?"'

The Keeper of the Treasury went promptly to the venerable fake sage and asked him the question as he had been directed. 'What is the proper punishment for an act such as you described?' he asked.

To this, the venerable fake sage gave a solemn reply:

'Cows and Brāhmaṇas are not to be slain,
nor women and children, nor one's kinsfolk;
nor those with whom we have broken bread,
and those who have sought sanctuary with us.

'In the case of women, despite the enormity of the crime committed, banishment is the only proper punishment.'

So, Padmāvatī was banished from the kingdom by her father, the king, who did so without investigating the facts of the case. The prince and his friend then mounted her upon a horse and returned with her to their own kingdom where her marriage to the prince was duly celebrated. As we have heard:

If an artifice is really well-concealed,
    even Brahmā, the Creator,
    cannot get to the bottom of it.
The weaver in Viṣṇu's guise loved the princess.

Without vigilant scrutiny do not act;
act only after full investigation;
lest you reap the fruit of bitter remorse,
like the Brāhmaṇa lady who struck her pet
    mongoose.[46]

Whatever deed Destiny has willed,
that deed will be as it has been willed;
nothing can be changed that has to be,
not even by the three-and-thirty Luminous Powers.[47]

Rāma could not see through the golden deer;[48]
to his palanquin Nahusa[49] yoked the Seven Sages,[50]
and Arjuna's mind was obsessed by the thought
of abducting the Brāhmaṇa's cow with its calf.[51]

In a game of dice, the son of Dharma[52]
staked and lost his four brothers and his queen.
At a time when catastrophe is poised to strike,
a man's judgement forsakes him, as a rule,
    even if he is virtuous and wise.

Deeply affected by the preceding events, the unfortunate king, Dantāghāta died of grief for the loss of his daughter. The mother mounted her husband's blazing funeral pyre and went straight to the world where Yama, god of death, holds his court.

Having related this tale the genie said: 'Now tell me, O, king, who is guilty of wrongdoing in this case? If knowing the answer you refrain from giving it, your heart will burst and you will die.'[53]

King Vikramāditya answered promptly: 'The king, of course, for he took a grave decision without due deliberation.'

The genie got his answer and got away, back to the śinśipā tree to hang there once again.

Thus ends the first tale in Śivadāsa's book, the *Five-and-Twenty Tales of the Genie.*

TALE 2

Of Mandāravatī and Her Three Suitors

Having bowed to the Muse, Sarasvatī,
goddess of wisdom and word incarnate,
goddess with large, lustrous lotus-petal eyes,
adorned with brilliant jewels, seated
eternally on the lotus-throne,[54]
I write.

Once again the king walked back to the śinśipā tree, placed the corpse on his shoulders and set out for his destination. As he was walking along, the corpse began his story-telling.

'Listen, O king, to this tale I tell,' and the genie began:

There is a city named Dharmasthala; there ruled the king, Guṇādhipa. A Brāhmaṇa named Keśava lived in that city. His daughter Mandāravatī, celebrated far and wide for her wondrous beauty, was ready for marriage. Three fine young Brāhmaṇas came to Keśava and asked for her hand in marriage. All three were equally qualified to be her bridegroom. Keśava became perplexed. In a dilemma, he said to himself: 'My only daughter and three suitors! To whom should I marry her? Whom should I reject?'

As he kept pondering the matter, it happened that Keśava's daughter was bitten by a venomous black serpent. Experts who could treat snakebites with spells and incantations were called in to cure the girl. But they examined her and declared: 'This maiden, bitten by a most poisonous black serpent will not live.' For as the texts state:

The fifth and ninth, the sixth and fourteenth days
of the half-month, and the eighth day as well,
are days set aside as fatal
for anyone bitten by venomous things.

For anyone bitten by a serpent,
Mars and Saturn are named unfavourable,
and eclipses as well are baleful, as pointed out
by astromancers well-versed in the texts.

Rohiṇī and Māgha and Āśleṣa,
Viśākha-Mūla-Kṛttikā and Ārdrā:
these seven stars[55] are inauspicious
for those suffering bodily hurt.

Sense-organs, lips, temples and frontal bone,
chin, throat, forehead and head and the twin thighs,
heart-navel-shoulder-belly, armpits and joints,
and the hands and soles of the feet as well:
    those stung in these spots will not live.

An old, neglected garden,
    or a cremation ground,
a lime-plastered building,
    or a burial-mound:
persons bitten in such places,
    go straight to Yama's abode.

Burning fever and sweating,
    vomiting and giddiness,
hiccups, paralysis of limbs,
    colic and loss of brightness:
these are the symptoms
    caused by a black serpent's venom.

Neck contorted, voice faltering,
wind in the belly backing up
    upward-pressing—
the patient dies, that is certain; why say more?

The Brāhmaṇa, Keśava, listened to the words of the healer and after his daughter died, carried her body to the banks of the river to perform the last rites. The three suitors came there to attend the cremation rites. One of them entered the funeral fire and perished; the second built a little hut for himself on that very spot and lived there; while the third suitor turned ascetic and went travelling to other lands.

One day, this ascetic arrived at a certain city and stopped in front of a certain Brāhmaṇa's house and asked for his midday meal.[56] The Brāhmaṇa householder said to him: 'Listen, ascetic, you have your food right here.'[57] The Brahmāṇi, mistress of the house, placed a seat for the ascetic and set food before him. As he was about to sit down to eat, the couple's little child started crying loudly inside the house. The lady of the house, the Brahmāṇi, lost her temper and picking up the child threw him into the blazing hearth.

At the sight of this devilish act, the ascetic refrained from eating. The host asked him: 'Look here, ascetic, why are you not eating?'

To this the ascetic replied: 'How can one possibly eat in a house where such monstrous acts are committed?'

The householder now went inside the house and brought forth a book. Opening the book, he recited some sacred words and restored to life that child who had been burnt to ashes. The ascetic, while watching this miraculous act of his host, the Brāhmaṇa householder, thought to himself: 'If only this book comes into my hands, I shall restore my beloved to life.' With this idea in mind, the ascetic stayed around out of sight. At midnight he quietly slipped inside the house and stole the book. Then he returned to the spot where Mandāravatī had been cremated.

The Brāhmaṇa suitor who had made that spot his habitation saw him and asked: 'Listen, friend, in your sojourn in other lands did you by any chance acquire any new knowledge?'

'Yes, I did. I acquired the knowledge of restoring the dead to life,' answered the ascetic.

'Well then, why don't you restore our beloved to life?' asked the other.

In reply, the ascetic opened his book and having recited the specific sacred words, sprinkled the dead girl's ashes with some water; and she was restored to life. The suitor who had immolated himself on the girl's funeral pyre, also stood up now, alive and well.

Now, all three suitors vying with one another for the girl's hand began arguing vehemently with their eyes blinded by rage.

Having related this tale, the genie said to the king: 'Listen, O king, tell me, whose wife should the girl rightfully be?'

King Vikramāditya replied: 'Well, listen, and I'll tell you:

He by whom the girl was restored to life,
    is a father because he gave her life.
He who died with her, is a brother,
    for he was born again with her.
But he who kept a place close to her
    and lived there,[58] is rightfully her husband.'

The genie heard the answer and was gone, back to that same place, to hang from a branch of the śinśipā tree.

Thus ends the second tale in the *Five-and-Twenty tales of the Genie* written down by Śivadāsa.

TALE 3

Of the Parrot and the Myna

I write, having bowed to Śiva, Supreme Lord,
the Luminous One, Lord of the ganas,
their stay and support; consort of Gaurī,
bright goddess, who bears on his head[59]
the holy river Gangā who rides
the sacred white bull, Nandi.

The king returned once again to the same place and slung the corpse over his shoulders; and, as he proceeded on his way the genie started to tell a tale. 'O, king, listen, I shall tell you a tale,' said the genie.

There is a city named Bhogavatī, ruled over by a king named Rūpasena. In his bright mansion lived a parrot by the name of Vidagdhachuḍāmaṇi, the crest-jewel of erudition. One day, the king asked the parrot this question : 'Sir Parrot, what subjects are you well-versed in?'

'I know all things that can be known, Your Majesty,' answered the parrot.

'Well then, tell me, is there a woman born who will be a perfect match for me as my wife?' asked the king.

'O, yes, my lord, there is,' answered the parrot. 'In the land of the Magadhas,[60] King Magadheśvara reigns supreme. His daughter, named Surasundarī will become your wife.'

And in Magadha, the princess sitting in her palace was

also talking to her pet myna, Madanamanjarī, love's flower-spray.

'Come, dear myna, tell me, is there a man born who will be a perfect match for me as my husband?'

'O, yes, Your Majesty,' said the myna. 'In the city of Bhogavatī rules King Rūpasena who will become your husband.'

Hearing the myna's words the princess became lovelorn, thinking only of Rūpasena.

As things turned out, an embassy of distinguished men had already arrived at Magadheśvara's court from King Rūpasena asking for the hand of the princess in marriage. The minister for war and peace presented them to the monarch on several occasions. The ambassadors requested the hand of the princess in marriage to their king; their request was accepted. Then on an auspicious day, King Rūpasena arrived at Magadha and the marriage was duly celebrated. The princess with her pet myna accompanied her husband back to his own kingdom. The king then placed the myna, Madanamanjarī, in the same cage with his pet parrot, Vidagdhachuḍāmaṇi.

The parrot saw the beauty of the myna and was smitten with love for her; and he said to her: 'Ah! My beloved! Let us enjoy love while fleeting youth still lasts. This is the best, the highest happiness for all living creatures in this world. For:

'Flower and fruit are superior to wood;
melted butter is finer than milk, it's said;
and oil is superior to the pressed oil-cake;
and further, it is better to choose love
    over good works and wealth.[61]

Once youth has flown, my timid one,
    life is vain, unprofitable

for sweet ladies who never know
    the joys of love offered by practised lovers.

All beings that live and breathe experience
    the carnal act of pleasure;
but it is some rare person who knows the secrets
    of the god whose weapons are flowers.

Where the make-up gets spoilt,
    adornments disarrayed,
consequent to the outpouring
    of profuse perspiration;
where indistinct sounds emerge,
    and involuntary murmurs;
where the tinkling of anklets is not heard;
    where it is not too long
    before all the senses come together
in one single experience concentrated,
    that, sweet ladies, I say
marks love's true enjoyment every time;
    and what's left out is a state of being
    that belongs in another world.'

The myna responded coldly: 'I am not one to love a man. Men are wicked; they are murderers of women.'

And the parrot retorted sharply: 'Women too are of bad conduct; they are liars who slay men; the reason being this:

'Women have innate flaws of character;
prone to falsehood, folly and audacity,
as well to deceit and cupidity;
    they are unclean[62] and ruthless.'

The king heard the two birds hotly arguing and quarreling with each other, and asked: 'Listen, you two, what is the reason for this argument you are having? Tell me.'

The myna spoke up: 'Your Majesty, men are wicked; they are murderers of women; and for that reason I shall never love a man. I can tell a good tale to prove my point:

'There is a city named Elapuram where Mahādhana, the President of the Merchant's Guild, lived. He had a son named Dhanakṣaya who married the daughter of Udbhata, President of the Merchant's Guild in the city of Puṇyavardhana. Having married her, he left her in her father's house and returned to his own city. In due course his father Mahādhana died. After that Dhanakṣaya lost all the wealth he had inherited by gambling, and his mansion as well.

'Then Dhanakṣaya decided to go to his father-in-law's house to bring his wife home. After staying for several days in his father-in-law's house, he decided to return home. He saw to it that his wife was decked out in all her jewellery, and started on his journey accompanied by her. Halfway, he turned to his wife and said: 'My beloved, listen, this place is full of dangers. Therefore, you had better remove all your jewels and give them to me.' She took off all her jewels and handed them over to her husband. And now Dhanakṣaya, with all the jewellery in his possession, also seized her fine outer garment and pushed her into a dry well overgrown with weeds. Then he took off and reached his own city.

'In the well, the lady kept sobbing and calling out for help. Fortunately, some travellers passing that way heard her cries and went close to the well. Seeing a lady in it who was weeping, they pulled her out and set her safely on the road. Sticking to that road, she turned back and reached her father's house where the whole family was surprised at seeing her return. They asked: "How is it that you have come back alone?"

'The lady replied: "On the way my husband was attacked and taken away by some robbers; they also took all my jewels. So I fled from them and came here. Whether my husband got away from them or not, I do not know; he may have been killed."

'Hearing her tale, the father grieved much and consoled his daughter.

'Now Dhanakṣaya lost all his wife's jewels in gambling. When several days had passed, he returned to his father-in-law's house. Even as he was at the door, he caught sight of his wife. His mind was in a turmoil of fear and doubts. "How on earth has she come here, when I had thrown her into a well?" he asked himself.

'Seeing him, his wife said: "Ah! My lord, do not be afraid." With these words, she led him into the house. Her father and the whole family rejoiced to see him and they greeted him.

'Dhanakṣaya spent several days there. Then one night, when his wife was sound asleep, he killed her in her bed and seizing all her jewels fled back to his own city.

'O, king, I tell you that I witnessed these incidents with my own eyes. Men are simply no good, my lord, look at it any way you like.'

Now the parrot spoke up.

'Among horses and elephants and goats,
in wood and stone and cloth,
among men and women and in waters,
there is difference—a great difference.'

The king listened to the parrot's comment and observed: 'Well, Sir Parrot, now you expatiate on the faults of women.'

'Yes, Your Majesty, pray listen,' replied the parrot.

'There is a city named Kāńcanapuram where Sāgaradatta was President of the Merchant's Guild. His son, Śridatta married the daughter of one Samudradatta, President of the Merchant's Guild in the city of Śripura. He returned with his bride to his own city. After a space of several days the bride was sent back to her father's house while Śridatta, having made arrangements to trade overseas, gathered all the merchandise needed and set out on a long journey. He was away for a considerable length of time. In the meantime his young bride was growing up in her father's home and soon she was in the first flush of youth. As it is well said:

'Budding youth lends a lovely charm
even to an ill-favoured form;
at the moment of rich ripeness
even the lime boasts of sweetness.

'The young girl used to go up to the terrace of her mansion and stand watching the royal highway. One day, she noticed a young man; their eyes met. Turning to her companion, she said: "Dear friend, listen; bring that young man here to me." The companion accordingly went down to the young man and said to him: "Listen, young gentleman, you appear to be the incarnation of the god of love himself! The daughter of Guild-President Sāgaradatta wishes to be with you in private."

'The youth agreed. "I shall meet her at your house tonight," said he. As it is said:

'The sight of a man freshly-bathed, perfumed,
clean and wholesome, makes women become moist
as an untempered jar filled with water;
    woman is a jar of melted butter
    and man the flaming energy of fire;
close to the fire the jar begins to drip;
the same happens when man and woman meet.

'The two young people met at the house of the garland-maker who was the girl's close companion. Love was born in their hearts. However, on one of the days following, the girl's wedded husband arrived at his father-in-law's house to take his wife home. Faced with the fact of her husband's arrival to take her, the girl became deeply troubled,

'"What shall I do? Where can I go?

Whom can I lean upon, alas?
No hunger nor no thirst—
no warmth nor no coolness—"

'She confided her troubled thoughts to her companion.

'There are, in life, several causes that lead to the downfall of women; they are the following: indulging in unbridled chitchat and idle gossip; possessing complete freedom permitted by the husband; undiscriminating social intercourse with men; travelling; staying at wayside places; and residing in foreign lands; ruin and disgrace of the husband; familiar contact with loose women and obsessive jealousy.

'The son-in-law had his evening meal and retired to the bedchamber where the girl was forcibly sent to him by her mother. She lay on the bed turning her face away from her husband. The more tenderly he addressed her, the unhappier she grew.

'Gestures speak of the tenderness
  the mind-born[63] god creates;
Glimpses of navel, arms, breasts and adornments,
  fidgeting with one's apparel,
binding the hair, letting it flow loose again;
arching of eyebrows, casting tremulous side glances:
  noisy sputtering, nervous laughter,
  rising from one's seat or the bed,
  stretching the limbs, and yawning,
pleading for small favours, for inconsequential trifles;
  enfolding the young bride in one's arms,
  on her upturned face kisses raining;
turning the back and throwing covert glances,
singing the praises of feature and form,
gently rubbing the ear: know these to be
  gestures of those in love:
  making of sweet speeches, offers of wealth,
singing of praises to gloss over defects—

She looks around, impassioned, she sees me—
ever-thoughtful, all disdain banished—
offering of lips and breasts, demure concealment as well,
beads of perspiration—the first advances—

'A woman cold to love and passion—
She turns away her face creased by knitted brows,
indifferent, discontent,
harbouring resentment,
she speaks harsh words, moves away impatient
of her lover's touch and gaze;
she flaunts the pride born of new-risen youth;
wipes her mouth between kisses;
leaps out of bed—[64]

'The young bride remained thus, lying on the bed with her face averted; as it is said:

'Sleep visits not the man impassioned,
even on a bed of fine silk cotton;
passion-free, he sleeps in comfort,
on bare rock, or even a bed of thorns.

'And the husband seeing that his wife was averse to his advances went off to sleep. When she was confident that her husband was fast asleep, the girl rose very quietly at midnight, slipped out softly and set out for her tryst. As she walked, she was noticed by a robber who began to wonder: "This young woman decked out in jewels—where is she headed?" And he followed her; as commonly understood:

'The woman who leaves her husband's side
and goes out of her house, elsewhere;
who sports constantly with her paramours

such a woman
is pointed out "The Wanton."

'Infatuated, she first sends a messenger,
her confidante, day after day;
and impetuous, she expressly fixes
some special spot or other for a tryst.
But alas! By a stroke of fate, she's denied
union with the man for whom she has pined.
Such a woman sage Bharata[65] types,
"The Deserted Lady."

'Unable to patiently bide her time
and wait for her messenger's return;
powerless to withstand love's feverous pain;
all a-thirst for love's delights, she sets out
greedy to feed upon her lover's lips:
Such a woman is typed by that best of seers,[66]
"The Audacious Lady."

'And that young girl's lover lay at the trysting place, dead, struck down by the royal guards under the mistaken impression that he was a robber.

'Were we to debate the merits
of lovers' union and lovers' parting,
consider the latter
infinitely better, here, in this world;
do not crave union with the beloved;
for, when my love and I are together,
she is but one, simply herself;
but, when we two lovers are parted,
she is the whole universe itself.

'And that poor girl enduring the pangs of separation

keeps embracing her lover's corpse. She will not accept that he is dead; but offers him perfumed unguents, saffron and sandal and the like, paan and supari and such other gifts of love; again and again, she kisses his lips tenderly. The robber stands at some distance watching all that is going on; and as he watches he thinks to himself.

'"She on whom my mind ever dwells,
    she is indifferent to me;
she deeply yearns for another,
    and, that other, is devoted to another;
what we plant yields fruit
    enjoyed by someone else or other.
Ah! The pity of it all! He and she,
    and Love; and this girl here and me!"

'As this was happening, a thought came into the mind of the yakṣa,[67] the Genius of the Woods, who happened to be sitting on a banyan tree there. "If I were to enter this corpse, I could enjoy sexual intercourse with this girl," thought the yakṣa.

'The yakṣa infused his spirit into the body of the dead lover and enjoyed sex with the girl, after which he bit off her nose and went away.

'The girl with her body drenched in her own blood went to her companion and narrated to her the whole train of events. The companion counselled her thus: "Listen, you had better go to your husband's bedside before it is daybreak and sit there weeping and sobbing and crying out loudly: 'Ayo! Ayo! I have been disfigured by this man.'"

'The girl followed this advice and seated beside her husband began howling loudly. Hearing the sounds of her wailing, her relatives came rushing in to the bedchamber; and what did they see but the young bride without a nose.

'Outraged they demanded furiously: "Hey! You wicked fellow! You perpetrator of senseless cruelty! What's this you have done? Why have you cut off our daughter's nose in this vicious manner when she has done no wrong?[68] Why?"

'Hearing these charges, the unfortunate son-in-law being at a loss for an answer, simply recited these verses:

'"Better trust a black serpent venomous;
or your bitterest foe brandishing a sword;
or a man whose wits are wandering:
    but trust not a woman's actions.

"Is there anything that poets[69] do not see?
Is there anything that crows do not eat?
Is there anything drunks do not babble?
Is there anything young women cannot contrive?

"Who knows, who can understand the reasons
    for the wild stampede of horses?
    And for springtime's sudden thunders?
For the failure of rains or their excess?
Or why women act or might act as they do?"

'The girl's family went straight to the royal halls of justice and handed over the son-in-law to the presiding magistrates who delivered their judgement: "This man is sentenced to capital punishment." As the unfortunate man was on the point of being taken to the place of execution, in came the robber and said emphatically to the magistrates: "Listen, honourable sirs, Royal Justices, hear me. This man does not deserve to be punished." He then explained by retailing before the justices the entire sequence of events of that night.

'The magistrates heard him and having duly deliberated over the case, set the son-in-law free; they also pardoned the robber. As it is said:

'The proper fostering of the virtuous,
and clear chastisement of villains,

this is the highest duty of rulers
in the worlds of the here and the hereafter.

'The proper protection of his subjects
is the ground and aim of Law for a king.
He who fails to protect goes straight to hell:
hence, it is imperative that subjects be protected.

'The fire that blazes up from the heat
of burning anguish of subjects,
not leaving unburned, the king's sovereignty,
his glory, noble dynasty,
and even his life, bring them all to an end.

'As for the young girl, she was mounted on a donkey[70] and chased out of the city.'

The parrot Vidagdhachuḍāmaṇi now concluded his tale with this comment: 'Your Majesty, this is how women are.'

Then those two birds, tellers of tales,
both shed their earthly forms as birds;
transformed into two Vidyādharas,[71]
shining with light, they straight ascended[72]
to the abode of the thirty-three gods.[73]

Having told this tale, the genie now asked: 'Tell me, O king; who is more prone to commit evil (man or woman)?'

And King Vikramāditya replied at once:

'Woman, and she alone deserves censure
here in this world of ours; not men, never,
for men are directed to and instructed
    in matters of good and evil.

The propensity for evil exists in greater measure in

women, whereas men are rarely guilty of serious wrongdoing.'

Hearing the king's answer, the genie left; it went back to that same śinśipā tree to hang there.

Thus ends the third tale in the work entitled the *Five-and-Twenty Tales of the Genie* by Śivadāsa.

TALE 4

Of Vīravara,[74] the Noble Warrior

I bow to Thee, Lord Ganeśa,[75]
mounted on a mole; great-bodied,
elephant-headed god,
Commander of the Ganas;
and Destroyer of Obstacles.

Once again the king took down the corpse from the śinśipā tree and slung it across his shoulders. As he was on his way to his destination, the corpse began a fresh tale. 'Listen while I regale you with a tale,' said the genie.

There is a great city named Vardhamāna where King Śūdraka ruled. Once he was seated in the Great Hall of Audience. Turning to the chamberlain, the king said: 'Sir Chamberlain, pray go and check if anyone is waiting outside the door to see me.' The chamberlain replied:

'Dripping with perspiration, soiled, covered with dust,
sadly lacking support, having no refuge,
here stands a host of supplicants at the door,
resembling patient oxen, O, godlike lord.'

Another day, a princely warrior from the southern land, named Vīravara, arrived at the Hall of Audience seeking employment with the monarch. He gained an audience. The king asked him: 'O, princely warrior, what order of payment do you expect per day?'

'Your Majesty, I expect to be paid one thousand gold coins per day,' replied Vīravara.

'How many elephants, horses and foot soldiers do you have to maintain?' asked the king.

'Your Majesty, we are only four; I, my wife and my son and daughter. There is no fifth body to maintain.'

Hearing Vīravara's words, all the personages present in the hall, princes, great warriors, heroes and ministers laughed. And the king reflected: 'I wonder why this man asks for such a large sum of money. On the other hand, this huge largesse might yet yield fruit some day, who knows.'

So, the king summoned the royal treasurer and gave him instructions: 'Give this man, Vīravara, one thousand stamped gold coins from the royal mint each day.'

Every day, after receiving his daily salary, Vīravara first distributed gifts to gods and Brāhmaṇas, to bards, strolling players, storytellers, dancers and those who put on shows, to the indigent, to the blind, and lame, to lepers and hunchbacks and all other supplicants; and only then did he sit down to eat. At night, sword in hand, he stood guard outside the royal bedchamber. In this manner when each night the king called out at midnight: 'Ho! Who is there at the door?' Vīravara always answered signifying his presence on duty. There is a well-known saying that runs like this:

Thus do the rich play with their retainers
consumed by hopes of advancement, calling out to them—
'Come here,' 'Go hence,' 'Fall down,' 'Get up'
'Speak,' 'Be quiet,' and so on.

He eats, but eats not in comfort,
he speaks, but not as he pleases,
unsleeping, he is not awake:

A servant! Does he truly live?

His own views he has to keep to himself,
he follows the bent of another's thoughts,
he has himself sold his body; so then,
where is there happiness for a servant?

Dumb through silence, yet, he is eloquent,
garrulous perhaps, idle chatter dispensing.
Timid from practising excessive caution,
disagreeable if displeased,
presumptuous when he is close by,
forgetful at a distance;
inaccessible indeed is the nature and practices
of those who serve others,
even to yogis with far-seeing, magical powers.

One day, at midnight, King Śūdraka heard the piteous sounds of a woman weeping in the burning grounds. Curious and concerned, the king called out: 'Who is there at the door?'

Vīravara answered at once: 'Your Majesty, I Vīravara, am here.'

'Hey, Vīravara, do you hear the sounds of some woman weeping?' asked the king.

'Yes, I do,' replied Vīravara.

'Well then, go to her and ask her why she is weeping. And return quickly and inform me,' ordered the king. As the well-known verse says:

A man is expected to know these well:
the servants he dispatches on missions;
his kinsfolk when there is a dire need of them;
    a friend at a time of distress;
the wife when faced with loss of rank and wealth.

Accordingly, Vīravara, following the direction of the sounds, set out for the burning grounds. And King Śūdraka, remaining incognito, followed him on that road mantled in darkness. There, in the burning grounds, he saw a woman weeping; her hair was floating loose and she was adorned with brilliant jewels.

There she was, dancing and leaping about,
gliding softly, then darting forwards,
weeping in sorrow immeasurable,
piteously, not shedding a single tear.

'Woe is me!' she cried, 'Oh! What misery!
What sort of sinful being can I be!
How my limbs shake and shiver repeatedly!
My whole frame, every single part of it,
trembles, convulsing uncontrollably!'

Beholding her, Vīravara asked: 'Who are you lamenting so woefully here?'

'Royal Glory am I,' she answered.

'If you are Royal Glory, why are you weeping like this?' queried Vīravara.

And she answered: 'On account of the displeasure of the goddess, on the third day, the king will be gathered to his forefathers; and I, I shall be widowed having lost my lord. I weep for this reason.'

'Is there a way, some means or other, whereby the king might live to be a hundred years?' asked Vīravara.

Royal Glory answered, 'O, king's man, if you sever the head of your son with your own hand before your tutelary goddess[76] and offer her the sacrifice, the king will live to be a hundred.'

When Vīravara heard this he set off immediately for his home. He woke up his sleeping wife and told her everything.

'And she, the wife with large lustrous eyes*
blessed with all womanly virtues and beauties,
possessing dignity and fortitude;
modest, with a gracious manner
and natural sweetness of speech;
mother of heroes, high-born, most beautiful,
possessing a deep navel winding inwards,[77]
full, firm breasts closely-set, fine thighs
tapered like an elephant's trunk—

'They are sons who are devoted to the father,
he is a father who cherishes his sons;
he is a friend in whom trust is reposed,
she a wife who provides peace and happiness.

'A disciplined son; learning valued for its own sake,
good health and the company of good friends,
a gentle wife who provides pleasant conversation:
these five pull sorrow out by its roots.

'Parting from the loved one, family disgrace,[78]
debts left unpaid, serving the wicked,
friends who turn their backs seeing one needy:
these five don't need the aid of fire to burn the body.

'Insolent servants, a miserly king,
knaves for friends, an ungracious wife:
these four are sharp darts that pierce one's head.

'Unburdening the heart to friends whose hearts are true,
confiding cares to a faithful servant,
and to tender women; telling one's troubles
to a master close to one's heart, a man finds relief.'

---

* The author does not clearly state who is speaking here—it could be the author, the narrator or Vīravara.

Why say more?

'For the sake of the king, subject am I now
to Death's dominion; that is most certain;
so, go, gracious lady, seek sanctuary
with father and brothers, O best of women!'

The wife answered thus:

'The father offers a measure,
measured is what a brother gives,
the son too offers a measure;
but a husband gives beyond all measure.
What woman will not honour her husband?

'What have I to do with a son?
My family, my kith and kin?
Neither father nor mother, but only you,
O, my lord, you alone are my sanctuary.

'A faithful wife am I, my lord,
and never shall I leave your side;
a husband is a woman's sole sanctuary;
this is the Law from time immemorial.

'A woman is not sanctified
by charitable works;
nor even by the observance
of religious fasts;
a woman becomes sanctified
by unswerving devotion to her husband.

'She is known as a truly faithful wife
who never forsakes her husband,
be he blind or a hunchback or a leper,
be he diseased or beset by misfortunes.

'This duty that I have thus spoken of
is the highest path a woman can take.
Women who follow any other way
go straight to the infernal regions.'

After hearing his mother's words, the son spoke up: 'If by my being slayed the king will be assured of a life of hundred years, what are we waiting for?

'Were the mother to feed her son poison,
or the father to sell him for gold,
the king takes all,
so why bemoan one's fate?'

For her part the daughter also expressed what ought to be. All four, having reflected well, proceeded to the shrine of their tutelary deity. The king well-concealed thought to himself:

'Each mind shapes its own thoughts, its own feelings;
whatever is going to be brings its own means as well.'

Vīravara stood before the Great Goddess, offered due worship, seized his sword and with the words: 'O, glorious goddess! By this sacrifice of my son, may the king live to be a hundred,' struck off his son's head and let it drop on the floor. Seeing her brother lying dead, his daughter drew her dagger and plunged it into her belly; and the mother killed herself. Vīravara looked down: his family was gone. He reflected thus: 'All of them, all three are gone forever. What reason is there for me to serve the king for a thousand gold pieces a day?' He then drew his dagger and severing his own head, let it fall on the floor.

The king, having witnessed the deaths of all four of them, thought to himself: 'For my sake this whole family has been destroyed. What use is my kingdom to me now?

'In a kingdom there is great unhappiness
    caused by anxieties over peace and war;
where fear of even one's own son is present,
    what happiness can empire hold?'

King Śūdraka drew his dagger and was on the point of severing his own head when the goddess spoke: 'My son, Śūdraka! I am pleased with your daring; ask for a boon.'

'Glorious Goddess! If you are pleased with me, pray grant that all these persons lying dead be restored to life,' pleaded the king.

'Be it so,' said the goddess.

The four dead persons were then restored to life by means of the Elixir of Life brought from the underworld.

Still unnoticed, the king returned to his palace. Vīravara went home with his family.

Next morning, at dawn the king was in the Hall of Audience; and Vīravara appeared there once again. The king asked him: 'Hey there, Vīravara, did you go out last night and investigate the reason for that woman's weeping?'

Vīravara repeated this verse in reply:

'By virtuous acts[79] does a man find
a master, generous and forgiving,
who appreciates the merits of another.
A retainer upright and accomplished,
who protects his king at all costs
    is hard to find, my lord.'

King Śūdraka gave half his kingdom to Vīravara. As the well-known saying goes:

Kings speak once; sages speak once;
    maidens are bespoke once;
these three are spoken once only.

Having related this tale, the genie put a question to the king. 'Tell me, O, king, of all these characters whom would you regard the most noble?'

'Why, the king, of course, he is the noblest of them,' answered King Vikramāditya.

'And why is that?' queried the genie.

'Servants give their lives for their masters; masters do not give their lives up for their servants. Because the king held his kingdom as a thing worth less than a bit of straw, and was prepared to give up his life, he is the noblest of them all.'

The genie got his answer and went back to the śinśipā tree to hang there once again.

Thus ends the fourth tale in Śivadāsa's *Five-and-Twenty Tales of the Genie.*

TALE 5

Of the Beautiful Mahādevī and Her Three Suitors

I bow to Pārvatī's son, awesome god,
Leader of the Ganas,[80] Dispeller of Fear,
pot-bellied, pendulous-lipped, elephant-eared.

Once again the king took down the corpse from the branch of the śinśipā tree and laying it across his shoulders proceeded on his way to his destination, when the corpse began his storytelling. The genie said: 'Listen, O, king, I shall tell you a story.'

There is a famous city known as Ujjayinī,[81] where King Mahābala ruled. His minister for peace and war, Haridāsa had a daughter, Mahādevī, who was very beautiful. She had reached the age of marriage. The father spent anxious days wondering how to find the best bridegroom for his daughter. And Mahādevī came up to him and said: 'Dear father, please marry me only to a man who is well-endowed with fine qualities.'

It happened that about that time, Haridāsa, the minister for peace and war was sent on a mission to the court of the sovereign of the southern lands.[82] He reached the capital and was granted an audience by the sovereign of the southern lands. The emperor said to him: 'Listen, Haridāsa, give me some description of the Kali Age.[83] And Haridāsa said:

'The present time is the Age of Kali:
men of truth are hard to find,
countries by excessive taxes are wasted,
kings are given over to grasping greed;
Gangs of robbers roam plundering the earth,
fathers fear to trust their own sons:
    Alas! It is an evil age.

'Passion for cruelty, proficiency in untruth,
dishonouring the virtuous, miscarriage of justice,
    indulging in rude behaviour,
    dishonesty even in revered preceptors;
graceful and charming talk to your face,
    censure and calumny behind your back;
in these many ways are manifested
    the powers of the great King of the Kali Age.

'The Law languishes in exile,
penances totter and fail,
Truth flees far, far away.
Earth's abundance is on the wane.
Kings are crafty and crooked,
Brāhmaṇas seized by lust and greed,
men are absorbed in dalliance with women,
while women are flighty and fickle;
texts sacred and secular float and drift
in different directions, in opposing contrarieties.
The good man is despondent
while doers of evil rise and flourish.
Such is the state of the world.
when Kali enters the stage.'

And there in the capital of the southern empire, Haridāsa was met by a Brāhmaṇa who requested him thus: 'Pray, give your daughter in marriage to me.'

Haridāsa replied: 'Sir, I shall marry my daughter only to

a man who possesses pre-eminent qualities.'

'Ah well; I possess inestimable qualities,' replied the suitor.

'Show me; give me proof,' remarked Haridāsa.

The suitor then displayed a chariot that he had made with his own hands, and said: 'Listen, this chariot travels in the sky and takes you to any place that you think of.'

'Oh, well then; come to me tomorrow morning with your chariot,' said Haridāsa.

The suitor went next morning in his chariot to Haridāsa as directed. Both of them then mounted the chariot and reached the city of Ujjayinī.

In Ujjayinī itself, a certain Brāhmaṇa came to see Haridāsa's son and pressed his suit for Mahādevī. 'Give me your sister in marriage,' he said.

'Sir, my sister shall be given in marriage to a man fully blessed with excellent qualities, not to just anyone,' replied the brother.

'I am versed in the arts of magic,' remarked the suitor.

'Well then, I shall give my sister in marriage to you,' said the brother.

Some time later, a certain other Brāhmaṇa went to see the mother and he requested the lady: 'Pray give your daughter to me in marriage.'

The mother provided the same answer. 'She shall be given in marriage to a man fully blessed with fine qualities; to no one else.'

'I am an expert archer who can shoot and hit any object by the mere sound even if the object is not within sight,' said the suitor.

'In that case, my daughter is yours,' replied the mother.

And thus, all three suitors were assembled in Haridāsa's residence and now they discovered that the girl had been promised to each one of them. All three were disconsolate, thinking: 'This is indeed some situation! Three suitors and one bride! How will this be sorted out?'

That very night, that girl of incomparable loveliness was carried away by some ogre to the Vindhya mountains.

Sītā,[84] exceedingly lovely
was by Rāvaṇa[85] abducted
from excessive pride;
from excessive magnamity
Bali[86] was bound into captivity:
excess invariably brings ruin in its wake.

In the morning the three suitors met at Haridāsa's house. The magic worker among them was asked a question. 'O, scholar in the magic arts, can you ascertain correctly what has happened to the maiden?'

He picked up a piece of chalk and did certain calculations. Then he said: 'An ogre has carried her off to the Vindhya mountains.'

The second suitor who was an archer who hit his target following the sound, spoke up: 'I shall kill that ogre and bring the maiden back.'

The third suitor now offered his chariot: 'Take my chariot, friend, and fly in it to save her.'

The archer mounted the chariot and flew off to the Vindhya mountains where he shot and slew the ogre and brought the maiden back safely.

The three suitors now began arguing hotly as to who should have her as his bride. The father was plunged into anxious thought: 'All three have been of help in her rescue; whom shall I give my daughter to in marriage? Whom can I reject?'

Having told this tale, the genie asked the king: 'O, king, tell me: of these three suitors, whose bride should the maiden be?'

'His, naturally, who slew the ogre,' replied King Vikramasena.

The genie demurred: 'But . . . . listen, all three suitors were equally well suited to be her bridegroom. Why do you pick the archer as the best bridegroom for the girl?'

The king answered the question thus: 'The other two men, the one versed in magic and the other in practical science were merely tools, helpers for the archer; how well it is said:

'Even the gods are wary of a man
in whom these six virtues are found:
firm resolve, daring and courage,
strength, intelligence and heroic valour.'

Having gained the answer to his question, the genie got away and hung once more on a branch of the śinśipā tree.

Thus ends the fifth tale in the *Five-and-Twenty Tales of the Genie,* set down by Śivadāsa.

TALE 6

Of the Young Bride Who Switched Heads

I bow to the God of Wrath, Ganeśa,
who bears a form awe-inspiring,
most majestic; Destroyer of fears,
Kindler of terror, Bestower of bliss.

Once again, King Vikramāditya took the corpse down from the śinśipā tree and slinging it across his shoulders started on his journey back. And as he proceeded, the corpse began its storytelling. The genie said: 'Listen, great king: I shall tell you a story.'

There is a city by the name of Dharmapurī; its king was named Dharmaśīla. He built a shrine to the goddess Ćandikā[87] and in front of the shrine a quadrangle and in its middle, a sacred pool. Daily the king offered due worship to the goddess before he touched a morsel of food. His minister said to him: 'Your Majesty, listen to what I have to say:

'Empty is the house where there is no son,
empty are the directions of space
    unpeopled by kinsmen;
empty is the mind of the ignorant;
    and to the poverty-stricken,
the whole world is one vast emptiness.'

The king heeded the words of his minister and began

to chant the praises of the goddess:

'Hail, hail to Thee, Luminous One!
    Ruler over Luminous Beings!
Adored by Brahmā, Viṣṇu and Indra![88]
    Gracious mother born of Śiva's body!
Hail to Thee! Source of Fortune and Prosperity!

Victory to Thee, O, goddess sublime!
Who is worshipped with blood-sacrifices!
Who joyfully accepts sacrifices!
Who wears the form of Time!
Who is wrathful as Time!
Dark Night! I bow to Thee.
Mounted upon a throne held up
by those noble who are now dead,
You are the very manifestation
of Śiva's awesome aspect;
Mantled in skins, adorned with skulls,
fierce goddess, four-faced[89] I bow humbly to Thee.

Goddess whose legs are straight and long
    as lofty palmyra-trees!
whose stupendous frame is stripped of flesh!
Devourer of flesh!
With hair streaming upwards
and eyes like blazing meteors,
goddess, patient, forgiving, I bow to Thee.'

The goddess was propitiated with such chants of adoration. And she spoke: 'O, best of monarchs, I am pleased with you. Ask for a boon; anything your heart desires.'

'If you are pleased, grant me the blessing of a fine and virtuous son,' said the king.

The goddess declared:

'You shall be blessed indeed, O, king,
with a son of great might and heroic valour.
Worship in my shrine with an oblation,
with flowers, incense and sandal salve,
with fine silk cloths and gold as best as you can.'

Thus spoke the goddess; and these things the king faithfully performed. A son was born to him. All the people came to have their ritual bath in the sacred pool and worship the goddess. And the goddess granted each one of them the wish they cherished in their hearts.

One day, a young prince from some neighbouring kingdom came to Dharmapurī with his friend to worship at the shrine of the goddess. As the prince sat there after duly worshipping the goddess, his eyes fell upon an uncommonly beautiful maiden, the daughter of one of the princes of the blood royal. He fell passionately in love; his mind was in a turmoil and he prayed to the goddess:

'Luminous One! Glorious deity! If I can only win this maiden as my bride, I shall offer worship to you with my head as oblation.'

Having sworn a sacred oath to this effect, the young prince returned to his own city, where he passed that whole day in torment. His friend went to the king and acquainted him with the condition of his son. The king then went straightaway to the city of Dharmapurī to the lovely maiden's father and asked for her hand in marriage to his son. The father consented and the young prince came to Dharmapurī. The marriage was celebrated; the bridal couple returned home.

Several days after the wedding, the young prince set out for Dharmapurī, accompanied by his bride and his friend, to visit his father-in-law. On the way, he came upon the shrine of the goddess. He said to his wife: 'My darling, stay right here for a brief while with my friend while I go inside the shrine and pray to the goddess.' He left her there and went inside. Taking his dagger out of his belt, he severed his head and dropped it on the floor before the goddess.

After a few minutes, the friend said: 'He has been gone a while; it is time for him to return; let me go in and check.'

As soon as he entered the shrine, the friend saw the prince there, lying dead. And at once he thought to himself: 'If I should now turn and go back I shall be accused by the world of killing the prince to get his wife.' Troubled, he severed his own head then and there.

The young bride waited; she wondered anxiously: 'Where have these two gone?' She entered the shrine and what did she see but two headless bodies. She was quick to arrive at her decision. 'Well, let me also die.'

She made a noose with one end of her upper garment and was about to kill herself when the goddess spoke:

'Daughter, no, do not commit a rash deed. I am pleased with your courage. Ask for a boon.'

'Glorious lady!' pleaded the young bride, 'If you are truly pleased with me, grant that these two men may live again.'

'Daughter, join the heads to the bodies, quickly,' ordered the goddess.

Hearing the divine words, the bride was in a flurry of excitement and joined her husband's head to the friend's trunk and placed the friend's head on her husband's shoulders. Both men stood up, alive and well, and started an argument over her.

Having related this tale, the genie said: 'Tell me, O king, whose wife is the lady now?'

King Vikramasena replied:

'Of all medicines, food is the best;
of all liquids to drink, water is the best;
    of all objects to enjoyment,
    woman is pre-eminent
    of all the body-parts,

the head is pre-eminent.'

The genie heard the king's answer and bolted, back to the śinśipā tree, to hang from its branches.

Thus ends the sixth tale in the *Five-and-Twenty Tales of the Genie* set down by Śivadāsa.

TALE 7

Of the Beautiful Tribhuvanasundarī, Beauty of the Triple World and Her Suitors

In contest or quarrel,
at the start of a journey
or cultivation of lands,
and at entry into any place,
remember Lord Vināyaka
think upon him with total devotion.

Once again, King Vikramāditya took the corpse down from the śinśipā tree, slung it across his shoulders and started walking. As he went along, the corpse began its storytelling. The genie began:

There is a fair city named Ćampakā, ruled over by King Ćampakeśvara. His queen was named Suloćanā and they had a daughter named Tribhuvanasundarī who was in the first flush of youth, ready for marriage.

Soft-spoken and steadfast,
smiling whenever she spoke,
never harsh or cruel,
attentive to the words of her elders,
modest and decorous;
blessed with natural beauty, sweetness and charm,

possessing dignity and courage,
lettered and accomplished, she was
the best among beautiful young women.

All those who were kings or princes on the face of the earth, wrote the praises of the princess on strips of silk cloth and presented them to her. Her father, the king, asked her: 'Dear daughter, does any one of these suitors please you?'

'No, dear father. Among all these suitors, I cannot find a single one who pleases me,' replied the princess.

'In that case, you should have a svayamvara,[90] our traditional ceremony of self choice for princesses when out of many kings and princes gathered in an open assembly, a princess makes her choice of a husband,' suggested the king.

'No, I will not have a svayamvara,' said the princess decisively. 'Choose for me a husband who has these three qualities, dear father: beauty, strength and learning.'

Four suitors from different countries came to Ćampakā, hearing about the resolve of the princess and the conditions she had laid down for a suitable husband for herself. They were brought into the Hall of Audience. To each of them, the king addressed this question. 'Tell us of your virtues and qualifications.'

One of the suitors said: 'In one single day, I can take in hand[91] five villages. One I shall give to Brāhmaṇas, one I shall dedicate to the gods, a third one I shall give to my kinsfolk and a fourth to my wives; the fifth I shall sell and use the proceeds for my food and flowers, paan and so on. In fighting battles no man can come remotely close to me. As for personal appearance, you see that for yourself.'

The second suitor now spoke: 'I understand the language of all creatures, of those that live on land or in the waters. In strength no man can come remotely close to me. As for my personal appearance, it is here before your eyes to see.'

The third suitor made his claim: 'I am well-versed in all the sciences; in strength no man can come remotely close to me. My personal appearance is for all to see.'

Finally, the fourth suitor spoke: 'I roam sword in hand; in battles I am invincible. My personal appearance is for the world to see.'

The king listened carefully to all their claims; he was lost in thought, perplexed. 'To whom shall I marry my daughter? All four of them possess the three qualities that she specified.' The king turned to his daughter and asked her tenderly: 'Dear daughter, whose wife would you like to be?'

The princess remained silent out of bashfulness.

Having related this tale, the genie said: 'Tell me, O, king, whose wife should the princess be?'

King Vikramasena replied: 'She ought to marry the Kṣatriya,[92] because he would be of the same warrior-class as herself.' For it is said:

> A wise man marries a high born maiden,
> even one ill-favoured, of his own class;
> not a woman of a lower class
> however beautiful she might be
> marriages are right between equals.

But the genie demurred: 'But the suitors are all of equal merit; why do you say that the princess should be the bride of the Kṣatriya?'

King Vikramasena explained: 'The suitor who would settle five villages in a day, is a Śudra; he who knew the speech of all living things is a Vaiśya; the third suitor, the learned scholar is a Brāhmaṇa. Therefore the Kṣatriya, the warrior, ought to marry the princess.'

Hearing the king's answer, the genie got away, back to the śinśipā tree to hang once again from its branches.

Thus ends the seventh tale of the *Five-and-Twenty Tales of the Genie,* set down by Śivadāsa.

TALE 8

Of King Gunādhipa's Gratitude

I bow to Bhāratī,[93] Word Incarnate,
who holds the lute and the book in her hands;
by her infinite grace is gained
unfailing eloquence of utterance.

Once again the king returned to the śinśipā tree, took the corpse down, laid it across his shoulders and started on his way back, when the corpse began once more its storytelling. The genie began:

There is a fair city named Mālavatī where King Gunādhipa ruled. A princely warrior from some distant land came once to the palace gates seeking employment in the king's service. Day after day, he walked on the paths of the pleasure gardens attached to the palace, but not once was he able to have a sight of the king. The money he had brought with him was spent during the course of the year during which he waited to see the king; the retainers who had accompanied him went away; he was left alone.

One day, the king went hunting and rode far out miles and miles. His retinue took another path. And right in the middle of the dense forest, the king found himself all alone. He had lost his way. 'How am I going to find my way back to the capital?' he reflected.

While he was lost in anxious thought, the needy Rajput prince who had come seeking employment, suddenly stood there before the king, bowing low.

The king asked in surprise: Hey there, brave Rajput, how did you get here?'

The prince replied: 'Your Majesty, I came in hot haste following your horse on foot.'

'Why do you appear so weak and dejected?' asked the king.

To this question, the prince replied with these verses:

'That we did not obtain our cherished wish,
is no fault of yours, great lord!
But the fruit of my own past ill deeds.
If the owl cannot see in the daylight,
is that any fault of the sun,
the god wreathed in golden rays?

'Springtime comes to green the groves of śāla trees:[94]
But, if the trees do not put forth leaves,
    is spring to blame?

'On the other hand, perhaps the attainment of prosperity is not in the cards for the poor.

'While I was as yet in the womb,
He who provided the milk, means,
    to sustain my infant years,
    is He asleep? Or dead?
That He provides me no means of livelihood?

'Good fortune dawns, and all flock to serve the man.
Once good fortune sets,
then most of these turn enemy.

'Far, far better is it to drink
the deadly poison that instantly kills,
than face the twisted knitting of brows
    of men with enormous wealth.

'Familiarity with young boys,
laughing for no good reason,
arguing with women,
serving despicable masters,
using rough and rude speech, riding an ass:
these six things bring a man into disrepute.

'Occupation, wealth and the span of life,
learning, the time and mode of death as well:
these five are determined for any man
while he lies yet in the womb.

'Service in the employ of a good master will in the long run bring its own rewards.'

The king remarked: 'Listen, good Rajput, I am famished.'

'Your Majesty, there seems to be no way of getting food anywhere here,' observed the Rajput. But from somewhere or other he managed to get two ripe Āmalaka fruit[95] which he gave to the king to eat. The king ate these and was satisfied.

'Now show me the way back to the capital, good Rajput,' said the king. And the Rajput guided the king through the forests. The king reached his capital and straightaway took the Rajput into his service and furnished him with fine clothes and jewels.

On a certain occasion, the Rajput was sent to the coast on business by the king. As he was sailing, he saw in mid ocean, a shrine of the goddess. There he saw a lady who was leaving the shrine after completing her worship of the goddess. He followed her. The lady turned and enquired: 'Gentleman, why have you come to this place?'

'I am here smitten by passion and wish to enjoy love's pleasure,' he answered.

'Well then, bathe in this sacred pool and enter my palace,' said the lady.

No sooner had he entered the pool than he found himself

back in his own city. He went to the king and related all the events in detail. The king then exclaimed: 'Let me go to that same place and see for myself.'

The king accompanied by his retainer, the Rajput, travelled to the ocean's edge and saw the shrine of the goddess. At that moment, the lady arrived at the shrine with her companions. When the lady had worshipped the goddess and was about to return to her palace, she saw the king and with him the retainer she had met before. She fell deeply in love with the handsome king and spoke to him in great tenderness: 'O, king, I am yours to command. Whatever you ask of me, whether it is proper or improper, I shall do it.'

'Well then, if you will heed my words, lady, then become the wife of this man, my retainer,' replied the king.

And the lady answered: 'O, king, I am passionately in love with you; how can I become this man's wife?'

'Remember what you said to me,' observed the king; 'You said this, my lady: "I shall do your bidding, even if it happens to be something improper." If you honour your word, then do my bidding: marry my retainer.'

She had to accept. Then and there, the two were married according to the Gandharva rites.[96] The king, with his retainer then returned to his own kingdom.

Having related this tale, the goblin asked a question: 'Tell me, O, king, between these two, the king and his retainer, whom do you consider the nobler man?'

'The retainer,' replied King Vikramasena.

The genie demurred: 'Why do you say this? Why, is not the king more noble when he had the chance to marry a fairy princess but gave her up and handed her over to his retainer as his bride?' exclaimed the genie.

'No,' replied the king. 'He who rendered assistance first, he is the nobler man.' As it has been said:

If the noblest among benefactors

performs a good and noble deed,
is that something to be applauded?
But, if someone who has cause to do harm
performs a good and noble deed
the virtuous praise him as noble.

Hearing these words, the genie went back to hang on the same branch as before.

Thus ends the eighth tale in the *Five-and-Twenty Tales of the Genie* set down by Śivadāsa.

TALE 9

Of Madanasenā Who Kept Her Vows

With supreme devotion having bowed
to the Muse mounted on a swan
and obtained Her gracious benediction,
I now narrate this tale.

Once again the king returned to the same place and took the corpse down from the śinśipā tree. Having slung it over his shoulders, he set out on the road; the corpse began its storytelling. The genie began:

There is a great city known as Madanapuram where King Madanavira ruled. In that city lived a merchant prince named Hiraṇyadatta who had a daughter called Madanasenā. One day, during the Spring Festival, she went with her companions to the great groves in the city, to amuse herself with her favourite sports. As it happened, the young merchant Dharmadatta, son of Somadatta, also came to those groves with his friend. When he saw the lovely Madanasenā, his heart became deeply disturbed with intense emotion. 'Ah! If only this maiden would become my wife! How fulfilled my life on earth could be!' he thought.

The night passed with the greatest difficulty as he lay tormented by not possessing the maiden he had fallen in love with. Next morning, at daybreak he resorted to the very spot in the groves where he had seen her previously. And there she was, alone, all by herself.

He took her right hand[97] and spoke earnestly: 'If you do not consent to be my wife, I swear I shall give up my life right before your very eyes.' For, as the poet says:

On your brow blazes this jewel[98]
shaped like an arrow's tip;
drawing taut the curved bow of your eyebrows,
I know not, fair maiden, whom you plan to strike.

O, what unprecedented art is this!
The archer's art, of that most glorious Power!
The god who wildly churns all hearts and minds;
whose arrows go straight to the heart
hidden deep within, piercing it;
but leaves the body whole, without a mark.

Madanasenā replied: 'Five days hence, the young merchant, son of the merchant prince, Āmadatta, is to wed me.'

Dharmadatta now burst out: 'I shall take you by force.'

'O, no, no, do no such thing; a virgin am I; you will be guilty of a serious offence if you touch me,' exclaimed Madanasenā.

'Nobly-born men do not force themselves
on a girl who in modesty
upholds her family's honour,
even if the breath struggles in their throats.'

To this appeal Dharmadatta replied:

'Why! Were there not beauteous women,
celestial, lotus-eyed, in the Realms of Light?
That its ruler, Indra, should seek out and force
Ahalya, Lady of Penances?
When Passion's fire blazes

in the heart's little hut of straw,
who pauses to weigh what is right, and what is not?
None, not even the wisest of men.'

'Ah! If such be the case, pray wait awhile. On the fifth day from today, my wedding will be celebrated. After the ceremony, I shall come straight to you. Only then shall I enjoy the embraces of love with my wedded husband.' And Madanasenā swore an oath to this effect.

When Madanasenā had given him her solemn promise, Dharmadatta released her. She returned to her own residence and he to his.

On the fifth day after this meeting, Madanasenā's wedding was duly celebrated. When her husband put his arms round her later that night, she stopped him.

'Why? Is there some reason for your not wanting me?' asked the bridegroom anxiously.

'Listen carefully to my words,' she replied. And she disclosed everything that had taken place when she was still an unmarried young girl.

'Well, if this is so, then go to him,' said the bridegroom.

As she was on her way to meet Dharmadatta, a robber saw her. The robber was overjoyed seeing this young girl, walking all alone; and he thought to himself: 'Ah! What a piece of luck! Now I shall grab all her jewels.' He addressed Madanasenā:

'Where, O, where are you going,
O, lady with beautiful thighs?'
'Where he lives, my heart's beloved,
dearer to me than my life.'

'You walk alone, tell me truly,
sweet maiden, are you not afraid?'
'Not at all, for Madana, Love himself,
with his feathered arrows, walks beside me.'

And Madanasenā apprised the robber of the preceding events. The robber let her pass in peace; he told himself: 'Oh, how could I even think of depriving her of her jewels when she is on her way, beautifully dressed and adorned, to meet her beloved, Dharmadatta, eagerly waiting for her in his bedchamber!'

When Madanasenā arrived at Dharmadatta's place, he looked at her in wonder and exclaimed:

'Ah! What do I see? Whom do I behold?
A Yakṣinī, genius of the woodland,
or else a Gandharvī, an aerial nymph,
one of the band of musicians to the gods?
A Kinnarī, spirit of woods and hills,
or Suresvarī, celestial lady?
A nāga maiden perhaps, a mermaid?
The daughter of some great sage,
or Siddha, perfected being
possessing superhuman powers?
Are you a nymph who flies by night?
Or Vidyādharī, a fairy
who assumes forms and shapes at will?
Are you an Apsarā, born of the waters
who dances in the hall of the immortals?
Or some wondrous creature that walks on earth?
    Or, are you a mortal woman?
Who you are, gracious lady, I cannot tell,
    or where you come from.'

To this Madanasenā replied: 'I am Madanasenā, daughter of the merchant-prince Hiraṇyadatta, the same girl whom you met once in the depths of the great groves; whom you seized by force; which act brought about the making of a solemn promise by her. I am that girl, now here. Though married, I have come to you. Do with me as it pleases you.'

Then Dharmadatta asked her: 'Did you mention all the

circumstances of our meeting to your wedded husband?'

'I told him everything,' she answered.

Dharmadatta then said:

'Adornment of the body unattired!
Eating a meal without melted butter!
Singing without sweetness of tone!
Making love without loving!
Oh! How absurd indeed!

'She loves you passionately,
and takes your all!
She loves you not, she is cold,
but she plagues the life out of you!
Oh! Women! Impassioned or passionless,
they are a trial and a tribulation indeed,
are they not?

'Any act that is audacious,
or unpredictable,
any act that is forbidden
or indecorous;
count on women to do just that:
where there are grounds to feel nervous,
how can you find pleasures amorous?

'At heart she is all poison no doubt,
outwardly, her appearance and conduct
ravishes the heart.
I say this in all sincerity
that young women, by nature,
are akin to the gunja berry.[99]

'They speak vivaciously with one man,
but look with amorous interest at another;

deep within the recesses of their heart, however,
they think upon and pine for yet another.
Who, in fact, is truly beloved
of any young woman?

'What is within the mind does not reach the tongue;
what is on the tongue comes not into the open;
what is openly said, they do not act upon:
strange indeed are the ways of women.

'The discerning and the intelligent,
the disciplined and the learned,
even the wise counsellor to kings—
like a puppeteer, women control these men,
make them act, the she-devils,
through continual practice perfecting their art.

'At the Beginning, the Creator did form
four ways, four expedients;
no fifth way did he create,
the way that young women follow.

'Oh, but why do I have to go on and on, at length? Suffice it to say this: "I shall not touch another man's wife."'

Madanasenā having heard his words, left quietly and on her way back stopped and related everything to the robber, who, commending her highly, let her go unmolested with all her jewels intact, to her husband's side.

Madanasenā related everything that had happened, in detail, to her husband; and then embraced him tenderly. As it has been said:

'Sweetness of tone is a koel's[100] true essence and beauty;[101]
Faithfulness is a woman's true essence and beauty;

Learning is the true essence and beauty of those ill-favoured;
and forgiveness the true essence and beauty of ascetics.'

Having narrated this tale, the genie said: 'Tell me, O, king, which of these three men is the most noble?'

King Vikramasena answered promptly: 'Why, the robber of course; he is the most noble.'

'Why? For what reason?' the genie questioned.

The king replied: 'Listen, the husband let Madanasenā go freely under the impression that she had given her heart to another man; the other man let her go free, out of fear of the king's justice; but the robber, what reason had he? None at all. Therefore, he is the noblest of the three men.'

Having heard the king's answer, the genie rushed back to hang once again from the branches of the śinśipā tree.

Thus ends the ninth tale in the *Five-and-Twenty Tales of the Genie* set down by Śivadāsa.

TALE 10

Of Three Very Delicate Queens

I bow to the Supreme
possessed of Infinite Powers,
The Ground of Creation wherein are upspringing
all the seeds of the universe,
That stands firm upholding the trident.[102]

Once again, the king went back to the same śinśipā tree, hauled the corpse down and placed it across his shoulders. As he walked along, the corpse began its storytelling. The genie began:

In the Gauḍa lands, there is a city named Puṇyavardhanam, ruled by King Gunaśekhara. In his palace lived the minister, Abhayachandra, a Buddhist votary. He initiated the king into the doctrines of Buddhism. All other beliefs and rituals and ceremonies such as the worship of Śiva, of offerings to the Wishing Tree,[103] gifts of land, gifts of gold, oblations to the ancestors, immersion of the bones of the dead in the river Gangā, and all other kinds of gifts and offerings whatsoever, were all completely dispensed with by the minister. The minister then addressed the king, thus: 'Your Majesty:

'Let the essence of the Teaching[104] be heard;
And heard, let it be reflected upon;
Whatever is contrary to one's well-being,
let that not be done to others.

The body is impermanent,
and greatness does not endure.
Death is forever present,
What the Teaching lays down ought to be done.
Brahmā-Viṣṇu-Maheśvara[105]—the Trinity,
they are not passion-free,
nor are they All-knowing;
they act according to earthly instincts:
love and hate, pride and anger, greed and folly.
By the gift of sanctuary one becomes
invincible, gracious, gentle,
a giver, an experiencer,
a treasure-trove of glory,
unblemished and long-lived.

There *is* no happiness in this world
and never had been or ever will be
that equals the happiness felt instantly
in giving sanctuary to living beings.

Those by whom the days, blade by blade of grass,
even leaf by leaf
are made to tremble, constantly in fear
and those too, by whom living things are
tormented—
Who more pitiless than they!

Those who slay a beast even as it holds
the grass between its teeth, such villains as these
who indulge in acts of depravity,
are they any better than wild tigers?

The impious who nourish their own flesh
with the flesh of other creatures
shall eat of their own flesh and that alone
when they are fallen into the lowest hells.

Those who inflict pain on living beings
even as they watch these writhing
in pain unendurable in these three worlds,
will themselves suffer all that pain.

Birth after birth will he be born
deaf or blind, maimed, dwarfish, diseased,
or full of sores, or a eunuch;
or brief will his life be on earth.

If ancestral spirits are gratified
only by feeding Brāhmaṇas well,
then, one man could be well-nourished, could
he not,
by melted butter ingested by another?

If giving gifts, or giving up a son,
frees a father of all his sins,
then, one man could gain Final Release, could
he not,
through the good conduct of another?

If a dead man becomes happy for a long time
because his bag of bones reaches Gangā's stream,
then, the tree burnt to ashes
should put forth green leaves if sprinkled with
water.

Drink! It drives out shame and wealth,
ruins the family, deranges the mind,
razes virtue, plunges people down headlong,
induces negligence, impairs memory,
destroys skills and learning, drives out cleanliness:
drink has a thousand, crooked, evil ways;
who on earth with any sense will take to it?

Never has there been an evil

greater than taking to drink,
nor shall ever be;
Never has there been any good
better than giving up drink
nor shall ever be.

Flesh does not grow from the ground,
it does not grow on trees, nor in the grass;
Flesh grows out of the procreative force;
therefore, flesh should not be consumed.

He who creates, he who destroys,
he who slays creatures, he who eats,
he who teaches, he who is taught,
these six are entitled to an equal share.'

Why speak at length? By sententious sayings as these, was the king initiated into the Buddhist teachings by the minister, Abhayachandra. Then, robbers and other evil men infested the kingdom, harassing the people. In the course of time the king went to his heavenly abode and his son, Dharmadhvaja became king. He soon drove the minister, Abhayachandra, with his whole family, out of the kingdom. The kingdom then became free of thorns.

On some occasion or the other, during the Spring Festival, the king emerged from the palace accompanied by the ladies of the inner apartments and resorted to the pleasure groves. A large lake came into view. As one of the maids in attendance plucked a lotus from the lake and presented it to the chief queen, the flower fell on the queen's feet and bruised them. Moonbeams falling on the body of the junior queen caused her skin to come up in blisters. The junior most queen having heard the sound of a pestle pounding in a house in the distance, began to suffer pain in her hands.

Having narrated this tale, the genie said to the king: 'Tell me, O king, of these three queens, which one is the most delicate?'

'Why, the queen who suffered pains in her hands, of course,' replied King Vikramasena.

Having heard the king's answer, the genie went back to the same śinśipā tree to hang there.

Thus ends the tenth tale in the *Five-and-Twenty Tales of the Genie,* set down by Śivadāsa.

TALE 11

Of King Janavallabha and His Fairy Bride

Having bowed to the Grandfather[106]
and the Great Lord,[107] I tell a tale
most interesting and curious
never told before.

Once again the king went back to that same śinśipā tree, took the corpse down ad bearing it on his shoulders started on his way, when the corpse began its storytelling. The genie began:

There is a city named Guṇapura, where King Janavallabha ruled. His minister was Prajnakośa who had a wife named Lakṣmī.

Once, the king began to reflect thus: 'What is the use of ruling a kingdom when it leaves no time for enjoying the company of beautiful women?' He, therefore, entrusted the burden of governing the kingdom to his minister, Prajnakośa, and spent his days without a care.

One day, when the minister had reached home after work, his wife observed: 'Why lord, you look worn out these days.'

'Night and day my time is taken up by the cares of government while the king spends his time in dalliance with beautiful women,' replied the minister.

'Why don't you take leave of the king saying that you are going on a pilgrimage?' suggested the wife.

The minister took his wife's advice and taking leave of the king, set out on a pilgrimage. As he sat by the seashore after worshipping at the holy site of Rāmeśvaram, he saw a wondrous tree rising from the waves. It had roots of gold; its branches were studded with rubies and fully covered with coral-sprouts. On top of this tree was a lady radiantly lovely, seated on a divan with down-filled cushions and she held a lute in her hands. She was chanting a triplet of verses:

Whatever seed a man sows, good or bad,
    in the Field of Action,
that will he always reap there itself,
    as fixed by Fate.

The entire world with all its orders of creation,
gods, demons, mortals, is dependent on Fate;
so, with every effort that a man makes,
let this thought be constantly borne in mind.

Whatever men have earned in former lives
    be it good or bad,
that alone is the cause of the spinning out
and drawing in of all creatures.[108]

Having chanted these verses, the lady disappeared with the tree in that very same spot into the waves. The minister marked this marvel. He then turned back and reached his own land. There he bowed to the king and then spoke deferentially:

'What is inconceivable may not be told
unless one has seen it with one's own eyes.
    If a monkey can sing songs,
    even the lower stone can grind.[109]

The monkey's prowess lies

in leaping from bough to bough.
But should he leap across the great ocean,
he is surely the source of prowess itself.'

Then he narrated to the king the events of his recent wondrous experience. No sooner had the king heard it all than he entrusted the burden of governing the kingdom to the minister and set out all alone for the seashore to worship at holy Rāmeśvaram.

He reached Rāmeśvaram and having worshipped there he sat by the seashore. Soon, he saw the Wishing Tree rising out of the waves with the beautiful lady seated on it. The moment he saw the tree, the king hastened to climb it and descend into Pātāla,[110] the underworld. The lady now asked him: 'O, hero! Why have you come here?'

'Tempted by your loveliness, I have come here to enjoy it,' replied the king.

And the lady replied: 'Well, then, if you undertake not to make love to me on the fourteenth day of the dark half of the month, you may marry me.'

'I promise,' said the king.

And with these words he made her his bride.

The fourteenth night of the dark half of the month now arrived. 'Listen, king; tonight you should not come near me,' warned the lady.

The king agreed. Then drawing his sword he stayed hidden in that same chamber. As the king was watching, he saw an orge coming towards the lady. The orge swallowed the lady. Seeing that, the king rushed out shouting: 'Hey! You vile ogre! You Slayer of Women! Where do you think you are going? Come, come and do battle with me.' For, is it not said?

We should be afraid so long as the thing
    we fear is yet to come;

Once it is here and faces us
the thing to do is to strike undaunted.

Drawing his dagger the king dispatched the ogre and pulled out the celestial lady from the ogre's stomach.

'Well done, O, hero!' exclaimed the lady. 'You have rendered me invaluable assistance.' As it has been said:

Emeralds are not had in every hill in sight;
pearls are not gained from every tusker[111] in sight;
sandal wood does not grow in every other grove;
noble men are not found by every hedge.

The king asked: 'Why is it that every fourteenth day of the dark half of the month an ogre comes and swallows you up?'

She replied: 'My father is a Vidyādhara. I am his dearly beloved daughter, Sundarī by name. My father would never have his meal unless I was there. One day, I failed to be by his side during his mealtime and in a rage he cursed me with the words: "On the fourteenth day of the dark half of the month, an ogre shall swallow you whole."

'I pleaded with him saying: "Dear father, you have laid a curse on me; pray bestow your grace on me."

'My father relented and said: "When some mortal, a heroic warrior comes and kills the ogre, you shall be released from the curse."

'Today is the day of my deliverance and presently I shall go to my father and kneel at his feet.'

The king made a request. 'If at all you value the help I gave you, then come with me first and after seeing my capital and my kingdom you may go to visit your father.'

'Be it so,' she said and with these words she led the king into the waters of a pool through her magic powers and submerged in the pool they both arrived at the capital of the king's realm.

The minister on seeing the king arranged for the city squares and markets to be festively decorated and held a great celebration.

With the full bodied sound of the five kinds of drums,
with minstrels singing songs of praise
and bards reciting ancient tales;
with the six different kinds of music
and the auspicious tones of Vedic chants,

all the citizens came to greet the king with auspicious tokens in their hands.[112]

After several days had passed the lady addressed the king, saying: 'Listen, O king, I am going to my father's place to pay my respects to him.'

And the king answered: 'By all means, go there.'

The lady meditated upon the magic spells she knew, but could not remember them.

The king remarked: 'What is the reason for your failure to call to mind the specific magic spells?'

And she replied: 'Having been a divine woman, I have now fallen into the human condition with my thoughts centred on human concerns. For that reason my magic powers have failed me.'

The king, hearing her words was transported with joy. He ordered a second celebration to be held in the city. As the festivities commenced, the minister, Prajnakośa, died, broken-hearted.

Having related this tale, the genie asked the king a question: 'Tell me, O king,' he said. 'Why did the minister die the moment the festivities in the capital commenced?'

King Vikramasena promptly replied, reciting these lines:

'A man of wholly virtuous conduct,

proficient in all the fields of knowledge,
long-suffering, having conquered anger;
a man contented and persevering,
one self-restrained, a liberal donor;
  a philosopher, illustrious;
a speaker of truth and self-possessed;
a man with a well-ordered mind,
one who acts above all
without a trace of self-interest:

'To such a minister, a king ought to be beholden, always.' And the king continued:

'The minister, Prajnakośa reflected: "Where a king is totally devoted, heart and mind, to his queen, and takes no thought for his kingdom, the subjects are helpless, orphaned; and the realm itself goes to rack and ruin. As the saying goes:

Pitiful is a man unlettered,
pitiful is conjugal love without offspring,
pitiful are subjects unsupported,
  pitiful too a realm anarchical."

'With these thoughts the minister died.'

Having heard this, the genie was gone.

Thus ends the eleventh tale in the *Five-and-Twenty Tales of the Genie* composed by Śivadāsa.

TALE 12

Of the Royal Priest Who Lost All

Having bowed in reverence to Sarasvatī,
The Word, rising from the Ocean of Nectar,
wreathed in garlands of billowing waves,
    I here arrange this tale.

Once more the king went back to that same śinśipā tree and hauled down the corpse. As he settled it on his shoulders and started walking, the corpse commenced its storytelling. The genie began:

There is a city named Ćūdāpura, ruled by a king named Ćūdāmaṇi. The Royal Priest was one Harisvāmi, son of Devasvāmi. In looks the Royal Priest was as handsome as Love, the dolphin-bannered god; in learning he was another Bṛhaspati, Preceptor of the Gods; in wealth he was Vaiśravana, the Lord of Riches himself. He wedded the daughter of a certain Brāhmaṇa. She was as beautiful as one of the daughters of the gods and her name was Lāvaṇyavatī, the maiden with the loveliness of lustrous pearls. They loved each other deeply.

Once, the couple were sleeping on the terrace of their mansion on a summer night. Seeing Lāvaṇyavatī sleeping naked, some Vidyādhara or other flying in the sky became enamoured of her beauty and swooping down, he picked her up in his arms and took her to his own palace in his aerial chariot.

When Harisvāmi awakened from sleep and sat up, he could not find his beloved wife. 'Where is she? Who has taken her away?' With such thoughts seething in his mind, Harisvāmi went searching in the entire city, but there was no trace of his wife. He returned to his mansion. He gazed on the empty bed, grieving and lamenting. 'O, my darling! O, faithful wife! My heart's beloved, dear as life to me! Abandoning me, where have you fled? Speak to me! Reply me!' Lamenting in this manner he fell down.

> 'Go, go, gentle breeze
> where my beloved is,
> caress her, then come, caress me.
> breathing that air, I shall live
>   until I see her again.'

Having lamented like this, Harisvāmi turned his mind to something else, the renunciation of the world.

> For many, for the most part,
> there is only one of two ways:
> Fine garments,
> or the holy man's patched old gown;
> a girl in hand, young and blooming,
> or, prayer-beads by Gangā's waters rippling.

'What use is this vain and profitless life of mine. Shall I therefore resort to a sacred ford, a place of pilgrimage and starve to death? Or shall I undertake austere penances?' thought Harisvāmi.

Having come to a decision, he put on the dress of an ascetic and left his home. As he was walking along, at noon, he reached some city or other. Making a bowl of palāśa leaves he went begging for alms. He entered the house of a certain Brāhmaṇa and called out: 'Give me alms.'

Oh! What a sorry turn-about!
Once, the two syllables, 'nā-sti,' 'nā-sti,'
—it is not, it is not—were, learnt and repeated;
now, it has come to saying two other syllables
—'de-hi,' 'de-hi'—'give me,' 'give me.'

A man struck a blow by Fate, does not give,
he does not eat or drink,
disoriented, he gathers things,
one thing after another:
just as a daughter, one's flesh and blood,
is really meant for another;
just as wealth in the house of a miser
is really hoarded for another.

The Brahmāṇi, the lady of the house, placed a portion of rice cooked in milk with butter and candied sugar in his leaf-bowl. Accepting the alms, Harisvāmi went to a pool nearby. He placed the leaf-bowl in the shade of a banyan tree there and went to wash his hands and feet in the waters of the pool. In a hollow in that banyan tree lived a large snake and the venom from its jaws dripped into the bowl of rice and the ascetic, Harisvāmi, inadvertently ate the poisoned food. As soon as he had eaten, Harisvāmi went into the Brāhmaṇa lady's house, shaking in all his limbs and unsteady. He exclaimed: 'Ha . . . ha . . . You have fed me poison, lady; I shall die presently.'

Even as he spoke these words, Harisvāmi dropped dead at the door of the Brāhmaṇa's house. The master of the house flew into a rage and threw his wife out, crying: 'Begone! Begone! You, murderess of a Brāhmaṇa!'

Having narrated this tale the genie asked his question: 'Tell me, O king,' he said, 'who bears the guilt of Brāhmanicide?'

King Vikramasena replied: 'Ah! Who is to blame? Listen,

I'll tell you. A snake bears venom in its jaws according to the laws of nature; therefore no guilt attaches to him, does it? The Brāhmaṇa lady, good-hearted offered the Brāhmaṇa good food, honouring him. So is she guilty of wrongdoing? No. The Brāhmaṇa ascetic ate the poisoned food unawares. Therefore, what can he be guilty of? Nothing. The guilt, therefore lies squarely on the head of the man who spoke so rashly, without thinking, without going into the matter.'

Hearing the king's answer, the genie went right back to the same śinśipā tree to hang from its branches.

Thus ends the twelfth tale in the *Five-and-Twenty Tales of the Genie* set down by Śivadāsa.

TALE 13

Of the Merchant's Daughter Who Loved a Robber

Salutations to Śambhu, the Beneficent,
    The Kernel of the Universe,
who maintains the world, who dissolves it,
who is the composer of the Cosmic Drama[113]
    and its stage manager.

Once again the king went back to the śinśipā tree, took down the corpse and as he slung it across his shoulders and started walking, it began its storytelling. The genie began:

There is a city named Ćandradarśanam, ruled by a king whose name was Raṇadhīra, steadfast-in-battle. In this city lived the merchant-prince Dharmadhvaja, banner-of-virtue. He had a daughter named Kṣobhinī. So beautiful was she that even the sun was enamoured of her. Growing up in beauty in her father's mansion, Kṣobhinī reached womanhood.

At that time robbers roaming around in the city nights, disturbed the peace. The leading citizens got together and petitioned the king: 'Your Majesty, the city is going to rack and ruin on account of the robbers.' The king heard their complaint and said, 'This problem will not continue any longer.' He detailed chariot after chariot of mounted guards to patrol the city at night. Even so, the city was not free of the menace of robbers. The citizens were in an uproar. So the king reassured them saying: 'I shall myself be at the centre of the city today at midnight and all alone I shall move around the streets.'

Later that night, as the king kept a lone watch moving around the centre of the city, he noticed a man. The king called out: 'Hey, fellow, who are you?'

'I am a robber,' answered the man; and he in turn questioned the king: 'And who are you?'

'I too am a robber,' was the king's reply.

The robber observed: 'Why, this is a piece of good luck, indeed. We two shall plunder the city together tonight.'

Having tramped through the city all night, the king went outside the city walls at daybreak with the robber and entered a well and reached a mansion underground. The robber left the king posted at the door and went inside. Then a servant girl belonging to the robber's household came out of the mansion and noticing the king standing there, exclaimed: 'My lord, what brings you here to the home of this evil-hearted man? Go quickly from this place before you meet your death here.' The king said: 'But I do not know the way out.' The girl then showed him the way and the king returned to his capital.

The next day, the king gathered his whole army in full battle and surrounded the well. The robber emerged from the well and slew large numbers of the king's men: warriors mounted on horses, warriors riding in chariots and foot soldiers as well. Then the king challenged the robber to single combat by wrestling and threw him down with great difficulty and then too only by resorting to a feint. The robber was bound fast with ropes and brought to the city where he was marched right round the city to the beat of drums that heralded an execution, and then led to the place of execution to be impaled. The whole city watched this, with people standing on their terraces and rooftops and murmuring: 'Look, look, this is the mighty robber who plundered our city.'

The daughter of the merchant prince Dharmadhvaja was

also watching. She saw the robber and fell violently in love with him. She went to her father and pleaded: 'Dear father, go to the palace, offer the king all the wealth you possess and get this robber released from royal custody.'

The merchant was aghast and he spoke severely: 'Listen, this robber destroyed the royal forces; he plundered the city; how can you think that the king will let him go?'

To this the girl replied: 'Dear father, if you will not have this man set free, I shall die.'

Hearing these terrible words, the poor merchant went to the palace and petitioned the king: 'Your Majesty, I offer you one hundred thousand pieces of gold if you will only set this robber free.'

'What?' exclaimed the king. 'This man plundered my capital; he destroyed the flower of my army; and here you are asking me to set him free; how can I do that?'

The merchant prince came back and told his daughter: 'The king will not set the man free.'

News of this came to the robber's ears. Learning of what had transpired, he first wept bitterly; then he laughed loudly; then he dropped dead.

When the merchant's daughter learnt that the robber was dead, she had firewood brought and a funeral pyre built. She sat on the pyre with the body of the robber on her lap and as she gave the order to have the pyre lit, the mother goddess appeared in the sky and spoke: 'Daughter, I am pleased with your daring. Ask for a boon; whatever your heart desires.'

The girl replied: 'Great goddess, if you are truly pleased with me, then restore this robber to life and let his body be whole, unblemished. And let him be my husband.'

'So be it,' said the goddess. The Elixir of Life was fetched from Pātāla, the underworld, and the robber restored to life. He married the daughter of the merchant prince and took her down to his mansion in the underworld.

Having narrated this tale, the genie said to the king: 'Tell me, O king, why did the robber at the moment of death first weep and then laugh? What is the reason for such behaviour?'

King Vikramasena promptly replied: 'Well, I know why the robber wept; the thought that passed through his mind at that point was this: "How can I ever repay him who was ready to give the king all his wealth to save my life?" He wept for that reason. Why did he then laugh? I know the reason for that too. He was thinking: "Mark! A woman's whim and her determination! Even at the moment of death, she is in the grip of passion!" As it has been rightly said:

'A man lacks all distinction, yet, Lakṣmī,
Goddess of Wealth and Beauty comes to him;
A man may be a knave, vile and churlish,
yet, Sarasvatī, Goddess of Art, is his;
women take pleasure in undeserving men;
Indra, the storm-god pours rain on the mountains.

'Who has seen or heard of these:
cleanliness in a crow, truth in a gambler;
patience in a snake, friendship in a king;
courage in a eunuch,
philosophy in a drunken sot; or,
a woman who is satiated with sex.'

Having heard all this the genie went away.

Thus ends of thirteenth tale in the *Five-and-Twenty Tales of the Genie* composed by Śivadāsa.

TALE 14

Of Mūladeva, Prince of Tricksters

Big-bellied God! Lover of Rich Sweetmeats![114]
I pray to you, dispel, O, Lord,
all impediments, at all times,
in all the works I undertake.'

The king went back again to the same spot and took the corpse down from the śinśipā tree. Laying it across his shoulders he started walking when it began its storytelling. 'Listen, O, king, while I tell you a tale,' it said. The genie began:

There is a city by the name of Kusumavatī; there King Suvićāra ruled. He had a daughter named Ćandraprabhā. She had just entered womanhood and was ready for marriage.

One day, during the Spring Festival she resorted to the pleasure groves with her companions to gather flowers. And at the very spot where the princess was, a young Brāhmaṇa, named Vāmanasvāmi came and stood. He saw her; she saw him too. Their eyes met and they gazed at each other.

The princess was smitten with love. Burning with love she managed to return to the palace with the utmost difficulty. As for the young Brāhmaṇa, he fell down at that very spot, overwhelmed by love. He was beside himself.

At that moment, along came that pair of confidence tricksters, Mūladeva and Śaśi. Mūladeva noticed the Brāhmaṇa lying on the ground and turning to his friend remarked:

'Hey, Śaśi, look, look at the state this Brāhmaṇa is in. As it is said:

'So long as showers of pinpoints of light
from lovely blue-lotus eyes do not alight on him,
wisdom born of learning assuredly arises
in the mind of an intelligent man.

'So long as arrow-glances fringed by those dark lashes
and released from the fully-drawn bow
of an arching eyebrow of charming women
do not fly, sounding sweet to the ear, straight to the heart
to wreak havoc on his fortitude;
so long as he keeps to the right way,
a man is master of his senses;
only then does he retain his innate sense of shame;
only then does he keep a firm hold on modesty.'

Mūladeva asked the prostrate Brāhmaṇa: 'Hey there, sir, Brāhmaṇa, how did you come to such a pitiful pass? Give me the reason.'

Vāmanasvāmi replied with these lines:

'Sorrows should be shared with someone
who can help to allay those sorrows;
But if a man can't do a thing to relieve them
why should he ask questions?

'Why these particular questions? The reasons for my sorrows are many. If you wish to do me a favour, then get me some firewood; what else?'

Mūladeva spoke soothingly to the young man: 'Well, well, friend Brāhmaṇa; refrain from such rashness. Nevertheless, tell me the reasons for your sorrow and I shall blow it out of existence.'

Vāmanasvāmi was encouraged to talk about his troubles. 'It is like this,' he said. 'I have fallen deeply in love with the princess; and I have got to have her, whatever it takes. Otherwise, I swear I shall enter the fire.'

Mūladeva said: 'Look, my friend, what on earth do you want with the princess? I shall give you enormous wealth; and you can have any number of women. Don't persist in such a stubborn attitude.'

And Vāmanasvāmi answered:

'No pleasure in this world, not even the Elixir of Life
exceeds the pleasure of making love with a woman,
whereby all the senses instantly realize
altogether, their fullest potential.

'Of all flavourful things, golden melted butter is the best;
the oblation is the best part of that melted butter,
offered into the Sacred Fire; of that oblation[115]
the essence is the attainment of Paradise;
and Woman is the quintessence of Paradise.

'An incomparable gem is Woman,
far above all precious gems.
For the sake of women do men crave wealth;
if one gives up women what use then is wealth?

'Nectar's bowl itself she is;
a veritable palace of delights;
Pleasure's own treasure-trove:
Ah! Woman! Who *did* form her?

'Riches are the fruit of good works;
happiness is the fruit of riches;
slender-bodied ladies are the source of happiness;
without them, where is happiness?

'The beloved has slender limbs,
a face lovely as a lotus,
and charmingly rounded breasts, full and hard,
tightly wedged against each other.
She is delicate as a Śiriṣa flower,
her arms are smooth and soft.
If a man does not embrace his beloved,
how vain and unprofitable is his life,
his birth in this world, his riches!

'The lover who does not know the taste
of a woman's lower lip, delicious
as a ripe berry, its ambrosial sweetness—
What on earth does he know? A mere beast!'

Mūladeva observed, thoughtfully: 'Well, if that is so, then get up, O Brāhmaṇa. Here, I give you the princess.' And he placed a tiny magic ball in Vāmanasvāmi's mouth. Vāmanasvāmi instantly became a very pretty girl, twelve years old. A second little magic ball he now placed in his own mouth, turning himself into a venerable Brāhmaṇa. Taking the girl by the hand, Mūladeva went to the palace. He gained an audience with the king who offered him a seat and accepting it Mūladeva bestowed his benediction on the king thus:

'He who traversed the triple world,
assuming the form of a dwarf,
who caused a bridge of boulders built
across the ocean by a host of monkeys
—O, what a wonder that was!—
Who held on the palm of one hand
—a marvel indeed—the lordly mountain,
to protect the herd of cows; may He,
that luminous Ruler of the Universe[116]
always protect you from dangerous ways!'

The king asked Mūladeva: 'O, Brāhmaṇa, where are you from?'

'Your Majesty, I live on the further bank of the Gangā and my respected wife is there even now. I have an only son, sixteen years of age; and one day my dear wife said to me: "Listen, O Brāhmaṇa, arrange for the marriage of our son." Therefore, I went to the houses of my kinsmen to ask for a bride for my son, but I was not able to find a suitable girl for him. So, I travelled to a distant land and having wandered around there, I finally found this girl and brought her to my son. He married her and took her to his own village. After several days, my son returned and sent the bride to her mother's home. When four months had passed my respected wife said to me: "Listen, O Brāhmaṇa, bring home the bride for the ceremony on the fourth day of the month." I went to bring the bride home. But even as I was nearing my home with my daughter-in-law, the village was subjected to a raid and my wife and son had fled, I don't know where. The whole village was in a state of great alarm and lawlessness. Thinking presently that the place was unsafe for such a pretty girl as my daughter-in-law, I was at a loss where to go. For this reason while I am engaged in rendering my home secure with the help of my son, let this young bride be here, protected with the greatest care and handed over to me on my return.'

The king reflected: 'If I do not do as the Brāhmaṇa wants, he may lay a curse upon me; who knows?' Marking how beautiful the young bride was, the king agreed. 'I shall do as Your Reverence wishes,' said he. And the old Brāhmaṇa, Mūladeva in disguise, left the palace leaving the girl in the king's charge.

Then, the king sent for his daughter and instructed her thus: 'Dear daughter, this young Brāhmaṇa bride ought to be protected with the greatest care in your apartments. Never let her out of your sight whether at mealtimes or at bedtime.'

The princess, mindful of the king's instructions, took the

Brāhmaṇa bride by the hand and led her to her own apartments in the palace. At night the two girls slept in the same bed, conversing with each other.

Once the fake-maiden asked the princess: 'Listen, dear princess, why do you appear so withdrawn and pensive? And so emaciated? Is there some secret sorrow lurking in your heart?'

The princess answered with these verses:

'When someone good is not there to whom
the sorrows of one's heart may be unfolded,
the heart leaps to the throat; and once again
the heart loses itself in the throat.

Few there are who appreciate fine qualities,
few offer their love to one who lacks wealth,
few there are to take care of the needs of others,
and few who grieve for the grief of others.

If with great difficulty, you obtain
the beloved whom you can cherish,
who is filled to overflowing with love for you,
you possess here, these three: happiness,
good companionship, Gangā.

O, Śankara! Do not create!
If create you must, not human births!
If births, not the experience of love!
If love's experience, not the grief of parting!

'Why say more? One day I went to the pleasure groves with my companions to amuse myself. There I saw a young Brāhmaṇa, handsome as the god of Love himself; our eyes met. But, I know neither his name nor do I know where he lives. That whole day my body knew intense torment. If he will only become my husband, then I shall live. This is the reason why I am so withdrawn and emaciated.'

Having heard these words of the princess, the fake-maiden said quietly: 'If I present your beloved to you, what will you give me?'

The princess replied: 'I shall be your slave for ever.' The fake-maiden then removed the tiny magic globule from her mouth and at once became the young Brāhmaṇa.

Seeing the man she loved standing there the princess became bashful. The Brāhmaṇa then made love to her. Every night from then on, Vāmanasvāmi became himself, a man, and during the day he turned himself into a young girl. In six months time the princess became pregnant.

One day, the chief minister invited the king and his family to his home for dinner. The princess accompanied by her companion, the fake-maiden, arrived at the chief minister's mansion, where his son saw the young Brāhmaṇa bride. Captivated by the girl's beauty, the chief minister's son declared straightaway: 'If this girl does not become my wife, I shall die.' And he pined away, soon reaching the tenth stage in the course of decline of a disappointed lover. He confided his grief to his best friend who straightaway informed the young man's father, the chief minister, who immediately sought the presence of the king and advised him of the situation.

'Your Majesty, pray give this young Brāhmaṇa bride to my son as his wife,' said the chief minister.

The king exclaimed: 'Is the wife of one man ever given in marriage to another? This is against the Law.'

The other ministers heard the king's statement and advised him as follows: 'Your Majesty, the chief minister's son is determined to die. If his son dies the chief minister will not survive him; and if the chief minister should die the kingdom itself will waste away and fall. Looked at from every angle, it is desirable to give away the young Brāhmaṇa bride.'

The king listened to the advice of his council and sent for the Brāhmaṇa bride and told her, 'You have to marry the chief minister's son.'

And the girl replied: 'But, Your Majesty, this goes against the Law, for I am already married.'

'Look, it is your duty to always ensure the protection of the kingdom; so, go to the house of the chief minister's son,' ordered the king.

The girl demurred and said again: 'Your Majesty, if I *have* to be given in marriage to the chief minister's son, I demand that, he on his part should carry out a condition that I shall lay down. After the wedding ceremony, he should go on a six-month pilgrimage to sacred places. Only then, after his return, can he consummate his marriage to me.'

The chief minister's son agreed and married the fake-maiden. Before he left on his pilgrimage he exhorted his first wife thus: 'Listen, see to it that while I am away on my pilgrimage, this new bride and you, both sleep at night in the same bed. Keep each other company all the time; you understand? And mind you, stay home; don't either of you go on visits to other people's houses.' Having strictly instructed his wife, the chief minister's son set out on his pilgrimage.

At night, the two wives slept in one bed and conversed with each other, exchanging confidences.

On one occasion the first wife started this conversation. 'Listen,' she said to her co-wife, 'I am devoted to my husband for sure; but I am not able to go out. My husband is not here and I am in the prime of youth. And you too, my dear friend, are no better off. What sins have you committed that Fate has led you here to my side? For you too have your own share of disappointment.'

The fake-maiden responded saying: 'Well, if it pleases you to fall in with a suggestion of mine, I shall turn myself into a man and make love with you.'

'What,' exclaimed the first wife. 'Are you pulling my leg?'

The fake-maiden at once removed the magic globule from her mouth and turned straightaway into a man and made love to the other girl.

And so the days passed with Vāmanasvāmi, the fake-maiden assuming a woman's form during the day and making love to the absent man's wife in his own person as a man at night. Strong love grew between the two.

But why say anything more? When six months were over, the chief minister's son returned from his pilgrimage. The two girls consulted each other anxiously: 'This mean wretch, the chief minister's son, is back. How can we now continue our life as passionate lovers?'

An idea flashed into the mind of the fake-maiden. 'Look,' she said earnestly. 'While the folks are engaged in welcoming the chief minister's son and performing various auspicious rites to celebrate his safe home-coming, let me assume my own form as a man and go out. I shall visit my benefactor, Mūladeva and acquaint him with the latest turn of events.'

Having decided that this was the best thing to do under the circumstances, Vāmanasvāmi became himself and went to consult that arch confidence trickster, Mūladeva. Mūladeva immediately swung into action. He turned himself into the venerable Brāhmaṇa and his friend Śaśi into his alleged son, a youth of sixteen. Leading his son by the hand he went to the palace.

He asked for an audience with the king. Being granted it, he bestowed the customary benediction on the king who offered him a seat and asked after his health and well-being.

'By God's grace, all is well,' responded Mūladeva in the customary fashion.

'And who have we here?' asked the king. 'Who is this youth with you?'

'Ah! This is my son, Your Majesty, whose young wife I entrusted to Your Majesty's care some time ago. Kindly hand over the young lady to me.'

The king replied in great consternation: 'O, holy Brāhmaṇa, do me the favour of listening to what I have to tell you.' And the king proceeded to acquaint the fake-Brāhmaṇa with all that had happened after he had left his fake-daughter-in-law in the king's care.

The fake-Brāhmaṇa pretended to be very angry. 'O, king,' he said hotly; 'What's this? How can such a thing happen? How can my son's wife be given in marriage to another man? I shall lay a curse upon you.'

'O, Brāhmaṇa, please do not be so angry with me,' pleaded the king. 'I shall give you whatever you ask for.'

And the fake-Brāhmaṇa, again pretending to be mollified somewhat, demanded: 'Well then, if you are prepared to give me whatever I ask for, then I demand that you give your own daughter to my son as his bride.'

The king discussed this demand with his council of ministers and fearing the Brāhmaṇa's curse, sent for the princess and made the formal offer of marriage to the Brāhmaṇa's son. The marriage of Śaśi, the fake-son of the fāke-Brāhmaṇa Mūladeva to the princess was duly solemnized in public. Śaśi and Mūladeva then took the princess home with them.

The young Brāhmaṇa Vāmanasvāmi had already arrived at Mūladeva's place.

A hot argument ensued. The rogue Śaśi announced vehemently: 'The princess is my wife.' The Brāhmaṇa Vāmanasvāmi countered this claim with: 'But she is carrying my child in her womb; therefore she is my wife.'

Mūladeva was totally powerless to sort this mess.

Having narrated this tale, the genie said to the king: 'Tell me, O king, whose true wife is the princess?

King Vikramasena replied readily: 'Why, of course, she is the wife of the rogue Śaśi.'

'Why so?' queried the genie. 'She carries the child of the young Brāhmaṇa in her womb. So, how is she not his wife?'

And the king answered: 'Look here, the young Brāhmaṇa entered by stealth; whereas, the rogue Śaśi and the princess were married before the whole world. Whether the child the princess gives birth to is a son or a daughter, that child will have the right to perform the last rites for the crafty Śaśi.'

Having heard the king's answer, the genie went back to hang again from the branch of the śinśipā tree.

Thus ends the fourteenth tale in the *Five-and-Twenty Tales of the Genie* of Śivadāsa.

TALE 15

Of Jīmūtavāhana and His Supreme Sacrifice

With absolute devotion I bow
to the mighty lord, big-bellied,
Ruler of Obstacles, displaying
an elephant's trunk and a single tusk.

Again, the king returned to that same spot, took down the corpse hanging on the śinśipā tree; and as he started walking with the corpse slung across his shoulders, it began its storytelling. The genie began:

On the celebrated mountain of eternal snows, known as the Himālaya, there was the King of Vidyādharas, named Jīmūtaketu, Cloud-Banner. Childless, he began worshipping the Kalpavṛkṣa, the Wishing Tree, to obtain a son. The tree spoke to him:

'I am pleased with you, O King of Kings;
and I have granted you a son
of supreme righteousness, O, king.
He will soon be born; rest assured.'

As a result of this boon granted by the Wishing Tree a son was born to the king. The birth of the little prince was the occasion for great celebration and King Jīmūtaketu distributed sumptuous gifts to his people. And when it was time for the naming-ceremony for the newborn child, the name of Jīmūtavāhana, Cloud-Rider, was selected. In the kingdom, everyone became devotees of Śiva; everyone joyously followed the path of the Law. And further,

Where the rule of Law prevails,
    people are law-abiding;
where there is misrule, people are lawless;
under a rule that is only middling,
people too are middling.
The world follows this rule:
like ruler, like subjects.

Revelling in a perpetual round
of splendid festivities,
devoted to being of service to others,
all dedicated to performing sacrifices,
all Śudras intent on dispensing charity,
the entire populace lived in amity,
free from the passions of hate and lust,
with no fear of natural calamities
nor indeed of invading armies,
with no fear at all of outlaws and robbers,
of stinging insects and venomous creatures,
or of deaths after incessant rain;
where the God of Rain showered his bounty as desired,
and the earth was perpetually green,
with cows yielding pailfuls of milk,
trees year-round fruit,
and women faithfully fulfilling all wifely duties,
here, King Jīmūtavāhana ruled
in whom all great qualities were found finely blended.

King Jīmūtavāhana also adored the Wishing Tree. And the Tree, being highly pleased spoke to the king:

'O, Jīmūtavāhana, ask for a boon,' said the Tree. And Jīmūtavāhana requested the Tree thus: 'O, Glorious Being! If you are truly pleased with me, banish, O, lord, all poverty from the face of the earth.'

'So be it,' blessed the Tree.

As a result of the gracious favour of the Wishing Tree, every single person on earth became possessed of wealth. No one cared a hoot for anyone; no one did anything. All remained living without putting their hand to any kind of work. King Jīmūtaketu, the father, and his son Jīmūtavāhana, both remained immersed in cultivating Virtue. The art of government and the duties of kingship were abandoned, totally.

The kinsmen of the king began to think and discuss the situation amongst themselves. 'These two kings, father and son have turned to the pursuit of Virtue and Virtue alone. It is bruited around and said openly everywhere in the realm: "Nobody does anything; no one lifts his little finger!" In these circumstances, let us fight them and seize the kingdom,' they talked like this amongst themselves.

Having decided to carry out their intentions, they came to the capital and surrounded it, laying siege to it.

King Jīmūtaketu, the father, consulted his son: 'My son, what is to be done?'

'Why, we shall fight them, of course, annihilate all of them and restore the greatness of the kingdom,' replied the son. However, the father demurred and said:

'Our bodies are impermanent
and wealth is transient;
we are forever face to face with death;
Virtue should be garnered.

Better milk than a hundred cows;

better one grain than a hundred;
better a prayer-seat than lofty mansions;
What remain are the highest glories beyond.

'Therefore, I shall not be guilty of the heinous crime of taking life. The great Yudhiṣṭhira was stricken by remorse after he had slain his kinsmen.'

'Well, if that is how you feel, then the only thing to be done is to hand over our kingdom to our kinsmen and retire to the great forests to perform penance,' observed Jīmūtavāhana.

Having taken their decision, father and son handed over the kingdom to their kinsmen and set out for the Malaya Mountains.[117] They selected a spot on the mountains, built a little thatched hut and lived there. There, Jīmūtavāhana met one Madhura, son of an ascetic who became his close friend and the two of them roamed all over the Malaya Mountains.

One day as he was roaming around on the mountains, Jīmūtavāhana came upon a shrine of the goddess. He saw a maiden seated before the goddess, playing on a lute. Her eyes fell upon Jīmūtavāhana. They fell instantly in love. With great difficultly, the maiden managed to tear herself away from that spot to return home, where she sat pining for the young man she had seen. Jīmūtavāhana also returned to his hut.

The next day, the maiden made it a point to visit the same shrine and worship the White Goddess.[118] Jīmūtavāhana also decided to visit that shrine at the same time. He asked the maiden's companion: 'Lady, whose daughter is she?'

The companion replied: 'She is the Princess Malayavatī, daughter of King Malayaketu.' And in return she asked Jīmūtavāhana, 'And pray who may you be, Sir, who seem to be the incarnation of Manmatha, God of Love? Where are you from?'

'There is a king of the Vidyādharas, Jīmūtaketu by name; I am his son; my name is Jīmūtavāhana,' replied the young prince; and added: 'Thrown out of power, the two of us, father and son have come here.'

The companion passed on this information to Malayavatī. Getting acquainted with each other, the two young people found themselves extremely tormented by the pain of love.

Princess Malayavatī now prayed earnestly to the White Goddess: 'Glorious Goddess! If I cannot have Jīmūtavāhana for my wedded husband, I shall slip a noose round my neck and hang myself.' And she set about making a noose to slip round her neck right there in the presence of the goddess, when the divine voice rang out: 'Dear daughter, I am well pleased with you; Jīmūtavāhana will be your husband; rest assured.'

All this time, Jīmūtavāhana had remained concealed and seen and heard what went on. He went back to the little hermitage he and his father had made, burning with love. The princess returned to the palace in a state of uncertainty, greatly tormented by love's wounding darts. She confided what had taken place in the shrine to her companion, who went immediately to the queen and reported everything. The queen decided to have a talk with King Malayaketu; she began: 'My lord, our daughter has blossomed into youthful womanhood and is ready for marriage. Yet, His Majesty has not thought of looking for a suitable husband for her.'

The queen's words started the king thinking: 'To whom should I offer my daughter in marriage?'

At that very moment, the Crown Prince, Mitrāvasu came in and spoke to his father: 'Your Majesty, I have some news. I have learnt that Jīmūtaketu, King of the Vidyādharas is here with his son, Jīmūtavāhana. It seems that they have been thrown out of their kingdom.'

Hearing the news his son had brought him, an idea struck the king. He said: 'I think it is a good idea to wed the princess to this Jīmūtavāhana.'

With these words he entrusted his son with an important mission. 'Look, my son, you better go to the hermitage of

King Jīmūtaketu and bring Jīmūtavāhana here to us.'

Commanded by his royal father, Prince Mitrāvasu went at once to the hermitage and requested an audience with King Jīmūtaketu. He formally offered the hand of his sister to Prince Jīmūtavāhana. The offer accepted, Jīmūtavāhana came to King Malayaketu's court and on an auspicious date his marriage to Princess Malayavatī was duly celebrated. After the wedding ceremonies, Jīmūtavāhana accompanied by his brother-in-law, Mitrāvasu, brought his bride to his father's hermitage. There Malayavatī bowed low before her parents-in-law.

Sometime later, Jīmūtavāhana went early one morning with his brother-in-law, Mitrāvasu, to walk on the Malaya Mountains. At a particular spot, they saw a large, white mound. Jīmūtavāhana, prompted by curiosity, asked his brother-in-law; 'Look, look, what is this?'

'Ah! This? This is a heap of serpent-bones. The Serpent Youths come up from their kingdom in the Underworld and Garuḍa, the Golden Eagle who is the King of Birds, eats them. He has eaten tens of thousands of these Serpent Youths; these are their bones that you see,' answered his brother-in-law.

Jīmūtavāhana listened attentively. Then he said to his brother-in-law: 'Listen, dear Mitrāvasu, why don't you go home and have your meal. I feel rather apprehensive that the hour of my morning prayers might soon pass.'

The brother-in-law started towards his palace; and Jīmūtavāhana walked onwards. As he walked, he heard the sound of an old woman weeping and wailing: 'O, my son; alas, my son.'

Jīmūtavāhana followed the sound and came upon the sorrowing lady. He questioned her. 'Listen, mother, why are you wailing like this?'

'Today is the day of death for my son Śaṅkhaćūḍa. Garuḍa will come here to eat him up; I weep out of grief for my son,' she replied.

Jīmūtavāhana promptly replied, consoling her: 'Listen, Mother, don't weep. Today I shall offer myself in your son's place as food for Garuḍa and thereby protect your son's life.'

The mother said in dismay: 'No, no, my son, don't do this. I look upon you as more precious than my son Śaṅkhaćūḍa.' At this moment, Śaṅkhaćūḍa arrived on the scene; he spoke these lines:

'Insignificant beings such as myself
rise and then fall away;
how often is a man like you born
who girds himself to protect others!

'To wish upon someone else what is hostile to one's own self! Oh! No! That is not the way of men of good conduct.'

Then Jīmūtavāhana countered these arguments:

'All creatures protect their own lives
by making use of the lives of others;
there is one alone who saves another life,
giving up his own: I, Jīmūtavāhana.

'I have given my word; it cannot be gainsaid. Now go back whence you came.'

Hearing this Śaṅkhaćūḍa went to worship the Lord and pray. And Jīmūtavāhana climbed the rock of slaughter and lay face down after laying aside his weapons. He saw Garuḍa come swooping down from the sky:

The son of Tarkṣa, the Primal Being,
he had vowed to annihilate the Snakes;
a bird of truly terrifying prowess;
his feet rested firmly in the Underworld,
his wings spanned all space, covering them;
in his belly the seven celestial planes,
in his throat, Brahmā's Egg, the Cosmos;

his two eyes were the Sun and Moon;
the point of his beak ten leagues in extent,
was open ready to seize; his whole form
awe-inspiring beyond all imagining;
Lord of the World of Birds, Tarkṣa's son
pecked him with the point of his beak.

Pecking a second time, he seized Jīmūtavāhana in his beak and flew up into the sky. As Garuḍa flew around wheeling in midair, eating him, a jewel marked with Jīmūtavāhana's name, and dripping with his life-blood fell on Malayavatī's lap. One look at that jewel all bloodied, and Malayavatī swooned away. In a moment, regaining consciousness, she ran to her parents and showed them this jewel belonging to her husband.

Her parents saw the jewel and crying out aloud they rushed to the rock of slaughter. Malayavatī swiftly followed them to the same spot. Śaṅkhaćūḍa also arrived there that very moment. He shouted, 'Set him free, set him free, O, Garuḍa. He is not your food; I am the Snake Youth, Śaṅkhaćūḍa; I am your food.'

Garuḍa heard him and was overcome by grave doubts. 'What! Am I eating some Brāhmaṇa? Or some warrior-prince? Alas! What evil have I done?' He was dismayed.

Garuḍa now questioned Jīmūtavāhana: 'Listen, maṇ, who are you? Why were you stretched out on the rock of slaughter?'

Jīmūtavāhana retorted: 'Do what you have to do; why do you bother over other matters?'

Garuḍa then exclaimed: 'O, high-souled man! Tell me, why are you sacrificing your life for another?'

Jīmūtavāhana replied with these lines:

'They provide shade to others
while they themselves stand in the sun;

they bear fruit for others,
those mighty trees, magnanimous.

'Rivers do not drink their own waters;
trees do not eat their own sweet fruit;
the raincloud does not pour its water for its own good;
to help others is the glory of the noble.

'Ground and ground again repeatedly,
sandalwood has a lovely fragrance;
chopped and chipped again repeatedly,
the sugar cane's stem is sweet to taste;
heated and heated again repeatedly,
gold gains a richer hue;
even as life draws to a close,
noble natures endure no change.

'Whether they are censured or praised,
by scholars well-versed in ethics;
whether Fortune stays with them
or leaves as she pleases;
whether death comes today
or in the years to come,
the steps of men of fortitude
never stray off the Right Way.

'They pay no need to others' possessions
but set their mind on their own actions;
evil are those seduced from right conduct,
saintly are the noblest of men.

'Dumb beasts live only to fill their bellies;
he truly lives who lives for others;
he deserves the highest praise.

'He who does not use his body
in the service of other beings,
why does he serve his own body,
day after day, the wretched fool!

What use is a well-fed body, strong and lasting long,
if a man does not help all living things?
though living, he is but a hollow man.

A life spent in the service of others,
that life is indeed true living.
Even a crow fills its belly,
but what kind of a life is that!

He who gives up his life for cows and Brāhmaṇas,
for his friends or for his master,
or in the service of women,
his is Final Bliss, whole and unalloyed.'

Then, Jīmūtavāhana fainted away from the wounds caused by Garuḍa's pecking. At that moment, his wife Malayavatī who had found the bloodied ornament with her husband's name on it arrived there with her family and companions, overwhelmed by sorrow. Seeing her husband lying unconscious, she called out to him piteously: 'Ha! Lord of my life! Husband! Ah! Noble soul who helps others! Ah! How magnanimous you are beyond compare! Ha! Lord dear to your people! Have pity on me! Reply me!'

Garuḍa, hearing the piteous lament of the princess, went down at once to the underworld to fetch the Elixir of Life and anointed Jīmūtavāhana's entire body with it. And the prince was healed and made whole.

Then Garuḍa said to Jīmūtavāhana: 'O, Soul of Magnanimity! I am amazed and pleased with your steadfast courage. Ask for a boon.'

And Jīmūtavāhana answered: 'Listen, Glorious Bird, if

you are in fact pleased with me, then grant me this: that from this day on you shall never kill and eat the Snakes; and that you will now restore to life all those whom you have in the past killed and eaten.'

'That is a promise,' said Garuḍa. With these words, Garuḍa descended once again to the underworld, fetched more of the Elixir of Life and brought every one of the dead snakes back to life. And he spoke again to the prince: 'Ah! Jīmūtavāhana! Listen to me; by my benediction, you shall rule as the Paramount Sovereign on this earth.'

Having bestowed his benediction on the prince, Garuḍa flew up to his own abode. Śaṅkhaćūḍa also returned to his own dwelling. Jīmūtavāhana now returned to the hermitage with his parents and his wife.

The Vidyādhara kinsmen of Jīmūtavāhana and his father having heard of Garuḍa's benediction and afraid of the wrath of the fabulous bird, came there. Falling at the feet of the prince they gave him back his kingdom.

Having narrated this tale, the genie said: 'Tell me, O, King; as between Jīmūtavāhana and Śaṅkhaćūḍa, who is the more magnanimous?'

'Why, Śaṅkhaćūḍa, to be sure; his magnanimity is greater,' answered King Vikramasena.

'Why do you say that?' questioned the genie.

The king replied: 'Because, having once left the rock of slaughter, he returned. Then he stopped Garuḍa from eating the prince, saying: 'Eat me'; by that, he forbade right at the start itself the death of another person in his place.'

The genie observed: 'You think so? Really? And what about the man who was ready to sacrifice his life for another? How can you declare that he is not the more magnanimous of the two? Answer me that.'

The king answered: 'In birth after birth into the world, it was always the practice[119] of Jīmūtavāhana to sacrifice his own life to save another's. That kind of sacrifice never troubled him; nor caused him harm. Moreover:

'Whoever observes the practice of giving,
of studying the sacred texts, of penance
by the repeated recollection
of such acts, will again perform the same act.

'Therefore, I declare that Śaṅkhaćūḍa's magnanimity is the greater.'

Having heard this, the genie returned once again to that same spot, to hang from the branches of the śinśipā tree.

Thus ends the fifteenth tale in the *Five-and-Twenty Tales of the Genie* set down by Śivadāsa.

TALE 16

Of Unmādinī's Fatal Beauty

I bow to the Luminous One, Sarasvatī[120]
worshipped by a multitude of poets; she
who dwells in the mine of gems, the ocean,
she who enjoys continually the fullness
of the nine moods and sentiments[121] of Poesy.

Once again the king returned to that same spot to take the corpse down from the śinśipā tree; and as he set out on the road back it started its storytelling. Then the genie said to the king: 'Listen, O, king; I shall tell you a tale.'

There is a fair city known as Vijayapuram. Its ruler was King Dharmaśīla. There a merchant prince named Ratnadatta lived. He had a daughter who was called Unmādinī or the enchantress, because she bewitched all who set eyes on her with her loveliness. Now, Unmādinī was in the first flush of youth ready to be given in marriage.

The merchant prince went to the king and said: 'Your Majesty, I have in my home a peerless gem of a maiden, my daughter. If it pleases His Majesty, he may accept her as his bride; if not I shall wed her to some other person.'

When the king heard this, he sent for certain celebrated men who were experts in judging the marks of beauty in women and dispatched them to judge the beauty of the merchant's daughter. When they arrived at the merchant's mansion and saw the maiden they were all enraptured with her beauty; for she had all the marks of beauty:

Large and lustrous expansive eyes,
a face glowing with the splendour of the moon;
the ears, what were they but the snares of Love!
Cheeks radiant as ćampaka blossoms;
the nose shaped like the pretty sesamum flower,
twin arching eyebrows bent like Love's own bow;
  teeth that dazzled like brilliant diamonds,
  a pair of lips red as richest coral;
gathered tresses gorgeous as the peacock's train;
the space of the throat charming as a conch
  shaped with its three graceful curves;
arms straight and graceful as Mādhavī[122] vines;
  hands glowing like rose-red lotuses
  with palms branching into slender fingers
    tapering to rosy fingernails;
breasts high, firm, well-rounded like shapely jars,
distinct, sweet as springtime and nestling close
like a pair of loving ćakravāka[123] birds;
the smallest waist, unsurpassed, easily clasped
within the circle of the fingers of one hand;
and, the charm of the navel, a perfect circle,
deep as a pool—Ah! Who has words to describe its charm—
bounded by three delicate folds of skin:
into which descends the fine line of down;
the belly's soft curve; ah! What artless grace!
the discs of the buttocks, those lovely planes
formed to be the seat of the god of love;
smooth thighs, tapered like a pair of plantain stems
that induce the longings of love in recollection;
the joints, sinews and veins, just right, supple,
possessing the resilient grace of young jasmine vines;
the feet, a pair of rose-pink lotuses,
well-matched, finely arched and equally placed;

their rosy toenails well-marked with pale half moons:
Thus did that maiden appear, blessed
with all the marks of beauty's perfection.[124]

Having seen such an exquisite form, the connoisseurs of feminine beauty, talked among themselves. 'If the king marries this beautiful maiden, he will be so lost in love for her that he will take no thought for the administration of the kingdom.'

With this thought uppermost in their minds, they returned to the palace and apprised the king of their assessment of Ratnadatta's daughter.

'Your Majesty,' they said, 'that maiden lacks all marks of beauty and therefore not fit to be His Majesty's bride.'

The king heeded their judgement and summoning the merchant prince told him that he would not marry his daughter.

The merchant prince having listened to the king's decision, offered his daughter in marriage to the commander of the Royal Forces, General Baladhara who came to Ratnadatta's mansion and was duly married to Unmādinī. Unmādinī lived in the general's mansion deeply resentful, brooding over the insult offered to her. 'So, the king rejected me saying that I lacked beauty,' she told herself.

One day it happened that as the king was on the royal highway he chanced to see Unmādinī standing on the terrace of her mansion. Gazing on her, he was greatly disturbed. As he reflected wondering whether she was a goddess or a mortal woman, he found himself falling madly in love with the unknown lady. With great difficulty he tore himself away from that spot and returned to the palace. After that, around midnight his body began to be racked with intense pain and suffering. The doorkeeper of the royal bedchamber noticed that the king was in great torment and asked: 'What is it that is troubling you, Your Majesty?'

And the king explained: 'My good man, this evening while I was out on the royal highway, I noticed an exquisitely lovely lady on the terrace of one of the mansions there. I wondered whether she was a goddess or an Apsarā or a Vidyādharī or simply a woman. But after setting eyes on her, I have fallen madly in love with this lady.'

'She is no goddess, Your Majesty,' replied the doorkeeper. 'She is a mortal woman all right. She is Unmādinī, the daughter of the merchant prince, Ratnadatta. In fact, she is the lady that Your Majesty turned down when she was offered in marriage to you, because you were under the impression that she lacked any beauty whatsoever. She is now married to General Baladhara.'

The king was taken aback. 'O, how have I been deceived by those connoisseurs of beauty, those celebrated judges of feminine good looks!' he exclaimed.

The king straightaway summoned those same men who were experts in judging the marks of perfect beauty.

'Listen, noble gentlemen,' he chided, 'you have all deceived me. That maiden you, who are experts, swore possessed not a single mark of beauty, is in fact a lady of exquisite loveliness in every limb; a goddess she is, descended from Svarga, the Realms of Light that is the abode of the Immortals. Such beauty as she possesses is not found among our mortal women.'

The judges of ideal beauty heard what the king said and agreed with him. 'Yes, Your Majesty, what you say is true. But there was a reason for the report that we submitted to Your Majesty stating that the maiden possessed no beauty at all.'

Now it came to General Baladhara's ears that the king was hopelessly in love with his wife. He came at once and said to the king: 'Your Majesty, I am your slave; and she, my wife, is my slave; and it is for her that Your Majesty is burning with passion. Command me, my lord, so that I may bring her to you.'

Hearing this the king became very angry. 'Is it the right conduct for men of virtue who follow the Law to approach another man's wife? Is it not said?

'He, and only he sees rightly, who regards
the wives of other men as his own mother,
the wealth of others as simply clods of earth;
and cares for all living things as for his own self.

'The preceptor chastises all persons,
the king chastises the wicked,
and Yama, god of death, son of the Sun,
judges all hidden acts of wrongdoing.'

To this the general replied: 'My lord, I give you my slave; how then can she be another man's wife?'

'What is against the accepted practices of society ought not to be done,' retorted the king.

'In that case, let me give her to the temple[125] where she will become a courtesan and then bring her to His Majesty's presence,' remonstrated the general.

'Now, listen to me,' reprimanded the king. 'If you dare make your chaste wife into a harlot, I shall punish you.'

The general now recited these lines:

'She, who is always honoured by the king,
and is greatly praised by the virtuous,
becomes desirable and sought after
and possessed of good fortune[126] as well;
whether she be a queen, or a princess,
or the daughter of the prime minister,
she has her husband in her power, even
if he has a harem of a thousand.'

Even as the general was making these comments, the king pining for Unmādinī had reached the tenth stage of unfulfilled love; as it has been described:

These are the ten phases that mark falling in love:
the delight of the eyes; constant thoughts of the person;
the birth of desire; loss of sleep; wasting away;
turning away from normal pleasures; loss of shame;
infatuation and obsession; loss of consciousness;
and finally death.

As well:

First come longings, then the yearning to see the beloved;
next, hot sighs are breathed out, then fever sets in;
in the fifth stage the limbs all burn,
followed by loss of relish for eating;
in the seventh stage, the limbs shake and tremble;
The onset of disorientation marks the eighth stage;
in the ninth stage life hangs in the balance;
finally, in the tenth stage, the lover breathes his last.[127]

A little later, the king expired. General Baladhara seeing the king dead went at once to consult his guru. 'Your Holiness,' he asked anxiously, 'at such a fateful pass what ought to be done?'

'Having worshipped the sun with an oblation the person should enter the fire,' answered the guru.

General Baladhara acted accordingly. His wife Unmādinī now asked the guru for advice. 'Your Holiness, instruct me in the duties of a wife,' she asked. The guru instructed her thus:

'She who follows her husband step by step
as he is carried to the burning grounds,
is a chaste and faithful wife; and she gains
the merit gained by performing the Horse Sacrifice.

With due rites a wife enters the holy fire
when her husband dies; than this no higher Dharma[128]
is known that virtuous women could practise.'

Unmādinī listened attentively to these words. She then took the ritual bath that purifies; dispersed charities and gifts and carried out other pious works. Having circled the funeral pyre she approached her husband's flaming body and uttered these words: 'Hear me, my lord; time and again in birth after birth I am your slave,' and she entered the flames.

Having narrated this tale, the genie said: 'Tell me, O, king, of these three persons, who is the most virtuous?'

King Vikramasena answered: 'The king is the most virtuous.'

'Why do you say that?' queried the genie.

'The king did not accept the lady even though she was offered by her own husband, voluntarily, because it was contrary to Dharma, the Law. A servant sacrifices even his life for his master and this was the dharma of the general. As for the wife she followed her husband in death, and this is the dharma of women. Therefore, for these reasons, I consider the king exceedingly virtuous.'

Having heard the king's answer, the genie went back to that same spot and hung from the branches of the śinśipā tree.

Thus ends the sixteenth tale in the *Five-and-Twenty Tales of the Genie* as set down by Śivadāsa.

TALE 17

Of Guṇākara and the Yogī Who Lost His Magic Powers

That Power which ordained Brahmā as the potter
within the cave of the Cosmic Egg;
that Power which cast headlong Viṣṇu
into the Forests of Mighty Perils
of His Ten Incarnations; that Power
which compelled Rudra to beg for alms
with the half-skull-bowl that served as hollowed palms
for food; that Power that perpetually spins
the Sun's Wheel in the heavens; to that Power,
the Cosmic Law, I humbly bow.[129]

The king returned once again to that same spot and took the corpse down from the śinśipā tree. As he placed it on his shoulders and began walking, the corpse started its storytelling with the words: 'Hear, O, king, while I tell you a tale.'

There is a city named Ujjayinī. It was ruled by King Mahāsena. In that city there lived a Brāhmaṇa named Devaśarma who had a son named Guṇākara. And he was an inveterate gambler. Whatever he could lay his hands on in his home, he gambled and lost. The family finally got together and threw him out of the house. Guṇākara set out for another land.

Having arrived at some land, he saw a deserted shrine and sat inside. There he met with a yogī[130] and bowed to him with reverence.

'Who might you be?' asked the yogī.

'A Brāhmaṇa from another land,' replied Guṇākara.

'Have you eaten?' asked the yogī.

'I am hungry,' replied the Brāhmaṇa.

'There is cooked rice in this half-skull-bowl; eat it,' said the yogī.

'I shall not eat my food in a skull,' replied the Brāhmaṇa.

In a state of profound meditation, the yogī reified an invocation. A yakṣiṇī who dwelt in a banyan tree materialized.

'Your Holiness, I am here. Command me,' said the yakṣiṇī.

'See that this Brāhmaṇa gets the food he desires,' ordered the yogī.

No sooner had she received the yogī's command than the yakṣiṇī created a splendid mansion. She led the Brāhmaṇa, Guṇākara into the mansion, set a fine feast before him, offered him a paan quid after he had eaten. Then she presented him with fine clothes and jewellery; next, she rubbed fragrant salves and creams made of blended camphor, musk and liquid sandal paste on his body. She then made love to him to his heart's content. At daybreak, the yakṣiṇī vanished and the Brāhmaṇa found himself alone.

He approached the yogī. Seeing him the yogī asked: 'Ah! Good Brāhmaṇa; you look dejected; why?' The Brāhmaṇa, Guṇākara replied: 'Without the yakṣiṇī, I shall die.'

'She is a luminous, celestial being; she can be summoned only through an invocation,' observed the yogī.

'O, great master, then pray instruct me in the esoteric arts; I shall diligently learn and master it,' pleaded the Brāhmaṇa.

The yogī taught the Brāhmaṇa a particular spell and instructed him as follows: 'Listen, Brāhmaṇa, stand in the middle of the waters and single-mindedly meditate on this spell.'

The Brāhmaṇa followed the yogī's instructions. He entered the waters and standing right in the middle, meditated on the magic spell. But the yakṣiṇī did not appear; all around him there seemed to be a maze of illusory images. He came out of the waters and standing before the yogī, exclaimed: 'Nothing, Your Holiness, I gained nothing.'

The yogī now said: 'Go, enter the fire.'

'Let me go and visit my family once; then I shall enter the fire,' said the Brāhmaṇa.

With these words he returned to his native land and went to see his family; he saw and met all his relatives. They threw their arms round his neck and wept with joy. His father said: 'Guṇākara, my child, where have you been all these days? How is it that you have forgotten your home? And it is said:

'By forsaking a wife faithful and devoted,
pious and of virtuous conduct, my son,
a man is guilty of a heinous act,
the act of destroying a child in the womb.

'No duty is more meritorious
than the duties of a householder;
    no happiness is greater
    than the joy a wife brings;
no place of pilgrimage is holier
than the space where parents dwell;
no divinity is greater than Keśava.[131]

'Men who despise their mothers and fathers
are vile, the lowest of the low;
    theirs is not the way up,
    so the Creator declared.

'The man who sees his wedded wife forlorn,
consumed by longing for the rites of love

and will not approach her despite her pleadings,
though she is most worthy of being loved,
is a man who sees with a Ćāndāla's[132] eyes.'

Guṇākara responded with these lines:

'Brimful of filth and impurities,
swarming with webs of worms,
    naturally malodorous
    and devoid of cleanliness;
a vessel of wine and ordure:
only fools revel in this body;
wise men abstain from its pleasures.

'Who is a man's mother, or his father!
    Who is his wife, or his son!
As we are born and born again
a man is linked in relationships
    with many different 'others'.

'Dead, only to be born again
born, I have to die again;
many different wombs have I seen,
a thousand—Oh! So many times.

'The body is formed, is it not,
of the mingling of semen and blood,
and perpetually filled with urine and excrement;
it is truly an unclean thing.

'As a pot filled with excrement
can in no way be clean outside,
so, the body remains unclean
however diligently it is cleansed.

'The body might be thoroughly cleansed

with the five products of the cow[133]
and with holy grass and water;
yet spotless and bright it is not,
any more than a piece of coal
however diligently polished.

'To performers of rites and ceremonies,
the divine is in the Holy Fire;
to visioning seers it shines in the heavens;
to shallow minds it is in images:
rapt in meditation, the yogī
sees the Supreme One within himself.

'But why expatiate thus on the theme? Listen to me, dear father, I have studied techniques of self-concentration and I shall not enter the life of a householder. I am now a yogī.'

With these words the Brāhmaṇa left forsaking family and home. He proceeded to the place where his guru, the yogī was; and in his guru's presence, he entered the blazing fire. As he did so he meditated on the magic spell to summon the yakṣiṇī. But she did not appear. His guru who also meditated on the same magic spell was unable to summon her either.

Having narrated this tale, the genie said: 'Now, tell me, O, king, why did the yakṣiṇī fail to appear?'

King Vikramasena answered: 'Knowing that the student of magic was meditating with a mind divided, the divine lady would not appear. For it is said:

'Single-mindedness leads to success;
a mind divided is foiled;
it is the arrow-maker who sees not
the army on the move.

'What renown for one wanting in self-denial?
What honour for one wanting in self-command?
What happiness for one wanting in right values?
What success for one lacking profound meditation?'

The genie retorted: 'Now, now, how can you call the student of magic a man with a mind divided, when he entered the fire at the mere saying of his guru?'

'For this reason that at the time he was instructed in the meditation on the magic spell, he left it halfway to go and visit his family,' explained the king.

The genie rejoined: 'In that case, why did the yakṣiṇī fail to appear when the guru himself meditated on the spell that would summon her?'

The king's reply was as follows: 'Listen, the "Spirit of the Spell" thought to herself: "How could the yogī impart the secret knowledge to such a pupil, a man with a mind divided?" This angered her and she failed to materialize.

'As a rule, in human beings
the intellect is shaped by action,
So, constrained by his actions,
what is the "rational man"[134] to do?'

Hearing this the genie left.

Thus ends the seventeenth tale in the *Five-and-Twenty Tales of the Genie* set down by Śivadāsa.

TALE 18

Who Is Prince Haridatta's Real Father?

I bow to Ganeśa, destroyer of all obstacles,
who at the beginning of all enterprises
is worshipped by even the Immortals.

Once again the king went back to the śinśipā tree and placed the corpse on his shoulders. As he set out on the road to the burning grounds where the necromancer, Kṣāntiśīla was waiting, the corpse began to tell a story.

The genie said: 'Listen, O, king, while I tell you a tale.'

There is a city named Kankolam where King Sundara ruled. In that city lived the merchant prince Dhanakṣaya whose daughter was Dhanavatī. She was married to one Gaurīdatta, a rich merchant and resident of the city of Alakā. After some time, she gave birth to a daughter named Mohinī. As soon as the child was born, the father died. The dead man's kinsfolk deprived Dhanavatī of all her husband's wealth and possessions right in the presence of the king, giving as reason the fact that she had no son to inherit the wealth. Dhanavatī had perforce to leave the city with her little daughter. She departed at midnight and on account of the pitch darkness she could not see her way. And she found herself in the burning grounds. There, in the burning grounds was a robber impaled on a pike. As Dhanavatī went up to him the robber, who was in extreme agony, addressed these verses to her:

'No one allots man his share of grief or joy;
How mistaken to think someone does;
O, body! You reap the fruit of deeds past!
You taste happiness, or, pay for the wrongs you did!

What is unplanned Fate brings to pass;
What is well-planned Fate undermines;
Fate alone puts in place those things
never thought of or even dreamed of by men.

The land, the place, the day, even the moment
where it has to happen, and how,
there, in that manner and no other
are the bonds of death inevitably tied.

Where death awaits, where sorrow waits,
where good fortune is, or imprisonment,
to that precise spot goes a man,
of his own will, urged by his own actions.'

Dhanavatī spoke to the man: 'Sir, who are you?'

'I am a robber, and here I am impaled on a pike; three days have gone by, but life has not left me as yet,' answered the man.

'Why is that?' asked Dhanavatī.

'I remain unmarried; if someone gives me his daughter in marriage, I shall reward him with one lakh of gold coins.'

'Done,' said Dhanavatī. 'I give you my daughter in marriage, O robber. But how can you beget a son?'

And the robber said in reply: 'Listen, when this wife of mine reaches womanhood, purchase the seed of some man for gold and let him beget a son on her. An excellent Brāhmaṇa youth will be led in the future to your presence, wherever you are. Give him gold, he shall beget a son on your daughter.'

Having said that, the robber was married to Dhanavatī's daughter by the Gandharva rites.[135]

'Lady, to the east is a banyan tree; as its base lies hidden one lakh of gold coins; take that,' said the robber to Dhanavatī. With these last words, the robber breathed his last.

Dhanavatī took the hoard of gold coins and returned to her own city of Kankolam. There she had built a splendid, white stucco mansion for herself. As the days passed, her daughter, Mohinī, grew up and entered womanhood.

Once, Mohinī, in the first flush of youth, stood on the terrace of her mansion watching the king's highway. A certain Brāhmaṇa youth was passing by and seeing him, Mohinī fell instantly in love with him. She turned to her companion and said: 'Dear friend, go, meet this young man and take him to my mother.'

Her friend went down, spoke to the young man, brought him in and ushered him into the presence of Mohinī's mother.

The mother, Dhanavatī, spoke gently to the young man: 'Listen, young Brāhmaṇa; my daughter is nubile. If you beget a son on her, I shall give you one hundred and one gold coins.'

'I shall do so,' agreed the Brāhmaṇa youth.

After his acceptance of Dhanavatī's offer, the young man was given a splendid feast that evening. He was offered paan and supari,[136] rubbed with fine creams, perfumed with liquid sandalwood paste and led to the bedchamber. He embraced Mohinī in love.

In the morning, Mohinī's companions plied her with questions. 'Tell us, tell us, dear friend, how did you and your beloved make love last night?'

And Mohinī responded with these lines:

'My sweet love on the couch beside me—
my waistband came unfastened on its own—
the jewelled belt unclasping—the lower garment
no longer secure sliding down somewhat—

to rest on my hips:—this much I know—
then, my friends—his limbs melting into me—
Ah! Lost, under love's enchantment—
Who is he? Who am I? And this?—
Is this love's ecstasy?—Or what—?
    I have no memory of anything.

'Brave, decorous as well, generous,
witty and polished in speech; free from guile,
kind and considerate in love; zealous
in safeguarding the honour of women:
can lovely young women ever forget
such a man? No, not even in succeeding lives.'

Mohinī conceived that same night, and at full term gave birth to a son. On the sixth day she had a dream at night; she saw a figure:

Matted hair twisted, coiled high on the head,
    and diademed with the crescent moon;
limbs dusted with ashes from funeral pyres;
wearing the white sacred thread and a garland of
                                        skulls,
    the waistband a twining white serpent;
seated on a white lotus; armed with a sword
and club with skull-shaped knob;
    the trident in the right hand—
joined to the hind parts of a beast, the figure
    appeared like World-Destroying Fire.

Such was the appearance of the ascetic she saw in her dream. In the morning she went to her mother and said: 'Dear mother, this was the dream I saw,' and described it.

The mother remarked: 'Dear daughter, your son will be a sovereign. Now, follow my instructions: place your son in a basket, together with one thousand and one gold coins and have him left at the palace gates.'

Mohinī had her baby son left at the palace gates in a basket together with one thousand and one gold coins.

The previous night the king had also been visited by a dream; he saw an ascetic:

Ten-armed, five-faced, copper-eyed,
exceedingly fierce in appearance,
with terrible tusks; triple-eyed, moon-crested;

and this ascetic addressed the king: 'O, king, at your palace gate a basket has been left with a little boy in it. This boy will be your heir and succeed as sovereign after you.'

The king was awakened by this dream. He confided it to his queen. And she advised him thus: 'My lord, send the lady who guards the inner apartments outside to the main gate, to see.'

The king sent for the doorkeeper and ordered her to check the palace gates. And when she went out and looked around, there at the gates was a basket with a little baby boy in it. The doorkeeper picked up the basket and brought it into the royal presence. The king turned over the coverlet and saw the baby and the thousand and one gold coins.

At dawn, the king sent for the experts skilled in judging signs and auspicious marks and showed them the child. The experts examined the baby with care and then exclaimed: 'Your Majesty, this little boy has all the thirty-two marks of excellence on his person.'

'What are these marks of excellence?' asked the king.

'The following,' they replied.

'Broad in three respects, deep in three as well,
elevated in six and short in four,
glowing a healthy red in seven,
long and fine in five:

'It is a mark of excellence in men

if the navel, voice and vital breath are deep,
and the thighs, forehead and face are broad;
if chest and shoulders, finger and toe nails
nose, chin and throat are raised and prominent.
It augurs well if the neck, back and shanks,
and the male member are short and shapely;
feet and hands, the corners of the eyes,
palate, tongue, lower lip, nails, having a rich red hue
undoubtedly ensure health and happiness;
persons in whom fingers and joints of fingers and toes,
hair, skin, teeth, are fine, will be free from misery.
A well-defined jaw and nose, expansive eyes,
long arms and well-defined space between the breasts,
these five marks of excellence are to be found
only in rulers of the earth.'

The king listened carefully to the considered opinions of the experts. He then removed a string of pearls from his neck and put it round the child's neck, and handed him to the Queen Consort. The queen placed the child on her lap and sat next to the king, on his left.

Following this, the citizens came with gifts and paid homage to the royal family. The king accepted the gifts of his people and then held a great celebration. The naming ceremony of the little prince was celebrated. He was given the name of Haridatta. By the time he was sixteen years of age, the prince had studied all the sacred and secular texts and had become accomplished in all the arts.

In the course of time the king passed away and Prince Haridatta was installed king.

One day, a thought flashed across the young king's mind: 'Of what use is my being born as a son when I have not worshipped at sacred Gayā and offered oblations to my parents and forefathers!' So he decided to journey to holy Gayā. There, he began the prescribed course of ceremonies done for ancestors. His guru spoke to him thus:

'The person whose heart melts with compassion
for all living things, gains wisdom
and Final Release as well. Of what use
are matted hair, ashes and tattered garments?

'A man might hold a trident in his hand,
    or shave his head;
he might dwell in a cave, or on rocks,
    or under a tree;
he might read the ancient texts
    or glean the essence of the Vedas;
but if his heart is impure, what use are these?

'Charitable works, worship of the gods,
    severe penances as well,
listening to revealed truths: unprofitable
are all such pursuits to one whose heart is not pure.

'Any act performed without faith
    or without worship;
any act done only for outward show,
    turns out fruitless;
    the ancestors do not attend.
The divine is not to be found in wood,
    or in stone, or in clay;
the divine exists in the mind and the heart;
    the mind and heart are its place of birth.'

The young king listened attentively to the words of the learned Brāhmaṇas and uttering the name of his father, offered the prescribed oblations with his own hand. Three hands now appeared to accept the oblations. Haridatta then looked around perplexed and exclaimed: 'Into which hand should I place the oblations?'

Having narrated this tale, the genie asked the king: 'Tell me, O king; which of these three hands has the right to accept the oblations?'

'The right to accept the oblations belongs to the hand of the robber,' replied King Vikramasena.

The genie however demurred; it said: 'Listen, the young Brāhmaṇa gave birth to Haridatta with his own seed; the king brought the child up. How is it that they are not entitled to the oblations?'

'Ah!' replied King Vikramasena. 'Listen, the Brāhmaṇa's seed was bought with gold; the king was also given gold before he undertook to care for the child. The child was borne by the legally wedded wife of the robber; therefore he is to be regarded as the legal father and consequently the one with the right to the oblations offered to ancestors.'

Once the genie had the king's answer to its question it darted back to the same spot, to hang from a branch of the śinśipā tree.

Thus ends the eighteenth tale in the *Five-and-Twenty Tales of the Genie* set down by Śivadāsa.

TALE 19

Of the Brāhmaṇa Boy Who Laughed Facing Death

At the commencement of studies,
in disputes and in battle,
when hemmed in by enemies,
on entering a new dwelling,
by meditating on Vināyaka,
Remover of Obstacles, with heart-felt devotion,
no harm will come to any enterprise:
    thus spoke the Supreme Goddess.

Once again the king returned to the same spot. He took the corpse down from the śinśipā tree and slung it over his shoulders. And as he set out on his way back to the burning grounds to meet Kṣāntiśīla, the necromancer, the corpse began its storytelling. The genie spoke: 'Listen, O king, I shall tell you this tale.'

There is a fair city named Ćitrakūtam, where King Rūpasena ruled. Once he went hunting. He went ahead of his army and soon lost sight of it. At noon, the king was fatigued; he chanced upon a lake. Dismounting, he led his horse to the shade of a tree to let it rest. He himself sat down in the shade to rest for a few moments. Then, he looked around and there, right at that spot, his eyes fell on the daughter of a sage, a maiden of exceeding beauty, who was engaged in gathering flowers. It was love at first sight and the king was overwhelmed by passion for the maiden. Having gathered flowers the maiden started to leave when the king addressed her thus: 'What strange behaviour on the part of Your Ladyship! Here I am, an unbidden guest[137] at your hermitage! Pray offer me due hospitality before you go, Your Ladyship; for:

'A man even of a lower class, who comes
to the home of one of the highest class
should be received with honour as prescribed.
All guests should be duly welcomed.'

Their eyes met. At that moment the great sage, father of the maiden, seeing what was happening, came there. The king, noticing the great sage, rich in penances, bowed with reverence. The sage pronounced his benedictions.

Then, that most excellent of sages addressed the king: 'How is it that you have come to this region all by yourself?' he asked.

'My fondness for the chase has brought me here,' answered the king.

The sage exclaimed: 'O, king, what makes you resort to such a heinous crime? Why? The truth of the matter is this:

'One man might be guilty of wrongdoing,
but the whole populace reaps the consequence;
they suffer the evil fruits, but are free of blame;
the guilt clings to the perpetrator alone.'

The king said: 'Reverend Master, be pleased to instruct me in the ways of right and wrong.'

And that most excellent of sages instructed the king.

'Deer live in the woods; they eat grass;
they drink waters unbelonging, unowned;

even so, they are slaughtered by humans:
who is to appeal to the world's conscience!

'Of all the many gifts that might be made,
this alone is the highest, the best;
to let all living things live free from fear;[138]
no other gift surpasses this.

'One and the same sacrificial rite entails
an entire host of expensive gifts;
one person fearful of producing fear, ensures
the safety of life of living creatures.

'What penance equals patience!
What happiness like contentment!
What gift equals the gift of learning!
What moral imperative greater than compassion!

'Mindful of the dictates of righteousness,
any guilty person ought to be spared
who folds his hands in utter wretchedness
and falls at your feet.

'Any one seeking sanctuary at the feet of others
from distress, or from fear should be protected
even at the cost of their own lives,
by men of disciplined mind and spirit.

'Not the gift of cows, not the grant of land;
not even the gift of food; these are not the best of gifts;
the gift beyond all gifts, as it is said,
is in this world the gift of sanctuary.

'The man who is just and pious,
who has conquered pride and anger,

who does not flaunt his learning,
who does not cause pain to others,
who is content with his own wife
and does not covet another's,
such a man has no fear in this world.

'Those who forsake their masters encircled by foes
and brought to a stand still in the thick of battle,
are men of evil conduct who without a doubt
go straight to the Bottomless Pit.[139]

'Those who hit a foe knowing him unarmed,
with hair dishevelled, garments in disarray,
are men of evil conduct who without doubt
go straight to the Bottomless Pit.

'Those who violate their preceptor's wife,
or their master's, or the wife of a friend,
are men lacking discernment who without doubt
go straight to the Bottomless Pit.

'He who fails to safeguard his kingdom
from harassment of robbers, and instead
uses his power to chastise those disciplined
who keep their vows, goes straight to the Bottomless Pit.'

The king listened attentively to the words of the sage and said: 'Your Holiness, from this day any increase in wrongdoing shall not prevail.'

The sage was highly gratified by the king's words; and that lord of sages said to the king: 'O, king, ask for a boon; whatever your heart wishes; I shall grant you that.'

'If you are pleased with me, Your Holiness, pray give your daughter to me in marriage,' requested the king.

Then that great sage bestowed his daughter on the king

who married her according to the Gandharva rites.

Placing his bride behind him on horseback, the king rode in the direction of the capital city ot his own kingdom. When they were halfway, the sun set. Somewhere in the middle of the forest, the king dismounted, tied his horse to a tree and with his bride lay down to sleep under a great tree. At midnight, a certain Brāhmaṇa ogre[140] arrived at that tree. He woke up the king:

'O king, I am going to eat your wife,' thundered the ogre.

'Oh, no, please don't do that; I shall provide you with some other victim for your meal; whatever you demand,' exclaimed the king. As it is said:

> In dire peril, one's wealth ought to be protected;
> at the cost of wealth, one's wife ought to be protected;
> one ought of protect one's self at all times
> even at the cost of wife and wealth as well.

'Well then, listen to me; if you sever the head of a Brāhmaṇa boy, seven years of age, with your own hand in my presence, I shall then let go of this lady,' was the ogre's response.

'All right, I shall do so. But you have to come to my city on the seventh day,' observed the king.

'I promise,' replied the ogre and returned to his own dwelling.

At dawn, the king reached his capital. There was a great celebration in the city. The king summoned the Chief Minister and told him everything that had taken place and asked for his advice. 'Honourable Minister, what shall we do now? On the seventh day the ogre will come here to claim his victim,' said the king.

'Pray, have no fear, Your Majesty; I shall do everything that needs to be done,' replied the Chief Minister.

Then the Chief Minister had the figure of a man made of solid gold costing many lakhs,[141] placed it in a cart and had it taken round on the four highways in the city to the beat of drums with the town crier proclaiming, 'If any Brāhmaṇa in the city is willing to give his seven-year-old son to the king who will then sever the boy's head, this solid gold figure worth lakhs will be given to him.'

In that city lived a decrepit and indigent Brāhmaṇa who had three sons. This Brāhmaṇa hearing the public proclamation said to the Brahmāṇi, his wife, 'Beloved wife; let us give the king one of our three sons and receive this gift of a golden figure of enormous value.'

'But I shall not give up my youngest,' replied the Brahmāṇi.

'And I shall not give up the eldest,' rejoined the Brāhmaṇa. The middle son who was listening, said: 'Well then, give me up to the king, dear father.'

The father said: 'Good; give yourself up, my son.' For it is said:

Greed is at the root of all sins;
bodily humours of disease;
fond affection of all sorrows;
Man is happy abandoning all three.

The middle son was therefore brought before the king by his father who was seized by greed. He accepted the golden figure and returned home. Then the Brāhmaṇa ogre arrived. The king honoured him, offering cooked rice, flowers, perfumes, incense, paan and supari, fruit, fine cloths; set other choice eatables before him; waved lights ritually as is done during the worship of divinities. Thus he duly worshipped the ogre and finally brought the young Brāhmaṇa boy as the victim before him. At the precise moment that the king lifted up his sword and severed the boy's head, the Brāhmaṇa boy laughed.

Having narrated this tale, the genie now addressed his question to the king: 'Tell me, O king, why did the boy laugh at the moment of his death?'

And King Vikramasena replied: 'Ah! Why did he laugh? I know the reason. The thought that passed through the mind of the boy as he was about to be sacrificed were these: "Aha! Look, look at the state of the world!

"In childhood the mother protects;
in boyhood the father cherishes;
but, in my case, alas! They destroy me,
who ought to be my preservers.

"Mother and father both offered me up,
a victim, gladly, willingly;
the king stands with uplifted sword in hand;
the divinity waits for the sacrifice;
who then has compassion for me?

"If a mother feeds her own child poison,
if a father sells his own son for gold,
if the king deprives me of all, my life,
What use is lamenting!"

'Reflecting thus the boy laughed.'

The genie heard the answer and fled to that same spot to hang from a branch of the śinśipā tree.

Thus ends the nineteenth tale in the *Five-and-Twenty Tales of the Genie* set down by Śivadāsa.

TALE 20

Of Star-Crossed Lovers

May Lord Viṣṇu who lost the crescent moon
to Lord Śiva, moon-crested, only to receive
rays of light multitudinous, streaming
from the full moon of Lakṣmī, His consort's face:
may He who holds the marvellous conch,
    Pānćajanya, preserve us all.

Once again the king returned to the same spot and having taken down the corpse from the śinśipā tree, placed it on his shoulders. As he set out on his way to meet the necromancer, Kṣāntiśīla, the corpse began its storytelling. The genie began: 'Listen, O, king to the tale I shall tell.'

There is a great city named Viśāla.[142] It was ruled by a king named Vipulaśekhara. In that city lived a merchant named Arthadatta, who had a daughter named Anangamanjarī. She was married to one Maṇinābha, a merchant belonging to the city of Alakā. Maṇinābha went over the seas to trade and he was away for a very long time. In the meantime, his bride remained in her father's house and as the days passed by she grew into womanhood.

One evening, she stood on the terrace of the mansion watching the great royal highway. She happened to see a young Brāhmaṇa named Kamalākara passing on the highway. His eyes fell upon her. With the meeting of eyes mutual love sprung up in their hearts. They stood still as if painted in a picture with their eyes riveted upon each other. Kamalākara with his mind in turmoil went slowly back to his own house accompanied by his friend. When he reached home he was beside himself with the pain of separation from his beloved. Sorrowful, he began lamenting:

'O, God of Love! Were you not burnt to ashes[143]
by the wrath of Śiva? O, fool!
Have you not suffered the pangs of separation
from Rati,[144] your beloved?'

And Anangamanjarī was in her room, chiding the moon thus:

'O, gracious moon! Born of the ocean's cold depths;
known the world over as the abode of ambrosia;
your brilliant rays streaming with the artless glory of vines
rival the beauty of garlands[145] of pearls.
The moonlight is your beloved consort;
your best friend is Love, of love all compact;
yet, indeed! Lord! What a blaze of sorrow
is here kindled! Why do you, O lord, burn me thus?'

Hearing Anangamanjarī bemoaning in this manner, her friend consoled her saying: 'O, my dearest friend, do not speak such words. Shame upon you to talk like this.'

Anangamanjarī's reply was:

'Across the waters on the other side of the pool
stays the ćakravāka, pining, giving out
his plaintive, love-lorn calls to his mate;
and she lives. The lotus ceases to mourn
at the close of night and laughs.
But, for one whose beloved is far away,
whose sorrow is destined to have no end,

who is overwhelmed having come within
the range of power of Love, the mind-born god,
how can such a person, a person such as myself live?

'O, my friend, I am well aware of the proprieties. But Love, the Mind-Churner, has made me shameless.'

Her friend, Malayavatī, advised her earnestly, saying: 'Be of courage; try to control your heart by your will, do not brush aside the modesty that keeps guard and prevents a woman from going astray; seek to hear your favourite stories. Be confident and composed, dearest friend.

'Ah! How in the twinkling of an eye
you have become the target of Love, the
Mind-Churner;
that hunter who draws his bow to its full extent
even up to his ear,
and discharges a swift stream of arrows!
And now you prate in this manner!'

Anangamanjarī answered:

'Irresistible are Love's five arrows:[146]
Fạr away is my best beloved,
and my heart is seized by intense longing;
deep and boundless is my love
and I am in the springtime of youth;
I draw my breath with intense pain.
The family is spotless,
but womanliness lays siege to fortitude.
Time is the bosom friend of Love,
Death waits in impatience.
All these many fires unendurable
raging now at the present time—
How can I bear them all, my dearest friend?'

Malayavatī now said: 'My dearest friend, wait, I shall blow away your anguish.' And consoling Anangamanajarī with these words, she went home.

Then Lady Anangamanjarī went ahead and having made a noose with one end of her upper garment, prepared to commit suicide. As she uttered these words: 'May he be my husband in my next birth,' and slipped the noose round her neck her friend, Malayavatī came rushing to her, crying out: 'No, no, O, my dear friend; no, don't attempt such a rash deed. If you die, what are you achieving? Nothing.'

Anangamanjarī answered: 'My dear friend, listen to me; what you say is perfectly true. But now my life hangs by a thread.'

'In that case, wait, wait for a short while while I run and fetch your beloved,' pleaded Malayavatī and hastened to the home of Kamalākara.

Kamalākara was also in a pitiable state, his limbs burning with the fever of love. His friend was sprinkling his body with drops of water mixed with liquid sandal paste and fanning him with the cool leaves of the plantain.

Kamalākara was speaking in weak tones: 'Listen, my friend, pray fetch me some poison so that I might drink it and die. For it is said:

'Where shall eyes that would be indulged and spoilt
    drinking the nectar of the beloved's face, now rest?
What is worth hearing that ears far distant,
    beyond reach of the music of her speech, to now hear?
How are these limbs that would encircle her
    in passionate embrace, to be now supported?
Faced by cruel parting from her—Ah! Misery!
    How desperate the state I find myself in now!'

Malayavatī went up to him and spoke anxiously. 'Oh! Kamalākara, I have come from Anangamanjarī; she has sent me to you. She sends you this message through me; I speak for her: "O, listen, lord of my life; grant me life."'

Kamalākara answered: 'Is she in the same situation as me, or not? Tell me. Is her life hanging by a thread as mine is?'

Malayavatī replied:

'She speaks of the moon as if it were the sun;
and the soft southern breeze as if it were the forest fire;
the lotus burns her life like a fiery brand;
the funeral pyre she counts as coolest snow.
Know this: to her such things are now like blazing fires
wreathing with flames her anguished mind and heart.
Alas! You have abandoned this gentle girl,
most unfortunate and miserable.

'Get up, Kamalākara; go to her while she still lives. Once she is dead what can you do for her?'

Kamalākara heard Malayavatī's words and trembling all over he rose with great difficulty from his couch. But when he reached Anangamanjarī's mansion, she lay dead. Seeing her lying lifeless, he died grief-stricken. Both were laid on the same funeral pyre.

In the meantime, Anangamanjarī's wedded husband arrived at his father-in-law's mansion. He heard Malayavatī weeping and went inside to the room where his wife lay dead. Even though he saw his wife lying on the funeral pyre with the arms of another man round her neck, so infatuated with the passion of love was he that he laid himself down on the same pyre and breathed his last.

The whole city was seized with amazement. They talked among themselves: 'Aho! Aho! Amazing! Amazing indeed! Nothing like this has ever been witnessed before! Nothing like this has ever been heard of before! That three persons should die for love! How strange indeed!'

Having narrated this tale the genie said: 'Tell me, O, king; of these three which one is blinded by the passion of love?'

'The husband, no doubt,' answered King Vikramasena. 'He is the one blinded by love. He saw his beloved wife dead for love of another man. Yet he felt no anger and gave up his life.'

The genie heard the king's answer and straightaway fled to the same śinśipā tree to hang from its branches.

Thus ends the twentieth tale in the *Five-and-Twenty Tales of the Genie* set down by Śivadāsa.

TALE 21

Of the Four Foolish Brāhmaṇas Who Revived the Dead Lion

To the Pillar in which is rooted the universe,
from which Pillar rises the triple-world.
To Śambhu, Giver of Bliss, I bow,
whose lofty head is kissed by the moon
set on it as a charming crest-jewel.

Once again the king returned to the same spot, took the corpse down from the śinśipā tree and settled it on his shoulders. As he started walking, the corpse began to tell a tale. 'Listen, O king, and I shall tell you a story,' said the genie.

There is a city named Jayasthala. It was ruled by a certain king named Vīramardana. A Brāhmaṇa named Viṣṇusvāmi lived in that city and he had four sons. One was a gambler, another a whoremonger; a third was an adulterer and the last son was an unbeliever. The father tried his best to instruct his sons.

'The dice brings all things to naught;
a man of good conduct should give it up.
As life is consumed by poison
so is good conduct by dice.
Dejection and disputes and brawls,

anger, confusion and calumny,
greed and sorrow and exhaustion;
    these are all the kinsmen of dice.

'The ears and nose of gamblers are lopped off;[147]
knowing this, virtuous men do not play at dice,
    a most deadly vice.

'In no time, harlots infatuate those who go to them;
men who wear Virtue's jewel with pride
    give harlots a wide berth.

'Kissing goodbye to truth and serenity,
to cleanliness, good conduct and moral imperatives;
to the observance of vows and religious rites,
voluptuaries freely enter the homes of harlots.

'To him who holds a harlot dear,
no one else in the world is so dear;
mother, father, son or daughter,
brother, sister, none is quite so dear.

'To unblushing paramours, good advice does not appeal,
nor reverence for parents and elders;
they love to lick the intoxicating slobber
off the faces of inebriate harlots.

'The learned hold that worldly sorrows
are the flowers born of adulterous love;
they fall into the Bottomless Pit
    its bitter fruit.

'A woman who hurts her loving husband
    will certainly play cat and mouse
will she not, with her paramour?

Given that the cat devours her own kittens,
is she one to let go of a mouse?

'The shame of riding upon an ass,
or serving as a sweeper in a potter's home;
the loss of manhood, public condemnation,
wretchedness, ill-luck: these are the consequences
of sleeping with the wives of others.

'Violating the wives of other men
is a horrendous crime, they say:
Shun a whore even at a distance,
terrible as a venomous serpent.

'Proud of their youth and obsessed with sex,
men who fail to acquire learning in youth
suffer humiliation in their old age,
their limbs freeze—burnt like frost-struck lotuses.'

The four sons then paid heed to their father's advice and discussed the matter among themselves. 'Listen, a man who is unlettered is like one dead though living; so let us go to other lands and acquire learning.'

Being of one mind each of the four brothers set out for a different country. With the passage of time having gained knowledge they arrived at the meeting place previously arranged. The eldest brother spoke first. 'Dear brothers, let us now do something to demonstrate our learning.'

One of the brothers then went searching in the forest and found the bones of a dead lion. Using his specialized knowledge, he assembled the bones to form the lion's skeleton while another brother employed his special expertise to clothe it with flesh, fat and body fluids, humours and the like. The third brother then furnished it with blood and skin and hair while the fourth breathed life into the assembled frame. The lion arose and killed all four and ate them up.

Having narrated this tale the genie said: 'Tell me, O, king, which of the four brothers is the biggest fool?'

'The one who gave it life,' answered King Vikramasena. 'For:

'Native intelligence is the best of all;
    mere learning is not;
far superior to book-learning is intelligence;
    devoid of native intelligence,
    people are utterly lost
    like these lion-makers.'

Having got his answer, the genie went back to that same spot to hang from the branch of the śinśipā tree.

Thus ends the twenty-first tale in the *Five-and-Twenty Tales of the Genie*, set down by Śivadāsa.

TALE 22

Of the Yogī Who Went from One Body to Another

To the Lord of the Triple-World,
All-Pervading, Consort of Parvati,[148]
to the Supreme Donor of Knowledge,
I humbly bow my head.

Once again the king went back to that same spot and took the corpse down from the śinśipā tree. Placing it over his shoulders he set out on his way to the burning grounds where Kṣāntiśīla was waiting. The corpse began its storytelling; and the genie said: 'Listen to me, O, king, while I tell you a story.'

There is a city named Viśvapuram where King Vidagdha ruled. In that city lived a Brāhmaṇa named Nārāyaṇa. He had studied and mastered the art of entering into the body of another. Once he sat reflecting upon his life. 'See how decrepit my body has become. Let me abandon this old body of mine and enter one youthful so that I can enjoy the pleasures of life.'

Then Nārāyaṇa entered into a youthful body, stood before his family and said: 'Look, I have become a yogī.' And he began to sermonize as follows:

'Dry up the waters of the pool of hopes

with the intense heat of penance;
  nurture what lies at its centre;
with harsh severity cleanse the body of its defects;[149]
dissolve its foulness in the Transcendent.

'The limbs droop; the hair turns grey;
the snout[150] lacks its bite;
an old man, walking with a stick—
yet he does not lay down the baggage of Hope.

'As long as he earns an income
the family pays him respect;
come old age and decrepitude;
no one in his home cares to speak to him.

'Different paths, different gods and gurus;
different service, different dress,
different ways of salvation:
Maya[151] alone unites all.

'Night comes round; then again the day;
the year comes around; then the month again;
  old again, a child again.
Time goes and comes repeatedly.

'Who am I? Who are you? What is this world?
Who grieves? And for what does he grieve?
  One comes; another goes.
Fitful is the understanding of all beings.

'The shaven monk wears matted hair;[152]
  the Brāhmaṇa turns Buddhist;
  the Sānkhya brings in god;
  agnostics grow in strength.
No one who dies can ever be born again;
  even so, cruelty[153] is the All-Slayer.

'A single self, many bodies;
a single truth, many follies;
knowledge is single, frauds many;
why have the learned fashioned
so many fallacies?

'Who am I? Whence come I? And how?
Who is my mother? Who is my father?
Life in this world is imagined as such, and such.
It is all a matter of dreaming.'

In this manner, the Brāhmaṇa Nārāyaṇa held forth. Then he made this pronouncement: 'Listen, all of you! I am setting out on a pilgrimage.'

His family rejoiced to hear this. Nārāyaṇa, having entered a youthful body, first wept, then laughed.*

Having related this tale, the genie said: 'O, king, now tell me; why did this man weep first, and then laugh?'

King Vikramasena declared: 'Listen; as the yogī was on the point of abandoning his old, decrepit body, he reflected: "Ha! In childhood this body of mine was nourished with tenderness by my mother. In boyhood it was cherished and reared with pride by my father. In youth it was the means to enjoy sexual pleasures and other delights and comforts. Now it is being abandoned." These thoughts made him weep. But a moment later he thought: "Ah! Now, I have a young man's body." And he laughed with joy. It is aptly said:

'To any one unmotivated by one or other of the four imperatives in life, namely, the desire and the will to acquire virtue, wealth, love, final release, life itself is devoid of meaning and purpose, like teats dangling from a goat's neck.'

Hearing the king's answer, the genie was once again

---

* This appears to be a scribal error in the Mss; comes in the wrong place.

back at the same spot to hang from a branch of the śinśipā tree.

Thus ends the twenty-second tale in the *Five-and-Twenty Tales of the Genie,* set down by Śivadāsa.

TALE 23

Of Three Rather Fastidious Brāhmaṇas

Mortals aspiring to compose great works
accomplish it by the grace of the Muse, Sarasvatī;
so let us adore her, the Goddess of Wisdom,
with unwavering contemplation.

Once again the king walked back to that same spot, took down the corpse from the śinśipā tree and as he set out on his way to meet the necromancer, Kṣāntiśīla in the burning grounds, the corpse began to speak.

'Listen, O king, to the tale I am about to tell,' began the genie.

There is a city named Dharmapuram. It was ruled by a certain king named Dharmadvaja. In that city lived a Brāḥmaṇa named Govinda, a scholar well-versed in the four Vedas. Four sons were born to him, named, Haridatta, Somadatta, Yajnadatta and Brahmadatta respectively, all scholars in Vedic texts. In the course of time, the eldest son, Haridatta passed away. Grief-stricken by the loss of his son, Govinda prepared to die. When news of this reached the ears of the Royal Priest, Viṣṇu Śarma, he came at once to Govinda and exhorted him thus: 'O, Govinda, listen to me:

'Misery is born the moment Man commences
within a woman's womb his sojourn on earth.
What untold misery for the babe in the womb,

drinking the blend of fluids in a woman's body
passed through the uncleanliness of the navel tube!

'In youth what bitter misery parting from loved ones!
And then, old age, sapless! Tell me, O, man,
    is even a scrap of happiness
    to be found in this maze of existence?

'Death, inevitable, strikes constantly:
within the womb and at the time of birth;
on the mother's lap, or in bed;
in childhood, in old age, in youth,
in the mature years of one's life;
    and in battle as well;
it strikes the rich man and the poor.

'On treetops, on mountain peaks,
in the clouds, on the ground,
    in waters as well;
    in a cage or a hollow;
even if you enter the Deep, Death waits.

'Death spares no one, whoever it is:
scholars learned in scared or secular knowledge;
men possessed of wealth with treasures of gold;
    warriors with strength of arms; or kings;
    men possessed of serenity
        and self-control;
    all those well, or ill; well-off or badly-off,
        living in happiness, ease and comfort,
            or in misery;
    like the forest fire, Death devours all.

'A span of hundred years is measured out for Man:
    of this half passes in sleep;
more than half of the remaining half

passes in childhood and old age;
what little remains is spent in sorrow,
the sorrows of illness and bereavement;
the hardships of service and other necessities.
In the wayward flow of the river of existence,
where is happiness for any living thing?

'Kṛṣṇa, the Finder of Light,[154] was his uncle;
his father, the great hero, Arjuna,
Conqueror of Treasures; yet, Abhimanyu lay dead.
Insurmountable indeed is Time!

'His home is filled with possessions;
Kinsmen are present in the burning grounds;
the body now belongs to the piled wood:
his virtues and vices go with him;
not mother or father, not son, nor kinsmen either.
Having led him into the Hall of Judgement,
to Yama,[155] his good deeds and bad leave him.

'Dawn breaks again; the star-spangled Night returns;
the moon rises once more; the sun comes up again;
what is that to Time? Youth flies. Even so,
the world understands not the tale that's told.

'Gone is great Māndhātā,[156] Lord of the Earth,
ornament of the Golden Age.
where is he[157] who bridged the great Ocean
and slew ten-faced Rāvaṇa, demon king?

'Gone are Yudhiṣṭhira[158] and the others,
and so will His Honour, the king;
yet this earth, rich and bountiful
did not accompany a single king;
you think she may go with you!

'Birds wander solitary in the skies, often in dire peril;
in the ocean's unfathomable waters fishes are caught
with hooks;
evil abounds in this world; why not goodness?
What good is it to be in the right place?
Even from a distance Time seizes all with
outstretched arm.

'What are possessions?
They are as dust on the soles of one's feet.
Youth rushes on, fleet
as streams down hills.
Man's existence moves back and forth
like an elephant's ears flapping.
Those who fail to follow Virtue with unwavering
mind
that unlocks the gates to the World of Light,
are in ripe old age stricken with remorse,
and burn in the flames of anguish.

'Think upon, Rāvaṇa:[159] Trikūṭa,
his fortress city impregnable,
the great Ocean its moat,
the rākṣasas his warriors, powerful demons;
hoards of treasures, his power;
Sanjīvanī, the magic art of restoring life
waiting, ready, on his lips:
that same Rāvaṇa lay dead.

'Mother, father, kinsman; wife, siblings,
what are they to us?
We go whence we came; so, why lament?

'No healing herb, no piety, no friend or kinsman,
can come to the aid of a man caught in the toils of
Time.

What was at dawn is not there at noon;
what was at noon is not there at night;
what was at night is no longer seen:
this world is a magician's trick!'

Govinda listened attentively and took Viṣṇu Śarma's advice to heart and, pondered over his words. He then decided to perform a sacrifice. As he began the rites he dispatched his sons to the edge of the ocean to bring back a turtle for the sacrifice. The three sons set out. At the shores of the ocean they met a fisherman.

'Listen, fisherman,' they said. 'Cast your net in the middle of the ocean and catch us a turtle. We shall give you a hundred and one coins stamped with the royal seal.'

The fisherman cast his net, caught a turtle and brought it to the three Brāhmaṇas. The eldest looked at his middle brother and said: 'Hey, brother, pick the turtle up and carry it.'

The middle brother now turned to his younger brother and said: 'Hey, brother, you carry this turtle.'

The third brother exclaimed: 'O, no, I shall not carry this turtle; it will make my hands stink. I am fastidious about food, you know.'

The middle brother said: 'And I, I am very fastidious about women. I shall not touch this fishy thing.'

The other brother, the eldest now said: 'I shall not touch this turtle. I am most fastidious about what I sleep on.'

The three brothers argued hotly amongst themselves as to who should carry the turtle. Continuing to argue they went to the palace and presented themselves before the king.

'What is the cause of your dispute, worthy gentlemen?' asked the king.

One brother spoke up: 'Your Majesty, I am very sensitive in the matter of food; so how can I carry a turtle?'

The second brother said: 'And I, Your Majesty, am really sensitive in the matter of women.'

The third brother swore saying: 'I am truly most sensitive in the matter of beds, Your Majesty.'

The king came to a decision. 'Well then, I have to first subject all three of you to a test,' he said.

The king set a test for the Brāhmaṇa who was finicky over food, first. Whatever fine foods had been prepared in the royal kitchen were served to him on a platter. The connoisseur of food took a bit of rice in his hand and as he lifted it to his mouth he smelt a disagreeable odour. He rose without eating and went at once to the king.

The king asked courteously: 'Well, Sir, did you enjoy your meal?'

'O, Your Majesty, how could I eat that food? It had such a foul odour.'

'O, really,' queried the king. 'Was that so? What kind of foul odour was it?'

'The fields where the rice was grown must have been close to the burning grounds, because I smelt the fumes of the smoke from the funeral pyres in the cooked rice served me.'

Hearing this extraordinary complaint, the king immediately summoned the Keeper of Stores.

'Sir, from which village did you purchase the rice for our kiṭchens?' he enquired.

'Your Majesty, this rice was sent by one of the royal tenants, and grown by him in his fields in the village lying on the outskirts of our capital,' answered the Keeper of Stores.

The king then dispatched a messenger to fetch the particular tenant who had furnished the rice to the palace. The tenant came. 'Sir, tenant-farmer, tell me, where exactly are the fields where you grew the rice that you sent to our royal stores?' asked the king.

'It is close by the city's burning grounds, Your Majesty,' replied the farmer.

The king was amazed by this piece of information.

'Indeed, O, Brāhmaṇa, you speak the truth. You really are fastidious about food.'

Next the middle brother was escorted to the house of a courtesan. Spies were then sent secretly by the king to observe what happened in the courtesan's house.

The Brāhmaṇa was welcomed with all due courtesies and was offered paan and supari, liquid sandalwood paste, oils perfumed and medicated with camphor, turmeric and other healthful and pleasant herbs. He went up to the couch and as he kissed the courtesan's mouth her breath exhaled the odour of a goat. Disgust crinkled his face and he turned his back to her and fell asleep. The spies concealed in the room watched everything.

Next morning the Brāhmaṇa went to the king who enquired: 'Hey! Brāhmaṇa, did you have a good night?'

'No; it was no pleasure,' replied the Brāhmaṇa.

'Oh! And why was that?' asked the king.

'Your Majesty, the woman's mouth smelled like a goat; I simply couldn't stand it,' replied the Brāhmaṇa.

The king sent for the bawd and questioned her: 'How did you get a daughter like this? Tell me the truth.'

'O, Your Majesty, it was like this. My sister gave birth to this girl. But my sister died of puerperal fever soon after and so I brought the child up on goat's milk.'

The king turned to the Brāhmaṇa and observed: 'well, you speak the truth. You are indeed a connoisseur of women.'

Then the king had a mattress made of finest silk cotton for the third Brāhmaṇa to sleep on and directed him to the bedchamber.

The Brāhmaṇa went in and lay down on the bed. But he did not have a wink of sleep all night. He passed the long night with great difficulty. In the morning, the king sent for him and enquired: 'Hey! Brāhmaṇa, did you sleep well?'

'O, no, Your Majesty, there seems to have been a coarse hair embedded in the middle of the mattress in the seventh layer of cotton. That caused such pain in my back that I could not sleep,' answered the Brāhmaṇa.

The king had the fine mattress ripped open and there it was, a coarse hair right in the middle of the seventh layer.

'Yes, you are indeed finicky about beds,' observed the king.

Having related this tale, the genie said: 'Tell me, O, king, of these three Brāhmaṇas, who was the most fastidious?'

'The man who was sensitive of beds,' answered King Vikramasena.

The genie fled as soon as he heard the king's answer.

Thus ends the twenty-third tale in the *Five-and-Twenty Tales of the Genie* set down by Śivadāsa.

TALE 24

Of Strange and Riddling Relationships

I bow to the Lord of Ganas over whose elephant cheeks
a throng of honeybees hover drawn by drops of ichor.
I bow to the Lord of Wishes[160] who grants
the fruits of our most cherished heart's desire.

Once again the king went back to take the corpse from the śinśipā tree. Placing it across his shoulders he started walking when the corpse began its storytelling. The genie said, 'Listen, O king, and I shall tell you a tale.'

There is a city named Prabhāvatī. A certain king named Pradyumna ruled there. His queen was named Prītikārī. They had a daughter named Ćandraprabhā and she was married to Vijayabala, King of the South. Ćandraprabhā bore a daughter named Lāvaṇyavatī.

Once, Vijayabala's kinsmen came in the quiet of the night and laid siege to the city. The king woke up his queen and said, 'My beloved, go out of the city with our daughter, while I do battle against the enemy. I shall return soon.'

Queen Ćandraprabhā hastily left the city with her daughter while the king, Vijayabala marched out to meet the enemy. A great battle was fought. King Vijayabala was killed.

The mother and daughter wandered on and soon reached

a lake. They stopped there briefly to rest and at the crack of dawn they left the lake.

A certain king from Kusumapura arrived at that same lake with his son while hunting. The prince noticed the lines of beautiful footprints by the lake's shore and pointed them out to the king: 'Look, look, dear father. Some queen and her daughter appear to have been here and gone onwards.'

The king examined the footprints carefully and exclaimed: 'Yes, my son; one has long feet and the other tiny feet. If we meet them, the lady with the longer feet shall become my queen; the other shall be your bride.' The prince agreed. Having settled the matter, the king and his son rode on and soon caught up with the queen and princess. They questioned the two royal ladies. Out of fear, Queen Ćandraprabhā told them everything not leaving out a single detail.

The king of Kusumapura exclaimed: 'A piece of good fortune, indeed! For you belong to the same warrior class, Kṣatriya, as ourselves.'

Though the truth of the matter was that the lady with the tiny feet was the mother and the one with the long feet was the daughter, the king declared: 'My son, I am taking the lady with the long feet.' As it has been said:

A woman can remain chaste, inviolate,
  if the place is not secluded,
  and the moment not opportune,
and no man is around desiring her.
  Only then, O, Nārada!

The son now took hold of the lady with the tiny feet as his own. Placing the princess and the queen behind them on horseback the king of Kusumapura and his son rode back to their own kingdom. On reaching the palace Queen Ćandraprabhā and Princess Lāvaṇyavatī were sent to the Royal Apartment as members of the harem. In time both mother and daughter gave birth, one to a son and the other to a daughter. Later, when the children grew up, they were married to each other.

Having narrated this tale, the genie put a question to the king. 'Tell me, O king,' said the goblin, 'what kind of relationship exists between these two?'

At this point, King Vikramasena made no reply.

Thus ends the twenty-fourth tale in the *Five-and-Twenty Tales of the Genie* set down by Śivadāsa.

TALE 25

The Epilogue and Conclusion

Seeing the king silent, the genie said: 'O, king, listen; I know that I have tricked you many a time; and that is why you now remain silent. Hear me now, O, great hero! I am mightily pleased with your courage and daring. I shall grant you a boon; ask.' Still King Vikramasena gave no reply.

The genie spoke again to Vikramasena. 'O, king; though you do not care to give me an answer, I say to you that I am pleased with your truthfulness and daring. I tell you now what you should do next and you should do as I say. Now go to the burning grounds with the corpse as arranged with the necromancer, Kṣāntiśīla. The naked monk will take the corpse and worship it with incense and sandalwood paste and other articles of worship. Then he will say to you: "Listen, O king, fall flat on your face and prostrate yourself on the ground with the eight limbs of your body touching the ground." Then, this is what you say to him in reply: "I do not know how to prostrate myself with the eight limbs of my body touching the ground. All who come before me prostrate themselves to do me homage. I have never prostrated myself before anyone. Teach me, O, Best of Ascetics! Show me first so that I learn to do it properly."

'When you say this to Kṣāntiśīla, he will at once show you how a proper and complete prostration is done. Then, immediately, draw your sword and sever his head at the neck. Offer his blood to me as an oblation. You shall gain the Eight Powers by this act. If you do not act as I tell you, you will be killed and the necromancer, Kṣāntiśīla will then gain the Eight Powers that he hankers after.'

Having said this the genie left.

King Vikramasena now carried the corpse to the burning grounds and set it down within the maṇḍala, the magic circle. The naked monk, Kṣāntiśīla, exclaimed delightedly: 'Well done, truly well done, O, great hero. You have performed a mighty penance.'

Kṣāntiśīla performed all the prescribed rites. He placed flowers and incense and other articles of worship and arranged the oil lamps and vessels containing various oblations within the maṇḍala and uttering potent incantations invoked the genie. Having called upon the genie to descend into the consecrated space and having performed all the necessary rites and ceremonies, Kṣāntiśīla, the naked monk turned to King Vikramasena and said: 'Now perform the complete prostration, O, king.'

The king recollected the instructions of the genie and said: 'Listen, yogī; I have never in all my life performed a full and complete prostration before anyone, never, not from the hour of my birth. I do not therefore know how to perform one properly. You show me first how it is done and I shall do it.'

Deluded by fate, the naked monk prostrated himself fully on the ground. As he did so, King Vikramasena drew his sword and chopped off the monk's head. He offered the blood flowing out of the skull as an oblation to the genie. Thus did King Vikramasena obtain the Eight Powers. And it is also said:

Pay a man back in his own coin;
do harm unto him who has done harm to you;
  I see no harm in that;
adopt foul means towards an evil man.

Then, the Gandharvas in the World of Light rained showers of blossoms on earth. The moon raised exultant cries of victory to the king. All the celestials made this proclamation: 'O, king, we are pleased. You shall possess the sovereignty of the whole earth. Ask for a boon.'

The king stated his wish. 'Grant that this work, the *Five-and-Twenty Tales of the Genie* may become celebrated and gain renown. By your grace may this Genie be my minister and carry out my edicts!'

Then, Brahmā-Viṣṇu-Maheśvara, descended
on earth, the Holy Trinity manifest,
bestowed high praise on him, the Lord of Men,
reverently bowing at his feet.

The Glorious Effulgence declared thus:
'A mighty lord, of my essence[161] you are,
a ray of light from me, born here, on earth;
Vikramāditya, Sun of Valour,
a monarch greater than ancient monarchs
who held dominion over the earth.
Vikramasena too are you named,
jewel of the lineage of earthly rulers.

'Enjoy the complete and continuing happiness and good fortune of the glory of the Vidyādharas.'[162]

Having obtained the benediction of Śiva, Foe of the Triple-City,[163] Vikramasena became the ruler who turned the Wheel of Empire.[164] Entering his capital he ruled with might and majesty, the possessor of Royal Glory.

Thus ends the twenty-fifth tale of the *Five-and-Twenty Tales of the Genie* set down by Śivadāsa.

Appendix

Tales from

The Five-and-Twenty Tales of the Genie

as set down by Jambhaladatta

Benedictory Verses:

1. Willed by the play of those stave-like arms,
the unmoving mountains whirl in response,
as the Great Lord[1] dances His Wild Dance[2]
marvellous:
the universe stands still wondering, awestruck
by those high-sounding tones, clamorous;
while the edges of the World-Snake's[3] thousand
expanded hoods
tremble beneath the burden of those stamping feet;
and the moon[4] rides high at the forest's fringes
of His matted locks, tawny as honey bees . . .
locks that twist and coil into garlands of lofty
waves.
May that dance bless you all with great good
fortune!

2. Having heard these tales of the goblin,
five-and-twenty,
filled with fine flavours,[5] from Varadeva's
lotus-mouth—
he who was Minister for Peace and War[6]—
Jambhaladatta in reverence for his preceptor
has set them down in words few but fitting
in order that these tales so fabulous
would always live preserved in men's memories.
Let all good folks hear them with keen interest!

3. Noble sirs! If to hear this tale you're all eager,
the likes of which has ne'er been told before,
why then, gentlemen, read it as it's written here.

PREAMBLE

Once, on this round earth, there ruled the glorious monarch, Vikramakesarī, Lion of Valour, supreme sovereign over kings; and he was celebrated as 'the jewel among monarchs'.

Earrings set with many different gems with the splendour of their blended rays shed lustre on his cheeks. His whole body shone, adorned by ornaments of various kinds. Learned in many sciences, the monarch was endowed with the finest qualities as the ocean is filled with the finest gems.

Like Kubera, God of Treasures, this monarch had amassed an incredible hoard of gems of various sorts: sapphires and emeralds, diamonds and lapis lazuli; rubies, pearls, and many other precious stones.

In each hill and valley on earth, in every direction of space, his glory sounded, sung exultantly by Vidyādharīs[7] skilled in music. Like Indra, Overlord of the Immortals, the monarch was blessed with the perfection of beauty of every limb and feature. Lord of the entire earth girdled by the four oceans, this mighty lord of men, surrounded by a host of vassal princes and by counsellors, passed his days in the enjoyment of that ineffable happiness that sovereignty brings.

Now, this is what happened. Every morning at daybreak, just as the glorious lord of heaven rose above the horizon wearing his garland of light-rays, at the very hour when the lord of the earth rose from his bed to wash his face, a certain anchorite,[8] named Kṣāntiśīla, sent through the chief royal bath-attendant, a marvellous bilva fruit[9] of rare colour and sheen. And each morning, the attendant would offer this fruit ceremoniously. The monarch would accept it each time graciously, admire its exquisite beauty and hand it back to the attendant. And in this manner passed twelve whole years.

Then, once it happened that the bilva fruit as it was being offered to the emperor as usual, slipped and fell from his lotus-palm on to the courtyard floor where it broke into pieces. Five priceless gems came out of its broken heart and rolled around on the floor. Seeing these priceless gems, the king was transported with delight and exclaimed: 'Ah! What a marvel indeed! In my whole collection of gems in which each gem has been sought for with great diligence and acquired, not a single one to compare with these gems in their rich and rare beauty is to be seen.'

The emperor was completely amazed as he looked at the gems rolling about on the floor; he now turned to the attendant and remarked: 'Listen! Water-carrier! Each morning you hand me one of these gorgeous fruits. Tell me; where do you find them?'

And the attendant answered: 'My lord, a skull-bearing anchorite, named Kṣāntiśīla, places one of these bilva fruits each morning in my hands wishing to gratify you.'

The king paused a moment; then he ordered the man: 'Go; bring all the other bilva fruits that you have brought me in the past for so many years.'

The water-bearer bowed and went out and soon returned with every one of the bilva fruits that had been kept in the royal store. The emperor had every one of these fruits broken open and looked at the heap of gems that rolled out. And he said over and over again: 'Ha! In my treasury of priceless gems not a single one can compare with these.' Then the emperor commanded: 'I wish to see the person who gives me these fruits, now, immediately.'

The attendant murmuring, 'As His Majesty commands,' ran to the outer gate and returned with the anchorite. He announced: 'Your Majesty; here is the skull-bearing anchorite who brings the bilva fruits; he waits at the door.'

'Usher him in,' commanded the emperor.

No sooner had the anchorite been ushered into the royal presence and seen the emperor than he thrilled with such fierce joy that the hairs on his body stood up stiffly, covering him as if with a coat of mail. Lifting his right hand straight up, he called down blessings galore on the emperor.

'Oh! Skull-bearer! Why have you been presenting me with these fabulous gems all this time under the pretext of offering simple bilva fruit? Noble soul! What is it that you want of me; tell me,' said the emperor addressing the anchorite.

'Listen, great king,' replied the anchorite. 'If Your Majesty be favourably inclined towards a stranger, then hear what I have to say in private, in secrecy.'

One glance from the emperor served to make his retainers and attendants withdraw to a distance; after which the anchorite spoke: 'I am Kṣāntiśīla, the skull-bearer, and a great magic-worker. This entire earth have I circled sunwise, searching for a person, very special, to assist me in certain magical rites done with a corpse; a person pure and virtuous, and highly accomplished. But I found him nowhere. Only when I arrived here did I see such a person, magnanimous and blessed with all imaginable virtues. If you pay heed to my words, then I shall disclose my cherished desire.'

'Speak freely,' said the emperor. 'Tell me what you desire and I shall make it come to pass.'

At these words of the emperor, the skull-bearer began: 'My lord, I ask for your assistance in rites to be performed using a genie that inhabits a corpse. If Your Majesty assents to my request, then I shall attain great powers; otherwise not.'

When the high-souled monarch heard this, he became determined to accede to the request made by the anchorite. Whereupon the anchorite again spoke to the king: 'If Your Majesty agrees to be my assistant in the rites, then I shall be able to gain the eight Siddhis,[10] or magic powers. To do this, I shall station myself in the burning grounds that lie south of the city, on the fourteenth day of the dark half of the month of Bhadrā.[11] Pray come to me at sunset on that day, at the burning grounds, unseen by anyone, Your Majesty. I shall explain my cherished wish to you the moment you come, for at that time, my purpose will bear fruit.'

The king, having listened attentively to the anchorite, gave his assent. 'So be it,' he said. 'Go your way and prepare to carry out your purpose. I shall meet you at that spot and make your wish come true.'

The king dismissed the anchorite with these words, and Kṣāntiśīla returned to his own place.

Come the month of Bhadrā, the anchorite arrived at the palace gates on the fourteenth day of the dark half of the month and sent word through an attendant to remind the king. King Vikramakesarī offered due worship to gods and ancestors and having transacted all the daily duties of administration, set out at dusk alone, unseen by a single soul, and armed only with his trusty sword. He came to the burning grounds to the south of the city where the anchorite was waiting for him and said: 'Here I am, O Skull-bearer; now disclose your wishes.'

Seeing the king there, the anchorite's eyes widened with great joy and he greeted the monarch with words of high praise.

'O, great monarch, you are indeed the best of men; a man of supreme virtue and courage in that you who are an emperor have come to me here in this place of cremation, alone, with only your sword for companion; and that too on this night, the darkest night of the month of Bhadrā, despite the deep and terrifying darkness. Your life here on this earth has achieved fulfilment.'

To these words, the emperor replied with becoming modesty: 'Be that as it may, O Skull-bearer! Tell me what it is that you desire so ardently. I have come fired by curiosity; what have I to be afraid of?'

Then Kṣāntiśīla replied: 'Listen, mighty monarch, I intend to perform the Rite of the Corpse and for this Your Majesty has to serve as my assistant. By performing this rite, I shall attain success and gain magic powers. When I acquire magic powers, Your Majesty will also gain those same powers.'

To these words, the king replied: 'Whether or not I gain magic powers is beside the point. You had better go ahead with your arrangements, O Skull-bearer. Only inform me what my part in all this is to be.'

The skull-bearer then said: 'By the river Ghargharā,[12] somewhat to the north grows a śinśipā tree.[13] On one of its upper branches hangs an unmutilated corpse. Take it down, place it across your shoulders, and bring it here quickly in complete silence disregarding what the corpse might say to you; for it will utter many clever, deceitful words. As soon as you arrive here with the corpse, I shall wash that corpse ritually within a magic circle constructed of diverse materials of worship; then I shall offer due worship to the divinities and utter a powerful incantation. By means of this rite, I shall accomplish my purpose and gain magic powers. You too, Your Majesty, will gain whatever you wish for.'

The king listened and following the anchorite's directions, came to the river-bank where he saw the corpse as described. The corpse noticed the king and seemed gripped by terrible fear. The moment the king came close and stretched out one hand to grab it, the corpse, inhabited by a genie, jumped up to the topmost branch and hung there.

King Vikramakesarī laughed heartily and addressed the corpse: 'Hey fellow! What are you but a corpse? Why are you running away? Now watch; I shall climb this great tree and take you down.'

The corpse, terribly frightened, kept leaping from branch to branch. But even as the corpse kept leaping from one branch to another, King Vikramāditya caught it while it was still on one branch and held on to it. Then slowly and carefully, the king crept up that great tree and with a single, sharp blow of his sword, severed the corpse from the branch it was clinging to and let it drop to the ground at the foot of the tree.

Now the corpse pretending to be badly hurt by the fall screeched loudly, making squeaky sounds—kichi-kichi-kichi. Changing its tone to one of plaintive pleading, the corpse now spoke humbly to the king: 'Listen, O, king; tell me, in what way have I offended you? Here I am, outside the pale of the living world, a miserable thing, unoffending and deserving of pity, merely hanging on to the branch of a solitary tree in an uninhabited wilderness. Why are you harassing me in this way? The bones in my poor frame are broken to bits from the fall.'

Hearing the corpse speak, the monarch answered: 'Indeed I am not to blame, O, corpse! This happens to be your fate, it seems. Do not be afraid. However, I *have* to carry you away, that is certain.'

With these words, the king climbed down the tree. But even as he stretched his hand out to pick it up, the corpse leapt up to the topmost branch of the tree and hung there. In this way the corpse repeatedly made things difficult for the king. After trying half a dozen times, the king paused to reflect how best to succeed in seizing and holding the corpse. Then, he again climbed up the tree, severed the corpse from the branch it was clinging to with one sharp blow of his sword, felled it to the ground and immediately jumped, falling on top of the corpse. Despite the fact that it started yelling loudly, the king raised the corpse onto his shoulders and started walking briskly towards the place where the anchorite was waiting for him.

The genie that lived within the corpse now spoke to the king, wishing to break his silence. 'Well, if you really have to carry me off like this, O King, let us at least pass the time as we go on our way, by telling each other riddling stories, shall we? By doing so, we shall not feel the weariness of the way too greatly. Your Majesty, it is I who will tell the tale. But you had better listen to it carefully, because the story poses a problem and you have to solve it. If you have the solution and knowingly refrain from telling it, you shall be guilty of wrongdoing. However, if in truth you do not have the solution, then no blame will attach to you.'

With these words, the genie begins his tale.

TALE 7

Of King Praćaṇḍasinha and his Friend the Skull-bearer

The genie heard the king's answer;
laughing loudly, left his shoulder,
he went back again in a great hurry
to hang from that same śinśipā tree.

As he was being carried along once more, the genie began another tale.

Your Majesty, (began the genie), a long time ago there was a city named Tāmraliptikā, ruled over by King Praćaṇḍasinha. There was a skull-bearing anchorite named Sattvaśīla for whom the king bore a deep affection. Once, the king entered a great forest with his friend, to hunt deer. Roaming around in the forest, the king became weary after a while and suffered acute hunger and thirst. To appease the king's hunger and thirst, Sattvaśīla gave him two marvellous Āmalaki[14] fruits to eat. Having eaten the fruit, the king, freed from the torments of hunger and thirst felt refreshed. And by this gift of two Āmalaki fruits, Sattvaśīla became dearer than life itself to his friend the king. King Praćaṇḍasinha spent his days in great happiness with his friend.

Sometime later, the king of Sinhala Island, having heard reports of the valour, nobility and high breeding of King Praćaṇḍasinha decided to give him his daughter, Kuvalayavatī in marriage. So an eminent emissary was sent in a ship laden with rich gifts to Tāmraliptikā to Praćanḍasinha, who, on receiving the emissary, ordered Sattvaśīla to go and inspect Kuvalayavatī's beauty.

Sattvaśīla in obedience to the king's orders went with the emissary from Sinhala Island. On the way, a wild storm blew up and the ship sank. As Sattvaśīla was swimming in the waters of the ocean, he saw rise before him, a jewelled mountain peak. On it there was an image of the goddess Pārvatī. A maiden whose beauty bewitched the three worlds was rising after worshipping the image and was leaving with her companion. Sattvaśīla fell violently in love with her.

Noticing the companion coming his way, Sattvaśīla spoke to her and conveyed his passion for the beautiful maiden. She listened to him and then said: 'Worthy gentleman, wait right here, while I go and acquaint my lady of your passion for her.'

The girl went to her mistress and told her of Sattvaśīla's infatuation. When the beautiful lady heard of the state of the shipwrecked Sattvaśīla from her companion's mouth, she laughed gaily and said: 'Go, my friend, tell the man that he should first bathe in the waters of the pool inside my palace and only then come into my presence.'

The companion went back to Sattvaśīla and said, 'First go and bathe in my lady's pool, O, best of men, and then come to see her.'

With great joy, Sattvaśīla plunged into the pool and when he arose, found himself in the pool in the pleasure gardens of his friend, King Praćanḍasinha. He sat on the edge of the pool with no other thought but of the beautiful maiden he had glimpsed and sat lamenting.

Now, King Praćanḍasinha's men noticed him sitting and pining and lamenting his fate and went at once to inform the king. 'Your Majesty,' they stated, 'that Sattvaśīla whom you ordered to go to Sinhala Island to note and report on the beauty of the princess Kuvalayavatī, is back here beside the pool in the pleasure gardens, weeping.

Hearing this the king was astonished and went to the pool's edge to see what the matter was. 'My friend, what's all this?' he asked Sattvaśīla.

On being questioned, Sattvaśīla blurted out everything from the very beginning. And the king, seized of the matter, joyously took ship, accompanied by his friend and went to the same spot where the marvellous events that Sattvaśīla mentioned had happened. And when he set eyes on that beautiful maiden, King Praćanḍasinha was overwhelmed with love for her. The maiden too fell deeply in love with the king the moment she saw him.

Though it was hard for her to bring herself to do this, the maiden honoured the king and offered due hospitality to him sending gifts through one of her companions. Then, she sent another of her companions to the king disclosing her love for him.

The king listened to the girl and replied; 'Go girl, tell your lady to give herself to me; go and tell her that.' The girl hurried back to her mistress and conveyed King Praćanḍasinha's demand.

The lady heard it and ordered her companion: 'Go, give this message to the king: "I offer myself; let the king do what he pleases with me."'

Obeying her mistress' command, the girl returned to the king's presence and delivered the message. The king listened and ordered: 'Let her come to me.'

Lāvaṇyavatī,[15] accompanied by her companion, came into the king's presence. Seeing her approaching, the king said: 'Lāvaṇyavatī, since you have given yourself to me, now you are mine to give to this man here, Sattvaśīla, my friend, who is dearer to me than life itself. If you disregard my words, it will amount to taking back a gift that you have made; you will then be guilty of grave transgression.'

To avoid the blame of taking back a gift, the maiden said: 'Do whatever it is that pleases you.' And by the king's command, she gave herself to Sattvaśīla, who spent days of ineffable happiness with her.

The king now addressed Sattvaśīla: 'The gift of a pair of Āmalaki fruits has gained you this peerless maiden, Lāvaṇyavatī; and Your Honour will acquire great merit in the life after.'

Sattvaśīla answered: 'Your Majesty! Through your favour, what is there that I might not gain!'

Then, Lāvaṇyavatī said once to Sattvaśīla: 'Listen, my lord; the great monarch Praćaṇḍasinha tarries here abandoning his kingdom. This is a grave offence. So, I have this to say: "Let us plunge into the magic pool and go home."'

'Now tell me, O, king! Of these two men, King Praćaṇḍasinha and Sattvaśīla, who is the nobler, the more magnanimous?'

'Oh! You genie, listen to me,' answered King Vikramāditya. 'The nobler man, the more magnanimous, is King Praćaṇḍasinha, without doubt. Because, he, King Praćaṇḍasinha, remembering the gift of two Āmalaki fruits he had once received, made a gift of an enchantingly beautiful girl that he was madly in love with, to his friend Sattvaśīla.'

Even as the king was speaking, the genie went back to the śinśipā tree to hang there once again.

This genie so cussed abandoned the king
who had broken his vow of silence by speaking;
away the genie fled to dwell on the branch of a tree.

Once more the king walked back uncomplainingly
even to the foot of that same śinśipā tree
that grew on Ghargarā's farther bank, solitary.

The Lord of the Earth, lost in wonder,
seized once more that sly, powerful creature
and slung him right over his shoulder.

King Vikramārka turned round and went on his way through the night compact of blinding darkness.

Thus ends tale seven in the *Five-and-Twenty Tales of the Genie*.

TALE 11

Of the Three Flower-like Delicate Queens

O, king, (began the genie), once, King Dharmadhvaja ruled over the kingdom of Kānćanapura. He had three queens, named Śṛṅgāravatī, Mṛgānkavatī, and Tārāvatī, all three richly blessed with youth and loveliness.

One day, the king accompanied by Queen Śṛṅgāravatī went to the pavilion standing on the edge of his pleasure pool. As he was making love to her, a water lily placed behind his ear dropped on the queen. Struck by the fall of the lily, the queen turned away and became unconscious. To revive her and dispel this calamity, the king arranged for an ongoing regimen of medical treatment. He gave away vast sums of money to Brāhmaṇas. As a result of all the merit accruing from the giving of charity, Queen Śṛṅgāravatī was with great difficulty restored to life.

Then, another day, the king accompanied by Queen Mṛgānkavatī, eager to sport with her, went at once to the jewelled pavilion in the palace; and he made love to her. And Mṛgānkavatī's whole body became crushed and bruised as it were when moonbeams fell on her. The king became deeply troubled and unhappy over this incident. He set in motion a complete system of medication for her; he gave away vast sums of money to gods and Brāhmaṇas; he had countless auspicious rites performed and recitation of sacred chants carried out for the well-being of the queen. And finally she managed to regain her health and life.

Yet another day, the king took Queen Tārāvatī and went there. He sported with her, dallying in love. And at that time, a sound was heard from the far distance, of a servant maid pounding grain. That very moment, the sound of the pestle caused the queen's whole body to break out into blisters. And the king, having recourse to the same means employed to restore Queen Mṛgānkavatī to good health, managed to restore Tārāvatī to health.

'Now, speak, O, king,' demanded the genie. 'Tell me, of these three queens, which one possessed limbs of unimaginable delicacy?'

'Ah, listen, Oh! You genie!' snapped King Vikramāditya. 'Surely it is Queen Tārāvatī, for her body broke out in blisters by the mere sound of a pestle in a mortar. The other two queens at least suffered the impact of some object.'

Even as King Vikramāditya said this, the genie went back to the śinśipā tree to hang on it once more.

Thus ends tale eleven of the *Five-and-Twenty Tales of the Genie*.

And that genie, carried along once more by the king, told another tale.

TALE 20

Of the Ascetic Who Entered the Corpse of a Brāhmaṇa Youth

Your Majesty, (began the genie), in the land of the Kaliṅgas there flourished the city of Yajnasthala. And there resided the Brāhmaṇa Yajnasoma. His wife was Somadattā on whom he begat a son named Brahmāsvāmī. Though he had complete mastery over all fields of knowledge, Brahmāsvāmī was cut down by the hand of Fate. The parents, bewailing his death bitterly, picked up his body and accompanied by friends and relatives, took it to the burning grounds to perform the last sacred rites.

A yogī who made the burning grounds his home, saw the body being brought there of a Brāhmaṇa youth of uncommon beauty and unparalleled learning in all the fields of knowledge, who had met an untimely death. And he cried out loudly in the most pitiful, high-pitched tones and began to dance wildly in frenetic excitement. Then, all of a sudden, he rose up, abandoned his old, shrivelled body and entered the body of the Brāhmaṇa youth. The dead youth at once sat up as if awakening from deep sleep. The joy of his parents knew no bounds. All the friends and relatives gathered there rejoiced. But Brahmāsvāmī, having regained life, gave up all comforts and desires and remained absorbed in yogic meditation.

'Why is it that the yogī, dweller of the burning grounds,

cried out wildly and then danced. Tell me the reason, Your Majesty,' asked the genie.

'Listen then, you, you genie,' said King Vikramāditya. 'The ascetic cried out loudly because he had to give up a body that he had possessed for a very long time. Then, seeing that he was giving up an old, shrivelled body for that of the Brāhmaṇa youth in which the finest qualities had found a home, he danced for joy.'

Even as the king said this, the genie was back again hanging on the śinśipā tree.

Thus ends tale twenty in the *Five-and-Twenty Tales of the Genie.*

Again brought back and carried along, the genie tells another tale.

TALE 21

Of How Four Merchant Princes Fared With the Courtesan

Your majesty, (began the genie), in the land to the south there reigned at one time, the great monarch, Vikramabāhu. In his kingdom was situated the fair city of Puskarāvatī where one Nidhipatidatta resided, a prince among merchants and owner of caravans whose wealth surpassed even that of Kubera the Lord of Wealth[16] himself. He had four wives whose names were Kāmasenā, Vāsavadattā, Kṣamāvatī, and Ćampāvatī. On these four wives he begot four sons: Ratnadatta, Maṇidatta, Kumāradatta and Kanakadatta.

Now the eldest of these, Ratnadatta, studied the Fine Arts. No one in this whole wide world was his equal in the field of music, dance and allied arts. The second son, Maṇidatta, studied the martial arts. No one in this whole wide world could equal his mastery of weapons of different sorts. Kumāradatta studied the liberal arts. No one in this whole wide world had his learning. And Kanakadatta studied the moral sciences. His equal in the knowledge of polity and statecraft and ethics was not to be seen. These four brothers who were endowed with all the finest qualities, who were radiant with beauty that put the god of love in the shade, who ravished the hearts of lovely, young women with their appearance and whose manliness was celebrated over all the known world, lived in great happiness with their wives enjoying all the good things of life. After some time their father departed to the other world. Soon after, by the play of Fate, though all four were one in mind and spirit, they were forced to separate on account of the bickering of their wives. The father's wealth amounting to crores was divided amicably among the brothers except for one item, three resplendent gems that remained in common, because their father, Nidhipatidatta had previously charged them thus: 'If at any time you four should separate, then, to which ever among you my dear friend, King Vikramabāhu, awards the gems, he alone will possess them.'

Recollecting their father's words, the four brothers proceeded to the king's court. Seeing his friend's sons before him, King Vikramabāhu enquired: 'Ah! You sons of my best friend, what is your purpose in coming to me?'

The brothers acquainted the king with their father's wishes. Beholding those three gems, the king, lost in wonder, reflected: 'These three resplendent, fabulous gems ought to be given to the one who proves to be the most resourceful of my friend's four sons. Therefore, it is imperative that their fitness be tested.'

Deciding that this was the right thing to do, the king addressed the four brothers: 'Listen, sons of my dear friend, let me state that you are not bound by any means to abide by any decision that I might make with regard to these gems.'

And they replied: 'Your Majesty, we shall strictly abide by your decision alone. For, which of us dares to disregard His Majesty's words?'

The king then said: 'Well then, let these gems remain here as your common property. Now, in the city of Kusumapura, lives a courtesan named Rūpavatī, whose beauty fascinates the three worlds. She gives herself to a man for one night on payment of one lakh of rupees. Not even for another lakh of rupees will she ever consent to grant a man a second night of lovemaking. These gems are his who succeeds in enjoying two nights of love in succession with that courtesan.'

The four brothers agreed to the king's condition and

asked: 'Your Majesty, who goes first? We await your command.'

'It is best to follow the order of seniority in age starting with the eldest,' advised the king.

So, Ratnadatta set out first for Kusumapura, appearing like Indra, Lord of the Immortals, taking with him an immense array of goods of many different sorts: a host of elephants and horses, jewels and priceless rubies, gold and precious gems. Reaching that city, he made a memorable commencement of his enterprise with a performance of dance, song and instrumental music and a display of his other accomplishments. He followed this up by sending a skilled emissary carrying gifts of goods worth a lakh of rupees to make Rūpavatī's acquaintance.

Rūpavatī, seeing that emissary approaching her, laden with rich gifts, began to reflect in amazement: 'Amazing! Such ardent expectation! Never has it been seen in any man!'

Gauging Rūpavatī's reactions correctly, the clever emissary began to instil trust in her, plying her with words sweet as nectar. Gaining confidence, he then addressed her: 'Rūpavatī! Let Your Ladyship deign to sport in love with His Honour, the most excellent Ratnadatta, a man who is like the god of love.'

And Rūpavatī answered: 'Indeed, how fortunate I am that a gentleman like him is enamoured of me. Pray bring him to me quickly, respected Sir. I shall make myself a worthy partner of his lovemaking. And when he has paid me one lakh of rupees, he shall enjoy the delights of love with me.' With these words, Rūpavatī dismissed him. And the emissary returned to apprise Ratnadatta of Rūpavatī's compliance.

The ecstatic Ratnadatta then went that night to the courtesan's house. Having enjoyed the most extraordinary kind of lovemaking with her, he then treated her to a display of jealously guarded secrets of his art so as to win a second night of lovemaking. Even gods and celestial singers and musicians descended on earth to see and hear Ratnadatta's performance of dance, song and the other arts that he was skilled in. After the performance Rūpavatī wept piteously.

'O, lady, dearer than life, what makes you weep for no reason?' exclaimed Ratnadatta.

'I weep, O, Lord of my life, knowing that there will not be another night of love with you who are the most excellent of men.'

'And why not?' queried Ratnadatta.

'I follow this practice; one night of love for one lakh of rupees,' replied the courtesan.

'I shall pay you three lakhs for the second night,' said the young merchant prince.

'No,' said the courtesan. 'Not even for a thousand lakhs will I give a second night of lovemaking. This is a solemn vow that I have undertaken.'

All efforts to make her yield failing, Ratnadatta, rejected, went out stunned and returned to his own land, most disconsolate. He went to the palace and reported what had happened to King Vikramabāhu, 'Your Majesty, who indeed might be the hero who can win a second night of lovemaking with this lady!' he said.

Now, Maṇidatta set out for Kusumapura with a vast treasure of gems and jewels and went straight to the reigning monarch and presented himself. Being informed of his arrival there, the king granted him an audience, provided him with all the means for fine living and set him up in a residence close to his own palace.

Meantime, an enemy ruler invaded the kingdom bent on conquering the king and having defeated the entire armed forces of men and elephants and horses, marched on to capture the king himself. At this point, Maṇidatta swore to the king: 'Your Majesty, I shall set out against this enemy king, defeat him in battle and bring him here before you.' Having sworn this oath, Maṇidatta met the enemy, defeated him and leading him into the king's presence handed him over.

And from that day on, there was not one single person in Kusumapura who was his equal as a man of valorous deeds. After performing many other deeds of heroism, Maṇidatta visited the courtesan and spent a night of lovemaking with her. But despite his extraordinary heroism, he was not able to win a second night with her. In great sadness, he returned and reported the outcome to King Vikramabāhu.

Kumāradatta next set out for Kusumapura and spent one night in lovemaking with Rūpavatī. But, he could not wrest a second night from her, even though he confided to her his desire for winning the three fabulous gems left by his father. Rejected, Kumāradatta also returned to his own land and reported the failure of his mission to King Vikramabāhu.

Now, Kanakadatta thought to himself: 'The brave and the beautiful have returned in despair. What can I accomplish going there? Even at the very start, there seems to be no promise of success. So, let me take just some provisions for the way and one servant alone to attend on me, go there and try to find out what this woman is up to.' Having made this decision, Kanakadatta travelled to Kusumapura and kept observing Rūpavatī's movements.

At one time, he noticed Rūpavatī going along the highway surrounded by a retinue of a thousand harlots. Kanakadatta stood gazing on her who looked like none other than a Vidyādharī in her dazzling beauty and then went up to one of the attendant harlots and enquired of her: 'Lady, who is this going on the highway?'

'Young gentleman,' answered the attendant. 'This is Rūpavatī herself, the courtesan.'

'Where is she going to?' enquired Kanakadatta.

'In a secluded part of the city, a lone female ascetic, named Puṇyaśarīra, who is her guru, lives in Śiva's shrine. And Rūpavatī always attends upon her, her guru, without fail,' she replied.

And Kanakadatta, pondering over this said to himself:

'My purpose is going to be accomplished; I know that. I shall therefore follow her.'

When Rūpavatī after conversing with the ascetic had taken her leave and was on her way home, Kanakadatta went into Puṇyaśarīra's presence and bowed reverently before her. The ascetic asked him: 'Who are you, Sir?'

'I am a warrior from another land,' he replied.

'Child, why have you come here?' enquired the ascetic.

'Mother, I have come to perform service to you,' answered Kanakadatta.

The ascetic spoke gently to him, soothing him with the nectar of her words and then gave him leave to depart.

Whenever Rūpavatī came there, Kanakadatta made himself scarce and waited elsewhere. In this manner, Kanakadatta attending to the needs of the ascetic stayed six months at the end of which the ascetic asked him one day: 'Child, tell me; why has Your Honour been performing such excellent service for me? I am pleased. Now, tell me what your cherished wish is. I shall make it come to pass.'

'Mother, this I have to disclose to you in private,' said Kanakadatta.

Then the ascetic sent away her attendants to a distance and said again: 'Now, disclose your cherished wish, my child.'

'Mother,' confided Kanakadatta to her, 'this lady Rūpavatī, who comes every evening to wait upon you, accepts one lakh of rupees from a man to make love to her for one night only. But she will not consent to give herself to him the next night; not even for a thousand lakhs. Why? It is to find out the reason for this that I remain here serving you.'

'Well, then, shall I ask her for the reason, the next time she is here? You better stay concealed in one corner of this pavilion and hear her reasons from her own mouth.'

And Kanakadatta was exceedingly pleased.

The following evening, Rūpavatī came as usual to the ascetic's dwelling. Seeing her arrive, Kanakadatta concealed himself carefully in one of the corners of the dwelling.

Rūpavatī having made obeisance to the ascetic remained there, carrying on an endless a conversation with her on many a subject.

Then the ascetic, seizing her opportunity, remarked to Rūpavatī: 'Daughter, I heard this as it made the rounds, passing from person to person; that you receive a lakh from splendid and distinguished men to grant them a night of lovemaking with you; but that you would on no account consent to a second night of lovemaking with any man. I wish to learn the reason for this. You have to give me the reason at all events. Only if you do so will I be pleased.'

'Oh, noble lady,' replied Rūpavatī, 'it is a secret matter that I am unable to speak of.'

'Now, daughter, if you refuse to tell me the reason, I shall be highly displeased with you,' exclaimed the ascetic.

Then, Rūpavatī said: 'Mother, if you insist that I must at all event give you the reason, then promise me that you will not tell anyone.'

The ascetic agreed: 'Daughter, if I ever disclose that reason to anyone, I shall become a promise-breaker.'

'Listen, then, mother,' said Rūpavatī.

'I am all attention. Let Your Ladyship begin,' replied the ascetic.

Then Rūpavatī begins to speak:

In the city named Padmapura, there once reigned King Praćaṇḍasena. I am the daughter of Vićitradatta, the king's minister for peace and war and I was dedicated to the worship of the goddess Gaurī and the observance of all rites connected with that worship. When the goddess was duly propitiated, she was pleased to grant me a boon: 'Daughter, through my grace, you shall be ever attended by good fortune. You shall be married to a man most worthy of you; and you shall possess the gift of memory of your previous births.'

Soon after, my father gave me in marriage to the king's

son, Prince Pratāpasena. On account of the benediction of the goddess, I became dearer than life itself to the prince. Once, the king dispatched my husband on a mission to drive back an enemy ruler. Since he could not endure even a moment's separation from me, my husband took me with him. Then, when that powerful enemy king fell upon him with force, terrified, my husband abandoned me who was dearer to him than life and fled for his life to another land. At that moment, I saw the enemy king who came up mounted on a she-elephant and a thought raced through my mind: 'Ha! Shame upon that man who abandoned me, a wife who possessed all the desired marks of beauty and fled. How will this enemy king who now has me in his power let me go, seeing my beauty that enchants the three worlds? My chastity is bound to be violated.' With these thoughts, I fixed my mind firmly on my lord, Pratāpasena, and abandoned my life.

At the moment of my death what I saw right in front of my eyes was the face of the she-elephant. For that reason I was reborn as a cow-elephant. Even in the form of a cow-elephant, I passed my days thinking only of my husband Pratāpasena. Rutting bull-elephants approached to mate with me, but I made every one of them back off disappointed, for I would not permit any courtship.

Now, one day, Pratāpasena who had become a tusker, met me during his season of rut. Through the gift of remembering my former existence, I recognized him immediately and yielded to him. From then on, I lived continually with him enjoying many pleasures.

Then it chanced that some elephant-catchers entered the forest one day and came upon us. Even then, though he was a tusker at that time, Pratāpasena abandoned me immediately and fled to another forest. I was caught by those elephant-catchers and presented to the king who made me the royal mount. One day the king mounted me and entered a forest to hunt. And then and there, I fixed my mind on my husband in the form of a tusker and instantly gave up my life.

At the moment of my death what I saw before my eyes was a doe and for that reason, I was born again, this time as a doe. And even after I had become an adult doe, I would not permit any stag to court me but lived in the constant thought of my husband.

Once, as I was roaming in the woods, I came across a buck. As the result of leading a life of purity, I knew at once that that buck was my lord, Pratāpasena. He had given up his elephant form and gained the form of a buck. And I gave myself to that buck and lived there in great happiness with him. But, alas, a forest fire sprung up one day devastating those woods and the buck abandoned me and fled to other woods. Unable to flee from the conflagration, I was burned alive with my whole being rapt in thoughts of my husband Praṭāpasena.

At the moment of my death beside a lake, I saw a female ćakravāka.[17] And because of that I was born again as a ćakravāka. But I would not mate with any of the ćakravākas there and remained pining for my own husband.

Then by a stroke of good luck, Pratāpasena, who had given up his existence as a buck to become a ćakravāka, approached me. United again with him, I spent my days in happiness enjoying love's delights with him. And once, we flew into a lake in the city of Kusumapura. One day, Pratāpasena noticed a group of fowlers coming to the lake. At once, he fled in fear abandoning me and I was caught by a fowler. However, concentrating my thoughts solely on my husband, I abandoned my life.

At the moment of my death, whom should I see but a superbly beautiful, young courtesan, swimming happily in the lake. So, I was born again, this time in the womb of a courtesan; and I remained in that city after reaching womanhood. And I reflected: 'How hard-hearted men are! How incapable of loving! In four births, one after the other, has Pratāpasena abandoned me who have been totally devoted to him! And he fled!' Anger rose in my heart and I took a stern vow: 'Men are fit to be enjoyed once only for one night; never should they be enjoyed again for a second night.

'Mother, this the reason,' concluded Rūpavatī.

The courtesan having thus let the ascetic into her secret, took her leave and departed with her retinue of a hundred courtesans. After a while, Kanakadatta bowed in reverence to the ascetic and obtained permission to leave. He disguised himself, and went around in the city entering the house of every single courtesan in Kusumapura with the sole exception of Rūpavatī's mansion. He did not sleep with any of them; instead he told them all this story:

'Listen, I am Pratāpasena, the son of Praćaṇḍasena, king of Padmapura. My wife was the daughter of Vićitradatta. Though I held her dearer to me than my own life, I once abandoned her through sheer terror of an enemy and fled. She died broken hearted and was born again as a cow-elephant. I too, having obtained the form of a bull-elephant, enjoyed great happiness with her until one day, terrified of some elephant-catchers, I fled, abandoning her. She was caught and fettered. Pining for me she died and was born a doe. I gave up my life as a bull-elephant in grief over her death and was reborn as a buck. I met her again and spent days of untold joys with her. But once again, caught in a forest fire, I abandoned her and fled in fear to other woods. But she still pined for me and died, to be born again as a ćakravāka. I also died and was reborn as a ćakravāka and met her once again to enjoy ineffable happiness with her. One day I took her along and flew to a lake in the city of Kusumapura where once I espied some fowlers and flew away in fear. My wife was caught by a fowler and fixing her whole being on me alone, abandoned her life to be reborn in a courtesan's womb. I too ended my existence as a ćakravāka and took my birth as a human being. I remain thinking of her and her alone.'

Kanakadatta wrote the whole story out on silken scrolls, handed them out to the courtesans and continued to live in that same city.

The story spread through the city, carried by word of mouth and finally reached Rūpavatī's ears. She sent for Kanakadatta and when he came, she made him recount the whole sequence of events in their entirety and then throwing her arms round his neck, began crying out so loudly that everyone there was dismayed. Love blazed in Kanakadatta's heart for Rūpavatī.

On her part, now convinced that she had at long last gained Pratāpasena's unfailing love and devotion, Rūpavatī freed herself of her stern vow and spent her days with Kanakadatta in the varied and countless joys of love.

When several days had passed, Kanakadatta said to Rūpavatī: 'Listen, my beloved, my city of Puskarāvatī is resplendent as Amarāvatī, the city of Indra. Let us go there; there I shall enjoy life's pleasures to the fullest with you who are dearer to me than life itself.'

'Lord of my life, I shall carry out your wishes, always,' answered Rūpavatī.

Kanakadatta, accompanied by Rūpavatī with all her wealth, travelled to his own land. On his arrival, he went straight to the king, and in secret reported everything that had happened.

Having heard Kanakadatta narrate the recent events, the king reflected: 'Amazing indeed! Many clever men have tried in vain to make love to Rūpavatī two nights in succession. Yet, this young man has brought her with him. Therefore, I shall make Kanakadatta my minister for peace and war.'

The king then awarded the priceless gems to Kanakadatta and bestowing many gifts on him, appointed him minister for peace and war.

'Now, speak, O king,' demanded the genie. In each of her former births, Rūpavatī knew her husband. Though she possessed the gift of remembering her former births, how is it that she failed to know who Kanakadatta really and truly was, as a result of which his falsely concocted story brought him success?'

King Vikramāditya replied: 'Listen, Oh! You genie! In every previous existence, Rūpavatī had sexual intercourse only with her wedded husband. The merit she earned through the purity of her conduct enabled her to know her husband. But once she was born in a courtesan's family, she became an unchaste woman. Therefore, even though she retained the gift of remembering her own former lives, she lost the power to recognize her own husband because she had slept with other men.'

Having contrived to break the king's vow of silence, the genie was back on the śinśipā tree hanging on it once again.

Thus ends tale twenty-one of the *Five-and-Twenty Tales of the Genie*.

TALE 22

Of How Mūladeva Obtained a Bride for Śaśideva

Your Majesty, (began the genie), in the city of Kuṇḍinapura, there once reigned a supremely virtuous monarch named Śvetaketu. He had a close friend in the merchant Śankaradatta, who was dear to him as life itself. This merchant, owner of great caravans, married Anaṅgasenā, daughter of Maṇidatta, another merchant in the same city. His life with her was one of great happiness.

Once, this merchant decided to go to far off lands to trade. He entrusted his family to King Śvetaketu and placing at the king's disposal a thousand armed guards for the protection of Anaṅgasenā whose beauty enchanted the three worlds, he strictly charged them to follow his instructions and set out. Twelve years passed and he did not return. Enduring cruel separation from her husband, Anaṅgasenā wasted away, appearing like the moon's slender crescent in the dark half of the month.

Now, the festival of the god of love fell on the fourteenth day of the month. Many men and women gathered there that day for the worship of the god of love. Maṇidatta's wife took this opportunity to advise her daughter: 'Dear daughter, you should go and offer worship to the god of love and pray for your husband, Śankaradatta's speedy home coming.'

Anaṅgasenā followed her mother's advice. Waited upon by a hundred serving maids and surrounded by her armed guards, she set out to worship the god of love. Having completed her devotions, she was approaching her father's mansion, when Śaśideva, that prince of rogues saw her and fell madly in love with her. With the greatest difficulty he managed to get away and then went straight to the city of Padmāvatī to seek his friend Mūladeva's help. He confided everything to Mūladeva who listened carefully and then said: 'My dear friend, Śaśideva, do not despair. I shall do everything in my power to obtain the lady for you.'

And Śaśideva observed: 'My lord, armed guards protect her. And further, her parents never slacken in their watch over her. Moreover, King Śvetaketu zealously provides protection for her. Therefore, how is it possible to reach her?'

'Why do you worry?' was Mūladeva's reply; and he went on to say: 'In that city lives a bawd named Kāmīkalpalatā.[18] She is one who can make even Arundhatī[19] stray from the straight and chaste path. Let us go and speak to her.'

Having come to this decision the two of them went and met the bawd. 'Ah! Śaśideva and Mūladeva, I too know Anaṅgasenā. But I tell you, the task is very difficult to carry out; however, let me try; I shall go and acquaint Anaṅgasenā of your love. However, the two of you should now leave and remain concealed while I shall engage in the constant worship of Śiva. When my powers become clearly manifest, I shall contrive a stratagem.'

The bawd then picked a pair of serving maids and began to devote herself to the worship of Śiva. After a while she became possessed of extraordinary powers. People began to say of her, 'This ascetic is omniscient.'

When these reports came to Anaṅgasenā's ears, she told her mother: 'Pray acquaint this ascetic lady about the matter of your son-in-law.'

The mother remarked: 'Daughter, good thinking.' She set out to see the bawd. She presented the sham ascetic with various offerings, bowed with reverence and laid bare her misgivings: 'O, Mother All-Knowing, my son-in-law has not come home in twelve years. What is the true import of it all? Pray tell me; I shall reward you with great wealth.'

'Ah! Yes. It is imperative that I should reveal the truth to you; no doubt on that score. Now, you go home. I shall meditate and then let you know the truth of the matter. But, I have to ask you to bring Anaṅgasenā with you when you next come.'

The next day, Maṇidatta accompanied by his wife visited the fake-ascetic bringing his daughter with him. Offering gifts to the bawd and bowing reverentially, he said: 'Mother, All-Knowing, here I am with my wife; we have brought Anaṅgasenā to Your Holiness. Pray, tell us the truth about Śankaradatta, Your Reverence.'

Being pressed by them many times, the bawd said: 'Maṇidatta, hear, your son-in-law has met and married over there a girl of enchanting loveliness.'

The grief-stricken parents now fell at the feet of that bawd who knew all and cried piteously: 'What can be done to induce Śankaradatta to abandon that girl and come back to us? Advise us, Your Reverence.'

The bawd replied: 'Maṇidatta, there is a magic spell; but obtained with infinite effort, it is impossible to give to another.'

Hearing her words, the parents exclaimed: 'Ascetic lady, listen to us; if Your Holiness does not impart this magic spell, Anaṅgasenā here will definitely die through separation from her husband. Her loss will certainly be our death; we shall surely die. And the blame for all our deaths will be yours then.' With these words the parents again fell at her feet.

Finally persuaded, the fake-ascetic said: 'There is one very great difficulty in the performance of that magic spell. Only if your daughter can perform that will the spell become effective.'

The parents declared vehemently: 'Whatever the injunctions are, Your Reverence, our daughter will carry them out; rest assured.'

Then the bawd took Maṇidatta's wife aside and exhorted her in secret: 'Listen to me. When a secluded pavilion is built, Anaṅgasenā will see there a man brought before her and at that moment, she should recite the magic spell. And every day she will enjoy the delights of union with that man. Only when that man takes on the appearance of Śankaradatta will her husband return.'

Maṇidatta's wife listened to it all and said guardedly: 'I have to consult my husband first.' She asked him; Maṇidatta readily agreed, saying: 'Beloved wife, do whatever needs to be done to bring our son-in-law back.'

On being informed of their readiness to follow her suggestion, the sham ascetic hesitated: 'So many armed guards stand at your gates that it is impossible for any man to enter when it is time for the recitation of the magic spell,' she pointed out.

Maṇidatta reassured her: 'Not a single soul will bar your way. I shall instruct all of them to that effect this very day. You will be able to come and go as you please, dear lady, with the greatest ease.'

Maṇidatta took his leave and had a pavilion built at once. The sham ascetic then went to the pavilion in a horse-drawn covered litter and taught the magic spell to Anaṅgasenā. After that the bawd, Kāmīkalpalatā, went there daily and remained conversing with Anaṅgasenā.

One day the sham-ascetic asked Anaṅgasenā in tones of concern: 'Daughter, why have you been reduced to such a state? Looking at you wasting away into incredible thinness through grief, I am deeply grieved. So, tell me why it is so, Your Ladyship.'

To this Anaṅgasenā replied: 'Mother, since the day my dear lord left to trade in far off lands, I have not set eyes even on the shadow of a man. Now, while repeating the magic spell, I see a man and fond memories of lovemaking with my husband come to mind.'

Hearing Anaṅgasenā's confession, the bawd said with

alacrity: 'If this is so, why don't you give yourself to this man?'

'If you think I should, O, lady, pray speak to that man,' replied Anaṅgasenā.

'Oh, I give that man to you. Your Ladyship will give and receive pleasure,' she replied.

'But let no one else know of this, respected lady,' warned Anaṅgasenā.

The bawd was delighted beyond measure. She met Śaśideva and gave him this secret information. When he heard it, Śaśideva became as one who had been restored to life; and from then on he made love to Anaṅgasenā continually in many different ways. And she too, forgot all about her husband Śankaradatta in the arms of that expert in the amatory arts, Śaśideva. As for the bawd, under the pretext of instructing Anaṅgasenā in the magic spell, she made her daily visits to the secret pavilion, going back and forth in order to enable Śaśideva to carry on his love-sports with Anaṅgasenā.

After some time, Mūladeva had a talk with Śaśideva: 'My friend, it is pointless to carry on like this living in this city. Therefore, let us take Anaṅgasenā and return to our own land.'

'Well, how do we manage this?' queried Śaśideva.

'Look,' pointed out Mūladeva, 'the lady hangs on your every word; is that not so? Whatever you ask her to do, she will do. So, let her come here in the covered litter. I shall think of something after that.'

Śaśideva went to Anaṅgasenā and conveyed to her what Mūladeva had told him. And she agreed willingly.

All on a sudden, Mūladeva appeared at the palace gates with a hundred-odd mercenaries. Seeing Anaṅgasenā seated inside the litter, he assumed Śaśideva's form and grabbing the hem of her garment, cried out: 'O, my wife, dearer to me than life! Where are you off to, running away like this?'

At once, the guards in charge of Anaṅgasenā's security

ran to Maṇidatta and reported her action. Maṇidatta hastened to the king and made his complaint.

Thinking that his friend's wife was being molested, King Śvetaketu had Anaṅgasenā brought to his side and then reprimanded Mūladeva: 'Oh, you knave! You shameless rogue! This! My friend's wife! Anaṅgasenā! And you address her as your wife! And lay hands on her! How dare you! Everyone knows Maṇidatta to be her father. How dare you speak like this? Leave! Be gone! Or, I shall kill you. See what I shall do; I swear here by my sacred thread;[20] I'll kill you. I, Śvetaketu, swear that I will.'

Then the knave, Mūladeva replied: 'Having been away from home a long time I saw this lady and seized her. I shall go now; but I shall definitely bring my own wife here and present her to the king. Only by that will this infamy of mine be driven out.' With such words did Mūladeva pacify everyone around and leave that place.

He then went straight to the bawd Kāmīkalpalatā and said: 'Mother, if you agree, I suggest that we now take Anaṅgasenā and leave this city.'

'Now, now, how is that possible?' she asked him.

Mūladeva observed: 'Mother, listen, she is so enamoured of Śaśideva that she will go with us if he asks her to. The problem is that she will then stand disgraced in the eyes of the world. It occurs to me that a dead woman has to be brought here by me. You anoint the dead body thoroughly with perfumes, sandal paste, yellow orpiment and such auspicious items, place it in the covered litter, honoured lady, and go with Śaśideva. Adorn the dead body with all of Anaṅagasena's jewels and lay it on Anaṅgasenā's bed, then you come back here. Śaśideva will set fire to the pavilion and return here with Anaṅgasenā. Then everyone who sees the corpse all decked out in Anaṅgasenā's jewellery will think it was she in fact. So, no one will say: "See, Anaṅgasenā ran away with her lover."'

Mūladeva's plan being carried out meticulously, Śaśideva

with Anaṅgasenā accompanying him returned to his own land with Mūladeva.

The next day, Anaṅgasenā's parents sat weeping bitterly, mourning her death. The king came there in person and out of his deep affection for his friend had the bones of the dead woman collected and sent for immersion in various sacred waters. As for the sham ascetic, she wept aloud crying: 'Alas! Alas! I cannot bear to stay here any longer. Now that my beloved pupil Anaṅgasenā is no more, I shall take myself to some other land.' With these words, she left for the city of Padmāvatī.

After some time Mūladeva, accompanied by Anaṅgasenā and Śaśideva came to King Śvetaketu's court at Kuṇḍinapura and presented Anaṅgasenā to the king; he said: 'Let Your Majesty look upon my wife who is the very image of Anaṅgasenā. Deceived by the extraordinary likeness, once formerly I laid hands on Anaṅgasenā.' Looking carefully at the lady the king was totally amazed: 'Amazing! Indeed, it looks as if Anaṅgasenā stands here in person before my eyes.'

Then bestowing gifts upon them he dismissed them. Anaṅgasenā's parents also gazed upon the lady, their own daughter in fact, and bestowed all their daughter's jewels on her. And they wept aloud.

The genie now addressed King Vikramāditya: 'Tell me, Your Majesty. Who had the sharper intelligence, the bawd, Kāmīkalpalatā or the rogue, Mūladeva?'

'Well, well, you genie!' replied the monarch. 'Mūladeva was the greatest trickster alive; his intelligence displayed itself everywhere, at all times.'

Thus, having played a trick on the king, the genie was back to hang on the śinśipā tree.

Thus ends tale twenty-two of the *Five-and-Twenty Tales of the Genie*.

The genie being brought back again and carried along, now began another tale.

TALE 23

Of the Ogre Who Ravaged King Arimaulimaṇi's Kingdom

Your Majesty, (began the genie), by the rippling waters of the river Narmadā[21] lay the fair city of Ekaćakravartī, where once King Arimaulimaṇi reigned. One day, a huge beast was seen swimming down the river's current. The citizens in their excitement slew it. Out of its belly came a maiden of enchanting beauty. The citizens all went immediately to the king and informed him of the marvel. The king hastened to the river-bank and greeting the maiden with many marks of friendship, enquired: 'Sweet maiden! Who may you be? Why have you been reduced to this condition?'

Asked thus kindly, the maiden replied: 'Your Majesty, I am Śobhāvatī, the daughter of King Nṛpamaṇimukuṭa. Once, I went down to the waters of the river surrounded by my retinue of a hundred companions to amuse myself in water-sports. This beast pounced on me and swallowed me whole. And I lived inside it as in a dream, not knowing who my father was or what my country was; not even knowing who I was. I knew not one single thing.'

Having listened to the maiden's words, the king told her: 'King Nṛpamaṇimukuṭa had already sent me an emissary sometime back about your marriage.'

The maiden listened and then said: 'What is Your Majesty's name?'

'I am King Arimaulimaṇi,' replied the king.

'Your Majesty, now my cherished desire is fulfilled.' The king became eager to marry her. Getting wind of this, an ogre appeared there disguised and shouted: 'How dare you take this maiden Śobhāvatī with you? My father and I will eat her; and if you wish to preserve your own life, you had better not marry her. Listen to me; my father exists in the shape of a shark and my mother in the shape of a sea-otter; while I myself exist in the shape of a giant lizard.'

The king flew into a great rage. He thundered: 'Go, go, you vile ogre. What can your father do to me?'

The ogre became furious. 'Go, go, you vilest of kings; we are Brāhmaṇa-ogres. How dare you speak so insultingly of my father? But let it pass. I shall not take notice of one offence.'

The king retorted loftily: 'A one-time offence! Enough of *that*! I shall insult your father one hundred times. Go away, you villain and do your worst.'

Blazing with anger the ogre rasped out: 'Vilest of kings! Better protect this kingdom of yours.'

Having spoken thus vehemently, the ogre informed his father of the matter; then, repairing to the city of Lankā, that ogre, Tālajaṅgha* summoned an assembly of ogres and returned to King Arimaulimaṇi's capital with his father. Assuming disguises, they began gobbling up whomsoever crossed their paths.

Next, the ogre Tālajaṅgha went to his mother and said: 'Mother Kumbodarī!** You assume the form of a harlot; go to that city and eat up all the men until the city becomes empty.'

Kumbodarī heeded her son's request and assuming the form of a harlot went to the city and stopped at the house of a bawd. The bawd enquired: 'Lady, who are you?'

'I am a harlot named Aphrodisia. May I stay in your establishment?' said Kumbodarī.

---

* Palmyrashanks

** Pot-belly

'Of course, you may, do stay in my house at your convenience,' said the bawd.

From then on, Kumbodarī took the men who visited her desiring intercourse to a secret place under the pretext of dalliance and quietly ate them up.

Now, it happened that one day, one Vidyādhara, son of the preceptor Vasudatta visited the harlot. Seeing that he was extremely handsome, Aphrodisia made love to him and continued to do so.

Once, on the insistence of his wife, Vidyādhara did not visit the harlot. The ogress, inflamed with passion, heaved great hot sighs and assuming the shape of Vidyādhara's mother, went to his house where she saw him engaged in making love to his wife. She became very angry and turning herself into a female honey bee buzzed around as if drawn by the fragrances of flowers in the chamber.

Vidyādhara noticed the bee and said to his wife: 'My darling, this bee should be driven away before it puts the lamp out by the incessant flapping of its wings.'

And his wife remarked: 'O, let it be, dear lord; she is here drawn by the fragrance and honey of the flowers; let her stay.'

But fearing that the lamp might be extinguished, Vidyādhara dealt the bee a sharp blow with the flat of his hand. The bee fell down stunned and remained unconscious; with great effort it managed to become all right. Then, Aphrodisia reflected angrily: 'Ha! Just let this fellow come to visit me again; I shall avenge this injury by drinking his blood and eating his flesh.'

The next night, Vidyādhara dropped off to sleep after having intercourse with the harlot. She then killed him and while he was being eaten, her husband Kharjūrajaṅgha* came there, picked the body up and took it to his own lair.

---

* Datepalmshanks

One of the citizens got wind of what the harlot was up to and reported her to the king. 'Your Majesty,' he said, 'There is an ogress living in our city disguised as a harlot; it is she who is eating all the men in our city. Vidyādhara too has been eaten by her.'

King Arimaulimaṇi went to her place and reprimanded her: 'Shame, shame upon you, you evil woman; you have eaten the son of a Brāhmaṇa. A citizen who saw this came and informed me of it.' He said.

The ogress replied: 'You have been rightly informed, Sir. I am the ogress, Kumbodarī; my husband is Kharjūrajaṅgha and my son Tālajaṅgha. You humiliated my son and took Śobhāvatī. Angered by that, my husband assembled the ogres to eat Brāhmaṇas.'

The king now ordered all his men: 'Kill this harlot; she is an ogress.'

But Kumbodarī resuming her natural form routed them all in no time and went to her husband's lair.

The king had perforce to send a suitable emissary to the ogre to pacify him and negotiate a truce. He bound himself by an oath to dispatch one person each day to the ogre. And time passed in this manner.

Once, the lot for that day fell upon a woman with an only son. With her son's death imminent, she began weeping. It happened that just then, Mahābala, a great monarch from another land came by and asked the weeping woman: 'Mother, why are you weeping?' She told him the whole sad tale.

King Mahābala said to her: 'Mother, I shall slay all the ogres and deliver your son. Now go and tell that to your king.'

She hastened at once to the palace and informed King Arimaulimaṇi who sent for Mahābala and spoke to him: 'My son, if you do this, I shall hand over this kingdom to you.'

Mahābala joyfully accepted the offer. He went straight

to the den of Kharjūrajaṅgha and beat him up. Aghast at the valour of Mahābala, the ogre cowered in terror: 'Spare my life, O, prince,' whimpered the ogre.

The prince said: 'All right, now swear an oath that you will not kill any living being; swear that you will not do any violence in King Arimaulimaṇi's kingdom.'

The ogre agreed and bound himself by an oath. Releasing him, Mahābala returned to the king.

Now that his purpose had been accomplished King Arimaulimaṇi showed scant respect to Prince Mahābala, who infuriated, spoke severely to the king.

'Well, well, your name of Arimaulimaṇi[22] suits you admirably, but in another sense. You are not a worthy king.'

With this harsh comment, Mahābala immediately went and released the ogre from his oath and then returned to his own land. And the ogre began eating the citizens in King Arimaulimaṇi's realm. The king accompanied by Śobhāvatī travelled to Mahābala's country. Mahābala welcomed him with all due honour and hospitality and the next morning asked King Arimaulimaṇi: 'O, king, why have you been reduced to such a state?'

The conscience-stricken king remained silent. Then the noble Mahābala with a little laugh, set out again and bound the ogre by an oath. Having done that, he gave his own elephants, horses, soldiers and equipment to King Arimaulimaṇi who had behaved rather shabbily, seated him on the throne and returned to his own land.

The genie said: 'Let Your Majesty speak. Tell me: who was responsible for the deaths of the citizens and of the Brāhmaṇicide of Vidyādhara? Was it King Arimaulimaṇi, or Mahābala or the ogre Kharjūrajaṅgha?'

King Vikramāditya replied: 'Listen, you, you genie; the guilt for the deaths of the citizens was entirely King Arimaulimaṇi's. Who else's?'

Having succeeded in breaking the king's vow of silence, the genie was back hanging from the śinśipā tree.

Thus ends tale twenty-three of the *Five-and-Twenty Tales of the Genie*.

As the genie was once again brought back and carried along, he tells another tale.

EPILOGUE

And the genie began: I was once a householder living in this kingdom, an oil-merchant by birth and profession. Once, Fate brought to my door a wise man 23 possessed of arcane and esoteric knowledge. He stayed with me several months, living in the small cell beside the shed built for sacrifices. Food in the shape of alms as prescribed was provided for him daily.

Later on, at the onset of the rainy season, the wise man decided it was time to travel to another land. He took me aside and spoke particularly: 'Good householder, listen; you have served us well continually and in many ways. For that reason, I am highly pleased with you. Come, I shall impart to you the knowledge of certain mysteries.'

He then deigned out of kindness to instruct me in the lore of magic; after doing that he extracted a solemn promise from me.

'Listen to me,' he exhorted. 'My former attendant who is like a son to me was to have come here in search of me during the rains, for I had promised to instruct him in the lore of magic. I have been expecting him and have waited till now. But it looks as if he will not be here to meet me before my departure from this place. If you honour your solemn promise to me, when this man does arrive here at your place in the course of his wanderings looking for me, you will without fail impart to him this knowledge that I have given you. He is a brother to you. Therefore, you are not to resort to guile and trickery where he is concerned. If you will not do as I say, you will certainly eat the bitter fruit of your wrongdoing in the shape of my dread curse which will doom you to a terrible death.' Having made this hard-and-fast compact with me, the wise man set out for another land; and as he left, he repeated his words: 'On no account are you to treat my advice as beneath notice.'

Having related these events, the genie fell silent. The king laughed and said: 'Hey there! Sir genie! Go on with the narrative.'

The genie too laughed and resumed his narration.

So, listen, O, king; when my guru had set out on his travels to another land, his pupil arrived at my place. He met me in my fire sanctuary and asked: 'Sir, that wise man who stayed here in this sanctuary . . . where is he?'

'He left to travel to another land,' I answered.

'Before he left, did he make any arrangements concerning me?' was his next question.

'O, no, none at all,' was my reply.

He cried out when he heard my words. 'Ha ha! O, misery! How am I betrayed!' Lamenting in this fashion he left, bereft of all hope.

After his departure, I remained in my house from that day on, sick at heart, constantly recalling my guru's injunction. And fully aware that I had transgressed my guru's express injunction, I remained tormented by acute anxiety caused by the sense of guilt festering within.

As this point in my life, Fate struck a cruel blow. Certain burglars who broke in and entered the palace, carried away a great many valuables and going into the royal stables also stole one of the king's horses, brought it to my house, tied it to the post at my gates and fled.

Next morning, the king learnt of the burglary and summoned the sentry. 'Hey, sentry, my treasury has been burgled; and one of the horses has been taken from the stables. Go and investigate. Make a thorough search and then come back without delay and report to me. Be quick, man, on the double. If you fail to discover the burglars and bring them into my presence, I shall round your family up and with yourself make mincemeat of all.'

The unfortunate sentry lost no time making a house-to-house search and seeing the royal horse at my gates, grabbed me straightaway and arrested me as the thief. He informed the king and showed him the horse. The king flew into a great rage and thundered out his command: 'Go, take him away and have him impaled.'

Bearing the royal command on his head, so to speak, the sentry went out and taking me to the outskirts of a village nearby handed me over to the executioners who raised me upon a pike. Impaled on the pike, I endured my existence solely through my acquired yogic powers, fixing my mind in profound meditation until my breath failed and my heart stopped. After that, possessed by a genie, I found myself on a tree growing on the banks of the Ghargarā straight in front, and rested there. Through the magic powers I had, omniscience arose in me.

As for that other pupil of my guru, he wandered from land to land and finally came to a shelter for travellers from distant lands that lay beside the shrine of the goddess Hingula;[24] there he saw the guru. He acquainted the guru with everything that related to his meeting with me. Deeply pained at heart by what he heard, the guru said to his pupil: 'That householder, the oil merchant, stole my knowledge of the arcane arts. However, he has reaped the fruits of his actions. And that man by virtue of the magic powers he had acquired, is now possessed by a genie and hangs as a corpse from a branch of a śinśipā tree that grows on the banks of the Ghargarā flowing through the kingdom of Mangalakoṭi. I am exceedingly pleased with you; you are our son. Since you have my benediction, good fortune and prosperity are yours for the asking. I grant you this boon by which through the instruction you will get from me, you shall possess supranormal powers. Possessing good fortune and supranormal powers and the ability to fly in the air, roam the world at your will and pleasure.'

The corpse desisted and paused. The king, having heard this tale, now asked the corpse once more in a voice indistinct and choking with joy. 'Listen, Sir Corpse; if you are pleased, then tell me the whole story, not leaving out one single, remarkable detail. And then advise me well as to what I should do now.'

The genie spoke to King Vikramāditya in earnest: 'Listen to me, O, great monarch! You are truly a god in essence, in human shape. Extraordinary virtues are yours from merit gathered in former lives. The fruit of that merit is the dawn of the good fortune that has led you here. Listen carefully and I shall tell you all.

'That pupil I have talked of was now instructed by the guru who was exceedingly pleased with him, as follows: "Now, you should go from here to the realm of the illustrious and most noble emperor, Vikramāditya; and to gain his favour, send him daily a bilva fruit with priceless gems concealed within. Follow this procedure for several days and when the emperor is favourably inclined towards you, get that noblest of men to promise you his assistance. With the help of the king, get hold of the genie-possessed corpse of that man skilled in esoteric arts and take it to the great burning grounds lying to the south of the city. Construct a magic circle there, place the corpse and the king at its centre and perform the Rite of the Charmed circle. Place your foot on the head of the corpse and offer the king as a sacrifice to the goddess; then place both your feet on the head of the corpse and recite the following mantra: 'Dread goddess, be pleased to accept my sacrifice of a living being! May great good fortune and supranormal powers be mine!' As you recite this prayer the goddess will pronounce her benediction on you."

'Then that man, Kṣāntiśīla, having received these precise instructions from his guru who was mightily pleased with him, came to you. He got you into his power through guile and used you to get me by these means. And now he will cut you down and gain suprahuman powers. I have informed you of these secret happenings in their entirety. Now it is for you to carry out whatever you think is right.'

The genie concluded his statement and paused.

The emperor's eyes dilated with fear; his eyes welled with tears of joy; he addressed the genie again: 'Oh, noble soul! Oh, omniscient one! Speak; advise me; what should I do?'

The genie noted the king's words and counselled him: 'Your unparalleled nobility gladdens me exceedingly. I shall acquaint you therefore with a secret method to achieve the end. First, you take me as arranged to Kṣāntiśīla waiting in the burning grounds. When you reach the burning grounds, Kṣāntiśīla's joy will know no bounds and he will exhort you in these words: "Hail! Great king! You have come. Now go, bathe quickly; then perform the due rites of worship to the deities; with you at my side I shall perform the rites of worship to the divinity, so that we two shall gain magic powers as I promised." Do as he says. Following his instructions, go to the holy pool of the goddess and have the ritual bath in its waters. When you return and face him, he will at that time give you his further instructions. He will say: "Now worship the divinity; I shall do the same." Again you will do as he says and worship the divinity. Once these rites of worship are duly completed, he will say to you: "Now go round the divinity sun-wise and make a complete prostration, stretched out full length on the ground, straight as a rod." And now—and mark my words carefully—be sure to make this reply: "I am a king; I wield the rod of justice; I am ever seated on the lion-throne; kings who rule over neighbouring kingdoms kneel at my lotus feet. Brāhmaṇas duly initiated into the proper performance of various rites and ceremonies, perform on my behalf all rituals and ceremonies of adoration of deities and divinities, offer oblations to my ancestors, do all the obsequial rites to the manes and the daily, prescriptive rituals of worship as well. By these means, the regular and perfect performance of all prescribed rites and ceremonies in my life is carried out. In my hands are always held the royal sceptre and the rod of justice. For this reason, it is not my office, it is not my duty or right, to perform various rites and ceremonies of adoration of divinities, of prostrating myself full-length like a rod and other similar acts. However, if Your Honour deems it a sacred injunction that I should prostrate myself full-length on the ground, then you have to teach me how a proper full-length prostration is done. Seeing you doing it, I shall do so likewise."

'Kṣāntiśīla will pay due regard to your words and prostrate himself full-length before the divinity. As he falls to the ground, his body fully stretched out, straight as a rod, sever his head that very instant with your sword; place both your feet on his head and the head of the corpse, shape your hands like a flowerbud, holding it over your head in the act of homage and chant these words to the goddess: "O, great goddess! May you be propitiated! Accept this sacrifice that I offer! By your grace, may the magic acts of Tāla and Vetāla[25] be mine for ever, utterly and inalienably!" This is the boon you shall ask for.' Having explained it all the genie now desisted.

King Vikramāditya, having heard the genie say all this was now in a state of ecstatic jubilation. With his heart overflowing with joy, he lifted the corpse on to his shoulders and set out to meet Kṣāntiśīla. When he saw the king coming towards him, the necromancer was transported with violent joy; he greeted the king profusely: 'O, king,' he said. 'You have actually made it to this place in just three watches of the night! Now hasten to the sacred pool of the goddess; bathe and return to me; and here within the space of the magic circle, perform along with me, the sixteen prescribed rites of adoration of the divinity. Your most-cherished wishes are about to come true. And my aim of which I have spoken, will certainly be well accomplished.'

King Vikramāditya went to the pool according to the words of the yogī,[26] bathed and returned. Stepping into the magic circle of worship, the king performed alongside the yogī the divine service with the materials that the yogī had collected for the sixteen rites of adoration, together with the appropriate chants of praise for each rite.

At the close of the service, the yogī spoke out clearly: 'O, king, make obeisance to the goddess with the full-length prostration.'

King Vikramāditya declared: 'I am a king who turns the wheel of empire.[27] All kings kneel at my footstool paying me homage. In particular, I bear the sceptre and rod; and in conformity with prescribed rules, I do not myself perform ceremonies for deities and the manes. All this is done on my behalf by a properly initiated Brāhmaṇa. So teach me how a full-length prostration ought to be made.'

Then, in response to the king's words, the yogī, impelled by Fate, himself made a full-length prostration. Seizing this opportunity, the king, standing by his side, drew his sword and cut the yogī in two. Placing both feet on both heads, the yogī's head and the head of the corpse, the king offered the goddess homage with hands folded in the shape of a flowerbud and uttered aloud these words: 'Hail! Hail! Mother of the Universe! Destroyer, Creator, Sustainer! Granter of boons! Accept this blood-sacrifice! Be propitiated! May great good fortune and supranormal powers be mine! Grant me this boon!'

And as the king fervently uttered this, deep-sounding, thunderously loud laughter arose within the shrine of the goddess; and a command came: 'O, king most noble and courageous! Live a hundred years! With glory unimpaired, turning the wheel of empire, may you enjoy the happiness that sovereignty brings! The magic arts of Tāla and Vetāla are yours utterly and inalienably!' With this benediction, the goddess vanished. Dawn broke. With his body pure and glowing, King Vikramāditya returned to his capital unseen by others and resumed his life. He exercised a sovereignty both powerful and noble. From that day on, he, Upholder of the Earth, was like one of the World-Guardians, as his life ran its course, smooth and ordered.

Thus ends the twenty-fifth tale in the text of stories known as the *Five-and-Twenty Tales of the Genie,* set down by the illustrious Jambhaladatta, Minister for Peace and War.

NOTES

Introduction

1. Edited in four parallel recensions by Franklin Edgerton, Harvard Oriental Studies, vol. 26, 1926.
2. The battle with Śalivāhana of legend; Śālivāhana was the grandson of a potter in Pratiṣṭhāna, born to his two-year-old daughter and a nāga prince of the underworld. Śalivāhana is Śātavāhana.
3. Nativity Tales—stories relating the miraculous birth of Gautama the Buddha, founder-teacher of Buddhism, and his successive rebirths as Bodhisattvas in human and non-human forms. The Buddha chose to be reborn repeatedly to teach, and guide man to salvation.
4. *The Seventy-two Tales of the Parrot.* The stories are told by a wondrous parrot to its young and beautiful mistress to keep her from straying while her merchant-husband was travelling overseas on business.
5. A finely structured book of beast fables, with a sprinkling of fairy and folk tales ascribed to Viṣṇu Śarma. See introduction, the *Pañcatantra* of Viṣṇu Śarma edited and translated by Chandra Rajan, Penguin Classics, 1993.
6. Kālidāsa used the Śakuntala story (*Mahābhārata,* I.62-69) in his great play, *Abhijñāna Śākuntalam.* The *Mahābhārata* has been consistently and heavily mined for its riches by later writers.
7. The *Jātaka Tales* would give a strong didactic twist to a story; e.g., the Valahāssa Jataka, similar in plot to Tale 8 in Śivadāsa's *Vetāla Tales.*
8. Intro. to the *Śukasaptati* by Pandit Ramakanth Tripathi, Chowkhamba, 1966.
9. This might be Gautamīputra Śātavāhana, the greatest ruler

of this dynasty, At the height of their power, the Śātavāhana rulers pushed up to the Narmadā valley, annexed Mālava and took over Ujjayinī, the capital of Vikramāditya.

10. Rajan, introduction, p.xx the *Panćatantra* of Viṣṇu Śarma, Penguin Classics, 1993.
11. Vidyādhara (vidyādharī, feminine) is literally one who possesses vidyā: Vidyā normally signifies knowledge; but earlier it meant knowledge of a special kind; esoteric knowledge; knowledge of magic. It also signified the scientific knowledge of ancient India in areas such as smelting and refining of ores, distillation, building of machines (yantra), perhaps even of flying machines; the kind of knowledge that would have been kept secret and imparted only to initiates and which must have struck the ordinary person as magical. This is the sense in which the word is used in the *Vetāla Tales*. In mythology, Vidyādhara—Vidyādharis, were semi-divine beings, with special powers such as the ability of flying through air, making themselves invisible, assuming different shapes at will. They were believed to be uncommonly beautiful and skilled musicians. Both males and females of this class of celestial beings were believed to bewitch and seduce travellers walking in lonely places. European mythology has similarly naiads, nymphs, sirens, mermaids and mermen, and fairies generally. Vidyādharas had their own splendid kingdoms and opulent cities in the Himalayan regions. With Yakṣas they are associated with Śiva, on whom they attended. Their Himalayan habitation lends credence to the supposition that in the very early history of the peoples of India, the term Vidyādhara—Vidyādharī, designated people of the Himalayan valleys who were different from the people of the plains and whose activities might have included mining for gems and ores, refining of metals, smelting and so on. Vidyādharīs were specially believed to have been very beautiful, lissom, enchanting (in both senses); and as inhabiting woods and groves, pools and streams.

They were skilled singers and were believed to fascinate passers-by with their beauty and singing.

12. I use the term 'saga' in preference to the commonly used word 'epic' because the word saga characterizes the work better. The *Mahābhārata* is essentially the 'tale of the tribe', to appropriate Ezra Pound's expressive phrase. Often a term taken out of a certain cultural context and literary tradition (the Western in this case) and applied in another (the Indian) *misleads* rather than leads the reader into understanding. This can and has led to misinterpretation and errors of judgement.

The Five-and-Twenty Tales of the Genie as set down by Śivadāsa

1. A tree that bears bitter berries, probably the neem whose leaves, twigs, flowers and berries have a medicinal use.
2. An ascetic has to begin all over again if his penance is interrupted.
3. Ascetics are often irascible and prone to utter curses.
4. Kumbhah has two meanings: a pot and a harlot's paramour.
5. Probably the simple structure of a thatched roof supported by four poles driven into the ground to serve as a shelter for farmers working in the fields.
6. Indra, Lord of the Immortals, attended by the apsaras who are celestial dancers.
7. The world of eternal light; abode of the Immortals.
8. Dharma, the Law of the Universe at its three levels, cosmic, natural and human. According to Dharma there is a fourfold division of a man's life. Each division is called an āśrama or station in life: the four are: the student's life involving education and professional training; the householder's life involving marriage, bringing up a family and fulfilling social and political

obligations; retirement and retreat into the forest; total abnegation of the world and its affairs.

9. The moon.
10. The lion.
11. A little water pot used in calculating planetary positions in order to draw a natal chart.
12. A child's head is shaved or its hair trimmed shortly after the first birthday, to ensure a new and healthy growth of hair.
13. A rite of passage that marks the end of one stage, namely, childhood and the start of another, boyhood which is the period of education.
14. A lacuna in the text.
15. The last rites are elaborate and continue over ten days and include the gathering of the bones, immersion of the ashes in holy waters, etc.
16. An auspicious mark of sandalwood paste blended with saffron, placed on the forehead of the participant/s in all rites and ceremonies, birthdays, marriage coronations.
17. Lakṣmī, goddess of wealth, good fortune, plenitude, beauty, sovereignty.
18. Dangers from enemies and lawless elements in the state.
19. Literally, lord of the ganas; the ganas are a troop of demigods, attendants of Śiva. Ganeśa is, in mythology, the son of Śiva; in metaphysical terms, an emanation, with certain recognizable functions, of Śiva as the Absolute and supreme godhead. Ganeśa—Ganapati, Vināyaka are other names or epithets—is regarded as the dispeller of difficulties, the destroyer of obstacles; and prayers are addressed to this godhead at the commencement of all enterprises, undertakings and courses of action to ensure success.

    In mythology, Ganeśa is pictured as elephant-headed, with a single tusk, pot-bellied, fond of good food, of rich sweets in particular. The association with rich food points to the origin of this godhead in an ancient harvest god.
20. See note 8.

21. At the end of time the world is dissolved back into its primordial state, by fire and wind and water; this dissolution is signified in Sanskrit by the term pralaya.
22. Digambara, 'clad in space' is the term used here; a term signifying a sect of Jaina monks but not exclusively.
23. The traditional welcome gift.
24. The term yogī is used in both in the Śivadāsa and the Jambhaladatta recensions for a magician; an ascetic who subjects himself to severe austerities over a long period not to effect the integration with Supreme Spirit, but to gain supranormal powers, the Siddhis, described in the frame story (pp.15-16).
25. The preceptor of the Immortals; also the name of a celebrated lawgiver who codified and formulated legal directives.
26. Yoginī—Dākinī, are terms signifying bands of female devotees of the mother goddess in her fierce, destructive aspect as Kāli. (Kāli is the feminine of Kāla, Time). They correspond to the Bacchantes of Greek mythology, the Maenads and Thyiades who are associated with the cult of Bacchus and its secret rites.
27. The fierce, destructive aspect of Śiva, the creative principle. In iconography and art, Bhairava is represented as wearing the symbols of death.
28. The great war of the ancient world known to the peoples of India around the beginning of the first millenium BC. It is the theme of the great epic *Mahābhārata*. The war was fought in the region around modern Delhi, between cousins, each vying for the throne and sovereignty over northern India and the territories contiguous on all sides. The two branches of the dynasty that fought this bitter war are known as Kaurava and Pāṇḍava; the former was the branch in power being the elder.
29. Karṇa and Śalva fought on the Kaurava side, the former being the commander of the imperial armies and the foremost warrior; the latter a powerful king and ally of the Kauravas.
30. The strongest warrior on the Pāṇḍava side, second of

the five Pāṇdava brothers, sons of Pāndu, who claimed the throne.

31. Brother of the reigning monarch. In the epic, Bhīma throws him down and slays him by tearing open his chest with bare hands and drinking his heart's blood. In the context of this passage in our text, the words Bhīma and Duhśāsana in the plural are used in a generic sense, perhaps for savages, outlaws and criminals who may have frequented burning grounds and performed ritual killings (cf. the ritual killings in Euripides' *Bacchae*).
32. The Daṇdaka was a vast region of forests stretching between the rivers Yamunā and Godāvarī in central India, inhabited and ruled by the very first nations of India, so to speak. Janasthāna was a powerful kingdom, part of an empire ruled by Rāvaṇa, probably lying on both banks of the Godāvarī. Khara and his brother were governors of Janasthāna and generals in Rāvaṇa's mighty army. Mārīća was Rāvaṇa's uncle who took the form of a golden deer to trick Rāma so that Sītā would be abducted (see note 48). Śūrpanakhā, literally, 'sharp-nailed' was Rāvaṇa's sister. She fell in love with Rāma in exile in the forests of Daṇḍaka; Rāma rejected her and passed her on to his brother who, enraged, cut off her nose and ears.
33. (See note 32).
34. Rāvaṇa was a powerful monarch in probably the region south of the Vindhya mountains in Central India (though tradition places his kingdom in Sri Lankā). He abducted Sītā, wife of Rāma, the hero of the epic, *Rāmāyaṇa* and was killed by Rāma. Lankā, the capital of Rāvaṇa's kingdom was burnt down.
35. Literally, Glory, one of the names or epithets of Lakṣmī, goddess of Wealth, Beauty and Success.
36. The writer, Śivadāsa, uses the term nāyikā, heroine.
37. An error: the city's name does not conform to what is conveyed by Padmāvatī's miming. 'Karṇa' is 'ear' and 'kubja' is 'crooked,' while 'abja' is 'lotus'. So the word should probably be 'Karṇābja'.

38. Literally, 'assaulting with the teeth'; perhaps the gnashing of his teeth itself terrified the king's enemies.
39. Literally, 'lotus-like', beautiful and fragrant as a lotus blossom. In iconography, Lakṣmī, goddess of wealth and beauty, also known as Padmāvatī, stands on a lotus.
40. A ritual bath is taken.
41. A poetic expression, 'giver of honour'; mānada is a term of affection and respect used between lovers.
42. Sweet, round balls made of milk, butter, sugar, nuts and flavoured with spices.
43. See note 26.
44. The maṇdala—a sacro-magical circle symbolizing the universe.
45. What is commonly known as the harem; a private and guarded set of apartments in the royal palace with its own gardens, groves and pools, where each queen and princess had her own suite of rooms.
46. The story of the weaver and the Brāhmaṇa lady who killed her pet mongoose are both in the *Pañcatantra* (see Rajan, *The Pañcatantra,* Penguin Classics, pp. 76-90, and pp. 400-401).
47. Personifications of cosmic and elemental forces such as dawn, fire, wind, sun, etc.; sometimes they are mentioned as thirty-three.
48. Rāma, hero of the epic *Rāmāyaṇa,* in exile in the forests sets out to catch a golden deer which Sītā desires to have as a pet; the deer is in fact Mārīča, (see notes 32, 33) who assumes this form to trick Rāma into leaving Sītā alone so that Rāvaṇa could abduct her.
49. An ancient mythical king of great merit and righteousness who became arrogant and lusted after the queen of heaven, the consort of Indra. He ordered the seven sages to bear his palanquin on their shoulders and commanded them to hurry. The sages cursed him.
50. The seven stars of the constellation Ursa Major; the first great sages born from the mind of the Creator; parts of the Vedas were revealed to them. The first mortals with the power to perform sacrifices to the gods, they were

apotheosized and became the stars of Ursa Major.

51. Kartavīryārjuna (Kartavīrya-arjuna), a king of the Haihaya dynasty ruling at Māhiṣmati on the banks of the river Narmadā, once went to the hermitage of the sage Jamadagni who feasted him with his whole retinue royally on a fabulous banquet provided by his celestial cow, Suśīlā, sister of the wish-granting cow Surabhi or Kāmadhenu. Lusting after this extraordinary cow, the king tried to abduct her and was cursed as a result.
52. The eldest Pāṇdava, regarded as the very embodiment of truthfulness, and a just ruler.
53. Evasiveness, prevarication, are character blemishes that are punishable. A curse like this one that the genie threatens the king with is a common motif in Indian stories.
54. The lotus is the symbol of the blossoming world.
55. The names in astronomy are: Aldebaran, Leonis, Hydrae, Librae, Scorpionis, Pleiades, Orion.
56. Ascetics and other holy men have no home or possessions. They eat once a day, whatever is offered by the lady of the house where they stop at the noon hour.
57. Indicating the veranda or front porch of the house.
58. The word niṣevitam is used here; it has a sexual connotation in addition to its normal meaning of dwelling in a place.
59. Śiva bore the tumultuous descent on earth of the celestial river on his head to break the force and let the waters flow gently down to the plains. The source of the river is in the Himalayas which is regarded as the temporal abode of the Supreme One, Śiva.
60. Modern Bihar; Magadha was the most powerful of the kingdoms of ancient India and the first to evolve into an empire comprising most of the subcontinent.
61. Dharma, Artha, Kāma, namely, Virtue, Wealth, Love, are the three goals in man's life on earth. To lead a *good* life, the claims of all these have to be borne in mind and balanced.

62. Lack of cleanliness in the physical and moral senses.
63. Love, Cupid, the Greek Eros.
64. This long verse passage does not appear to be directly related to the main thread of the story.
65. Bharata is the author of the *Nāṭya Śāstra,* a comprehensive treatise on dramaturgy and the allied disciplines of music and dance; he lists types of heroes and heroines and describes the techniques of representing the roles.
66. Bharata.
67. Yakṣas—spirits of woods and waters, usually beneficent but sometimes mischievous, even malevolent. Originally divinities worshipped by the ancient peoples of India, pre-vedic and non-vedic, yakṣas and yakṣīs (yakṣiṇīs), were beneficent spirits, givers of life, riches and plenitude. They became malevolent and turned against Man only when he broke the holy laws of nature. Yakṣas symbolize the forces and powers of nature and perceived as indwelling spirits in nature, in woods, trees, pools, and associated with fertility and plenitude. Described as uncommonly handsome, they were believed to assume shapes at will, even the shapes of trees, or peep out of the dense green foliage.

    Later, they were replaced by Vedic and Brāhmaṇic deities and fitted into the vast and complex mosaic of the pantheon, in subordinate stations: doorkeepers, guards, dancers and singers and so on.

    Kubera, their overlord became the Lord of Riches. His kingdom was located in the Purāṇas, in the Himālayan and trans-Himālayan regions; his treasures were guarded by the yakṣas. Kubera and his yakṣas as well as other celestials such as kinnaras, vidyādharas, nāgas, apsaras, are similar to the pre-Christian and pagan deities of European mythology: the Celtic fairies, gnomes, the Germanic lorelei, the Greek fauns, nymphs, dryads and so on.

    Kubera and yakṣas and other divinities noted here, are closely associated with Śiva whose temporal abode is the Himālayas. See a note on the vetāla for further information, p. lxiv.

68. Cutting off the nose was apparently an accepted form of punishment of a woman, for the crimes of adultery and murder. A woman could not be sentenced to capital punishment; disfigurement was prescribed in the law books.
69. The Sanskrit term kavi signifies primarily the visioning seer.
70. Disgraced and banished; this is a form of punishment meted to both men and women that we see in tales, especially tales whose provenance is southern India. The wrongdoer is seated on a donkey often facing the animal's tail, and chased out of the city gates. An added detail is sometimes present; the culprit's face is painted with black and red dots.
71. Vidyādharas a race of beings who possessed magical powers and/or scientific knowledge and skills which would have struck the common man as extraordinary and miraculous.
72. Apotheosis. To tell a tale and through the telling atone for some wrongdoing and gain release from a curse, is a common motif in the storytelling tradition of India. It is frequently found in the *Mahābhārata* and in later literature; the most celebrated use of this motif is in the *Kathāsaritsāgara* where it forms the theme and basis of the frame story.
73. See note 47.
74. The noble warrior.
75. See note 19.
76. Durgā, Śiva's consort and the war goddess, is the tutelary deity of warriors.
77. A deep, sunken navel is a mark of beauty in India; a protruding belly-button is not.
78. The term employed in this line, svajanāpamānam could also be translated as 'dishonoured by one's kin'.
79. Good works and virtuous conduct bring good fortune in a person's current life and in succeeding lives.
80. See Ganeśa, note 19.
81. Modern Ujjain in Madhya Pradesh. Ujjayinī was one of

the great cities of ancient India with a continuous history of centuries as the capital of rich and powerful kingdoms such as few cities have ever possessed. It was the second capital of the great empires for several centuries. During most of its history it was a cultural and commercial centre, the emporium of its time, for the trade-routes passed through it on its way to Arabian sea ports and to Alexandria and Rome. The city was long a centre of learning and intellectual activity; an observatory had been built there quite early in its history and the prime meridian passed through it. Sanskrit drama probably had its origin in Ujjayinī and Kālidāsa most likely lived and wrote there. It is regarded as one of the five hierophannic centres in the country and the great antiquity and sanctity of the shrine of Mahākāla lent it unusual religious significance. Mahākāla is an epithet of Śiva, in his aspect of cosmic time or eternity. Literally, the term means 'Great Time'.

82. Dakṣiṇāpatha—the land south of the Vindhyas.

83. The mythic history of India divides time on earth into four ages: Kṛta, the golden age; Dvāpara and Treta, the silver and bronze ages, and Kali, our present, iron age. The Sanskrit names are taken from the game of dice, Kali being the name of the losing throw.

84. See notes 32, 33 and 48.

85. See notes 32, 33 and 48.

86. Bali, a just and magnanimous ruler never turned away a suppliant. He was tricked by Viṣṇu who in the form of a dwarf asked for land covered by three small steps. When Bali agreed to give him the land, Viṣṇu assumed his cosmic form and covered earth and sky with the first two steps. Bali offered his own head for Viṣṇu to place his foot upon to take the third step and was pushed down into Pātāla, the underworld.

87. Ćaṇḍikā is one of the many names of the Mother Goddess. The names of epithets are descriptive of the different aspects, powers and functions of godhead. Ćaṇḍikā is the epithet conveying the fierce aspect of godhead that punishes evil.

88. Creator, Preserver, lord of heaven, as noted above (note 87); the One is signified by a word relating to a function.
89. The four faces, facing the four cardinal points, symbolize omniscience; the word 'four-faced' is a metaphor for the idea of All-Seeing.
90. Literally, self-choice.
91. The phrase is rather obscure; perhaps it means settling and cultivating.
92. The class of warriors and rulers.
93. Goddess of the Arts; the Muse of Poetry.
94. Sal, a lofty, timber tree.
95. Myrobalan; a green berry that is crunchy and slightly tart; when green used to make pickles.
96. A love marriage by mutual consent; it is legal and binding and carries all the rights and responsibilities of the Hindu sacramental marriage.
97. A significant action; the bridegroom takes the bride's right hand when he speaks the marriage vows.
98. A jewelled pendant worn by women on the forehead; it is attached to the hair by a chain running along the middle parting.
99. Tiny, poisonous red and black berries, used as the smallest weights by jewellers.
100. The Indian nightingale.
101. Rūpam, the word used means form, splendour.
102. The trident with its three lines is symbolic; it is the weapon of Śiva.
103. Worship of the Kalpaka tree, that grants wishes.
104. Buddhist doctrine.
105. The three aspects defining the three functions of the One.
106. Brahmā, the Creator.
107. Maheśvara, one of the epithets of Śiva; literally, the Great Ruler (of the universe, that is).
108. The process of creation and dissolution of the cosmos.
109. It is the upper of the two round stones that grinds flour.
110. Pātāla, the nether regions; it is not hell but regions where the kingdoms of the nāgas, great snakes and other beings

with wondrous powers, were situated.

111. It was believed that tuskers had priceless pearls embedded in their foreheads.

112. Flowers, grains of rice etc.

113. In Śaiva mythology, the process of creation-dissolution-re-creation is conceived of in terms of a play; the dance (or dance-drama) is the dominant metaphor in Śaiva metaphysics.

114. See note 19.

115. Butter melted and clarified is ghee used in food and as oblations offered in the Sacred Fire.

116. Lord Viṣṇu: three of the lord's avatars or incarnations on earth are mentioned in this verse. As Vāmana, he defrauded King Bali (see note 86) of his great kingdom—Bali was a threat to the gods because he was a just ruler; as Lord Rāma, he had the bridge built across the waters to reach Lankā and rescue Sītā by killing Rāvaṇa who had abducted her. As Lord Kṛṣṇa he protected his father's herds on the banks of the river Yamunā against the dangers of unprecedented rains by lifting up the hill nearby and holding it as a canopy over the herds.

117. The Western Ghats with groves of sandalwood trees.

118. Gaurī, the mother goddess, consort of Śiva; the word means 'The Bright Goddess'.

119. It appears from the context that Jīmūtavāhana was a Bodhisattva, an emanation of the Buddha.

120. The Muse; goddess of wisdom and learning.

121. Indian Poetics discusses nine rasas; rasas are modes with one or other of the primary emotions of love, laughter, wrath, fear, disgust (repulsion), valour, compassion and peace as the predominant mood that sets the tone of a piece of writing. The modes might be roughly listed as the following: the romantic, the comic, the awesome, the horrific, the grotesque, the heroic, the compassionate and the peace-bestowing.

122. Spring creeper, a variety of jasmine; it bears white, fragrant flowers.

123. Ruddy goose, also known as Brāhminy duck. These birds mate for life and are a paradigm in Sanskrit poetry for fidelity in love.
124. Certain old texts discuss the thirty-two marks of perfect beauty in men and women, as well as auspicious marks that auger greatness, sovereignty etc.; for instance, the sign of a wheel in the palm is the sign of sovereignty.
125. Temple dancers who sang and danced as part of the worship of a deity were often mistresses of princes and nobles and wealthy citizens. They were highly intelligent, learned and accomplished women. Being married to the deity these women did not or could not marry.
126. Fortune personified.
127. The *Nātya Śāstra* of Bharata enumerates the ten stages of love and describes how to depict the emotions on stage.
128. Duty.
129. The Power referred to here is the Law of the Universe in its moral and physical aspects which establishes and maintains Order and in the absence of which there would be chaos. Everything in the universe in bound by this Law, even the gods.
130. See note 24.
131. Viṣṇu.
132. An outcast.
133. Milk, melted butter, curds, urine and dung; the cow is sacred.
134. The ratiocinative part of the mind as different from the emotional.
135. See note 96.
136. See note 23.
137. A guest who comes unbidden; the Sanskrit term for such a guest is a-tithi (without a date). Not to extend hospitality to such a guest is a grave offence.
138. A-bhaya, without fear; the secondary meaning of the word is 'giving sanctuary'.
139. Any place of torment; Hell.
140. A Brāhmaṇa who leads an evil and depraved live is

doomed to become an ogre.

141. A lakh is one hundred thousand.

142. Literally, 'spacious,' 'expansive,' one of the names of the city of Ujjayinī.

143. The god of love, Kāma, tried to tempt Lord Śiva Himself, who was seated in single-minded meditation on Mt. Kailāsa in the Himālayas. The Lord opened His Third Eye (the eye of wisdom and of visioning) and a spark flew out and burnt Kāma to ashes. From that time, Love was known as the Bodiless.

144. Pleasure.

145. Hāra, the word used here describes a necklace of sixty-four, or 108 strings of pearls.

146. Love's five arrows: the red lotus, the aśoka flower also a deep red, the mango blossom, the spring jasmine and the blue lily.

147. A punishment for gamblers apparently, though I am unable to locate it in *Manusmṛti*. However the ethical texts do treat it as a terrible vice.

148. Literally, 'mountain-born' the Mother Goddess is the daughter of the Himāyalas, in mythology.

149. In yoga philosophy (one of the six systems of Indian philosophy) five blemishes or limitations of the personality are noted: ignorance, egoism, compelling desire, aversion, excessive attachment to mundane things and concerns.

150. A contemptuous word for the mouth.

151. Illusion, magic, sorcery.

152. Things are at sixes and sevens: normally a Buddhist monk is clean-shaven; a Brāhmaṇa wears a topknot; Sānkhya (one of the six systems of Indian philosophy) is atheistic and does not posit a gód, only matter and intelligence.

153. Himsa, cruelty is of three kinds; physical, verbal, mental.

154. Kṛṣṇa, an incarnation of Lord Viṣṇu who teaches the right path to Arjuna, in the Gita.

155. Yama, god of death and the final judge of all creatures and their conduct on earth.

156. Māndhātā, a mythical king born of his father without a mother and nursed by Indra, Lord of the Immortals,

conquered the whole world and ruled from sea to sea.

157. Rāma, hero of the epic, *Rāmāyaṇa*, lived in exile for many years during which his queen, Sītā was abducted by Rāvaṇa, king of Lankā. Rāma had a bridge built across the seas to reach Lankā to rescue Sītā and killed Rāvaṇa in battle.

158. The eldest of the five brothers, the Pāṇdavas, who fought their cousins for the sovereignty of India. Yudhiṣṭhira became the emperor.

159. See note 157. Trikūṭa was his fortress palace on a hill.

160. Ganeśa—see note 19.

161. Earthly rulers possessed the essences or the gods.

162. See note 71.

163. Triple-City; three cities of gold, silver and iron respectively were built in the sky, air and earth for the Titans. Śiva destroyed them.

164. Ćakravartī—Paramount Ruler, literally, 'one who turned the wheel of empire.'

Appendix

Tales from the Five-and-Twenty Tales of the Genie as set down by Jambhaladatta

1. Śiva the Absolute; the creator, preserver and destroyer of the universe. The word means 'auspicious,' beneficent.' Śakti, is the power of *Śiva*, the kinetic aspect of pure Being. Śiva-Śakti, Being—Becoming is one; the two different aspects of the creative principle.

2. The dance is *the* metaphor for creation-dissolution that symbolizes the rhythm, the eternal movement of the universe. The tremendous power of Cosmic Energy, Śakti, flows into time and space, shaped by the guiding principle, Śiva, into the patterns of dance that articulate the patterns of the life force, bringing the universe into

existence.

3. Śeṣa (the remainder) or Ananta (the endless), is the cosmic serpent that supports the universe on its manifold, expanded hoods. The serpent is a symbol of time in its eternal aspect. In mythology, Śeṣa is the king of serpents or Nāgas, living in Pātāla, the primeval space-ocean of undifferentiated potentialities of forms from which all creation emerges. At the end of time, the world-snake breathes out poison; the great deluge takes place; winds, waters, fire and poison destroy the creation which melts back into its primeval state into 'the waters' of the space-ocean. What remains is the creative principle, as well as the seeds of a new universe—śeṣa, the remainder.
4. The moon is Śiva's crest-jewel which he appropriated to himself when it rose among many other wondrous objects from the ocean that was churned at the dawn of time by the forces of light and darkness, the devas and dānavas (or asuras or daityas). Soma is one of the many names of the moon, soma being the sap of life extolled in the vedas. The moon is therefore a source of fertility. The sap of life is absorbed by plants from the moonbeams at night and enters other forms of life that eat plants and are in turn eaten by others.
5. Rasa is primarily taste, flavour, essence: in aesthetics, the term is used as the signifier for emotional states, for sentiments and moods. A work possesses a dominant mood, one of eight (then nine) rasas, which sets the tone of the work, with one or more rasas being subordinate, enhancing and giving depth to the work. Love, valour, anger, laughter, disgust, compassion, terror and wonder, and the ninth, serenity added later are the Rasas; from these, the following modes, erotic, heroic, passionate, humorous, pathetic, awesome and marvellous, derive. The ninth Rasa produces the mode of aesthetic joy (śānta) in which all the elements in a work of art are balanced.
6. The Sanskrit term is sāndhivigraha; the minister in charge of external affairs, or the Foreign Minister.
7. See note 11 of Notes to the Introduction.

8. The term used in the text is kāpālika, a skull-bearer. The kāpālikas were a sect of ascetics, devotees of Śiva, who carried a half skull as a bowl for food and drink. They were commonly regarded as a 'left-hand sect', that is, a heterodox sect.
9. The fruit of the tree, Aegle Marmelos, commonly known as woodapple. The ripe fruit, the size of a large apple or grapefruit has a delicious honey taste with a touch of tartness. The green fruit has medicinal uses in Ayurveda. The leaves, grey-green in colour are sacred to Śiva and offered in his worship.
10. Suprahuman powers, the eight siddhis: flying through the air; assuming shapes at will; power to become minute or enormous; light or heavy; controlling the minds and lives of others; not being controlled by others; becoming invisible.
11. The second month of rains, mid-August to mid-September; the months in the Indian calendar begin and end on the 15th day of the month according to the western calendar.
12. Literally the Gurgling River. Monier Williams identifies it with the Gogra, a tributary of the Gangā, and Apte with the Gangā itself. These identifications are perhaps incorrect, because the frame-story has as the protagonist the Emperor Vikramāditya (or Vikramakesarī) who ruled in Central India with his capital at Ujjayinī. The cycle of stories, therefore, might be presumed to be located in central India.
13. Dalbergia Sissoo. Its leaves and berries are bitter and acrid and used for medicinal purposes.
14. Myrobalan; Āmla in Hindi; a slightly tart and sweet fruit eaten raw or made into pickles.
15. Lāvaṇyavatī, literally, a maiden with the beauty of lustrous pearls; here it is used thus as an adjective; perhaps also as a proper noun, her name.
16. Originally divinities worshipped by the ancient peoples of India, the first nations, so to speak of the land, Yakṣas were regarded as beneficent spirits, givers of life and

plenitude of all kinds. They are forces of nature, indwelling spirits of woods and waters, spirits that assumed different shapes to manifest themselves to people. Later, they were replaced by Vedic, Brāhmaṇic divinities and relegated to subordinate positions in the vast and complex pantheon of god and demigod. Kubera, the Lord of Wealth, was the Yakṣa overlord; his kingdom was located in the Himalayan-trans-Himalayan regions. The Yakṣas were guardians of his immeasurable treasures; considered later as a class of celestial beings like the Vidyādharas (see note 7), Yakṣas were associated with Śiva who is called Yakṣarupa (with the form of a Yakṣa) and Kubera was regarded as a close friend of Śiva.

In the medieval period to which both the texts in this volume belong, there seemed to have appeared a tendency to view Yakṣas as malevolent or mischievous, and grotesque in appearance, as satyrs and gnomes in European mythology were. In their original connotation, the words yakṣa and yakṣi (feminine) signified nature-spirits like the pre-christian divinities and 'pagan' spirits of Europe, e.g. the Celtic fairies; the fauns, dryads and nymphs of ancient Greece.

17. Ćakravāka-Ćakravākī are generally known as sheldrakes, ruddy geese or Brāhmaṇy ducks. They mate for life and serve as symbols of connubial love and constancy.
18. Literally, The Wishgranting Vine. For lovers in desperate straits the go-between is the sole means of making their wishes come true.
19. Arundhatī in the morning star. In mythology, she is the wife of Vasiṣṭha one of the seven sages—saptarsi—apotheosized into the constellation of the Great Bear. Arundhatī is the model of unwavering chastity.
20. The sacred thread, worn over one shoulder crosswise, down to the waist, is first put on young boys at the rite of investiture. It is one of a number of 'rites of passage' in most societies in the ancient world; it signifies being born again, crossing over from childhood to youth. Performed around the age of seven (for Brāhmaṇas) and

a couple of years later for others, it marks the commencement of education and/or professional training, apprenticeship to a trade etc.

21. The river Narmadā or Rewā, rises in the eastern Vindhyas in central India and gathering the waters of many tributaries, flows across the peninsula in to the Arabian Sea.
22. The name Arimaulimaṇi compounded of the three words, Ari—mauli—Maṇi—, foe—head—jewel, can be understood in two ways: one who wears his foe as a crest jewel, or, one who is worn by his foe as a crest jewel; that is one who conquers or is conquered.
23. Jnānī, is one who possesses Jnāna, knowledge or wisdom. In the two texts in this volume, the word is however used to signify a special type of knowledge; the knowledge of and proficiency in magic, and possession of skills in soothsaying, casting spells, performing exorcism etc.
24. An aspect of the Mother Goddess, the tutelary deity of a tribe known as Dadhi-parṇa.
25. It is not quite clear what precisely these two terms signify; two kinds of magic power presumably, white and black magic.
26. A yogī is commonly a person who acquires extraordinary and suprahuman powers by virtue of performing yoga and/or severe austerities of various sorts. The powers so gained might be used for good, for the integration of the self with the over-self, the supreme spirit, this being the common meaning of the term. But the powers could also be used for the advancement of the person's self-interests in the material world, and acquisition of power, wealth, dominion. Kṣāntiśīla belongs to the latter category of yogīs. Power can always be used well or misused, as for instance, in the case of modern scientific knowledge, as in the control and use of atomic energy which can be put to destructive uses as well as constructive ones.
27. Ćakravartī, literally, one who turns the wheel of empire.

read more

PENGUIN CLASSICS

THE EPIC OF GILGAMESH

'Surpassing all other kings, heroic in stature,
brave scion of Uruk, wild bull on the rampage!
Gilgamesh the tall, magnificent and terrible'

Miraculously preserved on clay tablets dating back as much as four thousand years, the poem of Gilgamesh, king of Uruk, is the world's oldest epic, predating Homer by many centuries. The story tells of Gilgamesh's adventures with the wild man Enkidu, and of his arduous journey to the ends of the earth in quest of the Babylonian Noah and the secret of immortality. Alongside its themes of family, friendship and the duties of kings, *The Epic of Gilgamesh* is, above all, about mankind's eternal struggle with the fear of death.

The Babylonian version has been known for over a century, but linguists are still deciphering new fragments in Akkadian and Sumerian. Andrew George's gripping translation brilliantly combines these into a fluent narrative and will long rank as the definitive English *Gilgamesh*.

'This masterly new verse translation' *The Times*

Translated with an introduction by Andrew George

read more

PENGUIN CLASSICS

THE ANALECTS CONFUCIUS

'The Master said, "If a man sets his heart on benevolence, he will be free from evil"'

The Analects are a collection of Confucius's sayings brought together by his pupils shortly after his death in 497 BC. Together they express a philosophy, or a moral code, by which Confucius, one of the most humane thinkers of all time, believed everyone should live. Upholding the ideals of wisdom, self-knowledge, courage and love of one's fellow man, he argued that the pursuit of virtue should be every individual's supreme goal. And while following the Way, or the truth, might not result in immediate or material gain, Confucius showed that it could nevertheless bring its own powerful and lasting spiritual rewards.

This edition contains a detailed introduction exploring the concepts of the original work, a bibliography and glossary and appendices on Confucius himself, *The Analects* and the disciples who compiled them.

Translated with an introduction and notes by D. C. Lau

PENGUIN CLASSICS

THE BHAGAVAD GITA

'In death thy glory in heaven, in victory thy glory on earth.
Arise therefore, Arjuna, with thy soul ready to fight'

The Bhagavad Gita is an intensely spiritual work that forms the cornerstone of the Hindu faith, and is also one of the masterpieces of Sanskrit poetry. It describes how, at the beginning of a mighty battle between the Pandava and Kaurava armies, the god Krishna gives spiritual enlightenment to the warrior Arjuna, who realizes that the true battle is for his own soul.

Juan Mascaró's translation of *The Bhagavad Gita* captures the extraordinary aural qualities of the original Sanskrit. This edition features a new introduction by Simon Brodbeck, which discusses concepts such as dehin, prakriti and Karma.

'The task of truly translating such a work is indeed formidable. The translator must at least possess three qualities. He must be an artist in words as well as a Sanskrit scholar, and above all, perhaps, he must be deeply sympathetic with the spirit of the original. Mascaró has succeeded so well because he possesses all these' *The Times Literary Supplement*

Translated by Juan Mascaró with an introduction by Simon Brodbeck

PENGUIN CLASSICS

BUDDHIST SCRIPTURES

'Whoever gives something for the good of others, with heart full of sympathy, not heeding his own good, reaps unspoiled fruit'

While Buddhism has no central text such as the Bible or the Koran, there is a powerful body of scripture from across Asia that encompasses the *dharma*, or the teachings of Buddha. This rich anthology brings together works from a broad historical and geographical range, and from languages such as Pali, Sanskrit, Tibetan, Chinese and Japanese. There are tales of the Buddha's past lives, a discussion of the qualities and qualifications of a monk, and an exploration of the many meanings of Enlightenment. Together they provide a vivid picture of the Buddha and of the vast nature of the Buddhist tradition.

This new edition contains many texts presented in English for the first time as well as new translations of some well-known works, and also includes an informative introduction and prefaces to each chapter by scholar of Buddhism Donald S. Lopez Jr, with suggestions for further reading and a glossary.

Edited with an introduction by Donald S. Lopez, Jr

read more

PENGUIN CLASSICS

THE RUBA'IYAT OF OMAR KHAYYAM

'Many like you come and many go
Snatch your share before you are snatched away'

Revered in eleventh-century Persia as an astronomer, mathematician and philosopher, Omar Khayyam is now known first and foremost for his *Ruba'iyat*. The short epigrammatic stanza form allowed poets of his day to express personal feelings, beliefs and doubts with wit and clarity, and Khayyam became one of its most accomplished masters with his touching meditations on the transience of human life and of the natural world. One of the supreme achievements of medieval literature, the reckless romanticism and the pragmatic fatalism in the face of death means these verses continue to hold the imagination of modern readers.

In this translation, Persian scholar Peter Avery and the poet John Heath-Stubbs have collaborated to recapture the sceptical, unorthodox spirit of the original by providing a near literal English version of the original verse. This edition also includes a map, appendices, bibliography and an introduction examining the *ruba'i* form and Khayyam's life and times.

'[Has] restored to that masterpiece all the fun, dash and vivacity.'
Jan Morris

Translated by Peter Avery and John Heath-Stubbs

read more

PENGUIN CLASSICS

THE ODYSSEY HOMER

'I long to reach my home and see the day of my return. It is my never-failing wish'

The epic tale of Odysseus and his ten-year journey home after the Trojan War forms one of the earliest and greatest works of Western literature. Confronted by natural and supernatural threats – shipwrecks, battles, monsters and the implacable enmity of the sea-god Poseidon – Odysseus must test his bravery and native cunning to the full if he is to reach his homeland safely and overcome the obstacles that, even there, await him.

E. V. Rieu's translation of *The Odyssey* was the very first Penguin Classic to be published, and has itself achieved classic status. For this edition, his text has been sensitively revised and a new introduction added to complement E. V. Rieu's original introduction.

'One of the world's most vital tales ... *The Odyssey* remains central to literature' Malcolm Bradbury

Translated by E. V. Rieu
Revised translation by D. C. H. Rieu, with an introduction by Peter Jones

PENGUIN CLASSICS

THE ILIAD HOMER

'Look at me. I am the son of a great man. A goddess was my mother. Yet death and inexorable destiny are waiting for me'

One of the foremost achievements in Western literature, Homer's *Iliad* tells the story of the darkest episode in the Trojan War. At its centre is Achilles, the greatest warrior-champion of the Greeks, and his refusal to fight after being humiliated by his leader Agamemnon. But when the Trojan Hector kills Achilles's close friend Patroclus, he storms back into battle to take revenge – although knowing this will ensure his own early death. Interwoven with this tragic sequence of events are powerfully moving descriptions of the ebb and flow of battle, of the domestic world inside Troy's besieged city of Ilium, and of the conflicts between the gods on Olympus as they argue over the fate of mortals.

E. V. Rieu's acclaimed translation of Homer's *Iliad* was one of the first titles published in Penguin Classics, and now has classic status itself. For this edition, Rieu's text has been revised, and a new introduction and notes by Peter Jones complement the original introduction.

Translated by E. V. Rieu
Revised and updated by Peter Jones with D. C. H. Rieu
Edited with an introduction and notes by Peter Jones

PENGUIN CLASSICS

THE RISE OF THE ROMAN EMPIRE POLYBIUS

'If history is deprived of the truth, we are left with nothing but an idle, unprofitable tale.'

In writing his account of the relentless growth of the Roman Empire, the Greek statesman Polybius (*c.* 200–118 BC) set out to help his fellow-countrymen understand how their world came to be dominated by Rome. Opening with the Punic War in 264 BC, he vividly records the critical stages of Roman expansion: its campaigns throughout the Mediterranean, the temporary setbacks inflicted by Hannibal and the final destruction of Carthage in 146 BC. An active participant in contemporary politics, as well as a friend of many prominent Roman citizens, Polybius was able to draw on a range of eyewitness accounts and on his own experiences of many of the central events, giving his work immediacy and authority.

Ian Scott-Kilvert's translation fully preserves the clarity of Polybius's narrative. This substantial selection of the surviving volumes is accompanied by an introduction by F. W. Walbank, which examines Polybius's life and times, and the sources and technique he employed in writing his history.

Translated by Ian Scott-Kilvert
Selected with an introduction by F. W. Walbank

PENGUIN CLASSICS

THE PERSIAN EXPEDITION XENOPHON

'The only things of value which we have at present are our arms and our courage'

In *The Persian Expedition*, Xenophon, a young Athenian noble who sought his destiny abroad, provides an enthralling eyewitness account of the attempt by a Greek mercenary army – the Ten Thousand – to help Prince Cyrus overthrow his brother and take the Persian throne. When the Greeks were then betrayed by their Persian employers, they were forced to march home through hundreds of miles of difficult terrain – adrift in a hostile country and under constant attack from the unforgiving Persians and warlike tribes. In this outstanding description of endurance and individual bravery, Xenophon, one of those chosen to lead the retreating army, provides a vivid narrative of the campaign and its aftermath, and his account remains one of the best pictures we have of Greeks confronting a 'barbarian' world.

Rex Warner's distinguished translation captures the epic quality of the Greek original and George Cawkwell's introduction sets the story of the expedition in the context of its author's life and tumultuous times.

Translated by Rex Warner with an introduction by George Cawkwell

read more

PENGUIN CLASSICS

THE CONSOLATION OF PHILOSOPHY BOETHIUS

'Why else does slippery Fortune change
So much, and punishment more fit
For crime oppress the innocent?'

Written in prison before his brutal execution in AD 524, Boethius's *The Consolation of Philosophy* is a conversation between the ailing prisoner and his 'nurse' Philosophy, whose instruction restores him to health and brings him to enlightenment. Boethius was an eminent public figure who had risen to great political heights in the court of King Theodoric when he was implicated in conspiracy and condemned to death. Although a Christian, it was to the pagan Greek philosophers that he turned for inspiration following his abrupt fall from grace. With great clarity of thought and philosophical brilliance, Boethius adopted the classical model of the dialogue to debate the vagaries of Fortune, and to explore the nature of happiness, good and evil, fate and free will.

Victor Watts's English translation makes *The Consolation of Philosophy* accessible to the modern reader while losing nothing of its poetic artistry and breadth of vision. This edition includes an introduction discussing Boethius's life and writings, a bibliography, glossary and notes.

Translated with an introduction by Victor Watts

THE STORY OF PENGUIN CLASSICS

Before 1946 ... 'Classics' are mainly the domain of academics and students, without readable editions for everyone else. This all changes when a little-known classicist, E. V. Rieu, presents Penguin founder Allen Lane with the translation of Homer's *Odyssey* that he has been working on and reading to his wife Nelly in his spare time.

1946 *The Odyssey* becomes the first Penguin Classic published, and promptly sells three million copies. Suddenly, classic books are no longer for the privileged few.

1950s Rieu, now series editor, turns to professional writers for the best modern, readable translations, including Dorothy L. Sayers's *Inferno* and Robert Graves's *The Twelve Caesars*, which revives the salacious original.

1960s The Classics are given the distinctive black jackets that have remained a constant throughout the series's various looks. Rieu retires in 1964, hailing the Penguin Classics list as 'the greatest educative force of the 20th century'.

1970s A new generation of translators arrives to swell the Penguin Classics ranks, and the list grows to encompass more philosophy, religion, science, history and politics.

1980s The Penguin American Library joins the Classics stable, with titles such as *The Last of the Mohicans* safeguarded. Penguin Classics now offers the most comprehensive library of world literature available.

1990s The launch of Penguin Audiobooks brings the classics to a listening audience for the first time, and in 1999 the launch of the Penguin Classics website takes them online to a larger global readership than ever before.

The 21st Century Penguin Classics are rejacketed for the first time in nearly twenty years. This world famous series now consists of more than 1300 titles, making the widest range of the best books ever written available to millions – and constantly redefining the meaning of what makes a 'classic'.

The Odyssey continues ...